Keeping Up with the Kalashnikovs

Keeping Up with the Kalashnikovs

ROSS O'CARROLL-KELLY
(as told to Paul Howard)

Illustrated by

ALAN CLARKE

PENGUIN
IRELAND

PENGUIN IRELAND

Published by the Penguin Group
Penguin Ireland, 25 St Stephen's Green, Dublin 2, Ireland (a division of Penguin Books Ltd)
Penguin Books Ltd, 80 Strand, London WC2R 0RL, England
Penguin Group (USA) Inc., 375 Hudson Street, New York, New York 10014, USA
Penguin Group (Australia), 250 Camberwell Road, Camberwell, Victoria 3124, Australia
(a division of Pearson Australia Group Pty Ltd)
Penguin Group (Canada), 90 Eglinton Avenue East, Suite 700, Toronto, Ontario, Canada M4P 2Y3
(a division of Pearson Penguin Canada Inc.)
Penguin Books India Pvt Ltd, 11 Community Centre, Panchsheel Park, New Delhi – 110 017, India
Penguin Group (NZ), 67 Apollo Drive, Rosedale, Auckland 0632, New Zealand
(a division of Pearson New Zealand Ltd)
Penguin Books (South Africa) (Pty) Ltd, Block D, Rosebank Office Park,
181 Jan Smuts Avenue, Parktown North, Gauteng 2193, South Africa

Penguin Books Ltd, Registered Offices: 80 Strand, London WC2R 0RL, England

www.penguin.com

First published 2014
001

Copyright © Paul Howard, 2014
Illustrations copyright © Alan Clarke, 2014

Penguin Ireland thanks O'Brien Press for its agreement to Penguin Ireland
using the same design approach and typography, and the same artist,
as O'Brien Press used in the first four Ross O'Carroll-Kelly titles

The moral right of the author and illustrator has been asserted

Set in 12/14.75 pt Dante MT Std
Typeset by Jouve (UK), Milton Keynes
Printed in Great Britain by Clays Ltd, St Ives plc

A CIP catalogue record for this book is available from the British Library

ISBN: 978-1-844-88293-9

www.greenpenguin.co.uk

To Martin Codyre

Contents

Prologue

They look at me like I'm off my focking meds. JP points out that I couldn't pick Uganda off a map and I ask him why that's suddenly relevant. I couldn't pick Ireland off a map. Jesus, when would *I* have even *seen* a map?

'And anyway,' I go, 'I'm not suggesting that we focking walk there. We go online. We book four flights. We turn up at the airport. We get on a focking airplane. An hour of Jay-Z on the head-phones. A good romcom – something with Jason Bateman in it. Two or three gin and tonics and a bit of flirtatious banter with the flying waitresses. Three, four hours later, you're landing in Ooma Gananga.'

'Uganda,' Christian goes, as if not knowing the actual name of the country somehow proves JP's point.

I'm like, 'Whatever.'

Mr Munier, the dude from the Deportment of Foreign Affairs, puts the tips of his fingers together, smiles nervously and goes, 'I think what your friends are saying is that you don't know the first thing about the country. Look, we don't advise people *not* to travel to Uganda. It's a safe country – again, relatively speaking. What we *would* advise against is you suddenly arriving there and, well, what exactly *are* you proposing to do?'

I'm there, 'What I'm proposing to do is to look for our friend, find the fockers who kidnapped him and to bring them to justice.'

Christian rolls his eyes.

'You said that in a Liam Neeson voice,' JP goes.

I'm like, 'No, I didn't.'

'You did, Ross. Liam Neeson from *Taken*.'

I end up losing it in a serious way then – this is in the middle of this Munier dude's office, overlooking Stephen's Green.

'Fionn's been gone three weeks,' I go. 'And what have you done about it? The answer to that question would seem to be Sweet Foreign Affairs.'

I'm pretty proud of that as a line.

Mr Munier – he's from Cork, although he's actually sound, and probably in his late fifties – goes, 'Look, we can't stop you doing, well, whatever it is you're proposing to do. But if you suddenly land there and start . . .'

I'm there, 'Asking questions and decking people, where necessary.'

'You see, that could only harm the situation. You might even end up kidnapped yourselves. We'd strongly advise against doing anything so drastic – at least until we've exhausted the various diplomatic channels.'

'What diplomatic channels are we talking here?'

'We're liaising with the local authorities and various other parties on the ground. They believe that Fionn was taken for ransom. So the kidnappers are bound to make contact sooner or later.'

Oisinn is keeping very quiet, by the way. I mention that to him as well. He's sitting at the other end of this, like, boardroom table that we're all gathered around, his orms folded, saying – like I said – literally fock-all.

I'm there, 'Er, sorry, do *you* have an opinion at all?'

He's put on weight. That'll be the dinners my old dear is obviously feeding him. She uses a lot of, like, creams and cheeses in her dishes. She's an incredible cook, the raddled old soak.

Oisinn just shrugs. 'The Deportmment of Foreign Affairs say they're handling it,' he just goes. 'Maybe we should just accept that everything that can be done is *being* done.'

That's when I, like, seriously *seriously* flip?

'So we should all just sit around on our fat orses,' I go, 'eating crab ravioli with creamy truffle sauce and God knows what else?'

'What are you talking about?' he has the actual balls to go.

I'm there, 'You know what I'm focking talking about.'

He suddenly stands up, all six-foot-whatever of him. 'Do you have a problem with me?' he goes.

I walk down to the other end of the table, eyeballing him all the way, going, 'Oh, I have a problem with you alright.'

He's tapping my so-called mother. That's it in a nutshell. It's a focking miracle I haven't *already* decked him?

He's like, 'Well, what do you want to do about it?'

Mr Munier goes, 'Gentlemen! Gentlemen!' obviously not wanting to see blood spilled in his office.

I'm like, 'Two hits, Big O. That's all it'd take. Me hitting you. You hitting the deck.'

Oisinn looks me up and down. He should be scared, although he doesn't seem to be. He goes, 'Do you know what the hilarious thing is?'

I'm there, 'No, tell me, Oisinn. What is this so-called hilarious thing?'

'Why was Fionn even *in* Uganda?'

'Excuse me?'

'Why did he go there in the first place?'

And of course I straight away know what he's getting at. I look at Mr Munier, then back at Oisinn. 'He's a teacher,' I try to go – this is without actually backing down. 'He has a lot of information slash shit in his head and he happens to want to pass it on to other people. An opportunity came up for him to do just that in a foreign country.'

'He went because he had to get away,' Oisinn goes. 'He went because you broke up his marriage.'

'He wasn't even married, can I just point out? It thankfully never came to that.'

'Because you destroyed it.'

'Yeah, no, I tried to tell him that Erika wasn't right for him. Guilty.'

'And who were you to decide that?'

'Er, I'm *her* brother and I'm *his* friend.'

He laughs in my actual face. 'Some friend,' he goes – balls like focking watermelons, by the way. 'He only went to Africa to get away from the focking mess that you made of his life . . .'

'Again, I'd say it was more the opportunity to teach in a foreign country.'

'And all this anger that we're seeing now is actually just guilt. Because you know that, if it wasn't for you, he'd be married now . . .'

'Yeah, unhappily married.'

'The point is he'd still be here, still living in Dalkey, probably teaching in the Institute. Instead, he's tied up in some focking cellar, or in a cave, or in a jungle, God knows focking where, terrified out of his mind – and that, Ross, is down to you!'

I put my hand on his chest and I shove him backwards.

'Gentlemen!' Mr Munier goes, except *louder* this time?

And Christian suddenly jumps up and steps in between us. 'This isn't helping,' he goes. 'We're not going to get anywhere if we stort fighting amongst ourselves.'

It's Oisinn, can I just say, who ends up backing down first. A wise focking man.

'Christian's right,' JP goes. 'We need to come up with a plan.'

Of course, I'm not letting *him* suddenly hijack the meeting – it was, like, me who arranged it.

'Well,' I go, 'I'll tell you what *isn't* a plan? Sitting around and waiting for – no disrepect to you, Mr Munier – but this shower of useless focks to – what was that expression? – *exhaust their channels*? Because as far as I can see they've done basically fock-all so far, except make a bunch of phone calls.'

Mr Munier goes, 'What do you expect us to do?'

JP's there, 'Ross thought you'd send in a fleet of helicopter gunships and a crack team of highly trained operatives to locate and rescue him.'

Mr Munier laughs, then he cops the expression on my face and realizes that JP isn't joking. I really *did* think that.

'We, er, don't do that kind of thing,' he goes.

I'm like, 'I focking realize that now!'

'We're not the SAS.'

'Yeah, no, I copped that much when I walked through the door and saw all those people out there – again, I hate being a dick to you – with their sideburns and their Best for Men suits and their focking idiot bogman accents. I thought, yeah, no, making phone calls is what this crowd do and fock-all else. Pack of turnip rapists. That's why it's down to us. His friends. The people who played

4

rugby with him. And I'm only mentioning rugby in case these goys here have forgotten that basic fact.'

JP's there, 'We haven't forgotten, Ross.'

'I'm happy to hear it.'

'All we're saying is that marching into Uganda might not be the most sensible thing to do. We still don't know who's taken him. It could be, I don't know, a focking warlord or something.'

I'm there, 'Well, warlord or not, he's a big-time dick and he's getting decked. Of all the people he could have kidnapped, he picks Fionn. A dude who wouldn't hurt a focking fly. Actually, that was probably one of the things that stopped him being a truly great rugby player, even though this possibly isn't the time to point that out.'

They're all just staring at me. I realize I'm babbling. Maybe Oisinn is right. It possibly *is* just guilt?

'I, em, have another meeting,' Mr Munier suddenly goes, which presumably is Civil Service for thanks for dropping by and don't let the door hit you on the way out.

JP, Christian and Oisinn all shake his hand as they're leaving and tell him thanks for keeping us updated. I don't. I shake his hand and I go, 'I can't tell you how focking disappointed I am with this place.'

'Like I said,' he tries to go, 'it isn't the Pentagon.'

I'm there, 'You're focking damn right it's not.'

Afterwards, we end up standing around outside on Stephen's Green – we're talking me and the goys – discussing how we think it went.

I'm there, 'I still say we should go.'

Christian's like, 'Ross, I've got a baby on the way.'

Then JP's there, 'Yeah, no, so do I.'

I could say the same, except Sorcha doesn't want to tell anyone until she's broken the news to her old dear – and Honor, of course.

I'm there, 'So we just leave him to focking rot out there. Is that what we're saying?'

Christian goes, 'No. I'm saying we should sit tight – like Mr Munier said – until there's an actual ransom demand and we know something more concrete.'

JP's there, 'Actually, I was talking to Ewan and Andrea this morning.'

He means Fionn's old pair. They're massive, massive fans of mine – or at least they were before I destroyed their son's life. And very nearly their daughter's marriage. 'Jenny's coming over,' JP goes, 'this weekend.'

I'm like, 'Okay, who the fock is Jenny?'

'She's Fionn's girlfriend. She was the co-ordinator of this school-building project Fionn was working on over there.'

Jenny. I remember him mentioning her now, although I wasn't paying a lot of attention at the time. A project co-ordinator. She sounds like a focking dog. Erika was a rare nugget of gold for Fionn in a lifetime of panning through shit.

'She's been working to try to get him released over there,' he goes, 'but I think she's realized that she'd be of more use here, asking Enda Kenny and possibly even the EU to put pressure on the Ugandan Government to do something. I said to Ewan and Andrea that we'd definitely love to meet up with her to find out what we can do to help.'

I'm there, 'Does anyone fancy going for scoops?' because it's nearly half-two and I'm in the mood for a few Ken Earlys.

Christian says he has to get back to the shop. I'm hearing that that submarine sandwich place of his is not doing well. JP says that he and his old man are hosting another one of their famous distressed-property auctions at three.

Oisinn looks at me. His face has softened from a minute ago. He goes, 'Yeah, I'll go for a pint with you.'

But I'm like, 'Sorry, I'm actually choosy about who I drink with,' which obviously isn't true.

He's there, 'Look, I'm sorry. I didn't mean what I said up there,' and he sticks out his hand, suddenly wanting to be my bezzy mate again, as if an apology is suddenly enough to, like, square shit between us. 'No hord feelings.'

But shit can never be good between us. Not as long as he's knobbing *her*. So I keep my hand exactly where it is – in other words, in the pocket of my chinos.

I go, 'I'm giving this shower of Tipperary focking scarecrows four weeks to find Fionn and bring him home. If they don't, I'm going over there myself – kicking orse and taking names – with or without you goys.'

1. Hit Me, Baby, Three More Times

Empty the hoover bag. Defrost the fridge. Fix the wonky hinges on the cabinet where we keep the Villeroy and Boch glassware. Every time Sorcha opens her mouth these days, it's to give me a list of jobs that need doing. I'm pretty sure I remember this from the last time she was pregnant – it's what the experts call the *nesting* phase? It's all to do with mothers wanting to make sure that everything is absolutely perfect for their new arrival. It eventually passes, if you can ignore it for long enough.

'Did you put a new bulb in the sensor light at the front of the house?' she goes.

See, this is an example of what I'm talking about.

I'm stretched out on the sofa, in my baggy Cantos with the focked elastic, knocking back a couple of cans while watching a Johnny Sexton career-highlights reel on YouTube. She suddenly appears in the doorway of the living room, with my little granddaughter in her orms, screaming her lungs out, which is what she's been doing since pretty much five o'clock this morning.

I'm like, 'Yeah, no, it'll be done, Sorcha. It's definitely on the old bucket list.'

She's there, 'I can't get Rihanna-Brogan to settle today.'

I'm like, 'Where are Ronan and Shadden?' and I'm not saying it to be a focker. I'm genuinely wondering.

She goes, 'They're looking at schools.'

I forgot. They're both really serious about going back in September, except Castlerock won't take Ronan back because McGahy, the so-called Principal, thinks that having a student with a baby would have – what was it? – a morally corruptible influence on the rest of the student body?

So Ronan and Shadden are still looking for somewhere that'll take them – two single parents, still in their teens. And it's already

July, which means they're going to be dealing with the dregs anyway. Sorcha's deluded, though.

She goes, 'Shadden's going to call into Holy Child Killiney today and ask for the tour. I hope whoever shows her around mentions the thing in their mission statement about exploring one's talent to realize one's potential. I just think that's, like, *so* an inspiring quote.'

I'm like, 'Sorcha, is it not a bit late in the day to be thinking about the likes of Holy Child Killiney?'

'It's an amazing school, Ross.'

'I know it's an amazing school. But you've got to have your daughter's name down for that place while she's still a focking foetus. Don't get your hopes up is what I'm saying.'

She storts making nonsense-talk to Rihanna-Brogan then. 'Whassa matta wit you, liddew girl? Hmmm? Why are you cwying?'

I'm there, 'Okay, this sounds mad even as I'm saying it to you, but do you think she might be, like, homesick?'

'Homesick?' Sorcha goes. 'But this *is* her home now.'

'Yeah, no, but do you think she possibly misses being on the Northside?'

'How would she know the difference, Ross?'

'I would have thought the difference was obvious. And babies are sensitive – that's a thing you always hear people say. Meaning they pick *up* on shit? It's very much a different vibe over that side of things, isn't it? They've got, I don't know, smog and blah, blah, blah. I'm thinking out loud here, Sorcha.'

She's like, 'No, I'm pretty sure I know what's wrong with her.'

I'm there, 'What?'

She goes, 'Shadden's insisting on feeding her this . . . *baby food*,' dragging the words out of herself, like the girl is feeding her baby shit on a shovel. 'She buys it in Lidl, Ross!'

I'm there, 'A lot of people are shopping in Lidl these days, Babes. Ireland has gone to the dogs, in case you didn't notice.'

'I don't know why Shadden can't purée some avocado. Rihanna-Brogan is eight months old now – she should even be on finger food. Some sweet potato or butternut squash. There's, like, so much more goodness in it – especially if it's organic.'

'Babes, Shadden's from Finglas,' I try to go. 'She wouldn't have heard of sweet potatoes *or* butternut squash.'

That's actually true. I've been in Tesco's in the Clearwater Shopping Centre – every food item that isn't frozen or in a tin is in the Exotic Foods aisle.

Sorcha's there, 'That's why I have to advise her. I'm pretty much Shadden's legal gordian.'

She suddenly remembers something else. 'By the way, I was looking at your search history on the laptop.'

Jesus focking Christ. Is there a more terrifying sentence that a wife can say to her husband? I suddenly sit up.

I'm there, 'I, er . . . I was, em . . .' except, luckily, it has nothing to do with that Pilates porn site that JP's old man tipped me off about. Core Blimey dot com.

She goes, 'You've been watching that Liam Neeson clip a lot, haven't you?'

'Er, yeah, I suppose I have.'

'As in, like, two hundred and something views in the last week.'

'I didn't think it was that many.'

'You're obviously thinking about Fionn.'

'A bit . . . a lot . . . I'm half thinking of just going out there.'

'What, to Uganda? Ross, you couldn't pick Uganda off a map.'

'Jesus, why is everyone so obsessed with maps all of a sudden? Five years ago we were all buying aportments in places we didn't know existed. Can I just say one word to you? Camolin.'

Her old man bought two aportments down there. It's one of the reasons he's focked.

She's there, 'I'm just saying, Ross, it could be dangerous.'

I'm like, 'All I keep thinking is that maybe he's . . .'

'What?'

'You *know* what.'

'Ross, don't think that. Oh my God, *so* don't think it.'

'Well, why would they take the dude hostage and then not look for a ransom? It makes no basic sense.'

Sorcha's like, 'Ross, you're not going to do something stupid, are you?'

'I don't know. I might.'

'Well, I hope not,' she goes, putting her hand on her belly. It's three months and she's already showing – not hugely, but she's got a definite paunch. 'Because I'm kind of counting on you being around to help me raise this second child of ours.'

She broke the news to her old dear last night over the phone. Her old pair are in England on one of those bankruptcy holidays. Her old dear was obviously delighted with the news. But her old man, who's basically never forgiven Sorcha for calling off the divorce and getting back together with me, refused to even come to the phone. In the background, Sorcha heard him go, 'Well, that's that then! She's well and truly done it now!' and then she heard a door slam.

She said it didn't bother her, although when she got up for a hit and miss in the middle of the night, I heard her, like, sobbing through the wall of the *en suite*?

'Are you alright?' I go. 'As in, are you still upset about your old man?'

She's there, 'I'm not upset at all. I just think – oh my God – if my own father can't accept the choices that I've made in my life, whether he agrees with them or not, then I genuinely don't want anything to do with him. And I don't want him having anything to do with our baby. By the way, when are we going to break the news to our daughter?'

'Oh, shit,' I go, 'I forgot we had to tell her. Jesus, I'm not looking forward to that.'

Sorcha laughs. 'Oh my God,' she goes, 'why are we so frightened of her? This is, like, a seven-year-old girl we're talking about.'

And that's when Honor suddenly appears in the room. It's as if by talking about her we've somehow – I'm not sure if this is a word – but conjured her *up*?

Her opening line is, 'Can you shut that stupid baby up? Er, *irritating* much?'

'Honor,' Sorcha goes, 'that is not an appropriate way to speak about a little baby. Or any human being, for that matter.'

'Yeah, whatever. She doesn't belong here. She belongs in Finglas. That's why she's crying.'

See, I think there might definitely be something in that.

'She's crying because she's transitioning,' Sorcha goes, 'from milk to solids.'

Honor's like, 'Er, I don't *give* a shit? She's nothing to me. I just want some peace and quiet in my own home.'

'Of course she's something to you. She's Ronan's daughter. That makes her your niece.'

'Well, she's nothing to you.'

'She's my husband's granddaughter. That makes me . . .'

'That makes you the sad sap who's left holding her while her slapper of a mother goes back to school and pretends she never had a baby.'

She goes to leave the living room, except Sorcha's like, 'Come back here, Honor. Your father and I have something to tell you.'

I'm there, 'Er, I think it can maybe wait. You fire ahead, Honor – we'll tell you when you're in better form.'

Except Honor goes, 'What? What is it?'

Seriously. She's like a cross between a kid from *Glee* and a focking Chucky doll.

Sorcha goes, 'Something very, very wonderful.'

She's overselling it. There's no question of that.

Honor's there, 'This better not be what I think it is.'

She's a smort kid.

Sorcha goes, 'You're going to have a little brother or sister!'

Honor's like, '*Excuse* me?'

Sorcha comes over and stands next to me. All of Honor's hostility is coming her way and she obviously thinks it's something we should share. She lays her hand on my shoulder.

She goes, 'I'm pregnant, Honor!'

I actually hate myself for this, but I try to look like I'm not one hundred percent happy about the news myself.

'You focking idiot!' Honor suddenly roars. This time, it's directed at me.

Sorcha's like, 'Honor!'

'Pregnant!' she goes. 'How could you have been so stupid?'

Sorcha's there, 'Honor, it wasn't a complete accident. We're actually looking forward to it.'

'Whoa, whoa, whoa – don't tell me you're thinking of keeping it?'

Sorcha actually laughs. 'Well, of course I'm keeping it! Oh my God, what kind of question is that? Honor, it's a little life! I honestly thought you'd be delighted. I think you're going to make an amazing older sister.'

Honor's like, 'We've already got that baby,' meaning obviously Shadden's. 'We don't have room for another one.'

Sorcha's there, 'Honor, don't be silly. There's nothing *but* room in this house!'

'Hey, Honor,' I hear myself suddenly go, 'why don't I bring you to Dundrum right now and buy you loads of different shit that you want?'

She just, like, *glowers* at me?

'A baby,' she goes to me. 'At *your* age?' 'and then she storms out of the living room and back upstairs to her room.

Me and Sorcha just, like, stare at each other and neither of us says anything for a good ten seconds. Then I go, 'I don't know about you, but I think that could have gone a hell of a lot worse than it actually did.'

JP asks me how Sorcha is and I think, fock it, I might as well tell him.

She had this plan – once Honor, Ronan, Shadden and her old pair knew – that she was going to announce it on Facebook with a photograph of, like, a soother and then, underneath, the words, 'Coming in December 2012.'

Someone else did it. Michelle Monaghan, or possibly Kate Winslet.

Someone.

'Yeah, no, pregnant,' I go.

JP's like, 'Whoa!' and he genuinely means it. 'That's great news!'

Christian's there, 'Fair focks, Ross. Fair focks.'

And even Oisinn goes, 'Congratulations, Dude,' in a quiet voice and I just nod, like I don't a give a shit one way or the other what he thinks.

This is in, like, the Orangerie Bor, by the way, in the Radisson St Helen's. We're meeting Fionn's old pair and this supposed bird of his – Jenny whatever-the-fock.

'I'm just thinking,' JP goes, 'our kids are all going to be so close in age! Three boys is what I'm predicting. They'll be senior cup teammates – and the three of us will be watching from the sideline, like three old farts!'

I laugh then, because it's, like, an incredible thought, and I end up getting a bit carried away, because I clap my two hands together – totally forgetting the reason we're here – and I go, 'Let's get a bottle of Champagne – a big fock-off one, like it's 2004 again!'

Then I see Christian's face just fall, then JP's, then Oisinn's, and without even needing to turn around, I know that Fionn's old pair are standing immediately behind me.

'Celebrating something?' *he* goes – as in, like, Ewan.

Like I said, they *used* to be fans?

'Er, no,' I go, 'it was just a joke,' because there's no point in expecting them to be happy for me, especially when they've lost *their* son. Instead, I go, 'How's the form, Ewan? Andrea?' and I go to give *her* a hug, except her body just stiffens.

She goes, 'How do you *think* we are?'

I'm not getting a good vibe from them, especially *her*.

This Chinese bird, dressed in black, arrives over to where we're standing and I go, 'Can we get four pints of Heineken and whatever these two are having?'

Christian goes, 'Ross, I'm not really sure this is a drinking occasion.'

I'm like, 'Don't listen to him. He'll have a focking Heineken like the rest of us. And, like I said, whatever these two want – you're still a Dewar's man, aren't you, Ewan?'

The Chinese bird just stares at me like I'm talking in a foreign language. Which I possibly am to her. Some of them don't have great English.

Of course, I'm not ready for what ends up happening next.

'This is Jenny,' Andrea goes. 'Fionn's girlfriend.'

Can I just say, in my defence, that there was no mention of her being Chinese.

Of course, I end up falling to pieces. I'm there going, 'Oh . . . Er . . . Yeah, no . . . Er . . . I'm sorry! I thought you actually worked here!' and I can tell that the goys are really feeling for me. It could have been any one of us who made the mistake. I just happened to be the one offering to get the focking drinks in. People person and blah, blah, blah.

'Whoy would yoy thunk oy worked here?' Jenny goes, clearly not accepting my apology. 'What, because oy'm Oysian?'

She might be Asian, but she's got, like, an Australian accent. It turns out that she was born and raised in New Zealand.

I'm there, 'It was portly that, Jenny, and portly because you're wearing black.'

'So there's no royson whoy someone of Oysian descint should boy in a bar excipt to serve yoy Hoynikin, is that ut?'

Jesus focking Christ, I think to myself. Fionn really knows how to pick them.

'Like I said,' I go, trying to still sound reasonable, 'it was also the black shirt and trousers. A lot of lounge girls wear that kind of clobber and that's no offence to you.'

'What are yoy, some koynd of royshulust?'

'Okay, how exactly is that racialist?'

'Because yoy presoyme thut ivvery Choynoyse person yoy moyt is a waiter or a waitruss.'

'All I'm saying is that that's the way it usually is. And there's a lot of them in petrol stations as well.'

JP goes, 'Dude, you probably should stop talking now.'

Jenny just keeps staring at me. 'Oy'm sorry, Ewan. Sorry, Andrea. Whoy is thus idiut?'

'Yes, this is Ross,' Andrea goes.

And Jenny's like, 'Ohhh!' and then she just laughs, except in a really, like, bitter way, as if everything suddenly makes sense to her. Someone's obviously filled her in on a bit of my back story – possibly Fionn, possibly his old pair or possibly his sister Eleanor, who – you probably know – I had one or two scenes with when she was on a break from David, her then fiancé and now husband, the prick with ears.

Ewan makes the introductions. 'These are Fionn's friends,' he goes. 'Christian, JP and Oisinn,' and he ends up totally skipping me, although obviously we've already established who I am. 'I promised them that I'd keep them in the loop. I thought you might tell them what you told us last night.'

Andrea's like, 'Well, let's go and sit down first,' and that's exactly what we do. The seven of us end up sitting around this low table and Jenny takes a deep breath and then – in between giving me filthy looks – fills us in on the entire story of what actually happened.

'Fionn was toyching in a luttle vullage called Keenafwa, not far from Mbale, in Eastern Uganda,' she goes. 'We *boyth* were? It was an unbeloyvable ployce. I mean, the poyple there were amoyzing. You've niver seen smoyles loyk the smoyles on the foyces of the lycal kuds. They have nothung and yit you'd niver thunk it to *look* ut thum?'

I remember Sorcha saying something very similar the time she missed the exit for the Liffey Valley Shopping Centre and ended up in Lucan. Jenny goes, 'There's not a lot *in* Keenafwa? We taught the kiddies in, loyk, Nissen huts. Prefabs, moyd of, loyk, currugoyted *oyen*? And then when classes were, loyk, funushed, we worked on building the school. Fionn became pretty hendy wuth a trowel!'

We all laugh. I don't know why. Maybe it's the idea of someone we went to school with doing manual labour.

'It was haahd work,' she goes. 'Long doys. But, loyk, viry satisfoy-ing? Fionn especially loyked the fict that he was working in the soym area as an old proyst he used to knoy.'

'Father Fehily,' JP instantly goes. 'He coached us in rugby and, well, you could say life.'

She's there, 'Father Fehily – that was ut. Fionn loved the fact that a lot of poyple in Mbale remembered hum. On his doys off, he used to goy into the taahn and talk to the older poyple abaaht hum. He'd lusten to their stories. He faahnd a bar and on the wall there was a poyce of wood with something on ut that thus proyst used to soy – something about coal, oy thunk.'

'What else is a diamond,' Christian goes, 'but a piece of coal that did well under pressure?'

'That was ut. The man who oyned thus bar had it engroyved on a poyce of wood. Anyway,' she goes, becoming suddenly serious, 'Fionn was in Mbale the doy before he was toyken. He got beck loyte. He was toyred. Went to bid. The nixt morning, he was up early for school. Abaaht quarter-to-oyt, we heard a lorry approyching. Looked aaht and, royt enough, it was a flatbid truck – a Ford something or other. I don't knoy a lot abaaht trucks. There were sux of thum. Foyve min and a woman. Fionn saw the guns and he knoy straight away that thus was baahd. He told moy to run. He told moy to go aaht the beck door and to run as fast as oy could and doyn't look beck. But there wasn't toym. They suddenly burst in. Fionn stood in front of moy. He thought they were going to, you knoy . . .'

She suddenly storts crying. Andrea puts, like, a consoling *orm* around her?

'He thought thoy were there for *moy*?' she continues on then. 'But they came for hum. The woman – thus big, fet butch – she hut hum with the butt of her royfle. Brike his glawsus and oy'd soy probably his noyse as will. God, there was blood ivveryweer . . .'

I feel my fists suddenly tighten. I haven't wanted to deck someone so much since Fergus McFadden blanked me in Nando's in Dundrum two Valentine's Days ago.

'They put, loyk, a bag over his hid. Thin they toyed hum up. Hog-toyed, they call ut. Toyed his wrusts to his inkles and they carried hum off loyk . . . loyk a poyce of moyt.'

The tears stort really coming now and she ends up having to take a break from the story to get her shit together and mop up her face, while Andrea tells her how bascially *brave* she is? That's when a lounge girl suddenly appears and asks us if we want to order drinks. And of course, the most instantly obvious thing about the girl is that she's Chinese. And that she's also, like, dressed in black.

No one else seems to cop it, though. I catch Christian's eye and I roll *my* eyes in her direction, as if to say, 'Er, who's a racist now?' except he just gives his head a subtle little shake, as if to say, 'Don't go there, Rossmeister.' I can't be told, though. You might as well be reading *Ulysses* to a focking rabbit as talking to me sometimes. I end up having to try to draw everyone's attention to her.

'So,' I go, 'whereabouts in China are you from?' The girl – this totally focking random bird – is like, 'Xinjiang Province,' and I pull a pleasantly surprised face, as if it means something to me, which it obviously doesn't.

I'm probably one of Ireland's fifty stupidest people, bear in mind.

I'm there, 'God, there's a lot of you over here, isn't there? Especially, like, working in pubs and restaurants and shit. I'm just making that observation in a definitely non-racist way.'

Ewan interrupts my flow. 'Can I get a glass of 7-Up?' he goes. Andrea says she'll have a Diet one and so does Jenny, then Christian, JP and Oisinn all let me down by ordering Cokes. I suddenly realize I'm going to look like a total dipso if I'm the only one drinking at, like, half-twelve on a Sunday afternoon.

I think, fock it, and I order a pint of Hydrogen anyway.

'Has there been any word at all,' JP goes, 'from whoever took him?'

It's a good question. I probably would have eventually asked it.

'Noy, nathung,' Jenny goes. Andrea and Ewan both take a deep breath at the exact same time. There's no words to describe what they must be going through. The Chinese lounge girl arrives back with the drinks on a tray. As she puts my pint in front of me, I stort making conversation with her again, like the focking idiot that I am.

'So is there many of your crew over?' I go. 'As in, many of you from home? In other words, China.'

And that's when Jenny practically explodes. 'Will yoy stop talking about facking Choyna?' she goes.

I'm straight away thinking, *focking* China? Er, who's the racist now?

'Whoa,' I go, 'I'm only making conversation with the girl. The land of the billion welcomes – blah, blah, blah.'

'Does *hoy* have to *boy* here?' Jenny tries to go. She doesn't even, like, *look* at me when she says this? 'Fionn told moy some prutty turrible thungs abaaht hum and, frinkly, hoy's not the koynd of person oy want to spind moy toym araahnd.'

That hurts. That actually hurts.

Ewan goes, 'Well, he *is* Fionn's friend.'

But Andrea's on it like vomit.

She's there, '*Is* he, though, Ewan? Is he? Have you forgotten what happened on Fionn's wedding day?'

'Of course I haven't forgotten.'

'Have you forgotten what he did to my laptop computer?'

I took a shit in it, to cut a long story short – it's a UCD thing and it's callled a Waffle Press – although, in my defence, at the time, I thought it was someone else's computer.

She goes, 'I mean, *he's* the reason our son went to Africa in the first place.'

I'm wondering has everyone come to that same conclusion. JP decides to play the role of peacemaker. He's good like that.

'Ross,' he goes, 'maybe you should go.'

I'm like, 'Fock you, J Town. I'm only trying to make the point that I'm not a racist. And I don't appreciate having to constantly defend myself, especially when Fionn was practically like a brother to me,' and then I end up shouting it. 'A practically brother!'

The entire Orangerie Bor looks over. There's people there with their kids trying to enjoy a quiet Sunday lunch.

It's Christian then who goes, 'Ross, JP's right. Look, I'll give you a ring later and tell you the plan.'

I look around. Not one person at the table wants me there. So I just go, 'Fine,' and I stand up.

'Facking royshulust,' Jenny – under her breath – goes.

I'm like, 'I'm actually *not* a racialist?' and I pick up my pint and I storm out of there without even a backwards look.

Dordeen rings me while I'm doing sit-ups – Dordeen, as in Shadden's old dear.

It comes up as, like, a private number and I make the mistake of answering it – in a chirpy voice as well.

'Apologies for the heavy breathing,' I go. 'I was just exercising The Six.'

'Ine not fooken happy,' is her opening line – no hello, no how are you, nothing. She doesn't even tell me who it is ringing.

Unfortunately, I'd recognize that gravelly, Moore Street, cotton-sports-socks-tree-peers-for-your-yooro voice of hers in a focking hurricane.

I go, 'What are you not happy about, Dordeen?' like I actually *give* a fock?

'*We're* not happy' she goes. 'Me and Shadden's daddy. Ine just arthur been talking to him in the prison.'

I'm waiting for her to say something else, except she doesn't, so I go, 'I'm going to need some more information, Dordeen. You can't just tell me you're not happy and expect me to do something about it. I'm not the Deportment of Social Welfare.'

You have to go in hord on fockers like these. They think better of you for it.

'We're not happy,' she goes, 'wit Shadden going back to skewill.'

Seriously, how the fock did I end up with a family like the Tuites as my basically in-laws?

I'm there, 'You're not happy with, what, your daughter receiving an education? Wanting something from life other than selling focking fireworks from the inside of her jacket on Henry Street?'

She goes, 'She alretty has a job – as a mutter. And a mutter belongs wit her choyult.'

'Her *choyult* will be looked after.'

'That's reet – by Surrogate.'

'Her name is Sorcha and you know exacty how to pronounce it.'

'She's throying to take over.'

'She's trying to help out.'

'She's interfeerdon. And she's throying to send her to that skewill.'

'What are you talking about?'

'The Hoatley Choyult of fooken Kulliney.'

'It's a good school.'

'What, because it's posh?'

'Well, I'm talking more in terms of the Leaving Cert points table.'

'We're alretty sthruggling to wonderstand a woord she's saying.

She went to see her daddy in the chail last week and he had to keep aston her to repeat hoorself.'

'For fock's sake, she's only been living here two weeks.'

'That's alt it takes. We can alretty heerd it in her accent – even her brutters are saying it. We don't want Shadden forgetting where she kem from.'

She won't. Ten years in focking therapy couldn't erase those memories.

'Well, unfortuantely for you,' I go, 'we're Shadden and Ronan's basically legal gordians, so you don't actually *get* a say?'

'Ine still Shadden's mutter. And Shadden's still Rihadda-Burrogan's mutter, not that bleaten woyfe of yooers.'

'Dordeen,' I go, 'I hope this doesn't come across as rude, but if I wanted to spend my evening listening to focking scumbags shouting their mouths off, I'd stick on Ronan's *Love/Hate* box set.'

And then I hang up.

Sorcha says that breakfast is going to be eggs Benedict with New Orleans accents. Except I don't hear her. I'm staring across the kitchen table at her sister – whatever she's called – caught in the tractor beam of her Mahatmas, which I can see down the front of her nightdress. She's making sure I get a good eyeful as well, stretching first for the sourdough toast, then for the coffee pot, then for the baked grapefruit.

She smiles at me – it's like, a proper, *seductive* one? – and I smile back, probably like a focking simpleton.

'Oh my God, Ross,' she suddenly goes. 'What way are you staring at me?'

Sorcha, who's standing at the cooker, suddenly looks over.

I'm like, 'I wasn't – as in, I wasn't staring at you in any *specific* way?'

'Can you please stop looking down the front of my nightdress,' she goes. 'It's *actually* making me uncomfortable?'

Sorcha walks over to the table and puts my breakfast down in front of me with a bit of a thud. I'm pretty sure I'm not imaginging the thud.

'If you come down in the mornings dressed like that,' Sorcha goes, 'what do you think people are going to be staring at? The fock-ing Simplex crossword in the *Times*?'

The sister goes, 'I'm entitled to wear whatever I want without being objectified by your husband.'

'Go upstairs and put some clothes on.'

'Excuse me?'

'You heard me. You have work this morning, don't you?'

She works in Aldi, the one in the Beacon South Quarter.

'No, I don't,' she goes. 'I'm quitting.'

Sorcha's like, 'Do you have another job to go to?'

'Er, no – there's a *recession* on?'

'Exactly. That's why you're not quitting that job. As long as you're living under this roof, you're going to contribute. And as long as you're eating breakfast at this table, you're going to wear daytime clothes. There are small people living in this house now. They shouldn't have to sit there looking at . . . *those*!'

She means Biggie and Tupak.

The sister stands up, rolls her eyes and goes, 'Yeah, you're just jealous,' and she walks across the kitchen, then stands in the door-way for a few seconds, trying to catch my eye, then mouthing the words, 'Come upstairs,' to me.

I shake my head – Jesus, much as I'd love to – then I go back to my breakfast and she eventually focks off up to her bedroom, crushed, to put her Aldi skirt and blouse on.

'Oh my God,' Sorcha goes, 'that girl has got *such* an attitude problem.'

I'm like, 'Massive. Absolutely massive.'

'There's, like, no way she's living here without contributing, Ross.'

'Er, yeah, no, whatever.'

All of a sudden, Ronan and Shadden arrive down with Rihanna-B and Sorcha's face lights up. Mine possibly does as well.

Ronan's like, 'Alreet, Rosser?'

I'm there, 'Hey, Ro. And how's my beautiful granddaughter this morning?'

'Not a bodder on her now,' Shadden goes. 'But she's arthur been awake half the night again.'

Sorcha's going to say something. I can tell by her boat race.

'Shadden,' she goes, 'do you think it could be that she's hungry?'

Shadden's like, 'Begga peerton?' already on the big-time defensive.

I've always gotten on very well with Shadden. So has Sorcha. But Northsiders are like any wild animal. They're lovely right up until the moment they suddenly focking turn on you.

'I'm just saying,' Sorcha goes, 'I know she's having difficulty transitioning to solid food. Maybe those jars of baby food don't suit her.'

Shadden's like, 'There's nuttin wrong wit baby food.'

I get the sudden impression that her old dear has been in her ear.

'I'm not saying there's anything wrong with it,' Sorcha goes. 'I'm just saying that Rihanna-Brogan clearly doesn't like it. You might even try her on finger food. Some avocado or some mango.'

Shadden's like, 'Mango?'

'It's a fruit. You can buy them in most supermorkets here. At her age, she really should be self-feeding, Shadden.'

Again, Shadden takes definite umbrage. 'Soddy,' she goes, 'who do you tink you eer telling me what she should and shoultunt be eating?'

I'm thinking, Dordeen, you total focking shit-stirrer.

'I'm not telling you,' Sorcha goes. 'I'm just advising you.'

Shadden's like, 'Are you callin me a bad mudder?'

Ronan has to step in then. He goes, 'No one's calling addyone athin, Shadden. Alls the geerl is sayin is that *she's* rayized a babby. She's read all the bukes. Ine presuming you've read all the bukes, Sudeka.'

Sorcha's like, 'I have. And – oh my God – I wasn't saying you were a bad mother, Shadden.'

'There y'are, Shadden. She's oately offering you the bedefit of her expeerdience.'

Ronan manages to talk her down. For now.

'Let's all have some breakfast,' Sorcha goes, returning to the cooker. 'It's eggs Benedict with a New Orleans twist.'

Shadden looks at her like she's just been told to eat her grandmother's eye snot. 'I doatunt reedy eat much in the morden,' she goes. 'Usually it's just poddidge.'

Now it's Sorcha's turn to take offence. She's like, 'Excuse me?'

'Poddidge.'

'I think she's trying to say porridge,' I go. 'You *are* saying porridge, aren't you?'

Shadden's like, 'Yeah.'

I'm there, 'As in porridge that, like, prisoners eat?' Which is a bit insensitive of me, considering her old man's in the Joy.

She's like, 'It's not *joost* prisoners eerrit.'

'All we're saying is that it's a bit random,' Sorcha goes. 'I don't think we even *own* any?'

Ronan's like, 'You do. *We* bought some. It's in the secunt press theer.'

The second *press*. Jesus. Them living here is turning out to be a major culture shock for everyone.

Ronan pulls out this bag of Flahavan's, literally, porridge oats, measures some into a bowl, lashes some water in on top of it and then – I'm not making this up – puts it into the microwave.

Sorcha's feelings are hurt, but she tries not to show it.

'Oh my God,' she goes, 'how did you get on yesterday?' meaning down at Holy Child.

'I ditn't luff it,' Shadden goes. 'And thee dirrint want me in addyhow.'

Sorcha is obviously appalled by both of these pieces of news. She goes, 'What do you mean they didn't want you?'

'Thee said it was far too late to enrodle. Thee said they're full. It's grant. Ine arthur sayin to you I dirrint like it in addhow.'

Dordeen's been in her ear alright.

'Why,' Sorcha goes, 'what was wrong with it?'

Shadden's there, 'It's a bit of a snoppy skewill.'

'It's hordly a snobby school, Shadden. Did you know they have an African Immersion Programme?'

'Well, it doesn't mathor now. Thee said they're full.'

'I could make representations on your behalf,' Sorcha goes, trying to be nice, but at the same time maybe pushing it a bit. 'I became – oh my God – really good friends with a lot of girls from there when I did the Model United Nations and I used to be in the same book club as a woman who's on the board of management.'

That's when Shadden all of a sudden loses it. 'I doatunt want to go to that skewill,' she basically roars at Sorcha – eyes popping, teeth showing, the whole bit. 'Are you bleaten deaf or sometin?'

I'm like, 'Whoooaaahhh!'

And Sorcha's there, 'Oh! My God!'

'Mon,' Ronan goes, taking Rihanna-Brogan out of Shadden's hands and giving her to me, 'we'll leave the breakfast. We've a few utter skewills to look at tis morden,' and he basically bundles her out of the kitchen.

Shadden goes, 'Ine joost tired of her interfeerdon alt the toyum.'

And as he's going out the door, he turns around and mouths the words, 'Ine soddy,' to Sorcha.

Sorcha's left standing there in, like, total shock. Shadden and Ronan have only been living with us for a few weeks and this is the first time that Shadden's thrown a pissy fit.

And as one stroppy child leaves the room, another one enters.

Honor walks in – as usual, dragging her feet across the floor. She gives Rihanna-Brogan a filthy look – this is an eight-month-old baby we're talking about – then her little nose twitches, to try to work out what's cooking and whether it's worth eating.

Sorcha goes, 'It's eggs Benedict with New Orleans accents,' and, when Honor doesn't respond, Sorcha says it again. 'It's eggs Benedict, Honor, with New Orleans accents.'

Honor turns to me and goes, 'Can you tell that focking woman who you somehow managed to get pregnant that I'm not talking to her at the moment out of pure disgust?' And then she walks out of the room.

I'm thinking, this is some home that we're about to bring a new baby into.

'Well,' he goes, 'what do you think of James Reilly's current travails?' This is before I'm even in the door. 'I've just been on the phone to your godfather, in his current domicile of Florida, filling him in on what's been happening. I said, "Ross will have a take on this, Hennessy. Something suitably satiric, no doubt. You see if he doesn't!"'

I just, like, stare at him – I literally don't even open my mouth – but suddenly for, like, no reason at all, he bursts out laughing.

'You don't even *need* to say anything!' he goes. 'You've done it with a look! I'm going to ring Hennessy back this minute! Your best one yet! Oh, where would you and I be, Ross, if we didn't have politics in our lives?'

I just go, 'I need money.'

And he's like, 'Well, of course you do!' like there's no other reason I'd show up on his doorstep at ten-to-twelve on a weekday morning. 'First things first. Let's go and see what's in the safe, shall we?'

I follow him down to the study. Although that's not strictly true. I actually walk a couple of steps ahead of him. I'm obviously desperate for the shecks.

He bends down to key the code into the safe. He goes, 'How much are you looking for?'

'That all depends. How much is in there?'

'Something in the area of forty thousand euros, I think.'

'That'll do. For now.'

He takes it out and hands it to me, no questions asked – four wads of presumably ten Ks each.

'We're just finding it very expensive,' I go, for some reason feeling the need to explain it to him, 'running a big gaff, heating it, electricity, blah, blah, blah.'

'Oh, they're bloody well money-pits, those big houses.'

'Plus we've got Ro and Shadden living with us now, with little Rihanna-Brogan. And Sorcha's sister. Still haven't caught her name.'

'Oh, it's *all* expense – there's no doubt about that.'

'Plus, well, I might as well tell you, because a good few people already know – Sorcha's pregnant. With another baby.'

His mouth flops open. You'd nearly feel like throwing a live salmon into it.

'I'm actually pleased about it,' I go. 'I mean, it's definitely mine.'

I don't know why I decide to add that bit.

'Well, of course it's yours!' he goes. 'Who else's would it be? Oh, this is wonderful news! This is the best bloody well news that's come along in a long, long time!' and then he grabs me in, like, a clinch and I think, fock it, just let him be happy, and I pat him on the back a couple of times and when he pulls away from me I notice that he's got, like, tears in his eyes.

'You've made an old man very, very happy,' he goes. And then he storts shouting, 'Helen! Helen!'

She comes running – obviously thinks there's something wrong. She comes into the study. She cops me with the forty Ks in my hand. It's the first thing her eyes go to. She must think I'm a total focking leech. I stuff the bundles into my inside pocket.

'Ross has some wonderful news,' *he* goes. 'Do you remember I thought it odd, when they were here for dinner last weekend? I offered Sorcha one of your famous lychee bellinis and she responded like she'd been stung by a bloody well bee!'

'She's pregnant,' I go.

Helen's face lights up. 'Ross,' she goes, 'that's wonderful!' and she gives me the most amazing, genuine hug.

She's a great person. Way too good for him.

He goes, 'A little brother or sister for Honor! I'd imagine she's pleased.'

'Pleased wouldn't be the word I'd use. She's not talking to Sorcha and she's barely talking to me. She asked me this morning if I'd never heard of contraception. And then she said hashtag something – it might have been hashtag, too focking dumb to breed. Something like that.'

Helen and the old man listen to this with, like, shocked faces.

'Well,' the old man goes, 'I'm sure she'll come around. Especially when the baby's born.'

I'm like, 'I hope so.'

'Maybe don't leave the two of them together unsupervised, though.'

'I won't.'

'Not for a few years. You read of terrible cases. Do you know something,' he then goes, 'I think we've lived this day long enough without alcohol! What say we repair to the Four Seasons to celebrate your news with a glass or two of Veuve Clicquot?'

Of course, I don't need to be asked twice. I don't even need to be asked once.

'You'll have to pay,' I go, leading the way to the door, 'because I'm focking skint.'

He's there, 'But I've just given you forty thousand euros!'

I don't bother my hole even responding. It's beneath me.

Sorcha says she thinks she's going to have a hypnobirth this time, using visualization exercises and breathing techniques and possibly even essential oils rather than actual drugs to deal with the pain.

We're at the hospital for our ultrasound. Sorcha was, like, three months gone last week and today we're going to see our actual baby. I'm, like, excited *and* kacking it?

Honor, by the way, is sitting on the other side of the waiting room – she refuses point-blank to sit next to us – and she's turning the pages of an old *RSVP*, going, 'Sap . . . Sap . . . Sap . . . Desperate bitch . . . Desperate bitch . . .' and the bird on reception is looking at me as if to say, ' "You actually let your daughter talk that way?" '

I'm thinking, yeah, no, you try correcting her.

The nurse slash doctor slash whatever her actual qualification is comes out then, looks at her clipboard and goes, 'Sorcha O'Carroll-Kelly?' and we both stand up.

Sorcha makes the mistake of going, 'Honor, are you coming in with us?'

And Honor – this is unbelievable, even for her – goes, 'Er, *you're* the one who got knocked up. Don't try to involve me in your mess. And, hashtag, the world doesn't revolve around you and your foetus.'

Not surprisingly, there ends up being more than a few open mouths in the waiting room. She continues just flicking through the magazine, not even looking up.

'Honor,' Sorcha goes, 'you might feel differently when you see your little brother or sister on the screen.'

Honor's there, 'Yeah, I seriously doubt it.'

Sorcha just shrugs. There's nothing we can do about this kid, except count the days until she hopefully emigrates like the rest of her generation and then pray that the next kid turns out to be less of a bitch – or a bastard, if it's a boy.

'Okay,' Sorcha goes, 'we'll be out in a few minutes.'

The receptionist looks at us, her face all full of concern. She goes, 'You're not leaving her here, are you?'

And before either of us can answer her, Honor goes, 'Oh my God, what do you think I'm going to do to you? Do you think I'd waste my time and energy on you, you focking raddled old spinster. Hashtag, sad bitch. Hashtag, bag lady with a job. Hashtag, you'll die one day and no one will find your body for months.'

Me and Sorcha don't say anything. It's easier just to pretend nothing happened. We just walk into the little examination room and close the door behind us.

The nurse slash doctor – she's not *that* unlike Lucy Mecklenburgh – tells Sorcha to lie down on the examination table and pull up her top, which is what Sorcha then does. The bird – I'll just call her a bird, because I don't know what her actual job description is – puts this jelly stuff on Sorcha's stomach. Then she gets this, like, miniature paint-roller thing – I'm simplifying a lot of the terms here – and she rolls it back and forth over Sorcha's belly and, as she does so, she looks at this little TV screen to her left, which is turned away from me and Sorcha.

She doesn't say anything for a good, like, thirty seconds, to the point that Sorcha ends up going, 'Is everything okay? I'm not loving your silence?'

The bird goes, 'Em . . .'

And of course that sets me off then. I'm like, 'What's going on? What the fock is going on?'

The bird puts down the roller and goes, 'I just need to go and get a colleague,' and she leaves us – in the total focking dark, by the way.

Sorcha's suddenly having, like, palpitations.

'Oh my God, Ross,' she goes, squeezing my hand so tight that she's practically breaking my fingers, 'what's wrong with my baby? What's wrong with my baby?'

I'm there, 'It's nothing. I'm sure it's nothing,' even though I'm no more sure that our baby is okay than Sorcha is sure that Fionn is still alive.

A minute, maybe two, later the bird comes back with another bird, who I straight away suspect outranks her.

'What's going on?' Sorcha goes. 'Is there a problem with my baby?'

The bird gives her the roller treatment again and the more senior bird – who's nothing much to look at – goes, 'Your *babies*.'

We're both like, 'What?' at the exact same time.

'And there's nothing to worry about,' she goes, looking at the screen. 'They're doing great.'

Sorcha looks at me, her mouth slung open.

'Are you saying it's twins?' she goes.

And the bird turns the screen around to us and goes, 'No. I'm saying it's triplets.'

2. The Problem with Ezra Dumpling

If it's three girls, Sorcha says, she was thinking of either Ovesca, Marianie and Anahita; Chartreuse, Bahmanshir and Isabella, obviously after Isabella Thorpe; Maggia, Kilda and Aife with no o; or Senua, Giona and Anais with an umlaut over the i.

'Or maybe it should go over the A,' she goes, keying it into her phone when she pulls up at the next red light. 'Yeah, no, it looks more, I don't know, *symmetrical?*'

This is while we're on the way home from the hospital, by the way – we're talking literally forty minutes after we got the news and she already has the names possibly picked.

Personally, I'm still in, like, shock.

'If it's three boys,' I go, 'I was thinking either Brian, Jamie and Isa; Gordon, Jonathan and Leo; or even Isaac, Cian and Luke.'

Sorcha goes, 'Yeah, you can forget about that, Ross.'

'What?'

'We are not naming our children after random rugby players.'

'They're hordly random rugby players, Sorcha. I'd consider them very much personal friends.'

Honor suddenly looks up from her iPhone in the back. 'Yeah, right,' she goes. 'They don't even know who the fock you are.'

'Honor,' Sorcha goes, 'nice little girls do not use that word. And it's not the example I want you to set your little brothers or sisters when they arrive.'

I'm there, 'And get your focking facts right as well. They all know who I am. Jesus, I text Johnny on the morning of every big game. "Eat nerves, shit results." It's become a major port of his build-up.'

She has no answer to that. Instead, she goes, 'I've just been reading about a girl online who divorced her mother and father on the grounds that they were too stupid to properly parent her.'

The light turns green and off we go again.

'How are you going to feed us all?' she goes. 'Have you even thought about that yet?'

Sorcha's there, 'Don't worry, Honor. I don't expect you'll go hungry.'

And Honor's like, 'Do you think I'd believe a word that came out of your mouth? You're the one who's always going on about the planet being overpopulated. Now you're about to add three *more* people to the world?'

Three more people. When she says it like that, it puts the genuine shits up me.

Sorcha's like, 'Your father and I didn't choose to have triplets. That's just the way that nature has determined it.'

'Hashtag, liar,' Honor goes. 'Hashtag, phony. Hashtag, hypocrite.'

'I'm sure you'll feel differently when they arrive into the world.'

'Er, I'm not going to be *around*?'

'What do you mean, you're not going to be around?'

'I'm going to England to live with my Grandma and Granddad Lalor.'

That's definitely not going to happen. They focking hate her.

Sorcha's like, 'You're not going to England.'

Honor goes, 'I hate being part of this family.'

And I think, well, at least she's back talking to her mother again – that's definite progress.

'Anyway' she goes, 'I'm sure I'll be taken into care when you're eventually forced to admit that you can't cope. You'll probably have a nervous breakdown.'

Sorcha's like, 'Honor, don't even joke about things like that.'

'And I hope you'll be proud of yourselves when that day comes. The two of you. Dumb and focking Dumber.'

We pull up outside the gaff and get out of the cor. I open the front door and Honor pushes past me, into the hall and straight up the stairs to her room. Sorcha is bursting for a hit and miss – I remember that from the last time she was pregnant as well – and she heads for the toilet under the stairs, running with her two knees locked together.

I tip down to the kitchen and I make a pot of coffee, the whole time thinking about what Honor said. Three more mouths to feed. Three more human beings counting on me. The responsibility of that. And at the same time I know I haven't even storted to get my head around it.

My phone all of a sudden rings and it ends up being JP. I answer it, roysh, wondering at first whether Shoshanna has dropped, because she's actually gone a few days over her due date now.

But it's not that at all.

'Jenny had a call!' is his opening line.

He actually shouts it.

I'm like, 'What are you talking about?'

He's there, 'I'm saying Fionn rang her! He's alive, Ross!'

'What?' I go – and at the same time I laugh. 'Are you saying he's been released?'

He's there, 'No, they still have him. But they let him ring Jenny.'

'Jesus Christ,' I go. 'Is he okay?'

'He said he was fine. I mean, he wasn't allowed to tell her anything, you know, about his circumstances.'

'But he's *alive* – like you said!'

'Yeah, no, he's alive – she said it was definitely him . . . Ross, they want five million dollars for him.'

'Five million dollars? Five *million*? Dude, I'm not being a prick, but he's not worth that – as in, no one's going to pay that much for him.'

'Well, they want Jenny to put pressure on that charity they were working for to pay it. Uganda School Build – they're a South African crowd.'

'And will they?'

'No.'

'Why the fock not? I'm sure they're good for it.'

'They say if they pay one ransom, it'll make all of their employees a target for abduction. This is what Jenny's saying.'

'Fockers.'

'They do have a point, Ross.'

'Fockers at the same time. But at least he's alive. That's definitely a plus point, right?'

'Big time.'

'And did he ask for us at all, did Jenny mention?'

'I don't think he had time. They didn't have long to talk.'

'So he didn't tell us not to worry, it wasn't any of our fault that he went out there in the first place – blah, blah, blah?'

'Like I said, it was only about thirty seconds. He did say he was glad she was in Ireland – he said he was happy that she had good people around her.'

'Good people. That's a reference to us. That's a definite reference to us.'

'Anyway,' he goes, 'I'll let you know if I hear anything else.'

I hang up and I just, like, clench my fist. It's good news. We know he's not dead. And that's a hell of a lot more than we knew this morning.

The next thing I hear is screaming coming from the direction of the downstairs toilet. It's, like, Sorcha and she's going – like I said – 'Aaarrrggghhh!!! Aaarrrggghhh!!! Aaarrrggghhh!!!'

My first instinct – as you'd expect – is that it has something to do with the babies. I run out into the hallway just in time to see her literally fall through the door with her knickers around her knees, going, 'Oh my God! Oh my God! Oh my God!' we're talking proper, like, full-on *hysterical* here?

She falls into my orms. I'm holding her and I'm going, 'Sorcha, what the fock? What's wrong? Are you bleeding?'

But the babies are actually fine. She goes, 'It was a rat, Ross! A horrible rat!'

I'm there, 'A rat? Where? What are you talking about?'

'It was in the toilet!'

'*In* the toilet? We're talking *in* the actual bowl?'

She storts, like, sobbing then. 'I felt its whiskers touch my . . . Oh my God, Ross, it was horrible.'

'Sorry, Babes, I'm just trying to pull all the facts together here. You're saying that you were sitting on the toilet . . .'

'Yes.'

'Having a hit and miss . . .'

'Yes.'

'And you, what, *heard* something?'

'Heard it *and* saw it. And it wasn't something, Ross. It was a rat. There was, like, a splashing sound and I felt something tickle me . . . *down there*. I opened my legs and there it was, coming out of the water – oh my God, it was horrible – clawing at the porcelain, trying to get out.'

Jesus Christ. I think that might be the most disgusting thing I've ever heard.

I'm there, 'How the fock did a rat get in our toilet?'

She goes, 'He must have, I don't know, swum up the pipe or something. He was huge, Ross! And – oh my God – *so* disgusting!'

'So did he go back down the toilet?'

'No, he jumped out and ran into that hole in the wall behind the sink – the one I've asked you three times to fill.'

I sort of, like, peer around the door into the little bathroom. There's no evidence of a rat ever being there, aport from a bit of water on the floor and that could have been from Sorcha standing up mid-piss.

'Ross,' she goes, 'I know it's hord to believe, but a rat swam up into our toilet.'

But before I get a chance to say anything, Honor leans over the bannister and goes, 'Oh my God – she's already losing it! Hillair!'

'Tree?' Ronan goes.

I nod.

He's there, 'Tree little babbies?' with a big smile on his face.

He genuinely can't believe it, even though he's delighted – as was Sorcha's old dear when she rang her this afternoon. The two of them cried for basically an hour. Her old man still refused to come to the phone, though – the knob-end.

I'm there, 'I think we're both still struggling to get our heads around it – as in, what it's going to mean.'

He goes, 'Your life is fooked, Rosser!' at the same time laughing.

And I'm like, 'I know,' laughing, too. 'Five kids and one grand-child at the age of thirty-two . . . Oh, and a rat!'

'A what?'

'Yeah, no, it's nothing. Sorcha's convinced that a rat swam up the focking toilet while she was sitting on it this afternoon.'

'Ah, that dudn't happen, Rosser.'

'I know. It's one of those, what are they called, urban mists? I was thinking she might be in, like, shock or some shit – you know, from the news.'

'The female moyunt can be a sthrange thing, Rosser.'

He's wise way beyond his years.

I'm like, 'You're not wrong there, Ro.'

We're sitting at the table in the gorden, having a few beers, looking out across Killiney Bay and just, like, shooting the shit in the early-evening sun. I know he possibly shouldn't be drinking, what with him being only fifteen going on sixteen, but as you know, like the French, I've always believed that if kids are brought up with alcohol, they'll respect it.

Anyway, that one's definitely going to be his last, because he's had seven cans and he's throwing it down him like his focking bladder's on fire.

'Hee-er,' he goes, 'Ine soddy again – about Shadden kicking off like that. The way she spoke to Sudeka. She shouldna dud it.'

I'm there, 'She apologized, Ro, and it's forgotten.'

'Youse have been unbelievable, Rosser. Offering to moyunt Rihadda-Burrogan while the peer of us go back to skewill. We're veddy grateful.'

'It's actually a pleasure. We love having you here.'

'I think Shadden's joost skeered, Rosser.'

'Scared of what exactly?'

'Ah, skeered of hanton her thaughter over every morden to anutter woman to do the reardon. Skeered that she'll forget who her real mutter is.'

'That'll never happen.'

'Well, she's just woodied, is all. Bit padanoid. It's oatenly naturid-dle. I toalt her, Rosser. I says to her that Sudeka is hee-er to help – you have to steert thrusting her mower. The problem is Dordeen keeps getting insoyut her head.'

'Yeah, no, I had a call from her. Shouting the odds. Focking skank.'

'She keeps telling her that people from this side of the wurdled are diffordent to us and not to be turdening her back on her owen people.'

'Jesus Christ. Why does everything have to be seen from a gang warfare point of view?'

'Ine throying to tell Shadden the whole toyum, doatunt listen to her – or your auld fella, because he's in her ee-ur as well – they're only sturden things up. End of the day, she's her ma, but. I caddent come between thum. I've to walk the loyen – knowmsaying?'

I nod. I know only too well. He reaches into his pocket then and goes, 'Here, will we have a ballast of this?' and he holds up – I swear to fock – a joint the size of Fabien Pelous.

I laugh. I'm like, 'Is that, like, cannabis?'

'Cannabis!' he goes, mocking the way I say it. 'It's fooken hash, Rosser.'

'Haaash.'

'No, say it like this – hash.'

'Haash.'

'Hash.'

'Hash.'

'There you are – you've got it now.'

He lights it, takes a long blast off it, then offers it to me.

I'm like, 'Would you believe me if I told you that I've never actually smoked this shit before?'

He goes, 'Are you seerdious?'

'I'm focking deadly serious. I always just presumed it was something for, I don't know, the *poor*?'

'Just take it into ye, Rosser – hoalt it in yisser lungs as long as you cadden.'

Which is exactly what I end up doing, then I let it out. I can't believe my teenage son is showing me how to smoke hash.

'Jesus Christ,' I go, handing the thing back to him, 'it's no wonder they talk so slowly on your side of town.'

I think I'm possibly more shit-faced than he is.

He's there, 'It's veddy sthrong, this stoof. Gull knows a fedda brings it in troo Amsterdam.'

I'm like, 'Cool.'

I take another blast off the joint, then I look at Ro and I end up just smiling to myself. It seems like only yesterday that he was a kid, shouting, 'A. C. A. B.!' at the Liaison Gorda in Finglas. Now he's practically a man.

This is possibly the famous hash talking, but I think I've done an amazing, amazing job as a father.

'So what about you?' I go. 'Have you found a school yet?' Because it's nearly, like, August.

He's there, 'Ah, one or two. Thee said thee'd take me in Perez Berray.'

I'm like, 'Pres Bray?' unable to hide my disgust. I'd nearly rather he was in prison.

'The utter one,' he goes, 'is the Hody Choyult in Saddynoggin.'

I'm there, 'Jesus focking Christ. Is that it, Ro?' because this is a great kid we're talking about, with an IQ of something focking astronomical. 'I mean, Sally focking Noggin!'

'That's the hand I've been gibbon, Rosser. We just have to accept it.'

I go, 'Do you mind me mentioning, Ro, I'm unbelievably focking proud of you?'

See, it's fine to say shit like that to your kids, especially when you're pissed or, in this case, high.

I'm there, 'Look, I'm a typical Southside parent. If my kid took a shit in a cup, I'd say he was a genius. But I mean it. I'm definitely proud of the way you and Shadden are, like, making a go of things. The baby. Going back to school. Possibly college after that. Blah, blah, blah.'

He goes, 'We have responsibidities, Rosser. Know what I mean? We want to provide for ear thaughter – gib her all the things we nebber had groan up.'

I just shake my head. I focking love this kid.

'Jesus, Ro, when you talk like that,' I go, 'you make me want to face up to my own responsibilities.'

He's there, 'You probley shoultn't have any mower, Rosser. You're fooked, so you are!'

The two of us just crack our holes laughing.

The next thing either of us hears is Honor's permanently pissed-off voice go, 'What are you two laughing at?'

We both look around and she's suddenly coming down the gorden towards us with a face that would scare the flies off a meat truck.

I'm like, 'It was just something funny that your brother slash half-brother said.'

'Er, yeah,' she goes, stopping in front of us, 'like I'd even be interested. So where's the Old Woman Who Lived in a Shoe?'

That's what she's storted calling Sorcha. You'd have to say it's clever.

I'm there, 'She's having lunch with Claire from Bray of all places.'

I can feel a burst of giggles building up inside me, except it's never wise to let Honor see you laugh or in fact show happiness of any kind. She just stands there staring at the two of us. I watch her little nose suddenly stort twitching and that makes me want to laugh even, like, more?

'Oh my God,' she goes, 'are you two smoking hash?'

Ronan's there, 'No, it's, er, heerbs, Hodor.'

'That's right,' I go, still somehow managing to keep a straight face. 'Your old dear planted some, I don't know, rosemary and some possibly something else. There's all different types, isn't there?'

She goes, 'Do you know how working class that stuff is?'

We both just crack up laughing in her face.

Honor calls us losers – 'Er, *sad* losers?' – then turns and walks back to the gaff, stopping before she disappears inside, just to go, 'Maybe I'll ring the Drug Squad and then we'll see how focking funny it is.'

And, of course, that makes us even worse. We laugh for, like, full-on five minutes, slapping the table, tears rolling down our faces, until I'm seriously worried about us basically herniating ourselves. Eventually, we calm down and we sit there – father and son – just staring out at the Something Sea, drying our eyes and shaking our heads and just thinking about how focking great life can sometimes be.

Five, maybe ten minutes pass. Then I go, 'You know, she probably *will* call the Drug Squad?'

Ronan's there, 'I was thinking that,' and he stands up. His legs are like a newborn baby giraffe's. He goes, 'I'd bethor flush the rest of Gull's stash downt the jacks.'

Sorcha says she was thinking of making the theme of the nursery harmony. There's really not a lot you can to say to that at, like, nine o'clock on a weekday morning.

We're both staring into this massive, empty bedroom, where three cots are soon going to be, although I'm struggling to actually picture it. Either I'm still reeling from the news that we're having not one baby but three, or Ronan's hash has killed what few brain cells I had in my head.

See, it could be that my body's just not used to it – like the first time Ronan ate quiche and he went into anaphylactic shock.

Shadden suddenly joins us, little Rihanna-Brogan in her orms.

She's like, 'Howiya, Sudeka,' making the effort, in fairness to her.

Sorcha's like, 'Hi, Shadden.'

'Is this gonna be the noorsedy, is it?'

Sorcha's there, 'Yes,' because it's, like, the biggest bedroom *in* the gaff? 'I was saying to Ross, I was thinking of making the theme either harmony or consonance.'

'Be lubbly,' Shadden goes. 'Eeder of dose.'

I don't think she has a clue what Sorcha's talking about either.

Rihanna-Brogan storts suddenly wriggling, her two orms shot out in front of her. She wants to come to her granddad. It's a nice reminder to me that kids actually love me, with the obvious exception of Honor.

'Because this is the room in which we're likely to do most of our bonding,' Sorcha goes, 'it's important to keep the palette soothing and neutral, with the barest accents of colour, pattern and texture.'

Shadden's like, 'Are you gonna ast befowerhant if they're gonna be all boyiz or all geerlz or a mixchore?'

'No, I want it to be a surprise – don't we, Ross?'

It already is, I'm thinking. It already focking is.

'That's why I'm thinking of rich neutrals,' she goes, 'like grey, lilac and maybe some of the warmer *blues?*'

Shadden smiles – definitely pleased for us.

'I'm arthur been thinking,' she goes. 'I might take Rihadda-Burrogan off the jeers of baby foowut. Might steert gibbon her . . . what you said.'

It looks like whatever Ronan said to her did the trick.

'Sweet potatoes and butternut squash!' Sorcha goes, her day obviously made. 'I could purée some now – I mean, only if you want me to. And cooked lentils are also a really good source of – oh my God – loads of things.'

'Mebbe later,' Shadden goes. 'Ine gonna take her to see her utter grandda this morden.'

She means Kennet and she means in prison. Sorcha smiles sadly. It puts all her talk of consonance and warmer blues into prospectus, if that's the right word.

Shadden takes the baby off me and off she goes, to get the Dort and then the bus to the North Circular Road. What a focking world we live in, that's all I can say.

Sorcha links my orm, then lays her head on my shoulder. 'There's a girl in my book club – Sandrine – whose sister had triplets,' she goes. 'She says we're not going to know what hit us. As in, like, one is hord enough? I mean, look at Rihanna-Brogan when she has a bad night, Ross. Imagine what it's going to be like having three babies who all want to eat and sleep and have their nappies changed at different times of the day and night.'

'Ah, you'll cope,' I go. 'I mean, *we'll* cope.'

It's at that exact moment that there's a ring on the doorbell and I tip downstairs to answer it.

It ends up being a surprise – there's no doubt about that. It's Sorcha's old dear, with – I can't help but notice – two massive suitcases at her feet and then, standing behind her, a taxi driver who's looking to be paid.

She's like, 'Hello, Ross!' and she steps past me into the entrance hall.

I'm like, 'Er, yeah, no, hi,' definitely in shock.

Sorcha suddenly comes bounding down the stairs, going, 'Oh my God! Oh my God! Oh my God!' and she throws her orms around her.

From upstairs, I can hear Honor – at the top of her voice – go, 'Please, God, just give me one focking day without drama in this house.'

She has a point.

I pay the driver – eighty snots from the airport to the Vico Road – and I close the door.

'I'm going to stay with you,' the old dear goes, 'if that's okay. You're going to need a lot of help when the babies arrive.'

Sorcha goes, 'But what about . . .'

But she doesn't get to even say his name. Her old dear goes, 'I've left him, Sorcha. I've left him to his hurt and his anger and his bitterness.'

Sorcha's hands go to her face. She's like, 'Oh my God!'

'It's for the best,' her old dear goes, heading for the stairs. 'Now come on, show me your plans for the nursery.'

It's, like, Thursday night and I'm in Terroirs of Donnybrook, picking up a few tins of the Albert Ménès sardines that Sorcha likes, what with them being a vital source of something or other. The dude on the till is handing me back my credit cord when I suddenly get this, like, tap on the shoulder and I turn around to be greeted by a face from the past.

I'm there, 'Aaahhh!' the way you do when you can't remember someone's name. 'No! Waaay!'

'Speranza,' she goes, obviously familiar with the routine. 'Speranza Doyle,' and we do the whole air-kissing and oh-my-God-how-long-has-it-been thing.

Speranza is an ex of Oisinn's from back in the day. I think she may have even come to our debs. She's, like, freakishly tall – we're talking, like, six-three? – and I always thought she looked like Tiffani Amber Thiessen, especially when she made the effort.

There's, like, two specific things I remember about Speranza. One: not only did she have to spell out her name for strangers, like

43

a lot of South Dublin girls, but she also had to say, 'Yes, it *is* unusual! It was Oscar Wilde's mother's pen name!' every focking time, which always struck me as a lot of work. Two: she was always *that* girl at the porty, who got shit-faced way too early, storted walking around in her bare feet, then launched into, 'Suuum-mer-tiiime – and the liii-ving is eee-zyyy . . .' bringing the entire mood down.

I'm there, 'So what are you up to? God, it's been years.'

She goes, 'I know! I'm a doctor now! Qualified!'

'A doctor? Whoa! Well, I don't know if you've stayed in contact with Oisinn, but he's riding my mother these days.'

She seems a bit shocked by that line – I'm actually shocked to hear myself say it – so she pretends that she didn't hear it and instead storts asking about Fionn.

'I couldn't believe it when I saw it on the news,' she goes. 'I'm still struggling to get my head around it. It's like, Fionn? Kidnapped? It's, like, *so* random.'

'They want five million for him – that's the latest.'

'Five million?'

'Yeah, no, and that's, like, dollars?'

'Oh! My God!'

'The Deportment of Foreign Affairs have been no focking use, by the way. I could write a book about that place. They don't rescue people – did you know that?'

'Er, no.'

'That's just an example. You'd have to wonder what the fock they *actually* do.'

'Fionn gave me Irish grinds for the Leaving. He's the reason I got a B in honours.'

'He helped a lot of people.'

'I really liked him. If he'd made a move on me, I probably would have – you know? But he was way too much of a gentleman.'

'That's why he's only ridden three birds in his life. Well, four, if you count this Chinese slash New Zealand one who's suddenly appeared on the scene. She's not a fan, by the way.'

We end up talking about the dude for a good ten minutes in the middle of the shop.

I'm there, 'Well, at least he's alive – we know that now.'

'I saw his poor parents on the news,' Speranza goes. 'My mum and his mum were in the same Spanish cookery club for a year until my mum joined a different one with her sister in Enniskerry because it was handier in terms of distance.'

I nod. I don't know what to do with this information.

She's there, 'Why do bad things happen to good people?'

I feel my eyes suddenly fill up with tears, then she goes, 'Do you want to help me drink this?' and she holds up what I'm presuming is a bottle of wine, wrapped in green tissue paper.

And I go, 'Yeah. Yeah, I do,' and, before I know it, we're walking to her gaff halfway up Mount Eden Road, her banging on about how depressing life can sometimes be, and me with a bag of sardines swinging by my side, and I'm texting Sorcha to say that I ran into Rob and Dave Kearney on their way into Kielys – two big fans of mine – and we went for one and it's turned into a bit of a broccasion, as these things often do, so possibly don't wait up for me.

I'll probably never change.

We go into her gaff. It's nice inside. She's obviously doing well for herself if she's a doctor. She opens the wine in the kitchen, while in the living room, like an old pro, I recce the scene by testing the sofa for firmness. The pre-match rituals are always the same. She arrives into the room with two glasses of red and the bottle in the crook of her orm and she and tells me to make myself comfortable, which I do in a leather ormchair. She takes the sofa.

'So I heard about you and Sorcha,' she goes.

I don't know whether she means us breaking up or us getting back together. I keep my reaction neutral by pulling a hey-ho face.

'I can't say I was ever a fan of the girl,' she goes. 'She's, like, so self-involved and I'm not saying that to be a bitch. You're actually better off without her.'

I'm like, 'Hmmm.'

The conversation swings back to Fionn again. She asks me if I've ever read Brian Keenan's book, as in *An Evil Cradling*, and I tell her straight away no because I can state for a fact that the only books I've ever read are Ronan O'Gara's and Bernard Jackman's autobiographies twice each and also Alan Quinlan's and she says I should read it even though it'll really upset me and she stands up and picks it off a shelf and she says she actually re-read it after she heard about Fionn and she hands it to me and I tell her thanks and when she's not looking I stick it down the side of the sofa cushion.

She's throwing the wine into her. She goes to refill my glass, except I tell her no because I'm possibly going to drive, which is my subtle way of hurrying proceedings along. She smiles and says she saw a documentary once about the whole Twin Towers slash seven-eleven thing and in the aftermath of the terrible events and blah, blah, blah, people just storted having random sexual encounters with, like, total strangers they met in, like, Storbucks or the elevator in their building – grief sex, some psychologist called it.

She lets it hang there, then she knocks back what's in her glass and pours herself another and I think to myself, okay, I better make my move here before she storts singing 'Summertime'.

I move over to the sofa beside her. I sweep her hair back from her face, like in a movie, and I move in for the kill. She's a good kisser, to give the girl her due – she has a tongue on her that could pick the wallet out of your orse pocket through a wicker chair.

After five minutes, certainly no more than ten, she suggests we take the show upstairs, which I'm more than happy to do.

As she's sweeping the cushions and pillows off the bed to create room for us, she goes, 'Just promise me one thing.'

I'm like, 'Er, okay.'

'Please don't be gone when I wake up in the morning.'

'I won't be gone! Jesus!'

'Ross, please. It's the one thing I hate. It makes me feel . . .'

'Like a prostitute?'

'I was going to say cheap.'

'I get that from a lot of girls. Look, you don't have to worry. I'm not going to go sneaking out of here the second you're asleep, okay?'

'Okay.'

We end up doing the deed. If you're looking for juicy details, I'm going to disappoint you here. I've always been a firm believer that what happens in the bedroom should stay in the bedroom. All I'm prepared to say, just for the purposes of the story, is that she sits astride me and rides me like a stolen mountain bike, blinking furiously the entire time, muttering instructions in angry little snatches and honking like an injured goose.

She cheers herself right up – let's put it that way. Then, five, maybe ten minutes later, she climbs off me, rolls over and falls asleep from her, I don't know, exertions.

I decide, of course, that I need to get the fock out of there. I check my phone. It's, like, still only midnight. I peel the sheets off me as quietly and as gently as I can, then I pick my clothes up from where they landed.

I slip out of the room and I get dressed on the landing, then tip downstairs. I grab my bag of sardines from where I left them, hanging on the post at the end of the stairs, then I check out my reflection in the hall mirror – my hair could do with a cut – and I slip out the door, grinning like a focking hero.

I walk back to the Lambo, quietly congratulating myself on my exit. I check my phone and it's not even midnight. Sorcha will probably comment on how sober I am and I'll go, 'That's the Kearndashians for you – wussed out early, like they always do! I'd be better off boozing with your granny! Rob actually had a sherry – a Winter's focking Tale – and he made it last all night!' because she has a thing for the two goys and I like running them down any opportunity I get.

When I reach the cor, I get this sudden, horrible sensation that I've, like, forgotten something. I put my hand on my trouser pocket and I realize I must have dropped my wallet on the landing when I was pulling my chinos back on.

I think to myself, okay, do I really need it? I could cancel my credit cords. My Brown Thomas rewards cord – that information is all kept on computer. They could send me out another. But then I remember that the photo from the scan is tucked into the left-hand pocket. The photo of the three little babies growing inside of Sorcha and it's the only one we actually have.

I instantly know that I have to get my wallet back, which means manning up and going back to Speranza's gaff. First, though, I grab the tyre jack from the boot.

Thirty seconds later, I'm in the front gorden, trying to figure out is it easier to jemmy open a window or a door. I consider ringing Ronan, except time is *kind* of the essence here? So I stort working the flat end of the tyre iron into the crack between the window and window frame of the living room.

I'm sort of, like, pulling it towards me when I suddenly hear two things simultaneously. The first is the splintering of wood, which is a hell of a lot louder than I expected. The second is a man's voice behind me going, 'What the hell are you doing?'

I spin around and I notice Speranza's next-door neighbour – he's around my old man's age – standing there in his dressing gown, with a look of pure murder on his face.

'There's someone breaking in next door!' he shouts into the hall to, presumably, his wife.

I'm there, 'No, no, it's cool,' trying to get him to lower his voice, 'I actually know the bird who lives here,' except at that exact focking moment, her name decides to escape me. 'It's some famous poet's mother. It's not Spirogyra, but it's something very like it.'

'Call the Gords!' he shouts into the hall. 'Myra, ring them. He's got a bloody crowbar!'

It's actually a relief when the front door suddenly opens and Speranza – focking ridiculous name – steps out onto the front door-step to find out what all the shouting is about.

I notice my wallet in her hand.

'Do you know this chap?' the old dude goes. 'I caught him trying to force that window open.'

And Speranza looks me dead in the eye, slips my wallet into the pocket of her dressing gown and goes, 'I've never seen him before in my life.'

'Phone the Gords!' the dude shouts. 'Tell them to come now!'

I give Speranza a disappointed look, then I turn, and, with a sudden injection of pace that recalls me at my rugby-playing best, I run like fock back to the cor.

I'm in, like, Idle Wilde in Dalkey, making short work of a vanilla latte and a chorizo and pear panini, while at the same time checking out this bird, who's sitting on the other side of the café with, like, her *back* to me? What I'm checking out especially are her legs, which are incredibly tanned and they just, like, curve this way and then that, before finally disappearing into a pair of ankle-high chestnut Uggs.

My phone rings. It ends up being Sorcha.

'Ross,' she goes, 'can you talk?'

I haven't heard her this agitated since the time Alison Canavan skipped her in the Ten Items or Less queue in Marks and Spencers in Blackrock.

I'm like, 'What's Honor said or done now?'

'It's not Honor,' she goes. 'Ross, it's Shadden.'

I'm like, 'Shadden?'

I thought that shit between them was sorted.

She goes, 'She's chosen her school.'

I'm there, 'I take it from the wobble in your voice that she didn't change her mind about Holy Child Killiney.'

'Oh, it's not going to be Holy Child Killiney, Ross.'

'Okay. So where is it then?'

'Are you sitting down?'

'Sitting down? Jesus Christ, Sorcha.'

'Ross, she's going to Sion Hill.'

'Oh.'

'Sion! Hill!'

'Yeah, no, I heard you, Babes.'

'I mean, I'm not being a bitch, Ross, but we debated with them when I was in Mount Anville and they were, like, oh my God!'

'Yeah, no, I remember that about them.'

'I mean, *who* even went there? As in, what notable alumni do they have?'

'I couldn't tell you off the top of my head, Babes.'

'Oh my God, it's all beginning to add up.'

'What do you mean?'

'Well, first, she totally loses it with me about the baby food. Then she decides she wants to go to Sion Hill. I wonder is she maybe suffering from, like, post-natal depression?'

'It's not post-natal depression, Babes.'

'It certainly has all the hallmorks of it.'

'Dordeen's stirring her up.'

'What?'

'Dordeen. Her old dear. And her old man. Focking K . . . K . . . K . . . Kennet. They're telling her to remember who she is and where she came from.'

'That's horrible.'

'I know.'

'We've given her an opportunity to escape all of that – again, I'm not being a snob.'

'I know. But we might just have to accept this Sion Hill thing.'

'Excuse me?'

'Sorcha, it's *her* choice. Wrong and all as this sounds, we're not actually entitled to tell her that one school is better than another. If she wants to go to Sion Hill, that's her focking funeral.'

'I'm just hoping,' Sorcha goes, 'that whatever Shadden's going through, she gets over it quickly. I think Holy Child Killiney could be persuaded to take her after Christmas.'

Oh my God, this bird is now licking her spoon. She's skimming the froth off the top of her cappuccino or whatever the fock she's drinking and then she's rubbing the spoon down the tip of her tongue.

'Sorcha,' I go, 'I'll talk to you later,' and I hang up before she can say another word. The conversation was becoming a bit boring anyway and, as a life-long appreciator of beautiful women, I have to give this bird at the very least a pat on the back and a, 'Hell, yeah!'

So I stand up and I tip over. My opening line is, 'I wouldn't mind being that spoon right now.'

She turns around and looks up at me and I get such a fright that I end up nearly having a focking prolapse there on the spot.

It's my old dear.

I'm like, 'What! The fock?'

She's there, 'Hello, Ross! What are you doing here? And what an odd thing to say!'

I'm like, 'I didn't know it was . . . I thought you were . . . What the fock are you doing dressing like that in the first place?'

'Dressing like what?' she has the actual balls to go.

I'm there, 'Uggs and a denim mini . . . Jesus.'

'How I dress,' she tries to go, 'is really none of your business.'

I'm like, 'It is when it's all clobber that I love on birds. You know, I came over here actually wanting to . . .'

'What?'

'No, I'm not going to say it. I'd only end up giving you a swelled head. I know what this is about, can I just say?'

'Do you?'

'You're trying to dress younger to keep Oisinn interested.'

'Oh, is that it, well, thanks for telling me that, Ross, that's really nice to know.'

She's talking, for some reason, faster than usual.

I'm there, 'Yeah, no, that *is* it. To keep Oisinn interested. And the hilarious thing is that, when it comes to women, he's never given a shit about either looks *or* body. He actually prefers old dogs – the skankier the better. Ask him. He's got focking issues. Psychological. And I'm saying that as someone he took a bullet for on many, many nights out.'

'Are you going to just stand there hurling abuse at me, or are you going to sit down with me and have a coffee, it'd be nice to have a coffee and a catch-up, can I get you something, they do a fab-a-lous cappuccino.'

'I wouldn't have a coffee with you if you paid me. You look like shit, by the way.'

'Why, thank you, that's a lovely way to speak to your mother.'

'Yeah, no, I genuinely mean it. You look like a fire-damaged wax-work of Pete Burns.'

'Well, if you must know, Ross, we were at a party last night, a wonderful party, and it went on late.'

'What kind of porty?'

'It was a house party – a friend of Oisinn's called Donnacha.'

'Lives in Kilternan. Played centre for Clongowes the year we won

51

the S and I focking destroyed him. What, and you were at one of his porties?'

His porties are, like, famously mad. It'd be considered a quiet night if the Feds are only called twice.

'Yes,' she goes, 'I was at one of his parties and I had a wonderful evening and I really enjoyed myself and there's nothing wrong with that.'

I'm there, 'Why are you talking like that?'

'Like what?'

'Er, ninety to the focking dozen?'

'I wasn't, or I didn't think I was, or I wasn't aware that I was . . .'

'I can't believe you were at one of Donnacha's porties. People must have thought you were there to collect one of your kids, did they?'

'I was the oldest there, if that's what you're asking, and there's nothing wrong with that, there's no shame in it.'

'The oldest by a good thirty focking years, I'd imagine. Jesus, I'll never live this down. The only consolation for me is that it's not going to last long – you and Oisinn, I mean.'

'And what makes you say that, why do you think that?'

I actually laugh.

I'm there, 'You won't last the pace. Oisinn's a porty animal. Always was. What porties have *you* been to in the last twenty years? The Foxrock and District Residents Association Annual Dinner Dance?'

'I have more energy than you imagine, Ross, I'm more than capable of keeping up.'

'Look in the mirror, woman. You're focking wrecked. There's probably another porty tonight, is there?'

'Actually, there's a band he wants me to go and see with him at the Olympia and then – yes – there's a party in Blackrock, I think he said.'

'I can see you focking ageing even thinking about it.'

'I like being taken out, Ross, and I'm more than able for a late night or two, although I might take a nap this afternoon, my eyelids are suddenly very heavy.'

'A nap! The whole thing just gets funnier and funnier. Anyway, I'm out of here. And don't go thinking that you're somehow hot just because I came over here with the intention of trying to score you. You're bet into that skirt and you're bet into that top.'

I turn to walk away.

I reach the door, then I turn back – a busy café, remember – and I shout, 'It doesn't matter what you put on you, because you'll always look the same – two hundred pounds of ugly stuffed into a one-hundred-and-fifty-pound sack.'

I've said it before and I'll say it again. That woman brings out the best in me.

I step out onto the street. My phone suddenly beeps and it ends up being a text from, like, JP. It's, like, 'Ezra Dumpling born at 6 oc this am, 10lbs. Mother and son doing well.'

JP hasn't slept for forty-eight hours and yet I've never seen him look better. If you've ever had a kid, you'll know that feeling – especially after your first. You're high on, I don't know, happiness.

He'll be focked tomorrow.

He goes to give me a high-five, but he's getting a hug – I just think, fock it, he's earned it – and I'm there, 'Come on, J Town, bring it in – one size fits all!'

He goes with it, then just laughs. He's like, 'Ross, he's beautiful,' and his voice breaks, like a big focking girl's.

Again, you'd know if you'd been through it.

'What's the focking deal with the names?' I go. 'I take it Shoshanna chose them,' because they're a bit out there – even for this port of the world.

'Well, Ezra was her old man's name,' he goes. 'He died when she was a little girl.'

I'm like, 'Hey, sorry, Dude – no offence.'

'And Dumpling is what we used to call him when Shoshanna was pregnant with him. It was Dumpling because that's what he looked like in there – a big dumpling!'

I laugh along with him. I mean, it's shite-talk, but on days like today you can get away with it. The emotion and blah, blah, blah.

I'm there, 'Dude, they're not names I would have picked, but I genuinely couldn't be happier for you. And on top of the news about Fionn being still alive, I've actually got a really good feeling about shit.'

Christian and Oisinn suddenly arrive together – we're standing in a corridor in Holles Street, I should have mentioned – with Ross Junior in tow. *He's* carrying – I'm not making this up – a little pink plastic picnic basket with a smiley face on the side of it. It's basically a toy for a girl. There's shit I could say, but I don't.

'Hi, Roth!' he goes.

He's still got that focking lisp. *I thawt I thaw a puddy cat* and blahdy focking blah.

I'm there, 'Alright?' saying hello, but at the same not wanting to give him – what's that word that Sorcha is always using? – *validation?*

Oisinn and Christian both give JP a hug – big ones as well – and they say congratulations. Oisinn, I notice, has brought a bottle of Moët, which was a nice touch, the dick. He hands it to JP.

I go, 'That's from all of us, by the way. We all clubbed in.'

Oisinn says fock-all to contradict me. He knows he's on seriously thin ice with me anyway.

Instead, he watches JP examine the label on the bottle and goes, 'It's a double celebration. It's great news about Fionn – well, it's a lot more hopeful, isn't it?'

I'm there, 'Yeah, no, I've already covered that. And you'd want to tell that girlfriend of yours to stort dressing her focking age, by the way. I nearly tried to score her in Idle Wilde.'

He has no response to that, of course.

Christian decides to change the subject. It's not a day for haters.

'I really love the names, by the way,' he goes, because he's better at putting on an act than I am. 'And so does Lauren.'

And Oisinn's there, 'There's your full-back!' because that was the position that JP played back in the day.

Fock, he was a great full-back.

JP loves the thought of that. You can tell from the look on his face. He goes, 'Now it's up to Christian and Ross to produce the goods. We need a centre and an outhalf, goys!'

I love the way we're all ignoring the fact that Christian already has a son.

'By the way,' I go, 'I don't want to steal your thunder – big day for you and blah, blah, blah – but we're actually having triplets.'

Their jaws all just drop – even Oisinn's, in fairness to the orsehole.

'Oh my God!' Christian goes. 'Seriously?'

I'm like, 'Seriously.'

He shakes his head. He's like, 'Dude, your life is over.'

And we all laugh, even though I'm quickly realizing that it's probably true.

'Roth,' little Ross Junior suddenly goes, 'woulth you like a thandwidge?'

I'm there, 'What?'

He goes, 'A thandwidge.'

For fock's sake. He's talking about a focking imaginary one from his whatever-the-fock-it-is picnic basket. Fisher-Price or whatever.

'Ith Swith cheeth,' he goes, 'with pethto and thundried thomathoth.'

And *I'm* expected to just answer him?

'Jesus focking Christ,' I go – I end up, like, totally losing it. 'Everything doesn't have to be about you, you know? Focking ridiculous.'

Christian steps in between us. He ends up taking Ross Junior's side. Well, he has to, I suppose. He's his kid.

'Ross,' he goes to me, 'is that really necessary?'

I'm there, 'Well, he was pissing me off, Christian. I suppose I just snapped.'

'Would it kill you to just, like, play along?'

Little Ross Junior is looking up at me, big smile on his boat – it's impossible to offend him – offering me the invisible sandwich. I roll my eyes, then, like a tool, I end up taking it from him and I pretend to even eat it in, like, three fake bites.

He's like, 'Would you like thome tiramathu now, Roth?'

And Christian goes, 'Maybe Uncle Ross is full. He might have some later, okay?'

Oisinn rubs his two hands together and goes, 'So, are you going to show us this future Ireland number fifteen or not?'

And JP goes, 'Yeah, no, come on,' and we follow him down the corridor to the little private ward at the very end, where Shoshanna is sitting up in bed, with a little bundle, wrapped in a baby blanket, held tight to her chest.

She's like, 'Come on in, guys! Hey, little Ezra, are you ready to meet your uncles?' and she's including me in that, which is nice, because we've never really hit it off.

I'm like, 'Hey, we're not crashing in the middle of feeding time, are we?' because I've never really been that comfortable with the whole watching-women-breastfeed thing. 'I think I'd probably puke my ring up all over the floor.'

It's the kind of line that, in normal circumstances, Shoshanna would take offence at – except today she's in love with the world and that includes me.

She goes, 'Come on, Ross. Come and meet him,' and I walk over, closer to the bed. 'Do you want to have a little hold?'

I'm there, 'Er, yeah, no, cool,' because I think I'm on the record as saying that I actually really like babies and babies tend to be big fans of mine.

I take this little bundle in my hands – he weighs practically nothing – and I'm like, 'Hey there, little goy,' and I pull back the blanket to get a better look at his face and I'm like, 'Oh my God, he's absolutely . . .' and then I stop and suddenly I'm unable to say another word – as in, I literally can't talk. I'm just standing there, holding him, staring at his face, which is beautiful, don't get me wrong. But there's something about Ezra Dumpling that it's impossible to ignore.

He's black.

'Ross,' Sorcha goes, 'I really wish you wouldn't keep saying that.'

This is as we're driving along the famous Naas Road.

I'm like, 'What, about JP's son? His *so-called* son?'

She's there, 'If Shoshanna found out you were talking that way . . .'

'He's black, Sorcha.'

'You can't say that.'

'Black slash African-American slash whatever the proper non-racist expression is. He's not white – that's my point. He's not JP's.'

'Can I just remind you that you're supposed to be his friend?'

'Have a look at my phone there – it's in my pocket here. Go on, take it out.'

Which is what she ends up doing.

I'm like, 'Okay, check out the photo he sent out this morning. It should be the first or second thing in my inbox. The one of him in the little Leinster babygro.'

She calls up the photo and she just, like, stares at it for a good ten seconds and doesn't say anything until she eventually goes, 'Well, JP's quite dark himself, Ross.'

I'm like, 'Dark? Sorcha, the kid is black!'

She puts my phone back.

'Well,' she goes, 'I just think he's just dark. And I definitely don't think you should go saying anything, Ross.'

'As his friend, I think I'm going to have to.'

'Ross, I definitely don't think you should.'

I'm like, 'Where the fock is this place anyway?'

We're out shopping for a new cor, I should have mentioned, because Sorcha's old dear – very focking helpfully – pointed out this morning that we're not going to fit three baby chairs into my Lambo and we're certainly not going to fit them into this thing – we're talking Sorcha's Nissan focking Leaf.

'A cheaper solution,' Honor goes, from her seat in the back, 'would be to give these so-called babies to someone who *is* capable of looking after them?'

Sorcha's like, 'We've been through this, Honor. We are not giving them up for adoption. We're perfectly capable of raising them ourselves.'

'Yeah,' she goes, 'because you've done *such* a good job with me.'

She has a point.

Sorcha spots the place she found online – this, like, second-hand-cor showroom, if you can believe that. We pull in anyway and Sorcha is barely out of the front-passenger door when her eyes are suddenly set on this – okay, I'm just going to say what it is – it's a white Ford Transit focking minibus.

'You see,' Sorcha goes, peering in the window of the thing, 'this is exactly the kind of thing we need.'

Honor gets out of the Nissan Leaf and laughs in that cruel way of hers. 'Oh my God,' she goes, 'it's the kind of thing that builders go to work in!'

It's a pretty good description of it, to be fair to her.

I'm there, 'Babes, I was thinking more in terms of possibly a Volkswagen Transporter or – at a push – a Renault Espace.'

'They're not big enough,' she goes.

I'm like, 'You're only having *three* babies, Sorcha – not . . .' and I stort counting the seats. 'Eight, nine, ten, eleven, twelve. I mean, Honor's right. This is for driving people to building sites. Or the docks.'

'Yeah, do the maths,' Sorcha goes. 'You, me and Honor, plus three babies. That's six. Ronan, Shadden and Rihanna-Brogan makes nine. Then my mom and my sister.'

And it suddenly hits me again – like a big focking wave – what's about to happen to my life.

This dude – we're talking mid-twenties, gelled head, newsprint moustache, a pair of those glasses that turn into shades outdoors and a suit that probably fitted when it was bought for someone else – steps over to us, full of confidence.

'Hello, Madam,' he goes. 'Hello, Sir,' except he says 'Sir' like he doesn't really mean it. He says it the same way a bouncer would say it when he's trying to persuade a drunk to leave a nightclub – we're talking no sincerity whatsoever.

'Hi,' Sorcha goes. 'Can you tell us about this particular *model*?'

This particular model. She might as well have the words, 'Rob me!' tattooed across her forehead.

The dude smiles a big focking crocodile smile.

He's like, 'Of course, Madam. It's a Ford Transit Minibus. Classic body style with a seating capacity of twelve. You can see the configuration is two, three, three and four. Built with comfort, safety and dependability in mind. It's a very smooth drive.'

It's Honor who hits him with the first questions. 'Is it eco-friendly?' she goes. 'Because my mom gets very upset about people driving what she calls big gas-guzzlers – although that was before she storted doing her bit to overpopulate the planet.'

The dude just stares are her open-mouthed – like she's a focking dolphin reading the shipping news.

He's like, 'The, em . . . er . . . erm . . .' Honor has suddenly reduced him to, like, stuttering silence.

Socha goes, 'I'm still concerned about the environment, Honor, thank you,' and then she looks at the dude and goes, 'Actually, on that particular subject . . .'

'Er, yes,' he goes, trying to get his shit together. 'This particular, er, vehicle, Madam, contains the new fuel-efficient engine model that meets Stage V European emissions standards. It also has, em, Smart Regenerative Charging Technology, which only charges the battery when necessary, as well as Auto-Start-Stop, which saves fuel whenever you stop in traffic.'

That's good enough for Sorcha. She nods, already ninety percent convinced.

'What's on the clock?' I go, knowing that the answer is probably going to be horseshit either way.

He's like, 'Er, sixty thousand kilometres.'

I laugh in his face.

'Yeah, no,' I go, 'you've obviously wound it back, haven't you? You should be wearing a balaclava, you focking thief.'

'No,' he goes, 'it's only three years old. It belonged to a special needs school. They only sold it because they needed a bigger bus.'

Honor goes, 'Oh! My! God!'

And Sorcha suddenly turns on her. 'Honor,' she goes, 'don't you dare say whatever it is you're about to say!'

Honor laughs. She's like, 'Oh! My! God!'

'Honor,' Sorcha goes, 'I mean it. I don't want to hear whatever it is you're thinking!'

The special needs history of the minibus is eventually what

clinches the deal for Sorcha. She mentions to the dude that she has a second cousin with special needs – 'even though, thankfully, it's only mild autism?' – and that she was also really, really, really good friends with a girl in UCD who was blind.

Of course, the dude doesn't give a fock one way or the other, although – in fairness to him – he makes a pretty good job of pretending he does. And why wouldn't he? Sorcha ends up agreeing to pay sticker price for the focking thing and that's without even consulting with me.

The dude goes inside to fix up the paperwork.

Honor is standing there, shaking her head, going, 'I can't believe you've just agreed to pay eighteen grand for – oh my God – a special needs bus. Hashtag, lollers! Hashtag, never live it down! Hashtag, hillair!'

I'm there, 'She's being a bitch, Sorcha, but she has a point. I mean, you're the one who's always banging on about money. How can we suddenly afford eighteen Ks?'

Sorcha goes, 'We'll just sell one of our existing cors.'

Of course, I don't get a chance to ask her which of our two cors she's talking about selling. The dude comes out with the various bits of paper that he wants us to sign.

Sorcha looks at him and goes, 'Do you, like, *buy* cors as well?' and I watch his eyes turn to the Leaf – a focking electric cor – and what he's obviously thinking is, 'You've got to be ripping the piss.'

But then, without saying a single word to me, Sorcha goes, 'Because my husband is getting rid of his Lamborghini.'

The mother of my first-born rings me while I'm in the hallway of the gaff, opening my post – my replacement ATM and credit cords.

Her opening line is, 'C'mere to me, you.'

I'm there, 'Tina, could you not try kicking off a conversation for once with a simple focking hello.'

'I want a woord wit you.'

'Yeah, I gathered that. I'm familiar with the way phones work, Tina.'

'Ronan's heert is burroken.'

I'm like, 'Broken? Why? What are you talking about?'

'He wants to go back to heez oawult skewill.'

'Yeah, no, they won't have him back, though. Your ex has seen to that.'

I'll never let her forget that she had a thing with McGahy.

I'm there, 'Anyway, he's talking about possibly Pres Bray now.'

'He dudn't want to go to Perez Berray.'

'Look, I'm not exactly happy about it either. I mean, personally, I wouldn't board a focking dog in that school, but that's only because there's bad blood there going back to my rugby days. The point I'm making is that Ro doesn't have a lot of options.'

'We're going to speak to Tom.'

'We?'

'Heez peerdents.'

'Do you not think it'd be better coming from just you? You two have got your whole history.'

'You're Ronan's fadder. You're coming wit me.'

'Fair enough.'

'Ine arthur makin an appointment for Friday morden.'

I'm about to tell her that I'll check the diary, except she's already hung up. And that's when I suddenly hear piercing screams – two sets – coming from the kitchen.

I race down there to find – I'm not inventing this – Sorcha and her old dear literally standing on the kitchen table, screaming their lungs out.

'We saw it,' Sorcha somehow manages to go. 'I told you I didn't imagine it.'

I'm like, 'What? What the fock are you talking about?'

'It's a rat!' her old dear goes. 'A rat! Eeeuuuggghhh!!!'

'Mom put her hand in the vegetable tower,' Sorcha goes, her hand clamped over her mouth, like she thinks she might vom. 'And it was in there.'

Her old dear's like, 'A big black thing – God, it was as big as a Jack Russell – just staring up at me, eating a potato!'

★

Andrea answers the phone. She sounds like she might have been crying. Of course, I end up putting my foot in it by going, 'Whoa, someone's coming down with a cold!'

She goes, 'Who is this?'

I'm like, 'Yeah, no, Andrea, it's Ross?'

There's, like, total silence on the other end, which means I end up having to talk again.

'Look, I'm sorry about that day in the Radisson,' I go. 'There was a lot of emotion in the room. I possibly didn't handle it very well. I know Jenny definitely didn't. Jesus, where does Fionn keep digging them up from?'

She's like, 'What do you want, Ross?'

I'm there, 'Yeah, no, I was actually just ringing to find out if there is any news?'

'No, there isn't – is that everything?'

'I was just going to say, I'm beginning to regret not going over there to look for him. I was the one gagging to go – I don't know if the goys mentioned – until that carrot-chomping fockwit from the Deportment of Foreign Affairs talked me out of it. Maybe if I'd gone with my gut instinct, I'd have your son home by now and I'd be the hero. I suppose we'll never know.'

Totally out of the blue then, she goes, 'Don't ring this number again.'

And I'm so caught on the hop, roysh, that I end up going, 'Is the landline better for you?'

She ends up totally losing it with me. She's like, 'Don't ring me! Don't ring my husband! Don't ring any member of my family! Stay away from us!'

I'm there, 'Andrea, you used to be a big supporter of mine – can I just remind you of that?'

'You made him go.'

'Hey, let's not stort throwing around accusations.'

'He only went to get away from you.'

'Again, I'd like to think he went for the whole experience of working abroad and helping people thing.'

'Do you know what I dreamt last night? That he was buried alive.

That he was buried under the ground and he was calling for me, his mother.'

'I'm presuming that's why you're upset today.'

'If they kill him, Ross, it's on your head.'

'Don't say that. Andrea, I'm the one who was thinking of going over there to look for him, remember. I still might.'

'I said it to Ewan this morning. I said if we never see our son again, it'll be Ross O'Carroll-Kelly's fault.'

And before I can say another word in my defence, she hangs up.

The Kind Heart 3000 is the last word in humane vermin entrapment technology – or at least that's what the dude in Woodie's in Sandyford told me, slightly overselling it, I would have thought. It's basically just a cage with, like, a *door* at either end?

Sorcha seems pleased with it, though. She's sitting on the low stepladder in the lorder, reading the instructions to me.

'The highly sensitive trip plate,' she goes, 'is designed to torget the specific weight and shape of the rat, while the solid galvanized steel construction results in a secure capture, with no shorp edges to horm the animal if he or she struggles to escape.'

She cocks her head to one side and goes, 'Awww!' because she's caring like that.

I'd have poisoned the little focker, so he's getting off lightly.

'By the way,' she goes, 'you're not doing anything on Saturday, are you?'

I'm like, 'Er . . .'

'Garret and Claire have invited us to theirs for a borbecue.'

'A borbecue?'

'Yes.'

'In Bray?'

'Yes, in Bray.'

'Yeah, no, it's a pity,' I go, 'but I'm actually busy that day.'

She's there, 'Busy doing what?'

The girl is like Poirot. Focking dogged.

'Saturday?' I go. 'Errr . . .' but I'm just not able to come up with something in time. 'What's the focking occasion anyway?'

She goes, 'They're leaving, Ross.'

I'm like, 'Leaving?'

'I know. It's very sudden, isn't it? They've decided to, like, *emigrate?*'

I actually laugh. I'm like, 'What country would want that pair of focking saps?'

I hate Garret and Claire, even though I've ridden *her* more times than I've had coffee.

'Canada,' Sorcha goes. 'And don't be mean, Ross. They're my friends.'

'Hey, don't get me wrong, I'm delighted they're going. I hope they never come back.'

'They're fed up with this country.'

'Well, the feeling is definitely mutual.'

'I think the banks just – oh my God – point-blank refusing to give them the money for their organic café in Bray was the last straw for them.'

This was the famous Wheat Bray Love they wanted to open on the Quinnsboro Road. Telling them to go fock themselves might be the most sensible thing anyone in an Irish bank has done for about thirty years.

'I'll definitely be there,' I go. 'If only just to make sure they don't have any second thoughts. I'm actually beginning to feel a lot more positive about the future of this country now that I know they're going. It's like a weight has been lifted.'

She's like, 'Well, I'll feel the same when we capture this rat. I mean, I love all creatures, but we can't have it in the house. They've been known to attack babies. It might even attack Honor.'

I laugh. I'm there, 'Yeah, it would take a brave and foolhardy rat to do that.'

Then Sorcha laughs.

It's nice that we can laugh about our daughter, even though what we're actually laughing about is what a horrendous wagon she's turned out to be in spite of us basically spoiling her since she was born.

I throw in a few strips of bacon, which rats apparently love, then I pull back the lever and that's the trap set.

★

'The Principal can only give you a few minutes,' McGahy's secretary tries to go. 'And he's running about half an hour behind schedule today.'

I'm like, 'Focking spare me, would you? It's August. What's he doing – playing Tetris?'

I hate being a dick to her because she looks like Kaley Cuoco – or an Irish country version of her, if you can imagine such a thing.

Then I think to myself, do you know what? I'm not sitting here like a tool waiting for him to decide when he's ready to see us. Our appointment was for ten o'clock and I'm going in there right this second. So I end up morching straight past the secretary one, with Tina following close behind me.

I give the door some serious shoulder and McGahy looks up from his computer, pretty much soiling himself with the fright I end up giving him.

'Caught you focking slacking,' I go, then I laugh.

He wasn't doing anything, by the way, just tapping away on his keyboard.

'I tried to tell them you were running late,' the secretary goes, trying to cover her hole.

He's like, 'It's fine, Margaret, thank you,' and then he sad-smiles Tina – doesn't even look at me, by the way – and goes, 'Please, take a seat.'

We both sit down opposite him.

Tina, by the way, hasn't bothered her orse getting dressed up. 'Jeans and runners?' I actually said to her when I saw her stepping off the number ten bus. 'Would you not have made the focking effort?'

I should be relieved, I suppose, that she's not in her pyjama bottoms.

McGahy has the balls to go, 'Today is a very busy day for me, so if we could just . . .'

Tina's like, 'You know why we're hee-ur.'

He's there, 'Of course. Well, as I outlined in my letter . . .'

'How deer you – arthur what we had together – send me a lehurr to say my son wadn't welcome back to heez skewill.'

'You dick,' I go, because I want him to know I'm here as well.

'The board of management requires us to communicate all such decisions in writing,' he tries to go. 'Our relationship – past relationship – has nothing to do with this, Tina.'

She goes, 'Ronan will be steerting back hee-ur next munt – and dat's all there is to it.'

He sort of, like, laughs to himself, in a really, like, *condescending* way?

'The governors have made their decision,' he goes. McGahy looks at me, possibly half expecting me to drag him across the desk and slap him around the head. I'm Finn McFocking Cool, though.

I go, 'Did Ronan not win Student of the Year two years ago?'

He's there, 'Yes, he did.'

'Okay. And weren't you the one who suggested he sat his Junior Cert a year ahead of the rest of his class?'

'Yes, that's also true.'

'So how is it not in the interests of the student body that he comes back here?'

'Because the governors and I are worried that having a classmate who is a father at – what, fifteen years of age? – would have a morally deleterious effect on his peers.'

I end up suddenly losing it. I sit forward in my seat, point at him and go, 'That's my son and my granddaughter you're talking about. I should drag you across this desk and slap you around the focking head for that.'

Tina goes, 'Ross, keep your mout clowized.'

'Morally dooby debious,' I go. 'You've got some focking balls, McGahy.'

'I said shut your mout!'

McGahy has a little smile to himself. He's in his element seeing me get smacked down.

'Look,' *he* goes, at the same time standing up and walking around to our side of the desk, to let us know that our audience with him is over, 'Ronan leaves this school with our best wishes. And if he needs a reference for his next school . . .'

That's when Tina hits him with it.

'Sure you might be luken for a refordence yisser self, Tom.'

He smiles – or tries to.

He's like, 'What?'

'Ine just arthur been tinkin,' she goes, 'since you're such a stickler for the rewils, you'll probably be teddin the boawurd abou rus, woatun't ye?'

He's there, 'Er . . . er . . . er . . .'

'Because accorton to your conthract of employument, you could be sacked for habben a sexual relationship with the mudder of a studunt. Gross misconthuct – idn't dat what you toalt me?'

'Tina, look . . .'

'Idn't dat the reason we had to keep eer afeer a secrit? Ine shewer the gubbenors would be veddy intherested in heardon all abourrit.'

'Please,' he goes, his cough definitely softened, 'this is my career.'

'And dis is moy son!' Tina goes. 'And beleaf you me, he's a lot mower impowertant to me than your bleaten cadeer.'

I underestimate Tina sometimes. She might dress like an office cleaner working for four yoyos an hour, but she's a focking tigress when it comes to protecting her son – well, *our* son.

'Do you need toyum to tink abourrit?' she goes.

McGahy's like, 'Er, er, n . . . n . . . n . . . no. Look, I'll make Ronan's case to the board again, this time a little more volubly. I'm sure I can sway them. And we'll, em, see him back here in the first week of September.'

Tina stands up. I stand up, too, and we just morch out of there, because there's nothing else that needs to be said, although on my way out the door I'm unable to resist telling McGahy that he's a knob with ears.

Outside in the cor pork, Ronan is waiting for us. Which is a surprise. He's supposed to be back in the gaff. He couldn't wait to hear, I suppose. He stares at me with a big look of hopefulness on his face.

I'm there, 'Well, you're not going to Pres focking Bray, Ro, I can tell you that! You're back in! You're back in Castlerock!'

He runs at me and he throws his orms around my waist and goes, 'You're the man, Rosser! You're the fooken man!'

And while it's a very nice thing for me to hear, I end up having to

69

go, 'It wasn't all down to me, Ro. Your mother played a definite blinder.'

'Oh! My God,' Chloe goes. 'I heard you racially abused Fionn's girlfriend!'

This is while I'm horsing into a burger and Jenny – the bird she's talking about – is standing, like, ten feet away from us, being hugged, first by Sophie, and then by Amie with an ie, who is telling her that she's – oh my God – *so* brave, and that Fionn is – oh my God – *so*, so lucky to have a girlfriend like her working so hord for his release.

I wouldn't be so sure. Looks-wise, I'd say she's only a six or a six and a half at best.

It was, like, Christian who suggested bringing the girl along – as Fionn's friends, he said, we should be making a fuss of her while she's in Ireland – and Sophie and Amie with an ie are certainly doing that.

'I didn't racially abuse her,' I go. 'Jesus Christ, I can't believe that's the story doing the rounds. I tried to order drinks from the girl, if you must know.'

Chloe's like, 'Oh! My God!'

'I don't know why Fionn's old pair didn't warn us that she was Chinese.'

'*Warn* you?'

'Well, give us a heads-up in advance.'

'Maybe they don't agree with defining people by their ethnicity. Because that's *actually* racist.'

'Well,' I go, 'I genuinely believe that mistaking her for a lounge girl wasn't racist, so let's just agree to differ.'

I look up at the sky, hoping it suddenly pisses rain on Garret and Claire's big day.

I shove the rest of my burger into my mouth and I go into the kitchen to grab one of my beers from the fridge.

Sorcha and Lauren are sitting at the kitchen table talking babies and all the rest of it. Sorcha is telling Lauren about her old man basically not giving a shit that she's pregnant with triplets.

She goes, 'He just can't accept that I'm not his little princess anymore and that's his biggest issue. But I'm – oh my God – finished with him, Lauren, and I actually mean that.'

Lauren nods, really, like, sympathetically. I love Lauren, even though she wouldn't be a major fan of mine. She's actually getting ready to drop herself – it couldn't be more than a few weeks away.

Sorcha gives me a little smile. She looks incredible today. Pregnancy really suits her and I'm not saying that to be a wanker.

I grab my beer and I head back out to the gorden to look for Christian. I've been trying to get him on his own all day to talk to him about JP and the whole black baby thing.

Garret is standing over the borbecue, flipping Tesco's own-brand burgers and unspecified chicken body ports from fock knows where. And he's, like, holding court – *supposedly*? Christian and one or two others are listening to him, banging on, full of himself. He's drinking some piss that I've never even heard of – it's called, like, Spalt or Splonk or something like that – and he's going, 'I'm really into my craft beers these days.'

The goys are all just nodding, like he's *not* full of shit?

He's going, 'I genuinely don't know how you drink that stuff,' and what he's talking about – if you can believe this – is Heineken. 'It's just chemicals. Here, taste this,' and he offers Christian his bottle and Christian, like a dope, takes it and knocks back a mouthful.

'It's very low in alpha acid,' Garret goes – you can picture him, I'm sure, with the goatee and bits of wool up and down his wrists and the focking board shorts and the Birkenstocks. 'It's something I've basically studied, to the point where all I need to do is smell a particular beer and I can straight away tell you the actual terroir of the hops. As long as it's craft beer.'

Christian nods and goes, 'I mean, you can definitely taste the difference.'

I can't tell you how disappointed I am in him.

Garret goes, 'That's what's known as toasted cereal depth. Seriously, do yourself a favour. That stuff you're drinking – like I said, chemicals. By the way, is there any news on your man?'

Christian's like, 'Who?'

'That poor fucker who got kidnapped.'

'He has a focking name,' I suddenly hear myself go. 'It's Fionn.'

Garret just shrugs. 'Okay,' he goes, 'Fionn, then. Is there any word?'

Christian's there, 'Nothing since that one ransom demand. Jenny's trying to arrange a meeting with Enda Kenny, to possibly put the pressure on – see can something be done, I don't know, internationally.'

Garret just pulls a face and goes, 'Well, hope for the best but expect the worst – that would be my advice.'

I'm like, 'What the fock does that mean?'

He goes, 'I'm just making the point. It costs money to keep a hostage alive. They've got to feed him. They've got to pay people to guard him. If they think there's no hope of getting money for him, they'll cut their losses and shoot him in the head.'

I get this unbelievable urge to suddenly deck him – to take out all my frustrations on him by laying him out lengthways here on the focking patio.

But that's when Claire suddenly appears, claps her hands together and goes, 'Okay, everyone, listen up. Can everyone come out to the garden, please? Sorcha and Lauren, come out. Garret and I just want to say a few words of goodbye to you all.'

'Okay,' Claire goes when everyone is standing on the lawn in, like, a focking circle around them, 'as most of you already know, for the past year and a little bit, Garret and I have been trying to open an organic bakery and coffee shop on the Quinnsboro Road. Our dream was to provide Bray with a place where people could finally source breads and cakes that were baked with only the most wholesome ingredients, because we genuinely, genuinely felt that it was needed. Unfortunately, because of the situation with the economy, the Irish banks are just not lending at the moment.'

Garret goes, 'And don't believe the corporate bullshit on the ads. As soon as they find out you're from an SME, they do not want to know.'

Claire's like, 'And that's why we're leaving this country to start hopefully a new life for ourselves in Canada. We haven't given up on our dream of opening a café called Wheat Bray Love. It's just that Bray's loss is probably going to end up being Toronto's gain.

Thank you all for coming. Garret, do you have anything you want to say?'

'Just that this country is fucked,' he goes. 'A thousand people emigrating every week and I wouldn't focking blame them. It's *genuinely* fucked. And I'm not being a dick here, but I actually feel sorry for those of you we're leaving behind. Christian, do you want a real beer or are you going to keep drinking that piss?'

And that's when suddenly, without any, like, pre-warning, I end up totally losing it. You'd have to say that Garret has definitely had it coming. It's been building up to this for a long, long time.

It happens too quickly for him to even react. I walk straight across the gorden with my fist cocked and ready to fire. There's, like, a look of confusion on his face as I drive my knuckles into his jaw. It's a perfect punch. Even the noise of it. Boomf!

And it's very much a case of lights out.

I hear Sorcha scream and maybe one or two others as well – definitely Claire – as Garret collapses like a Scottish scrum. I hear myself shout, 'You and your focking craft beers!' and my voice sounds suddenly like a crazy person's voice and not like mine at all.

One or two of Garret's mates grab me and bundle me into the kitchen, through the gaff and out the front door. I'm there going, 'I'm not going to hit him again. He's already decked.'

Ten, maybe twenty or thirty seconds later, Sorcha storms out of the house and walks straight past me. She doesn't even look at me. She doesn't say a word – that's how, like, pissed *off* she is?

Garret's mates let go of me.

Other people are suddenly spilling out of the gaff as well, a lot of them giving me serious filthies or telling me that, whatever he said about Ireland, he didn't deserve that.

I watch Sorcha get into the cor. She sits into the driver's seat and doesn't move. She just, like, waits for me. I give myself twenty or thirty seconds to catch my breath and get my courage up, then I go over and I open the front-passenger door.

'What the fock?' she goes, before I've even sat into the thing. 'You nearly broke Garret's jaw!'

'He described Heineken as piss,' I go. 'You know how loyal I am to it and how many years I've been drinking it.'

She goes, 'You did *not* hit him because he described Heineken as piss, Ross. What the fock is going on?' and then suddenly, in the space of, like, two seconds, her voice goes from mad as a focking meat axe to suddenly concerned.

The reason, I realize, is that I'm crying. And not only crying – we're talking, like, properly sobbing, like an actual *baby*?

Sorcha takes my hand in hers.

'Ross,' she goes, 'what's wrong? Come on, tell me.'

And I'm there, 'He said they're probably going to kill Fionn.'

'We've been through this. They're not going to kill him, Ross. He's worth too much to them alive.'

'He said they'd cut their losses if they thought no one was going to pay the five mills.'

'Well, whatever he said, Ross, you know how much I abhor violence. One of Honor's middle names is Suu Kyi.'

'But if they do end up killing him, Sorcha . . .'

'Ross, stop thinkng like that. They're not going to.'

'I'm saying if they do, then it'll be my fault.'

3. 'Now It's Us, Now It's We'

I ask Christian if we're all going to just ignore this thing and he asks me – I shit you not – *what* thing?

I'm like, 'Er, the fact that little Ezra Dumpling is more Jay-Z than JP.'

It's a cracking line – even I have to admit it.

'He's definitely dark,' he goes. 'But then JP is pretty dark himself.'

He's slicing a baguette lengthways as he says this, then he smears one side of it with pesto.

I'm like, 'Pretty focking dark? Dude, it's a black baby!'

Christian finally just nods.

'Yeah, look,' he goes, 'it did cross my mind as well. That day at the hospital. I didn't know where to look when you handed him to me. I just thought . . . Well, I don't *know* what I thought.'

'So whose baby is it?'

'I've no idea.'

'Do we know if she was seeing someone else at the same time as him?'

'That I don't know either.'

'Dude, what are we going to do about it?'

'We're not going to do shit, Ross, because it's none of our business.'

He looks at the customer – this cranky-looking focker, who I'd say is in his early twenties – and goes, 'Sorry, what else did you say you wanted on it?'

'Yeah, tomato,' he goes – and he says it with a bit of a tude as well. 'And mozzarella.'

He's wearing a Leinster jersey – he must be in DBS – but he obviously has no idea who the dude making his sub used to be. Probably can't name a single player outside the current squad. Christian actually apologizes to the little scrote, then puts the mozzarella and tomato on the baguette, like the true pro that he is.

He goes, 'By the way, Ross, I was talking to Ewan and Andrea last night.'

I'm like, 'Andrea? She's not a fan of mine these days. She said one or two things. I'm happy to let them slide, because she's upset. So have they heard from Fionn again?'

'No, but they had a call from some crowd in England. I think they're called the Walsk Group. Something like that.'

'And who the fock *are* they?'

'They're private security consultants. They specialize in, like, anti-terrorism, hostage negotiations, that kind of thing. I looked them up. They've got a pretty impressive client list. A lot of big multinationals use them. Seems to be mostly ex-services personnel working for them – SAS, that kind of thing.'

I get suddenly excited. I'm there, 'You see? This is what should have happened weeks ago. None of this channels of communication horseshit. Send in men with focking guns.'

'Well, we don't know if that's going to happen,' Christian goes, cutting the sub in two. 'Someone's coming over next week to talk to Ewan and Andrea. And to Jenny. And, well, they've asked me and JP to be there, too.'

I'm there, 'Well, you can count me in as well.'

'Er, the thing is, Ross, I think Ewan and Andrea want to keep it small.'

'You can save your focking breath, Christian. I'm going to be there.'

The dude waiting for his lunch rolls his eyes and goes, 'Yeah, I didn't ask you to cut it in two.'

I feel like grabbing him by the back of the neck and smashing his head on the focking counter.

But Christian's like, 'I'm so sorry. I'll stort again.'

He's there, 'No, don't bother – I'll take it. Otherwise, I'll be here all focking day.'

And that's when the phone in the shop suddenly rings.

Christian goes, 'Ross, would you mind answering that?'

I don't mind – mainly because he's my best friend and I'd do any-thing for him – but I make sure to keep staring this prick of a customer out of it as well.

I answer the phone, going, 'Hello, Footlong, Chatham Street.'

The voice on the other end goes, 'Who's that? Who the fock is that?'

It's Lauren and she sounds pretty worked up about something.

I'm there, 'Hey, Lauren – it's the Rossmeister. How the hell are you?'

'I'm in focking labour!' she goes. 'Tell Christian to get down to Holles Street! Now!'

I hang up and I'm like, 'Christian, Lauren's having the baby – go, go, go!'

His mouth drops open and he tears off his apron. He's there, 'Ross, will you look after the shop for me?'

And I'm like, 'Of course I focking will! You just go and do what you have to do!'

Off he runs. The dude in the Leinster jersey shakes his head and goes to follow him out the door.

I'm there, 'Whoa, Dude, where are you going?'

He's like, 'Er, I'm standing here for the last ten minutes, listening to you two having a chat.'

'His wife's about to drop.'

'Why should I care? I only have forty minutes between lectures.'

Dumb Blonde School – I'm a great reader of people.

'I'll tell you what,' I go, an idea forming in my mind, 'you're actu-ally right. You've been focked around grandly here today, so I'm going to give it to you for free.'

He's like, 'What?' suddenly all ears.

Students love free shit.

'That's how much your custom means to us,' I go. 'You shouldn't have had to wait as long as you did. Ten minutes is a disgrace. Yeah, no, you're getting this on the house. As a matter of fact, grab a packet of Hunky Dorys there behind you.'

He doesn't need to be told twice. He turns around to grab the crisps. The second he does, I open one half of his submarine sambo, take a big focking sniff, then I let a humungous flem-globber fall from my mouth onto it.

'Thanks very much,' he goes, turning back to me.

I'm there, 'Not at all. It's the least you deserve. You know that goy who just ran out the door, the dude who owns this place?'

'Er, yeah, what about him?'

'You know he could have very nearly gone on to play for Leinster himself.'

'What, in rugby?'

'Yes, in rugby. In fact, it's a miracle that he never did.'

He has the balls to actually laugh. '*Could* have played for Leinster?' he goes. 'Anyone could say that.'

So I'm there, 'Do you know something? You've really been jerked around here today. As a matter of fact, grab a free drink there to wash it down.'

'Really?'

'Big time. Go and help yourself.'

The focking dope does as well. He walks over to the fridge and takes out a bottle of 7-Up – not a can, by the way, a focking bottle. I open the other half of the sandwich, I do another big snort – a much deeper one this time – roll it around in my mouth, then drop it on top of his tomato and mozzarella. I close it up again, then I wrap it up for him.

'Thanks,' he says to me – I end up having to laugh – on his way out the door.

And I'm like, 'Dude, believe me, the pleasure was mine.'

Sorcha's old dear is waiting for us in the hall when we arrive home from Superquinn. I can tell from her boat race that she's got something to tell us.

'You had a visitor,' she goes, 'while you were out.'

I look at Sorcha – her face full of, like, *hope?*

She's there, 'Dad?'

But her old dear goes, 'I'm sorry, Sorcha, no – it wasn't your father.'

'Oh,' she goes, crushed. 'So, like, who was it then?'

I *instantly* know?

I'm like, 'The rat.'

Sorcha's old dear goes, 'I came downstairs this morning to make Honor's breakfast and he was in the trap. Come and see.'

We follow her down to the lorder, where, as it turns out, Honor is getting acquainted with the thing, talking to it through the bors of its little prison, telling it not to be frightened.

Sorcha can hordly bring herself to look at it.

The thing is focking massive – they weren't wrong when they said it was the size of a small dog. It's black with, like, little roundy ears, dork, beady eyes and it's making one hell of a noise, screeching at a really high pitch and chewing madly at the sides of the cage.

'Honor!' Sorcha goes. 'Come away from him – he's probably full of disease.'

'It's not a him, it's a her,' Honor goes. 'And don't be such a sap. We need to feed her.'

She opens the fridge, pulls out a head of broccoli and storts dropping little – I think they're called, like, *florets*? – into the trap for her.

The rat takes each one in her two front paws and literally just shoves it into her face, letting her big, shorp teeth hack away at it inside her closed mouth, while bits of food spill out of the sides and dribble down her chin and neck.

It's a bit like watching my old dear eat an Avoca Handweavers Rice Krispie cake.

Next, roysh, Honor grabs a salt cellar, one with, like, a little teat at the top of it, rather than one that's full of holes. She fills it up with water, then tips it upside down through the roof of the trap and – incredibly – the rat stands up on her hind legs and storts sucking the water out of the thing.

Honor goes, 'Oh my God, you're a thirsty little girl, aren't you?'

My phone all of a sudden beeps. It's, like, a text message.

It's like, 'Oliver Fionn Ford born @ 5.23 this am. Lauren v tired but v happy!'

My face obviously lights up.

'What is it?' Sorcha goes.

I'm like, 'Christian and Lauren had a little baby boy this morning.'

'Oh my God, that was a long labour.'

They're calling him Fionn – well, as a middle name.'

'Oh, that is so a lovely thing to do.'

'Oliver Fionn. Yeah, no, I'm delighted for Christian. Hopefully, the baby is his now.'

'Ross!'

'I'm serious. After the whole JP thing, it'll probably end up being Indian or focking Japanese.'

Sorcha tells me I shouldn't joke about things like that.

The rat suddenly finishes drinking and I go, 'Okay, I'm going to bring this thing off to release it somewhere.'

And that's when Honor says it. 'You're not,' she goes. 'I'm keeping her.'

I'm there, 'Excuse me?'

She's like, 'I want you to go to that pet superstore in Sandyford and get, like, a proper cage for her and some bedding and a water bottle. Go now, will you? Don't just stand there with your focking mouth open.'

Sorcha, by the way, doesn't say a word.

I'm there, 'Honor, you can't keep a rat as an actual pet. They carry fleas and I'm presuming all sort of diseases.'

'Yeah,' she goes, 'if you really cared about fleas and diseases, you wouldn't be sending me to a national school in Ballybrack.'

She has a point.

I'm there, 'You're going to a national school in Ballybrack because you were expelled from your last school and no one else would take you.'

There's still no back-up from Sorcha. She seems to be in an almost trance.

Honor looks through the little bors and – in the sweetest voice you can imagine – goes, 'Come on, Pippa, I'll show you your new home!' and she picks up the trap by the handle and carries it outside to the tool shed.

I look at Sorcha and I'm like, 'Don't tell me you're cool with this.'

She goes, 'Well, maybe she could keep her for a trial period. Provided she doesn't bring her into the house.'

'Sorcha, it's a rat.'

She looks at her old dear and goes, 'It's the first time in her life that I've ever seen her show concern for something other than herself.'

We're possibly *all* a bit in shock?

I look at Sorcha's old dear, expecting back-up. I'm there, 'But what about, I don't know, diseases and blah, blah, blah.'

Sorcha's there, 'We'll tell Honor not to handle her. And when she's visiting her to wear rubber gloves and that little breathing mask I bought during the worldwide SARS scare.'

I'm like, 'Sorcha, I definitely don't think this is a good idea.'

But Sorcha's old dear goes, 'I've never heard her speak nicely like that before – to anyone or anything.'

And Sorcha's there, 'I'm thinking it might bring out the whole nurturing side to her personality. It might help her accept the fact that she's going to have three little siblings.'

Which means her mind is made up. We're adding a focking rat to our ever-swelling number.

Ronan's old school uniform doesn't fit him anymore and it's kind of, like, *hilarious*? The sleeves of his blazer only reach about two-thirds of the way down his orms and the hems of his trousers are riding a good four inches above his shoes.

'It's fowerteen munts since I had irron me,' he goes, although I still can't believe how much he's grown in that time. And neither can Sorcha. We're sitting at the kitchen table, watching him parade back and forth in front of us, me knocking back coffee, Sorcha eating a breakfast of dried beans and lentils, which she says she's planning to do for the duration of her second trimester.

He's there, 'Would I gerra way wirrit – just for the foorst few days?'

'Oh my God, I'd love to say yes,' Sorcha goes, 'but, Ronan, you can't go back to school looking like that.'

Then she has an idea. 'Ross,' she goes, '*your* old Castlerock uniform is upstairs in the wardrobe.'

Which is true. I had this idea in the back of my head that I was going to possibly frame it and hang it up in a room alongside some of my old jerseys and photographs of me in my glory days. It was going to be an actual Ross Room.

It might seem petty to bring it up now, though.

'Yeah, no,' I go, 'you can definitely try it on. It's in the second wardrobe from the left in our dressing room.'

Off he goes to get it.

'And will you knock on Honor's door and tell her that it's half-past-seven?' Sorcha shouts after him.

Honor just so happens to walk into the kitchen at that exact moment, dressed for school and carrying – this is a surprise to pretty much everyone – Sorcha's old piccolo.

She goes, 'Mom, can I borrow this?'

Sorcha's face lights up. It's always been, like, Sorcha's dream that Honor would one day take up an instrument. In fact, she used to stick the business end of the thing in Honor's mouth when she was a tiny baby to try to awaken the desire in her to make music.

That's how *she* put it, by the way?

Sorcha's there, 'Are you saying you *want* to play the piccolo?'

Honor's like, 'Yes.'

'I thought you said it was sad – for saps and retards.'

Honor just shrugs. She goes, 'I've changed my mind. I want to play for Pippa.'

I'm like, 'Pippa?'

She goes, 'It says on the Internet that rats like music.'

Sorcha smiles.

She's there, 'Okay. Do you want us to sign you up for lessons – the same place as I went?'

She goes, 'I'd love that,' and then out to the tool shed she goes to see her little friend.

'Oh my God!' Sorcha goes. 'I always wanted a daughter who was musical!'

Shadden arrives in, dressed in her Sion Hill uniform, with little Rihanna-Brogan in her orms. It's maybe the first time that it properly hits me – that she's basically a child *with* a child?

Sorcha asks her how they slept.

Shadden goes, 'We slept right troo. There wadn't a bodder on Rihadda-Burrogan all neet – it's like she knows we've a big day ahead of us today.'

I can see what Sorcha's thinking. That'll be the sweet potatoes and whatever else she's giving her.

'I was going to maybe try her on some finger food during the day,' Sorcha goes. 'Maybe some pear slices and some halved blueberries – *if* that's okay with you?'

Shadden goes, 'It's foyen, Sudeka – you're the one's gonna be looking arthur her,' and as she says it, roysh, I can see the definite sadness in her eyes.

Sorcha nods, then stands up.

'Well,' she goes, 'sit down there and I'll get some of this famous porridge that you seem to love.'

Outside, we can hear Honor playing the piccolo – or at least blowing into it and trying to produce actual notes.

Ronan steps back into the kitchen wearing my old blazer and trousers. They fit him perfectly.

'Now that's better!' Sorcha goes, measuring the oats and water into the bowl. 'Oh my God, Ronan, you look *so* like your father when I first met him!'

Ro looks at me. 'You doatunt moyunt,' he goes, 'if I weer it?'

I'm like, 'Yeah, no, I was going to hang it up in one of the spare rooms upstairs, which was going to be a sort of tribute room to my rugby. But it's cool.'

We all sit and eat our breakfast together, which is nice.

'Shadden, you must be so excited,' Sorcha goes. 'Oh my God, I always *loved* the first day back at school, didn't I, Ross?'

She did. She was a focking sap, even then.

She's there, 'All those brand-new copies to fill. The smell of the books. New shoes to break in. Do you know what Shakespeare play you're going to be doing?'

Shadden's distracted. She's like, 'Er . . . *Mack Bett*.'

'Oh my God, I love that play, even though *I* did *Othello*. You should definitely watch the movie version – even the modern-day one, set in Melbourne. Sam Worthington is in it, who was also in *Avatar*.'

I look at Shadden and I realize that she's not even listening. She's staring at little R&B, sitting in her high-chair, hitting the table tray in front of her with the palm of her hand and laughing. And all she can obviously think about is that, in a few minutes' time, she's going to be saying goodbye to her daughter for the first time in the nine months since she had her.

Sorcha hasn't copped it, though, and she continues just babbling on.

'I know you're only going into fifth year,' she goes, 'but you should definitely try to cover everything on the syllabus by next May. That means that in the year of your *actual* Leaving Cert, you'll basically be *re*-reading everything? I did that and it gave me a definite advantage.'

Ronan realizes that Shadden is about to burst into tears, so he stands up and goes, 'Mon, Shadden – we'll wander dowin for the Deert.'

Shadden stands up as well. She's barely even touched her porridge. 'Joost let me say goodbye to her,' she goes, then she picks little Rihanna-Brogan out of her high-chair and she holds her close to her, the tears suddenly streaming down her face.

Sorcha finally cops that Shadden is upset and she stands up, her face full of concern.

'Shadden, she'll be fine with me,' Sorcha goes. 'And she'll be – oh my God – *so* excited to see you when you get home from school.'

Shadden's eyes are still full of tears, but she nods like she understands. She goes to hand Rihanna-Brogan over and Sorcha goes to take her, except it's like Shadden's hands are suddenly paralysed. They refuse to let go of her daughter. And suddenly she's hysterical.

'No,' she's going. 'She'll forget me, so she will! What if she forgets me?'

Ronan goes, 'Mon, Shadden,' peeling away her fingers, one by one. 'Mon, you'll see her in anutter few hours.'

Ronan puts his orm around his girlfriend, and then, with his *and* her schoolbags slung over his two broad shoulders, he walks her out of the house and down the Vico Road in the direction of Killiney

Dort Station, talking softly to her, telling her that she'll always be Rihanna-Brogan's mother, telling her that this is for the best.

'He's changing every day,' JP goes.

He's talking about the famous Ezra focking Dumpling. And it's all I can do to stop myself from going, 'He hasn't changed into a white baby yet, has he?' because, even though it kills me to see one of my best friends in the world – a former teammate, don't forget – taken for a fool by a bird, I still have to be careful how I *handle* it?

I don't want to lose him as a mate, which I could easily do if I end up saying the wrong thing. For instance – Dude, that baby is black.

So I just go, 'Yeah, no, that's great, JP. I'm focking delighted for you.'

He's there, 'Do you know something, Ross – I used to listen to you talking about Ronan and Honor and it was like you thought you actually invented fatherhood. Like you were the only one who'd ever been through it. And the thing is, I totally understand that, now that I'm a dad myself.'

'Hmmm.'

'I remember you used to say it was the most important thing in the world.'

'I possibly exaggerated that.'

'Well, I'd go even further and say it's the *only* thing!'

'Let's not go making big statements. There's other stuff. There's loads of other stuff.'

'Nothing that really matters, though.'

'Er, there's *rugby*? I've a very strong feeling that Leinster could make it three-in-a-row this year. Don't put all your eggs in one basket is the lesson I'm trying to teach you. In case it all turns to shit later on.'

He's not listening, though. It's like he's still *high* on it all?

He goes, 'I look at him lying there, totally helpless and I think, I would do literally anything to make sure he's warm and fed. And I genuinely would, Ross. I'd sweep the roads. I'd clean toilets . . .'

Like I said, he's talking out of his hole. It's a relief when we finally pull up outside Fionn's old pair's gaff.

Ewan and Andrea are pretty surprised to see me standing on their doorstep, although disgusted is another word. 'What the hell is *he* doing here?' is Andrea's actual opening line.

JP rushes to my defence and I'm saying fair focks. 'Christian couldn't make it,' he goes. 'Lauren's just had a baby. They had another boy.'

Andrea just shrugs like she can't see the connection between the two things – me being there and Christian not.

I go, 'Look, I'm sorry about the last day. You were upset. And I accept that, deep, deep down, you don't actually blame me for Fionn going to Africa in the first place . . .'

Ewan – in fairness to him – is there, 'Let's not have this conversation on the doorstep, shall we?'

He opens the door wider and in we go.

I end up getting the exact same grilling from Jenny when I step into the living room – and from Fionn's sister, Eleanor, and her husband, David, who are sitting around waiting for this dude from England to arrive. I think I mentioned that I gave Eleanor my A game while she and David were having a few pre-marital jitters.

'What are yoy doying here?' it's Jenny who goes. 'Oy doyn't remimber yoy being invoytud.'

'Look,' I go, 'I know that pretty much everyone in this house has an issue with me. Either you think I'm a racist, or you blame me for Fionn leaving Ireland in the first place, or you hate me for maybe taking advantage of a situation to seal the deal with Eleanor there and blah, blah blah. Whatever way you feel about me, I still regord Fionn as a very good friend of mine and I'm sure he feels the same way about me. And just to let you know, Christian's wife, Lauren, had a little baby boy yesterday morning and his middle name is going to be Fionn. I know that has fock-all to do with me, but I'm just throwing it out there as a positive.'

Before anyone has a chance to react to my little pep-talk, the doorbell rings and Ewan goes back outside to answer it.

'Oy doyn't want to hear a word out of yoy,' Jenny goes, 'whin this goy cams un.'

I've always found Australian slash New Zealand birds to be very aggressive.

I'm just like, 'Yeah, whatever,' at the same time thinking, yeah, you've known Fionn for, what, four or five months? I've known him since we were, like, fourteen years old. I gave him his first official wedgy. One of his balls went up inside him and a nurse had to knead his groin for ten minutes before it dropped back down. In other words, we go way, way back and I'm not going to be told when I can and can't talk, especially by a basic blow-in.

In they come, first Ewan, then this dude – Fred Pfanning, he turns out to be called. And, it has to be said, he's a hell of a lot older than I expected him to be. At a guess, I'd say we're talking early sixties, although he clearly keeps himself in shape. He's got less meat on him than a runway model's conscience and he's incredibly tall – maybe even six-foot-five – with grey hair ported to the side, a thick grey moustache and a set of teeth that'd put the focking shits up a seal colony. He's wearing a purple polo-neck, tucked into grey slacks with razor creases and he talks like one of the airmen – I don't know if you remember them – from *'Allo 'Allo!*.

'Hellay,' he goes, hand out. 'Fred Pfanning is the name . . . Hellay. Yes, Fred Pfanning . . .' as Ewan leads him around the room, making the introductions.

'These are two of Fionn's oldest friends,' Ewan goes and it's nice to get that acknowledgement. It's a genuine boost. 'JP and Ross.'

'JP and Ross,' the dude goes. 'Yes, very good. I'll remember those names.'

Andrea offers him tea or coffee, but he looks at his watch and goes, 'Nay, nay, thank you. I had a coffay four ars agay. Knay your optimum caffeine level. A lesson I learned during the Falklands Conflict. To my eternal cost. Tell me something about Fionn.'

He sits down, so we all do as well.

I go to say something, except Andrea gets in before me, then I think, fair enough, she's his mother – she knows him a bit better than me.

'He's a lovely boy,' she goes. 'He's caring and considerate.

Incredibly smart. He got the maximum points possible in his Leaving Certificate. He could have done literally anything . . .'

Fred sort of, like, twirls his finger around his temple. 'I'm processing all of this,' he goes. 'I'm processing it.'

Jesus, he's as nutty as focking parrot shit.

Ewan goes, 'Caring is probably the quality we'd most like to emphasize. He has a good, good heart.'

Out of the blue, I suddenly go, 'He also played rugby. He was a winger, even though he possibly lacked the pace to become, say, a Denis Hickie or a Shane Horgan. I think the rugby thing is definitely worth mentioning, though, because it'd be a major port of his whole CV.'

Everyone just stares at me like I've just said, 'I think I'll pull my trousers down and take a shit in the stove burner there.'

'I don't like this one,' Fred goes, pointing at me. 'Ross, isn't it? I'm rather a good judge of character and this chep strikes me as an all-round bed egg.'

No one says a word in my defence, by the way. In fact, Jenny goes, 'He's also a racist.'

'Hmmm,' he goes. 'Thet, I'd wager, and a lot more besides. What I'd like to knay about Fionn is his likely psychological state at this time. Is he mentally strong, would you think? Is he resourceful?'

'Oy would soy *definitloy?*' Jenny goes. Like I said, the girl hasn't been in his life a wet focking day. 'Knaying him loyk oy doy, oy would soy he's coypen okoy – probably a lot bitter than moy,' and then she bursts into tears and Eleanor ends up having to put her orm around her to, like, *comfort* her?

'If there's a positive in all of this,' Fred goes, 'it's thet the motivation for the kidnapping is criminal rather then political. We're not dealing with the Lord's Resistance Army or any of these other fections. These cheps aren't fenetics. Don't get me wrong – they're dangerous. But they're purely in it for the money. I understayend they're looking for five million dollars. I also gether that they're not gaying to get it. As time goes on, they're gaying to become more and more desperate and, inevitably . . . well, they're gaying to make mistakes.'

Me and JP look at each other. We're both obviously thinking the same thing – that could be good news *or* bad news?

Ewan goes, 'Can you help us?'

Fred doesn't give him a straight answer. He gives him the company profile. 'The Walsk Group, of which I am a director, has thirty yurrs of experience,' he goes, 'in operating in some of the world's most troubled regions – Irawq, Efghenisten, Somalia, Eastern Georgia, South Sudan, the Horn of Efrica at the time of the war between Ethiopia and Eritrea. A major part of what we do is to offer security to personnel working in areas where they've been told not to be. But very awften, people call us when things gay wrong. We specialize in hostage negotiations and I'm rather proud to say that we have never hayended over as much as a brass farthing in rayensom money.'

There's, like, a pause.

'But I won't lie to you,' he goes. 'What we do *is* expensive.'

'How much?' Andrea goes.

I was going to ask it, but – again – I decided to leave it to her.

'To take on a job like this, we require a non-refundable advawnce of one hundred thisind pindes sterling . . .'

Andrea looks at Ewan. She goes, 'We have some savings.'

The dude isn't finished 'Plus a success fee – payable on the safe return of your son into your care – of five hundred thisind pindes.'

My mouth drops open – wide enough for a lion tamer to stick his focking head in there. A hundred Ks, plus another half a mill. But Ewan doesn't need to even think about it.

'We'll sell the house,' he goes.

Andrea nods. She's like, 'Of course we will.'

And then Eleanor looks at David and she's there, '*We'll* sell ours as well.'

The girl looks well, it has to be said. I can see the full outline of her mamms through her black fitted shirt.

David nods and goes, 'We'll put it on the market tomorrow. There's about eighty thousand euros worth of equity in it.'

Jesus. That's both their homes gone in twenty focking minutes. Who needs a recession with dudes like Fred Pfanning in the world?

JP catches my eye, possibly wondering the same thing that I'm wondering – are they being taken for a ride here? Is this dude even for real?

'I've hayendled more than a hundred cases like this,' he goes, as if reading our minds, 'and I'm heppy to report that I've successfully extrected the target in eighty-six percent of those cases. There's a list of testimonials on the website.'

Ewan looks at Andrea, then back at Fred. 'We'll need some time,' he goes, 'to come up with the hundred thousand. Like I said, we have savings and, um, some money that my mother left us, which is in a bank account that, well, we can only get at it with a month's notice. And I have a life assurance policy that I could possibly cash in.'

Fred stands up. We all stand up.

'I *would* say take your time,' Fred goes, 'but I'm quite certain you don't need me to impress on you the urgency of acting quickly in this case.'

Ewan's like, 'Yes, of course. I'll speak to the bank. They might let us have it sooner.'

But I feel the need to suddenly say something. It's like I suddenly *have* to? It's pretty obvious that Fionn's family would do anything to get their son back. But someone has to look out for their – I'm going to say consumer *rights*?

'So how does it work?' I go. 'You send in a crew to stort cracking heads?'

He's like, 'Crecking heads, as you call it, is thenkfully seldom necessary. Old-feshioned detective work and patient negotiating skills usually kerry the day. And I'm more than familiar with Ugenda, its criminal gengs and its terrain.'

'You?'

'Yes.'

'On your own?'

'Yes, on my own.'

He turns around and shakes hands with Fionn's old pair, then with Jenny, and he tells them not to worry, he'll bring Fionn home and to call him when they're ready to wire the cash. But I'm still not a happy rabbit.

'Whoa, back up the hord drive,' I go. I grab him by the top of the orm, because he was trying to get out the door without answering the hord questions. 'These people have just agreed to hand over every cent they own in the world. They're prepared to even sell their gaffs. I think they're entitled to gun-ships and tanks and all focking sorts. And you're saying *you're* going to handle it yourself? Er, no disrespect to you . . .'

I give his orm a squeeze. There's literally no muscle on his bones. It's like holding onto the pole while standing on the Luas.

I'm there, 'But what exactly are you going to do if it all kicks off?'

I don't see the punch coming. That's because it doesn't travel far. Three or four inches at the most. He hits me square in the chest and, I swear to fock, it's like Cian Healy has just thrown a focking Dort carriage at me. I can't breathe – in *or* out. I can't move. I'm left just standing there with a shocked expression on my face.

Fred puts one hand on my shoulder and the other between my legs and he lifts me up like a shop dummy, turns me upside down and literally body-slams me down onto Fionn's old pair's living-room floor.

I'm pretty focking sure I've got the pattern of the corpet in reverse on my back.

I'm left just lying there, gulping for air, looking up at Fred's upside-down face looking down at me. He goes, 'Thet is what I do, old chep, when it awl kicks awf.'

Sorcha asks me if I've thought about whether she should have a vaginal birth or a Caesarian. This is while I'm eating a toasted ham and cheese sandwich. I drop it onto the plate.

'Sorcha,' I go, 'you definitely pick your moments.'

She's like, 'It's something we should definitely discuss, Ross.'

'But not while I'm having my lunch.'

She's down on the kitchen floor with Rihanna-Brogan and they're just, like, rolling a ball backwards and forwards to each other. Sorcha reckons it helps babies develop co-ordination and teaches them about taking turns when they're playing.

She goes, 'Good girl, Rihanna-Brogan! Who's the good girl?

Hmmm?' and then she turns to me and, in a totally different voice, goes, 'Well, pardon me, Ross, for wanting to involve you in the decision as to how your children enter the world.'

I just sigh. I'm like, 'Okay, what are the pros and cons?'

She's there, 'Well, obviously, this is all just hypothetical. A lot depends on how the babies are positioned in the uterus in the final weeks, especially the one that's closest to the cervix . . .'

I push the plate away. That sandwich is not going to be eaten now.

'Generally,' she goes, 'for triplets, they do prefer you to schedule a C-section. But I've been reading one or two books that say that in carefully selected cases, multiple vaginal deliveries may actually be safe.'

'Okay.'

'I'm just saying that I'm going to talk to the midwife about it. If it's at all possible, I'd like to give birth naturally . . . Good girl, Rihanna-Brogan. Oh, your mommy is going to be so proud when you show her what you learned today! So proud!'

Sorcha's old dear arrives into the kitchen. She's tearing up a piece of paper, which she then drops into the old Brabantia.

Sorcha goes, 'I'm just saying, Mom, that I think I'm going to have a natural birth, if it's at all possible. The problem with having a Caesarian is that your body doesn't know that it's, like, *had* a baby? I've read that in loads of different places. If you want to, like, properly bond with your baby or babies, then it's best to have them the way nature intended. It's what I did with Honor.'

I'm about to go, 'Yeah? And how did that work out for the two of you?' when I suddenly notice that Sorcha's old dear is upset about something.

I'm famously useless when it comes to crying women – despite years of exposure to them – so I use my eyes to draw Sorcha's attention to it.

'Oh my God,' Sorcha goes, jumping to her feet, 'what's wrong?'

Her old dear's like, 'Nothing.'

'What was that . . . Oh my God, what was that piece of paper that you put in the bin?'

'It was a letter. It doesn't matter.'

'A letter? A letter from whom?'

I never really know when you're supposed to say 'who' and when you're supposed to say 'whom'. I sometimes wonder does anyone *actually* know? The rule seems to be that you just go with whatever feels good. I'm a definite 'who' man.

'It was from your father,' she goes. 'He wants a divorce.'

Sorcha's like, '*Excuse* me?'

She's there, 'Now don't overreact, Sorcha,' even though she's the one making a big deal of it.

Sorcha's there, 'He wants a divorce on the grounds that, what, you wanted to spend time with your daughter who happens to be pregnant with triplets?'

'He wants a divorce on the grounds of abandonment.'

'Abandonment? Hang on, are you saying that was an *actual* solicitor's letter?'

'Sorcha, stop shouting.'

'Oh! My God! Show it to me!'

Sorcha makes a grab for the bin. Her old dear stands in her way.

'I want to see it,' Sorcha goes.

Her old dear's like, 'I've torn it up and that's that. As a matter of fact . . .'

She takes the top off the bin and pulls the bin bag out of it. Then she opens the back door and brings it outside to throw it into the wheelie bin.

Sorcha lays her hand on her bump. 'Oh my God,' she goes. 'Ross, my parents are getting divorced! My parents! Are getting divorced!'

I love Sorcha, but she can be a serious drama queen. As can her old dear, by the way. She suddenly comes running back into the kitchen, going, 'Something's going on! In the tool shed!'

I'm like, 'What do you mean?'

'There's screeching.'

'There's always screeching. There's a focking rat in there.'

'It's a different pitch. And it's more, oh, I don't know, insistent.'

Out we go to investigate – me, followed by Sorcha, with Rihanna-Brogan in her orms, followed by Sorcha's old dear.

When we reach the tool shed, I just throw the door open,

although I do step back at the same time, not knowing what to expect.

Sorcha's old dear ends up being right. Pippa is making strange focking noises. I reach around the door for the switch and I flick on the light. We stort creeping slowly towards the workbench that her cage is sitting on.

Sorcha's old dear cops it pretty much straight away.

'She's in labour,' she goes.

I'm like, 'What?'

Sorcha says the same thing as me.

She's there, 'What?'

We all take another step closer. Pippa's body is swollen like a focking Galia melon. I'm thinking, why didn't any of us notice?

She suddenly gets up on her tiptoes and something small and pink appears through a hole just under her tail. It's a focking rat baby. She squeezes it out of her, her head tucked between her two front legs to watch it drop.

It's, like, pink and hairless and half the size of my finger, its little eyes shut tight, blind to the world. Pippa storts licking the thing clean. Look, it quite possibly *is* a miracle, but at the same time it's focking disgusting.

Sorcha and her old dear are both going, 'Oh my God!' although it's impossible to know whether it's in a good way or a bad way.

That's when the second head appears.

I'm like, 'Oh, for fock's sake! This is . . . Jesus!'

This one slides out a bit easier. I suppose the first one dug the focking tunnel. Pippa gives rat baby number two a good old sniff and takes her tongue to it as well.

'There's another one,' Sorcha's old dear goes. 'How many do they have?'

Sorcha goes, 'I think they have, like, a whole litter.'

I'm there, 'How many is in a litter?'

She's like, 'I don't know.'

The answer is fifteen – well, at least that's in Pippa's case. We stand there for an hour and a half and we watch her squeeze them out, one by one, then lick them all over. Then, when it's finally finished, she lies down on her front, focked from all the effort, while her full rugby team of rat babies clings to her fur – for presumably, like, warmth.

Rihanna-Brogan smiles and claps her two little hands together.

Sorcha looks at me, her face all pale. She blows hord and I realize that one thing is for certain. She's changed her mind about having a vaginal birth.

Honor asks me what the fock we're doing here and by here she means my old man's front door. It's just a short detour on our way home from her piccolo lesson in the Royal Irish Academy of Music.

'It's Helen's birthday,' I go.

I've brought her a bunch of irises, which are her favourite flowers, and the new JK Rowling, which I heard her say she wanted to read.

Like I said, I'm a huge fan and she's always been a major defender of mine.

'She's not your mother,' Honor goes.

I'm there, 'I know she's not my mother, Honor. But she's engaged to my old man, which means one day she's going to be presumably my stepmother.'

Honor sighs – bored.

'Just promise me we're not going to stay long,' she goes. 'Pippa needs me.'

Pippa and her babies. Honor is smitten with them, by the way. When she came home from school and saw those fifteen tiny little rats – blind and hairless, and pink like uncooked cocktail sausages, I think she fell in love.

Which is unfortunate, because Sorcha – having told Honor that she could keep Pippa – has finally come to her senses and decided she now wants both mother and babies gone. She also wants *me* to break the news to our daughter, a job I've been building myself up to and then bottling for three days now.

The old man opens the door.

'Well, hello there!' he goes – top of his focking voice. 'My son and heir and my beautiful granddaughter! Oh, look, you've got your little flute with you!' because he sees the little case in her hand.

Honor's there, 'It's a piccolo.'

He goes, 'A piccolo! Wonderful! Are you going to play us a tune? Perhaps "Happy Birthday" for my intended!'

'No, because I've been playing for the last hour and my larynx is sore.' She walks straight past my old man into the gaff. 'Anyway,' she goes, 'we're not staying long.'

I look at the old man and smile, as if to say, kids, huh?

He invites me in. 'We were just about to have birthday cake!' he goes.

I'm like, 'Coola boola,' and I follow him down to the kitchen.

By the time we get there, Honor is showing Helen photographs of the rat litter on her iPhone. Judging by Helen's expression, she's no longer in the humour to eat cake.

'I have to get back to them,' Honor goes. 'That's why it's just a flying visit.'

Helen sees the flowers and the book and she's delighted. 'Ross,' she goes, 'that's terribly thoughtful of you!'

I hand them to her and we sing 'Happy Birthday'. Well, me and the old man do. Honor rolls her eyes and tells us we're lame and also saps. Then Helen cuts the cake. It turns out to be a Black Forest, which I actually love.

'Any word from Erika?' I go. 'As in, for your birthday?'

She's in, like, Buenos Aires with that focking showjumper she ran away with. I wouldn't even consider showjumping an actual sport.

'No, nothing,' Helen goes, smiling sadly. 'She has her own life to lead. Your father and I just have to get used to that fact.'

The old man goes, 'What kind of a girl considers her mother not worth a phone call even on her bloody well birthday?'

'She'll get in touch when she's good and ready, Charlie.'

Honor goes, 'Okay, I'm bored now. Can I get back to my babies?'

Five hundred yoyos for a cor seat. Five hundred yoyos. For a cor seat. And we need three of them.

You do the math.

'There's cheaper ones,' I try to go. 'Why do we have to buy the most expensive?'

Sorcha's there, 'I'm going to leave you to think about what you've just said,' and then, literally five seconds later, she goes, 'Oh my God, look, Ross, it can also be used as an extended rearward-facing seat. And it's got an impact shield rather than a horness when facing forward.'

I've finally done the math, by the way. It's fifteen hundred yoyos. I just hand her my plastic.

'We'll get these back to the minibus,' she goes, 'then we might come back to look at cots.'

My bank account got skimmed once and they didn't go through my money half as fast as my wife. I should have focking married *them*.

She knows that's what I'm thinking as well, because she goes, 'This is for your children, Ross!' and then she goes off to pay.

That's when I cop JP's old man. Or actually he cops me. He sort of, like, sidles up to me, looking majorly hassled, and goes, 'What am I supposed to buy this fucking kid?'

He has, like, a babygro and one or two other bits in his hand.

I'm like, 'Dude, who knows. Who focking knows. Congratulations, by the way. The whole grandfather thing and blah, blah, blah.'

He just laughs. 'Yeah,' he goes. 'I'm a grandfather – fucking sure I am,' and then he stares at Sorcha – she's making baby-related small talk while the bird behind the counter swipes my cord – and goes, 'I hear she's having triplets.'

I'm like, 'Yeah, no, I still haven't got my head properly around it.'

'Three,' he goes, still staring at her – mostly at her orse, I notice. I know what he's going to ask before he even asks it. 'Has she decided . . .'

'It's going to be a Caesarian,' I go.

He nods, thoughtfully. 'It'd have to be,' he goes. 'You know, triplets would make a real fucking mess down there.'

I'm like, 'Yeah, thanks for that, Mr Conroy.'

'Be like throwing a rucksack into Busárus.'

'And thank you for that image.'

'So what the fuck is going on with my son?'

'What do you mean?'

'What do I mean? What do you think I mean? He thinks that *he's* that baby's father.'

It's actually a relief to hear him say it. I'm there, 'Are you saying you think he possibly isn't?'

'Jesus Christ,' he goes, 'the baby is black.'

'Well, JP's pretty dark himself.'

'Is that supposed to be funny?'

'No, it's just what a lot of people are saying. I don't know, have you mentioned it to him?'

'I've tried to. In a roundabout way. So has his mother. You know what JP's like. You say the wrong word and he's liable to never speak to you again.'

'Yeah, no, I know.'

'Him and his fucking principles. Look, I'm an estate agent. I've sold thousands of people in this country into a lifetime of mortgage servitude for the privilege of living in a giant fucking pigeon loft on the side of a motorway. I lie for a living. I do it well. But I can't keep looking at that baby and telling my son, "He's got your eyes" and "He's got your smile."'

'He looks fock-all like him. I was actually the first one to say it, in fairness to me.'

'He either doesn't see it or he doesn't fucking want to see it. The other thing is, if anything happens to JP, this kid is next in line to inherit. And I don't know who the fuck his father is!'

'Well, what are you going to do?'

'Nothing. Because you're going to do it.'

'What?'

'You're going to sit him down and you're going talk to him.'

'Errr . . .'

'That's it. It's decided. You're doing it.'

'Dude, what makes you think he'd listen to me?'

'Of course he'd listen to you,' he goes. 'My son would walk through a fucking wall for you.'

I'm like, 'Would he?'

I don't know why I'm so surprised. It's nice to hear it all the same.

He's there, 'You were the captain of his team.'

I'm like, 'But that was, like, years ago.'

He goes, 'Your captain at school is your captain for life.'

It was one of Father Fehily's expressions. It was actually the last thing he said to us before he died.

Jesus, this dude definitely knows what buttons to push with me.

'Okay,' I hear myself go. 'I'll be the one who says it to him.'

Sorcha goes, 'Have you told Honor to get rid of those rats yet?'

I'm watching my DVD of the Leinster v Northampton miracle match.

I'm there, 'I'm still kind of working up to it, Babes.'

She goes, 'What does that mean?'

'It means she's going to be upset. And when she's upset, she tends to lash out and say hurtful things to me – especially about my rugby.'

She's there, 'Your *rugby*?' and she shakes her head, to make it appear like I'm being ridiculous.

I'm there, 'The girl knows how to really wound me, Sorcha.'

She goes, 'Go and tell her, Ross. She's in the tool shed now. I want them gone by today.'

'Again, I'd prefer to just . . .'

'Ross, do it now!'

I have no choice. I get up from the TV and I go outside. I end up standing around for a good four or five minutes to try to work up the courage to tell my daughter that I have to release her beloved pets into the wild.

I finally head for the tool shed, thinking, okay, if I can face down a stadium full of haters back in the day, then I can face the wrath of Honor.

She doesn't seem to notice me at first, she's so lost in her own little world. She's, like, chatting away to Pippa and the little rat babies through her breathing mask and she's dropping little cereal clusters through the bors of the cage and telling them all how beautiful they are.

I'm there, 'Hey, Honor.'

I hear, like, a sniffle and that's when I realize that she's already crying.

I go, 'Honor, what's wrong?'

Without even looking at me, she's like, 'I know what you're going to say.'

'What?' I go. 'What do you think I'm going to say?'

She takes off her mask, turns around to look at me and goes, 'You're going to tell me I have to get rid of them.'

Her eyes, I can see, are filled with tears.

I'm there, 'How did you know?'

She's like, 'I just knew she'd change her mind. And she didn't have the focking guts to tell me herself either.'

I end up having to just sigh. I'm there, 'Yeah, no, that's true. She definitely bottled it. But you do understand, don't you? No one's denying that you're great with them. But it's what you might end up catching off them.'

She just nods – her face a mess of snot and tears – and goes, 'I want to be there, when they're being released.'

I'm there, 'Of course. Actually, can I just say, I genuinely didn't expect you to take it this well. I thought you were going to stort slagging me off about Leo Cullen calling me Rod instead of Ross coming out of Marco Pierre White's.'

She's like, 'No, I understand. You've got the babies to think about.'

'Yeah, no, that's your mother's line all of a sudden.'

She just nods. I'm actually a great father. I should be teaching this shit in a classroom.

I'm there, 'Will we do it now?'

She wipes her face with the palm of one of her yellow rubber gloves and goes, 'Where are we going to release them?'

'I was thinking maybe Bray. That place must be full of them.'

I pick up the cage and that's when she says it – again, this is, like, totally out of the blue. She's like, 'Daddy, I don't have any friends.'

Jesus Christ. My hort literally breaks. I put the cage down.

I'm like, 'What are you talking about? You've got loads of friends,' but at the same time I'm hoping she doesn't ask for names, because I literally can't think of one.

'I don't,' she goes. 'Other mums and dads tell their children to stay away from me, because I'm horrible.'

I crouch down and I'm like, 'Come here – you're not horrible. Jesus Christ, Honor,' and I pull her close to me and that's when the tears really stort to come. She just, like, cries and cries and cries into my shoulder, until I end up actually crying *myself*?

'You're the only person who actually likes me,' she goes.

I'm there, 'That's a nice thing to say. I do like you.'

'You're the best dad. You're the best dad in the world.'

I'm like, 'That's a boost. That's a serious boost.'

At the same time, through my tears, I'm looking at Pippa and her little rat babies and I'm thinking, Okay, what's the actual horm here? Okay, there's Weil's disease and possibly plague – but I can't deny that a definite change has come over Honor since Pippa entered her life. She's turned into a little softie and – much as I hate patting myself on the back – a total daddy's girl.

I'm there, 'Okay, what if I told you there was a way you could possibly keep them?'

Honor pulls away from me and just, like, stares at me with her eyes and mouth wide open. The wonder on a child's face is one of the most beautiful sights in the world.

She's there, 'I thought that focking bitch said I had to get rid of them?'

I go, 'She did. But we don't have to tell her.'

'But she'll find out.'

'Not if we move them down to the old coach house, she won't.'

The old coach house is, well, literally that – this sort of, like, out-building at the bottom of the gorden, where the original owner of the gaff – in nineteen hundred and something – used to keep an actual stage coach. Sorcha refuses to go in there because there was a story, from the time she was a kid, that the place was haunted by the ghost of a headless something or other. He presumably tried to go under a low bridge, the stupid fock.

Anyway, the point is that from the time Sorcha heard the story, she never darkened the door of the place again – and neither did her old dear or her sister.

'The old coach house?' Honor goes. 'Isn't that supposed to be, like, haunted?'

I'm there, 'You don't believe in all that, do you?'

She laughs. She's like, 'No!'

I'd say if ghosts do exist, they frighten each other by telling Honor O'Carroll-Kelly stories.

She goes, 'I'm going to need more cages – they're going to have to be separated once they've been weaned.'

I'm like, 'You seem to know very much what you're doing.' I know she's spent hours online, basically reading up on the little fockers and their habits.

I'm there, 'We'll tell your old dear that we're going off to release them, then we'll swing into Sandyford and get those new cages – is that okay?'

She nods. She's like, 'Thank you, Daddy.'

I pick up the cage, then she slips her little rubber-gloved hand into mine and we carry Pippa and her fifteen rat babies down to the coach house, Honor actually skipping – I've never known her to skip before – and me feeling like suddenly the best father in the world.

'He picked him up,' JP goes – he's focking loving telling the story. 'Ross, what weight are you?'

I just, like, refuse to answer. I wouldn't give him or the rest of them the pleasure.

'Say, thirteen stone,' he goes. 'And bear in mind, this is, like, an old man we're talking about – sixty-one, sixty-two. He picks him up like he's a fourteen-year-old Romanian gymnast and he slams him down on the living-room corpet.'

They all laugh. Everyone. We're talking Shoshanna. We're talking Christian. We're talking Jenny, who actually witnessed it. We're talking JP's old pair. We're talking Chloe, Sophie and Amie with an ie.

I'm there, 'Well, if it had been a rugby match, it would have been classed as dangerous play. Because if you lift a player off his feet, you have to make sure that you deliver him safely to the ground again. Those are the focking rules.'

JP goes, 'What's that got to do with anything?'

'I'm just making the point that if it had been an actual match situation, he would have been red-corded and possibly banned for six months.'

'But it wasn't a match situation. And you got owned. By an old man.'

They all crack their holes laughing again. I end up just shrugging. There's shit I could say, but I don't. It's JP's day.

We're in Kielys, by the way, to supposedly wet Ezra focking Dumpling's head.

'So when is this dude going to Uganda?' Christian goes and everyone – and I mean *everyone* – looks at Jenny, like she's got the exclusive rights to talk about the situation, even though I've had focking toenail infections that have lasted longer than her relationship with Fionn.

She goes, 'Ewan and Andrea noyd another woyk or toy to come up with the monay. Andrea's selling her caahr.'

It's a Honda Civic, but it's 06. I don't know what the fock she'll get for it.

'This Fred soyms pretty hipefill abaaht foynding hum, thoy. He's got a lut of experience in gitting poyple aaht of hustige situoyshions *aloyve?*'

Chloe and Amie with an ie tell her that she's – oh my God – *so* courageous, while Shoshanna rubs her back in, like, a comforting way, her new bezzy focking mate.

'Oym troying to git a moyting with Inda *Kinnoy?*' she goes. 'Oym hoyping he can put prishure on the Ugandan Government throy the E Yoy? Oh, and oym goying to be on the *Loyte Loyte Shoy.*'

'Oh my God!' Chloe goes.

'Yeah, it's in a capple of woyks. Oy just thunk it's soy important to koyp Fionn's noym in the noys, so poyple doyn't *forgit* hum?'

Yeah, there's no focking danger of us forgetting him, I think about going, except I don't get the chance to. Because I notice JP's old dear staring at Shoshanna, obviously thinking, How could you do it to him – as in, let him think that he's a father when he's basically not?

And that's when I happen to look at JP's old man and I notice that he's just, like, glowering at me – basically urging me, again, to have a word with his son.

I just nod.

He mouths the words, 'Fuck's sake!' at me and I decide that if I'm going to do this thing, I need one or two straighteners first.

I go up to the bor. I order a double brandy and Christian suddenly appears at my elbow.

'Jesus,' he goes, 'what's that for?'

I'm there, 'Courage.'

'Courage?'

'I'm going to say something to JP.'

'About what?'

'For fock's sake, Christian – about that baby being . . .'

I suddenly have to be careful with my words because the borman who's serving me is *also* black?

Christian goes, 'Ross, I'm really not sure that's a good idea.'

I'm there, 'Somebody has to say something. He's bonding with that kid and it's not even his.'

'We don't know that for sure.'

'Well, you seemed pretty focking certain the last time I spoke to you.'

'I'm just saying, Ross, what are we basing this on?'

The borman raises his eyebrows at me. I decide that a double isn't going to do the job. I push the glass back across the bor to him.

'Put two more in there,' I go.

The dude turns around to the row of optics.

Christian's there, 'Come on, Ross. Answer me. You're going to tell him it's not his baby. What are we judging it on?'

I go, 'I'm judging him on the colour of his focking skin, Christian. He's focking black. He's not Irish. And I just think what's happening is wrong.'

The next thing I hear is a bird's voice behind me – Australia slash New Zealand – go, 'Yoy facking pruck.'

I quickly spin around. It's Jenny. She's just, like, staring hord at me, mad enough to stick the wine glass she's holding into my actual windpipe.

I'm like, 'Jenny, I think you might have possibly got the wrong end of the stick there.'

She goes, 'You facking . . . facking pruck!'

Everyone is suddenly looking over, including Shoshanna, JP and all the rest of them.

'What's going on?' it's JP who goes.

I'm there, 'I, er, think Jenny might have possibly misheard something. It's cool. Go back to your conversations and let's all forget it ever happened.'

'Oy dudn't mishear innnythung,' she has to go. 'He sid something abaaht this gintlemun behoynd the baaah.'

The borman suddenly looks at me, confused.

Jenny shakes her head. 'Oy can't even repoyt ut,' she goes.

Shoshanna's like, 'Was it racist?'

Jenny nods. 'Oh, ut was roysust alroyt.'

The borman asks me what the fock I said. He has a Dublin accent, which comes as a bit of a surprise.

I'm there, 'I wasn't talking about you.'

Christian, by the way, doesn't offer me a single word of back-up, even though he's my witness.

'You sid you were jadging hum boy the colour of his skun,' Jenny goes. 'You sid he dudn't belong here.'

'I said he wasn't Irish,' I hear myself suddenly go. 'And I wasn't talking about *him*. I was talking about . . .'

I look around at JP's old man. Un-focking-believable – he has the balls to actually look away.

'Who?' JP goes. 'Who were you talking about?'

I just think, Fock it – I'm going to have to say it here.

I go, 'I was talking about your baby. Your so-called baby.'

JP and Shoshanna both screw their faces up. Shoshanna's like, 'Okay, *what* does he mean by that?'

Focking American. Actually, I hope *that's* not racist.

'That baby is black,' I go. 'Black, or *a* black – or whatever the PC expression is.'

JP's there, 'Black? Ross, what the fock are you talking about?'

Again, I look at JP's old man and – I swear to fock – he's actually checking out his fingernails. Everyone else is either looking at their shoes or their phones or their drinks and I suddenly realize that I'm on my Tobler here.

I knock back the four shots of brandy in one go. Then I'm like, 'Dude, I'm sorry to be the one to have to tell you this. I'm not saying anything that the rest of these fockers aren't already saying behind your back. That is not your baby.'

I watch his eyes fill up with tears. Deep down, he possibly already knows anyway. But now it's been confirmed by, like, an independent *witness*? I've hurt him. I realize that. Possibly more than I've ever hurt any of my friends, with the exception of obviously Christian when I gave his old dear the treatment.

'Get the fock out of here,' he goes, under his breath.

I'm like, 'Dude . . .' because I love him like a brother, bear in mind.

But Shoshanna steps between us and goes, 'You heard what he said. We are done with you, Ross.'

Lauren pulls a face. She's like, 'Rats?' and then she literally shivers at, like, the *mention* of the word? 'I'm terrified of them. I really am.'

Sorcha's there, 'Well, Honor was very sad saying goodbye – weren't you, Honor?'

This is, like, a week *after* the event?

Honor just shrugs. 'It just wasn't practical,' she goes, 'not with all the diseases they carry and three little babies coming into the house.'

She's good. There's no doubt about that. I suppose she has the background in acting.

I'm there, 'Well, they seemed definitely happy when we released them back into the wild, didn't they, Honor? Pippa actually stopped and looked at you – didn't she? – as if to say, you know, thanks for looking after me and my babies so well and I'm really going to miss you.'

I'm overcooking it. I realize that. Honor just closes her eyes and shakes her head, disappointed with me. Then she goes back to her iPhone.

We're in Lauren and Christian's gaff – the little townhouse they're renting in, like, Booterstown. It's pretty tiny – it's only got, like, two bedrooms – and they're definitely going to have to find somewhere bigger, what with having another kid in the house.

Lauren's holding little Oliver Fionn and Sorcha's holding little Rihanna-Brogan and it's suddenly all baby talk again. Lauren says she's been walking around in a daze since Oliver arrived – 'I'm, like, a total mombie!' – and Sorcha says she thinks she's going to wear a maternity belt for the third trimester, because her back is already – oh my God – killing her.

I feel this sudden need for male company. Christian should have been home from work, like, an hour ago.

'How are things between you and Shadden?' Lauren goes. 'Any better?'

Sorcha's there, 'Most of the time, it's fine. Then she suddenly blows up for – oh my God – absolutely no reason. Ross thinks Kennet and Dordeen are stirring things up.'

'I don't think it,' I go. 'It's a fact.'

'I'm still convinced it's post-natal depression. There's times when everything I say seems to be the *wrong* thing?'

'Speaking of saying the wrong thing,' Lauren goes, 'I heard you disgraced yourself in Kielys last week.'

She's talking to me, rather than Sorcha. I don't know if it's necessary for me to add that detail.

Sorcha looks at me, then back at Lauren. I never told her what happened. Some of us don't have to spill every single detail of our lives to our wives – unlike Christian, who can't hold his piss.

'He told JP that Ezra wasn't his baby,' Lauren goes. 'He told him in front of the entire pub that the baby was black.'

Sorcha's mouth drops open and her eyes pop like she's on a focking rollercoaster. She's like, 'Ross, I told you to stay out of it.'

Except Lauren – this is a genuine surprise to me – goes, 'Well, for once in your life, Ross, I think you might well have done the right thing.'

I'm there, 'Really? Jesus, that's a good thing for my ego to hear, Lauren,' although at the same time I'm worried that with her next sentence she might take it *back*?

'Someone had to say it,' she goes. 'It's beyond ridiculous. Everyone's looking at this baby and they're telling JP that he's the image of him. And JP must know – that's the awful thing. I mean, wasn't Shoshanna's last boyfriend black?'

I'm like, 'What?' because that's definitely news to me.

'Yeah, she was with this guy – he was from, I don't know, wherever. They were both studying at the Royal College of Surgeons. I mean, that's why she was *in* Ireland in the first place.'

I'm there, 'What was his name?'

Sorcha's like, 'Ross, look, you said your piece. Now, I think you really *do* need to stay out of it.'

Lauren goes, 'I don't know his name – as in, he was off the scene when she met JP. Or we presumed he was. There may have possibly been an overlap.'

That's when little focking Ross Junior decides to make his entrance. He's like, 'Hi, Roth!' and I notice that he's carrying – oh, for fock's sake – his little pink picnic basket again.

I'm there, 'Yeah, hi, Ross.'

The kid is a focking attention junkie. He'll almost certainly end up in musical theatre. Or a serial killer. Although you can't say that, of course, because Lauren is famously touchy.

He goes, 'The thoup of the thay ith okth thail.'

Focking this again, I'm thinking.

I'm there, 'I think I'm, er, okay for soup, Ross. Maybe your little brother would like some,' trying to subtly direct the heat away from me.

'Oliver doethunt drink thoup, Roth! He drinkth milk from my mommyth breatht.'

Jesus focking Christ.

'That's right!' Lauren goes, like it's an okay thing for a five-year-old boy to just blurt out.

The kid goes, 'Jutht like I thid. I thucked milk from my mommyth breatht, too – thidn't I, Mommy?'

Honor looks up from her iPhone and goes, 'Okay, *someone* needs to talk to that child about boundaries. Hashtag, Norman Bates much?'

I possibly shouldn't have let her watch that movie.

Before anyone can react, though, Christian suddenly arrives home. It's, like, hellos all round – an air-kiss for Sorcha and a really nice high-five for me – then he tells Lauren that he's sorry he's late, but he had a bit of paperwork to do after he closed the shop.

I can tell straight away that something's wrong. I know Christian like I know myself. I was an outhalf and he was my inside centre – that's just the way it works, my friends.

Sorcha screws up her face, like she smells something bad. She *does* smell something bad. Rihanna-Brogan's shat her pants – well, her nappy. You can't be pissed off with her, though. She's still a baby.

Sorcha goes, 'Ross, would you . . .' and she hands her to me.

Lauren is like, 'You can change her in our room, Ross. There's a towel laid out on the bed.'

Christian says he's going to grab a shower, then he follows me upstairs. When we walk into the bedroom, I turn around to him and I'm like, 'Okay, spill.'

He's there, 'What?'

'Dude,' I go, 'you couldn't keep a secret from me if you tried. We had a psychic connection on the field and it'll be like that for life, for better or worse. Now, come on, what the fock?'

He leans up against the wardrobe. He looks like shit. 'They're taking the franchise off us,' he goes.

I'm like, 'Whoa! Who?'

'Footlong. I had a letter. By registered post this afternoon. All written in focking legalese. Ordering me to close the shop.'

'I mean, why? As in, what the fock?'

'They said they found human matter in one of our sandwiches.'

Uh-oh.

I'm like, 'What?'

'They sent in, like, a mystery shopper,' he goes. 'Oh, just some randomer. Head office sends them into shops every so. often to make sure that franchise-holders are maintaining standards. Quality, taste, cleanliness. It's a corporate thing. And like I said, they said there was human matter in one of our subs.'

I can't even look at him.

'Human matter?' I go, laying Rihanna-Brogan down on the bed and whipping the shitty nappy off her. 'That sounds a bit, I don't know, random.'

'I've been on the phone to New York all afternoon – that's why I'm late – asking them, you know, what that even means. Human focking matter. They said it could be anything, from a fingernail, to snot, to saliva.'

I just nod, with my big concerned face on me. I'm there, 'And are they going to, like, DNA test this so-called human matter?'

He's like, 'Why would they do that?'

'I don't know. To find out who it belonged to – to maybe try to pin it on someone specific?'

'It's not focking *CSI*, Ross. They don't give a fock who it belongs to.'

'Well, that's something at least. Dude, it sounds to me like you'd be better off just accepting this thing and moving on with your life.'

'How can I move on? Me and Lauren sank all of our life savings into that focking shop. Jesus, I signed a five-year lease on the unit – what am I going to do with it?'

'I don't know. What about a Centra? Chatham Street seems to be one of the few streets in Ireland that doesn't actually have one.'

He's there, 'I still don't know how I'm going to break the news to Lauren. Jesus Christ, Ross – we've lost everything.'

And all I can think is, Oh fock.

4. Quizzy Rascal

I follow the sound of Honor's piccolo down to the bottom of the gorden, then I end up standing at the door of the coach house for a good five minutes, watching her play, in total awe.

The Royal Irish Academy of Music. Only the best for my little girl.

When she's finished, I stort clapping and she turns around and sees me for the first time.

I'm there, 'Well done,' except she just, like, *shrugs*?

'It was only "Frère Jacques",' she tries to go, refusing to accept the compliment. That's one way in which we definitely differ.

I'm there, 'They seemed to be really enjoying it.'

She goes, 'I told you, rats love music.'

She puts the piccolo down, then storts moving from cage to cage – she has them separated into, like, six groups – and she pushes little bits of food between the bors and chats away to them, through her little breathing mask, like they're actual children.

I crouch down to her level and I stare into one of the cages with her. I'm like, 'It's like the Pied Piper, isn't it? The Pied Piper of Blahdy Blah?'

They're all getting big as well, even though they're only, like, six weeks old. All their eyes are open. And they've all got, like, hair.

I go, 'The focking size of them! What's that you're feeding them?'

She shrugs. 'It's just dog kibble,' she goes, like it's the most natural thing in the world to know this shit. 'And I put a little bit of saffron on it, because they like the taste.'

I'm like, 'Saffron? Jesus!'

It's nice and focking toasty in here, by the way. I notice she's brought out the two portable radiators that we bought for the triplets' nursery. I'll buy two more before Sorcha cops it. Let's be honest, I'm pretty much putty in my daughter's hands.

'I'm very impressed,' I go.

She's like, 'Thanks,' and she seems to genuinely mean it.

I pick up a stack of A4 printouts that she has on this, like, table – it's as thick as the 01 phone directory. I just know that she's read every single page.

'You've definitely done your homework,' I go. 'You genuinely seem to know what you're at. And what's that in the bottom of their cages? As in, what are you using for bedding?'

'It's just, like, torn-up bits of newspaper and then, like, wood pellets – the same ones we use in the stove burner.'

'And what do they do?'

'They absorb moisture. Otherwise, it would – oh my God – stink in here.'

I'm there, 'And to think, your old dear was actually worried about you keeping them. That just seems laughable now. You've certainly proved yourself to me.'

She goes, 'I love them.'

'I can see it.'

'I love them like you love your rugby tactics book.'

It's the first time she's ever called it that – usually it's either my 'sad book' or *Dickhead's Diary of Delusion*.

'Yeah, no,' I go, 'that's probably a good comparison alright. Anyway, you don't need me breathing down your neck. I'm going to leave you to it. I'm proud of you, Honor.'

I'm on my way out of the coach house when – this is totally out of the blue – she goes, 'I hope they find your friend and that he's alive.'

I'm like, 'What?'

'Fionn,' she goes. 'I know you're worried about him. I hope he's okay.'

I feel like nearly bursting into tears.

I'm like, 'So do I, Honor. Thanks for saying it.'

It's, like, Thursday night and I'm in Kielys, having a drink and considering ringing JP, wondering has he maybe calmed down yet, when all of a sudden, for whatever reason, I turn to discover Hennessy standing at my elbow. He's home from the States.

Of course, I get a sudden attack of the verbal squits.

I'm like, 'Hey, Dude – good to see you. How long are you going to be home for? Are you going to any of the autumn internationals? How's things in Florida? I'd say you're possibly playing a lot of golf out there and I'm judging that by your tan.'

He just stares at me – he doesn't even break eye contact when he lifts his brandy glass to his lips and takes a sip. He talks when he's good and ready. Hennessy only ever talks when he's good and ready.

'I'm home for a few weeks,' he goes, 'to see my new grandson and to sort out this shit with my daughter's business.'

I'm there, 'Yeah, no, Christian mentioned something about it to me. Human matter. Jesus. I don't know if there's any coming back from something like that. I certainly wouldn't eat in there again and I played rugby with the dude.'

'Are you involved in this somehow?'

'What?'

He raises his voice then. He goes, 'I said are you involved somehow? Do you know something? Something I should know but don't.'

'Er, no. Definitely no. Why would you think I was involved in it somehow?'

'Because you're jibbering away like a fucking rhesus monkey and you've got a look on your face that tells me you do know something.'

'Dude, I genuinely don't know what you're talking about.'

He goes, 'If I find out you are involved in this somehow, you can be sure of this – I will fucking crush you.'

I'm walking past Sorcha's sister's room when she all of a sudden calls me from inside. She's like, 'Ross!' in that sweet little butter-wouldn't-melt way of hers.

I poke my head around the door. She's sitting on the end of her bed.

'Oh my God,' she goes, 'don't look so frightened. I was just going to ask you to help me take off my Uggs.'

I'm there, 'What?'

She's like, 'Er, help me take off my *boots?*'

I roll my eyes, then in I go – warily, I might add.

She goes, 'I just don't have the strength to do it myself today.'

She holds up her left leg. I bend down and I cup her calf in my left hand, then with the other I grab the heel of her boot, pull it off and drop it to the floor.

'So what do you think of my mom and dad getting divorced?' she goes. 'Oh my God, it's, like, *so* hilarious.'

I'm there, 'I don't know. Sorcha seems pretty upset by it.'

'Oh, please! This is, like, typical of my dad. He just hates losing. He didn't want his precious daughter to get back with you because he thinks you're a complete waste of human life . . .'

'Thanks for that.'

'And now she's knocked up with triplets, he knows that there's no going back for her. She's trapped.'

'Again, this conversation isn't exactly doing a lot for my self-confidence.'

She lifts up her other leg and I take that boot off, too.

She's like, 'You know what's going to happen, of course?'

I'm there, 'What?'

'The second Sorcha goes into labour, he's going to come running over here.'

'He can't. I mean, he has to stay in England because of the whole, like, bankruptcy thing, doesn't he?'

'He won't give a shit about that. He'll want to be with his precious little angel – you watch.'

I actually don't think so. Not this time.

I stand up and I go to turn away. As I do, she storts – I swear to God – unbuttoning her shirt and going, 'Ross, can you have a quick look at my breasts.'

I'm there, 'I don't want to look at your breasts,' hating myself for saying it, but at the same time surprised that I'm capable of being such a gentleman.

'I don't mean in that way,' she goes. 'I think I've got a problem with one of my implants.'

Before I get to utter a single word of objection, she's whipped off her shirt and unhooked her bra and I'm left standing there, just staring at her torps.

'Is one of them lower than the other?' she goes. 'I've been looking at them for so long, I can't even tell anymore.'

I'm there, 'Errr . . .' because I'm still in a bit of shock here.

'Oh, for God's sake,' she goes, 'you've seen them often enough. Enough with the little-boy-lost act. Does the left one look a bit saggy?'

'My left or your left?'

'My left.'

I go, 'Er, yeah, no, it does,' because it *actually* does?

She's there, 'I focking knew it!' sounding seriously pissed off. 'God knows what that's going to focking cost me. Do you think the VHI would cover it?'

'Er, I doubt it.'

'Plan B plus options.'

'Like I said, I don't think so.'

'Again, this is my so-called father's fault for being too much of a scabby bastard to pay for a proper aug.'

Strictly speaking, her old man didn't pay for her breast job – and I'd usually be the last one to defend him. He gave her ten Ks to supposedly travel around Australia for the year. On the day she arrived in Sydney, she checked into a private clinic and ordered the biggest pair of jahoobies they had in the place, then phoned her old pair and told them she needed another ten Ks – unless they wanted their youngest daughter sleeping rough in King's Cross.

'And of course now,' she goes, 'he's going to say he doesn't have the money to get them fixed, which is focking typical of him.'

I don't really know what else I can contribute to this conversation, so I go to leave and it's as I turn around that I notice Sorcha's old dear standing in the doorway, watching her daughter putting her bra back on, while her other daughter's husband watches.

She's like, 'What's going on here?'

Talk about giving a dog a bad name.

Quick as a flash, I go, 'I was, er, using *her* en suite. Yeah, no, there's a floater in ours that just won't flush.'

I've never really been what you would call son-in-law material. She seems to buy it, though.

Then, Sorcha's sister – why does no one ever call her by her name? – goes, 'Don't rush to judge people, Mom – just because your own marriage is in ruins.'

They're some focking family.

I tip downstairs to see Sorcha. Before I've even reached the door of the living room, she roars my name. She's like, 'Ross!'

I step into the room.

'Nothing happened,' I go. 'We've established that.'

She's like, 'What are you talking about?'

'Nothing. Continue.'

She's sitting in my favourite ormchair in her dressing gown and slippers, with her two feet up on the old antique pouf. I notice that she suddenly looks very, very pregnant.

She goes, 'Come on, are you watching this?'

It turns out to be the *Late Late Show*. I forgot it was even Friday. That can happen when you do fock-all all week.

I sit down.

She goes, 'Is Honor down in that coach house again?'

I'm there, 'Errr . . .'

'I heard her down there playing her piccolo. I really wish she wouldn't go down there, Ross. It's eerie.'

'Eerie?'

'I've told you the stories.'

Tubs has the old sad face on him, just so you know not to be expecting focking laughs from the next item.

'My next guest,' he goes, 'is living through what can only be described as a waking nightmare. Exactly one hundred days ago today, her boyfriend, Irishman Fionn de Barra, was kidnapped while working as a teacher in Uganda . . .'

I'm wondering what tune the Camembert Quartet will play. Either 'Africa' or 'China Girl' would be my bet.

'Ever since then,' Tubs goes, 'she has campaigned tirelessly for his release – both here and in the Ugandan capital of Kampala.

Ladies and gentlemen, would you please welcome my next guest, Jenny Hongxia.'

I laugh out loud. It's just a funny name, that's all.

Out she comes from behind the screen. In the end, the Camembert goys don't play anything. It's not the time to be ripping the piss, I suppose.

Tubs walks over to greet her. He gives her a hug – warm, but at the same time not lecherous, and I'm saying that as someone who's always struggled to find that particular biting point.

'Oh my God,' Sorcha goes, 'I've got the exact same velvet dress – see does she say if it's by Dagmar.'

I'm there, 'I doubt if that's going to come up, Sorcha.'

'Well, it's *by* Dagmar – that's what I'm telling you. She actually looks really, really well.'

Sorcha's right. She does, even though I've never really been that into Chinese slash Japanese birds and I don't mean that in a racist way. Although I'd definitely ride Michelle Yeoh if it ever came up. Which it may not.

And Devon Aoki.

They both sit down. Tubs gives her a bit of blah before he gets down to the serious business. He tells her she's very welcome to the show and asks her how she's bearing up, like a good pro.

She goes, 'Oy'm okoy – considering *ivverythung?* Oy have to soy, the Irush poyple have boyne ibsoloytly amoyzing – that's in terms of boyth the support they've guven moy and their offers of, like, prictical *hulp?*'

Tubs goes, 'Tell me about Fionn? What's he like?'

I'm pretty sure Tubs met him once or twice in Finnegan's.

'Obviously oy'm *boyussed?*' Jenny goes. 'But to moy, he's, loyk, the swoytust goy you're ivver loykloy to moyt. He's, loyk, unbeloyvably ginerous. Oy moyn, that's whoy he was aaht there in the first ployce – to hilp poyple liss fortunate than humsulf. Virry generous and virry guving. Virry warm. He's just the moyst incridible person oy've ivver had the fortune to knoy . . .'

Her voice cracks.

Sorcha goes, 'Oh my God, she's so, so brave.'

Tubs nods and goes, 'And you were talking about getting married?'

I'm like, 'What?' and I actually shout it at the screen.

'Yes,' Jenny goes. 'We're, loik, virry much in love? Oy moyn, oy've nivver boyn a bug believer in that oydea that there's only, loyk, one person in the world for yoy? But that's exickloy hoy oy filt when oy mit Fionn. Within, loyk, toy doys, I knoy he was the one for moy. And oy knoy he filt the soym woy. Mitter of fict, on the doy he was toyken, we were actually in bid, talking abaaht gitting engoyged.'

'You focking idiot!' I suddenly go. Again, I roar it.

Sorcha's there, 'Ross!'

I'm like, 'Sorry, Babes. It's just that's one thing that's always pissed me off about Fionn. He always shows his hand too early in relationships.'

'Ross, don't be so hord. They're in love.'

'He only knows her a wet day. Six months ago, he was in love with Erika. The love of his life, he said. I remember he thought *you* were the love of his life – remember that? Now it's this bird. He always jumps in with both focking feet.'

'I just think Jenny really *gets* him.'

'He could never be an orsehole to women. That was always one of Fionn's biggest failings. Telling her that he loves her after, what, a few weeks? Focking ridiculous nonsense.'

'Well, I think it's lovely.'

'I'm only thinking about him, Sorcha.'

Tubs – his voice all serious – goes, 'Do you remember the day he was kidnapped?'

Remember it? She focking better. It was only, like, three months ago.

She goes, 'Yeah, oy moyn, oy've been reluving it ivvery doy sunce it happened. Tin *toyms* a doy. Like oy sid, we were in bid, just talking abaaht just *us* royly. Fionn had to git up because he was toyching that morning. Abaaht a quarter-to-oyt, we heard a lorry approych-ing. Looked aaht and there wus a flatbid truck aahtsoyd with all these, loyk, poyple on the back of ut. And oy could till straight awoy thit they had, loyk, guns . . .'

'Her shoes are a bit too clunky for that dress,' Sorcha goes. 'She should have gone for something a bit more strappy-strappy.'

I'm there, 'I honestly don't know what Fionn sees in her. And that's me being genuine. He's been with way nicer, and I don't just mean Erika. Who was that bird from Alex? She was a keeper.'

'Aoibheann Lysaght?'

'No, I mean she was literally a keeper. She played in goal for Three Rock Rovers.'

'Oh, Jeanette Osborne.'

'Jeanette Osborne! A serious focking looker! Fionn was seeing her, what, two weeks, then he springs it on her one night that he thinks he's in love with her. The next day, she kicks him into touch.'

Sorcha goes, 'If I remember correctly, Ross, the reason they broke up was because she did the dirt on him with you.'

'She wanted fun – she came to me.'

'Because whenever Fionn found happiness with a girl . . .'

'It was always the wrong girl.'

'You had to sabotage it – like you always do.'

'I was saving him from himself. That's why I got in there. And now it's this one. Focking Jenny. And this time he doesn't even have the excuse that she's good-looking. And, again, that's not racist.'

'I think she's lovely. She's one of those girls who definitely makes the most of herself.'

I try to look at her objectively. She's got good skin, I suppose. A nice enough smile.

She's on the screen going, 'Fionn told moy to run. He told moy to go aaht the beck door and just, loyk, run as fast as oy *could*? Then they burst in and, loyk, the woman oy told yoy abaaht, she hut hum with the butt of her royfle. Smished hus glawsus and probabloy brike his nyse as *will*? Thin they put, loyk, a beg over his hid, toyd hum up, then carried him off loyk . . . loyk a poyce of moyt.'

That dress really shows off her appetizers as well.

Sorcha goes, 'Oh my God, she's, like, so, so strong. I've actually got a bit of a girl crush on her – aport from obviously the shoes.'

And that's when I suddenly realize – and, in my defence, it comes as a bit of a shock to me as well – that I've got a sword on me here that'd make Zorro turn and run.

'Oh my God,' Sorcha goes. 'Did you hear about Lauren and Christian?'

I'm there, 'Er, no,' playing the innocent.

I've just finished fitting the cor seats into the – as Honor calls it – special needs bus, so I'm pretty pleased with myself.

She goes, 'I knew there was something up with Christian when he came in from work that night . . . Ross, they've had to close the restaurant.'

I'm like, 'I wouldn't have classed it as a restaurant, Babes. I think it'd be more of a *sandwich* shop?'

'What does it matter what it's called? They've been shut down. They said they found, like, human matter in one of the subs.'

'Yeah, no, Christian did mention something about that to me alright.'

Sorcha, by the way, has Rihanna-Brogan lying on her back on the ground. She's holding her right wrist and her left ankle and she gently brings them together across her tummy until they touch. Then she does the exact same thing with her left wrist and her right ankle.

I'm like, 'What are you doing, by the way?'

She goes, 'It helps develop co-ordination in babies and strengthens nerve communication between the left and right side of the brain. It encourages them to walk earlier.'

I love my wife, but she has an awful lot of shit in her head.

She goes, 'You know Lauren's dad is home? He's – oh my God – determined to fight it.'

'Yeah, no, I met him in Kielys.'

'They won't even tell them what they found in the sandwich or even when they found it.'

'I think they should just leave well enough alone. Accept that it wasn't to be.'

'No way. I was saying to Lauren that if they could a least find out *when* it happened, then they could check the CCTV video.'

'What?'

'They have a security camera in the shop. They have to for the insurance. I said if they give you the date, then at least you can check the tapes for that day to see if anything, like, *untoward* happened?'

Oh, for fock's sake.

I'm like, 'I still say they should maybe cut their losses. A Spar with a deli counter. Selling chicken dippers and possibly wedges to people falling out of the likes of Neary's. That's where the future is.'

'Well, if anyone is capable of getting to the bottom of it, then it's Hennessy. When he gets his teeth into something, he's like a dog with a bone.'

I suddenly go, 'Anyway, I, er, think I'll head into town for the afternoon. One or two things to do.'

Sorcha's there, 'No, you won't. Look at the time!'

'What do you mean?'

'You've got to collect Honor from school. It's already after two.'

'Can you not do it?'

'Ross, I'm heavily pregnant with triplets! I can't fit behind the wheel anymore.'

It's true. She's fat as a focking fool.

I'm there, 'Okay, *I'll* go.'

She's like, 'I can come with you, if you want. We can push the front passenger seat right back.'

'No, no, I'll go myself.'

I point Sorcha's Nissan focking Leaf in the direction of Bally-brack. Fifteen minutes later, I'm pulling up outside St Aileran's. Honor is standing in the cor pork, her nose – as ever – stuck in her focking phone. I pull up, then I get out to tell her I'm here, because she hasn't actually noticed.

Mr O'Focking Fathaigh, the school Principal – the Príomh Oide, as he calls himself – intercepts me on the way over to her.

'Ross,' he goes. 'Can I speak with you?'

Naturally enough, I'm straight away on the defensive, obviously thinking the worst.

'Dude,' I go, 'whatever she gets up to while she's here is your responsibility. You only have her for six hours, can I just remind you? We have her for the other however many.'

He laughs. I think he thinks I'm ripping the piss. I'm not actually prepared for what he *does* end up saying?

'I know Honor came to this school with, shall we say, an *interesting* backstory?' he goes. 'Which is why I thought it only fair to tell you that her behaviour this term has been absolutely exemplary!'

I'm there, 'Exemplary?' no idea what the word even means.

'Her teacher tells me that she's been very much a model student. Polite. Attentive. She can't believe the change that's come over her. I wish we could say the same about all of our students.'

All of a sudden, I hear chanting – a big group of boys in a huddle, going, 'Fight! Fight! Fight! Fight! Fight!' egging on two girls – neither of which is my daughter, I'm happy to say – who are literally tearing each other's hair out in great handfuls.

It's very much a knacker school.

He's like, 'I'd better go and break this up,' and off he goes.

I call Honor. We get into the cor – me in the front, her in the back. She prefers the back, she always says, because she likes the feeling of being chauffeured.

I'm there, 'Your ears must have been burning there, were they?'

She goes, 'What are you talking about?'

'Yeah, no, I'm just saying that Mr O'Fathaigh said you've been very well behaved this year. The words *model student* were mentioned.'

'I still hate this school.'

'But you're not causing major trouble on a daily basis like you were last year. I'm paying you a compliment here, Honor.'

'You know I have to sit beside a boy all day whose father is unemployed?'

'There's lot of people who are unemployed, Honor.'

'What if it ends up lowering my educational expectations?'

I laugh. She can be very funny when she's not being a complete bitch.

I'm there, 'I wouldn't think it would, Honor. I mean, *I'm* technically unemployed.'

'That's different. You're rich unemployed.'

She has a point. I suppose I'm out of work in the same way that JP McManus is out of work.

I stort the engine.

'And speaking of money,' she goes, 'I need three new cages.'

I look at her in the rearview mirror. I'm like, 'Three more? Why?'

'Some of them are fighting,' she goes. 'It says on the Internet that if they're fighting, you have to separate them – otherwise they'll kill each other.'

'Okay – again, you seem to know what you're doing, so that's cool. We'll pick them up later.'

'And more kibble.'

'More kibble – cool.'

I point the cor – so-called – in the direction of town. Honor goes back to her phone and she doesn't look up again until we're going over Leeson Street Bridge. She has a sense that we should be home by now, then realizes that we're not.

She's like, 'Oh my God, where are we going?'

I'm there, 'I have to pop into town to quickly do something.'

'What's so urgent? I want to go home to Pippa.'

'I, er, have to check on Christian and Lauren's sandwich place.'

'It's closed down.'

'Yeah, no, I know. I just said I'd check whether the alorm is going off and blah, blah, blah.'

She stares at me hord in the rearview mirror until I have to eventually look away. She knows me well enough to know when I'm up to something.

I throw the cor in the Stephen's Green Shopping Centre, then we walk down towards Chatham Street together.

All the way, Honor keeps going, 'Oh my God, what are you going to do?' and it's like she's actually getting a kick out of it. It's focked up, roysh, but I think she actually admires that side of me.

We go to the front of the shop. It's all locked up. Inside, it's dark. There's a sign in Christian's handwriting Sellotaped to the inside of the window, and it says, 'Closed Until Further Notice'. I put my nose against the glass and I can see the security camera pointing down at the counter.

Yeah, no, I'll have definitely been caught on tape gobbing on that focker's sub.

'Come on,' I go, 'let's check around the back.'

Honor's like, 'Oh my God, you *are* up to something!' and she follows me down the laneway – or, actually, she *doesn't* follow me? She runs about three steps ahead of me, she's so excited.

I check out the back of the building.

Focking bingo!

There's an open window. It's, like, upstairs and I'm pretty sure it's the window to the toilet in Christian's old office. He used to always keep it open. He can be focking rotten at times. He's got some kind of gluten issue and I'm saying that as his friend.

I go, 'Look, Honor, I hate myself for this, but I actually need your help.'

Honor laughs. She's like, 'Okay, what are you talking about?'

I grab one of those humungous black dumpsters and I wheel it over to the back of the building, then I shove it up against the wall, directly under the window.

I'm there, 'Do you think if I stood on this thing, and I lifted you up onto my shoulders, you could squeeze in through that window up there?'

See, she's actually small for her age. But she's also clever.

She goes, 'Okay – and why would I want to do that?'

I'm there, 'There's thirty or forty video tapes on a shelf behind your Uncle Christian's desk. I've seen them there.'

'So?'

'I want you to fock them down to me, one by one.'

Her face suddenly lights up. She's like, 'Oh! My God! It was you!'

I'm there, 'What?'

'I heard Mom talking about it. You were the one who did a shit in someone's sandwich!'

'I didn't do a shit in it, Honor, so get your facts right. I did a gobber. And the focker deserved it because he was disrespecting Christian at the time. Talking to him like he was dirt.'

'Hill! Air!'

'And I'm pretty sure I was caught on video doing it as well.'

'Oh my God, this is so lollers!'

'So are you going to help me or not?'

'What, to destroy the evidence?'

'Yes.'

'That depends. What's in it for me?'

Shit.

'Er, the cages,' I try to go. 'I'll get you those new cages you asked me for – as many as you want, in fact.'

She's there, 'You've already promised me the cages.'

'Well, what do you want then? Jesus Christ, what are your demands?'

'I want a thousand euros.'

'Honor, you're seven years old. I'm not giving a seven-year-old girl a thousand euros. I'll give you five hundred euros.'

'Eight hundred.'

'Seven fifty.'

'Okay, seven fifty.'

We shake on it. I lift her up onto the lid of the dumpster, then I climb up myself. I pick her up and I lift her onto my shoulders, sitting at first, then, once we've steadied ourselves, she stands up. She reaches the ledge quite easily. I'm about to give her one or two instructions – once a captain, always a captain – except she doesn't need them. She pulls herself up onto that ledge, then she disappears, head-first, through the window, like – well, like a rat, basically, disappearing into a hole.

When I hear her go, 'Oh my God, the focking smell!' I know it's the right place.

Anything is liable to set Christian off. Sausages. Bread. Some specialist even told him to go off the beer, the focking lunatic.

Once she gets over the hum, Honor gets straight to work – fair focks to her.

Literally thirty seconds later, the first five video tapes are dropped from the window. I catch two or three of them. The second one to drop into my hands is dated Wednesday, 12 September – the day that little Oliver was born. I'm good at remembering birthdays, in fairness to me.

I snap back the plastic flap, then I stort pulling out the tape, metres and focking metres of it, and I snap it in about thirty places, to make sure it can never, ever be seen, while at the same time, even more tapes – fifty, maybe sixty – come raining down on me from the window, a few of them hitting me on the head, although I don't *give* a fock, the rest of them smashing on the ground.

After, like, three or four minutes, Honor sticks her head out of the window. She's there, 'That's all of them.'

I'm like, 'Trash the place a bit.'

'Excuse me?'

'Trash it – as in, make it look like a *burglary*?'

Christian's right. I possibly do watch too much *CSI*.

I hear various drawers opening and things crashing to the floor, then – Jesus focking Christ – actual glass breaking. I get the impression that she's kind of enjoying herself up there.

Maybe five minutes later, she appears at the window again and throws one leg out, then the other and sort of, like, sits on the ledge. I hold up my two orms and she drops into them.

I feel shit about what I've just asked her to do, although I still see myself as an amazing father who just happens to be having an off-day.

She goes, 'Oh my God, you are *so* bad!' and she says it – like I mentioned – with definite approval in her voice.

I'm there, 'No, Honor. I don't ever want you to think that that kind of behaviour is acceptable,' doing the whole responsible father thing. 'But sometimes when we don't want to face up to our responsibilities, we have to resort to extreme measures.'

I jump to the ground, then I lift *her* down. I throw open the skip, then I stort gathering up the video tapes and focking them inside for the bin men to take away. Honor even helps me.

'So bad,' she keeps going, with genuine affection. 'I am *actually* impressed.'

I'm stretched out on the sofa with Sorcha, watching *The Great British Bake Off*, wondering am I the only one to notice that Mary Berry looks like Brian Ormond dressed as a woman on *Anonymous*. That's when Sorcha, without even saying a word, grabs my wrist and lays my hand on top of her bump.

I feel it straight away – a kick.

'They're lively tonight,' she goes.

I'm there, 'I know we don't know if they're going to be boys or girls or a mixture of both. But there's a definite future number ten in there!'

She smiles at me. It's a nice moment, that's all I'm saying.

She's like, 'Are you excited?'

'Yeah, no, I am,' I go, 'although I'm still a bit, I don't know, in *shock*? I haven't properly come to terms with it yet.'

'I know what you mean. And yet I've got this weird feeling that the biggest shock has yet to come. What would you think of Christmas Day, by the way?'

'What do you mean?'

'The midwife said that – all things going to plan – I can elect to have the Caesarian at any time between the twentieth and twenty-ninth of December. So what would you think of the twenty-fifth of December?'

'Yeah, no, I'm cool with that.'

'It'd be nice for them to have their birthdays on Christmas Day.'

'Be fewer presents, I suppose.'

'Did you really just say that?'

'I was really just thinking out loud, Sorcha. *Processing*, I've heard it called.'

She's there, 'Oh, by the way, keep Hallowe'en Night free, will you?'

I'm there, 'Why, what's on?'

'A table quiz.'

'Fock! Are we really that old?'

'Don't be like that. It's in Kielys. Everyone's going to be there.'

'Okay, you had me at Kielys.'

'Jenny's hosting it.'

'Oh, for fock's sake.'

'I know you're not a fan, Ross.'

'That's the understatement of the century. What's it even in aid of?'

'I think she feels bad that Fionn's parents are about to hand over their life savings to this man who's supposedly going to find Fionn. I think she wants to feel like she's making a contribution, too.'

I'm there, 'Well, fair focks would be my attitude, even though I think Fionn's punching way below his weight there.'

'Ross, that's an awful thing to say.'

That's when my phone suddenly rings. At first, I consider *not* answering it? But then I look at the screen and I notice that it's Oisinn and it just strikes me as instantly odd that he'd be ringing me, since we're barely even on *speaking* terms these days?

Then I think it might be news about Fionn.

'Answer it,' Sorcha goes.

So I do.

I'm there, 'Hello?'

He's like, 'Ross!'

I go, 'Yeah, no, what the fock do you want?'

'Shit.'

'Dude, what? Is it something to do with Fionn?'

'No, it's not Fionn. It's just . . . Shit the bed, there's no easy way of saying this . . . Fionnuala's out cold, Ross.'

I laugh.

I'm there, 'Ah, now you're bringing me back to my childhood. Just drag her pathetic carcass into the shower and hose her down with cold water. She'll be sober again in about, oh, fourteen hours?'

'Ross,' he goes, 'I think your mother's OD-ed.'

I'm like, 'On what?' and then it suddenly dawns on me – the reason she was talking ninety to the focking dozen in Idle Wilde that day. I stand up. I'm like, 'Dude, you've *got* to be shitting me!'

He's there, 'I wish I was, Ross . . . God, I wish I was.'

I go, 'This is what it was leading to, Oisinn. She's practically focking sixty.'

Sorcha's looking at me in total shock.

She's like, 'Ross, what's wrong?'

Oisinn goes, 'Ross, please. I need someone with a cool head. Because I'm kind of losing it here.'

I'm there, 'Forget it. Ring an ambulance. Or a focking hearse. You decide which.'

'Ross, please!' he goes – and this next bit is unbelievable. 'We played rugby together.'

I'm just like, 'You can't play the rugby cord with me anymore, Dude,' and I hang up on him.

But of course he can play the rugby cord. That's just an unfortunate fact of life.

Sorcha goes, 'Is Fionnuala okay?'

I consider telling her that she's storted taking coke, except in the end I don't. Sorcha has a lot of respect for the woman, even though it's based on nothing. And despite everything the old dear has put me through, there's a port of me that wants to protect her – I'm going to use the word – dignity.

'She's shit-faced and she's fallen down the stairs,' I go. 'Oisinn said she's pissed herself and everything, the gin-soaked bitch. I have to go out.'

Paul Hollywood is telling some bird on the TV that her macaroons are shit.

'Do you want me to come with you?' Sorcha goes.

I'm like, 'No, no, it's cool. I won't be long.'

I stop at the door and I look back at her. 'You know,' I go, 'sometimes I wish I never played rugby . . . But then, even as I'm saying that to you, I know I don't mean it. I'll be back in hopefully an hour.'

I point Sorcha's cor in the direction of Foxrock, genuinely not knowing what kind of scene I'm about to walk in on – and hating the two of them for making me do it.

I pull into the driveway, then I get out of the cor. I walk up to the front door and I don't even bother my hole knocking. I put my foot to it. Six or seven hord kicks and it gives way with the sound of, like, wood splintering.

The joke is, of course, that I actually have a key. But, like I said, I'm pissed off and I need to take it out on either someone or something.

I tip up the stairs. I hear Oisinn's voice – all small and girly – coming from the old dear's bedroom. He's going, 'Is that you, Ross? Ross, is that you?'

I push the door.

He's like, 'Oh, thank God!'

I'm not prepared for the sight that greets me and I end up having to turn away for a few seconds.

The old dear is collapsed on the bedroom floor and she's wearing – I shit you not – a red, PVC body suit. A focking gimp costume, basically. Oisinn is wearing – oh, Jesus suffering fock – a red mankini and a set of nipple clamps, which he quickly whips off when he catches me staring at them.

I check out the old dear's dressing table and there's, like, a small hill of white powder in the middle of it, with a rolled-up fifty-yoyo note and her Superquinn Reward Cord beside it.

I'm like, 'For fock's sake, Oisinn!'

He's there, 'Dude, I'm sorry.'

'*That* shit? She's an old woman.'

'I know. She said she always wanted to try it. She said she's always been curious.'

'And you were happy to get it for her? You're un-focking-believable.'

He goes, 'I don't understand it. One minute she was standing there, chatting away, the next she was on the floor. I mean, she didn't even take much.'

I'm there, 'Didn't take much? She's got nostrils like a focking Derby winner. Of course she took much.'

'It was one line. Two at the very most.'

I pick up the fifty-yoyo note and I stick it in my pocket, just out of habit. Then we're both standing there, just looking down at her.

Oisinn's like, 'Ross, what are we going to do?' and I know we're both suddenly thinking about that scene from, like, *Pulp Fiction*.

I'm there, 'I'm trying to remember – was it Uma Thurman?'

'Uma Thurman! That's it. Isn't it supposed to be a shot of adrenalin to the hort or something?'

I'm like, 'Yeah, good luck finding that!'

He goes, 'Ross, I'm going out of my head here.'

So I grab the old dear by the legs and I'm like, 'Let's just go with my original idea,' and I stort dragging her across the floor of the bedroom towards the bathroom, memories of the night of my First Holy Communion coming flooding back.

I make sure to hit her head off various items of furniture on the way there – the leg of the bed, her night stand, the door frame, twice – and then Oisinn helps me lift her big fat cadaver into the jacuzzi and we turn her onto her front, because I don't want to drown her, tempting as it is.

I put her head under the cold tap and I'm about to switch it on when something suddenly hits me.

'Where's her orse?' I go.

Oisinn's like, 'What do you mean?'

I'm there, 'My old dear has an orse like a focking rhinoceros. It's where they mine all the fat to inject into her face. Except it's suddenly gone. There's no actual orse here.'

'I don't know what you're talking about,' he goes.

I tell him to get me a scissors, which he does. Then I stort cutting her out of the PVC suit, from the bottom of her neck downwards. When I reach the small of her back, I put down the scissors and I just rip the rest of the suit open, like you would a packet of Doritos.

And the mystery is suddenly solved.

The two sides of the suit fall away to reveal that, as well as the gimp suit, my old dear is wearing, not one, but two pairs of Spanx.

I actually laugh.

'She didn't focking OD,' I go. 'You're not going to need that ambulance.'

Oisinn's like, 'Oh, thank God! So what happened?'

I'm there, 'She's double-bagged it, that's what.'

He's like, 'What?'

'She's double-bagged her orse. That's the real reason she passed out. It was fock-all to do with coke. She cut off her own blood flow.'

I switch on the tap and I give her a blast of cold water on the back of the head. She suddenly jolts back to life, as if she's been given an electric shock.

She's like, 'Oh my God! What happened? What *happened*?'

Oisinn goes, 'It's okay, Fionnuala. I'm here! And so is Ross.'

I'm like, 'Yeah, unfortunately.'

She goes, 'Oisinn! I don't know what happened! I felt suddenly faint!'

She doesn't say a word of thanks to me, by the way. And neither of them apologizes.

Oisinn helps her up, out of the jacuzzi and back into the bedroom. And the old dear goes straight for the dressing table and goes, 'I think I'll have a couple of toots – might wake me up.'

I end up just shaking my head, then just leaving them to it, Oisinn telling her that he thought he'd lost her and the old dear looking around for something to hoover up with.

And one thing is instantly clear to me. I need to break these two up – we're talking once and for all.

I'm in the Stephen's Green Shopping Centre and I'm passing that little croissant place when I spot a familiar face wrapping itself around, I don't know, a *croque monsieur* or something.

I'm thinking, okay, how do I know that dude? And it bothers me to the point where I end up standing there for a good five minutes, just staring at him and racking my brains. And then it suddenly comes to me. It's Mr focking Munier from the so-called Deportment of Foreign Affairs.

It's, like, so random seeing him out of context like this – like when you were at school and you happen to see one of your teachers out one weekend loading bags of, I don't know, bork mulch into the boot of his cor.

I tip over. The plan is to make some crack about him being from the country – 'I didn't know they did bacon and cabbage sangidges in here!' – but I don't get it together in time.

So instead I just go, 'Ah, look who it is!'

I look down and he has a bag from Best Menswear at his feet. You couldn't make this shit up.

He doesn't recognize me at first. He's like, 'Errr . . .'

'Ross O'Carroll-Kelly?' I go. 'A friend of Fionn de Barra? The dude who's still missing somewhere in Um Blom Blum?'

He's there, 'Oh, yes, you're the fella thought we were going to send in the SAS!' and he has the balls to actually laugh.

I'm like, 'Well, what did you *actually* do, since we're on the subject?'

He tries to go, 'Well, we're still monitoring the situation. We're liaising with the local authorities on the ground . . .'

I just cut him off. I nod at the shopping bag and I go, 'Is that a new sports coat you bought?'

He has no answer to that. My old man calls the civil service the Stationery Agricultural Complex.

'Monitoring the situation,' I go. 'I'd say whoever's holding Fionn is shitting bricks. They're going, "Some bogmen in Ireland are monitoring the situation – I think we may have bitten off more than we can chew." '

He's there, 'Like I told you, we're unfortunately quite limited in what we can do.'

'Never a focking truer word,' I go. 'Well, the good news is that Fionn's old pair have hired a professional.'

They've managed to get the sheks together. The word is that Fred is heading out there next week.

'What do you mean by a professional?' he goes.

I'm there, 'An actual security company. I think the word consultancy was even used. Someone who knows what they're doing, in other words.'

'I'd be very careful engaging these freelancers. There's a lot of, shall we say, rogue elements working in that area.'

But I'm just there, 'Well, we've tried it your way and look where it's gotten us. Er, *nowhere*? Maybe it's time for the rogues to take over. Enjoy your bacon and cabbage sangidge.'

Sorcha is sitting on the floor of the kitchen, with her back to the dishwasher and her two feet raised about twelve inches off the floor.

Of course, I make the mistake of asking her what she's doing and she says she's trying to tone up her pelvic muscles, because she keeps having little involuntary releases every time she laughs or sneezes.

She means of, like, *piss*?

I wonder, after the triplets are born, will I ever go back to fancying Sorcha again. I'm worried that maybe I know too much.

We've the house pretty much to ourselves. Ronan and Shadden are on their mid-term break and have taken Rihanna-Brogan to the zoo. Sorcha's old dear is seeing her solicitor about this supposed divorce. Her sister has a hospital appointment and Honor is down in the coach house playing the piccolo to her rat mates.

'Oh my God, listen,' Sorcha goes. 'It's *Allegro*.'

The tune comes drifting up the gorden to the gaff. She's good on it – there's no doubt about that.

'It's Vivaldi,' Sorcha goes. 'It's on my *Greatest Classical Album in the World . . . Ever!* CD.'

I'm there, 'Yeah, no, I thought I recognized it.'

'I wish she wouldn't spend so much time down there in that coach house, though.'

'She likes it down there.'

She's there, 'It's creepy, Ross. In fact, I think I'll go down there and tell her to come up to the house,' and she goes to stand up.

'No!' I go, probably a bit too eagerly as well.

I put my hand on top of her head and push her back down.

She's like, 'What are doing?'

And I'm there, 'Yeah, no, I was just going to say, you know, maybe we should just leave her to it.'

'Leave her to what?'

'I just mean, you know, let's give her a bit of space. I mean, I told you what Mister O'Fathaigh said – she's really behaving herself these days. Or least she's not being as much of a bitch as she used to be.'

'Oh my God,' she goes, 'I have to show you her end-of-term report cord. It arrived this morning. Her teacher described her as mannerly and co-operative.'

'Jesus.'

'I know. I feel terrible, but I actually rang the school to find out if they'd sent me out the wrong report.'

'And they hadn't?'

'No.'

'Did she maybe hack into the school's computer system and change it? I'm just trying to cover all the angles here.'

'I thought that as well. But again, no. They've got nothing but good things to say about her. It's like she's had a total personality transformation, they said.'

'Yeah, no, that's basically what the headmaster said to me. So why don't we just leave her alone?'

'Do you know what, Ross, maybe you're right.'

She goes back to clenching and unclenching and I realize that I have to leave the room. I tip out to the hall and that's when Sorcha's sister comes through the front door. I can tell from the way she's effing and blinding that she's not a happy camper.

'I was focking right,' she goes. 'One of my implants *has* ruptured.'

That's obviously why she was at the hospital. The penny drops.

I'm like, 'Jesus! How did it happen?'

She goes, 'There was a focking flaw in it.'

'Could you not, I don't know, bring it back?'

'What, to Australia?'

'Oh, yeah, I forgot you got them there.'

She shakes her head and laughs at – I don't know – the injustice of the world. 'Do you know how much they want from me to fix it?'

'Er . . .'

'Five! Grand!'

'That sounds like a lot.'

'Where the fock am I going to get five grand?'

'I don't know. Maybe work and save up – I know that sounds ridiculous coming from me.'

'Do you know how much overtime I would have to do in Aldi to make five grand?'

I'm there, 'No,' and in a way I don't want to – I'm comfortable not knowing about that whole PAYE side of life.

'And until then,' she goes, 'what, I'm supposed to walk around with two tits pointing in different directions?'

She storts walking up the stairs.

One of the elements of my play that's still talked about to this day was my ability to spot an opening when none appeared to *be* there? And it's a quality I've carried with me into everyday life.

'I'll give you the money,' I automatically go. 'I'll give you the five grand.'

She stops, five stairs up, then turns around.

She's like, 'Why?'

I'm there, 'Well, it's like you said, how long would it take you to earn that?'

'No, what I mean is, what's in it for you? Free goes?'

'Free goes? Jesus Christ.'

'Well, what then?'

'Well, as it happens, there *is* something you can do for me?'

'What is it?'

'I want you to seduce someone?'

'*Seduce* someone? What do you think I am, a hooker?'

'I didn't say that.'

'Who?'

'A friend of mine.'

'Which friend?'

'Oisinn.'

'Which one is Oisinn?'

'Big goy. Curly, blond hair.'

'He's actually kind of cute.'

'That's amazing, because it's usually only dogs who like him.'

'And why am I *seducing* him exactly? And that's not to say that I'm going to do it.'

'Well, as you know, he's doing a line with my old dear. Actually, he's doing a lot of lines with my old dear.'

'And you want to break them up?'

'I know it sounds possibly immature, but yeah.'

'So, what, I get him into bed and you arrange for your mother to walk in on us – is that it?'

'I haven't worked out the finer details. As a plan, it's only just come to me. But something like that.'

'And you'll pay me five grand?'

'Are you saying you'll definitely do it?'

'Of course I'll definitely do it. It'll be the easiest money I've ever made.'

What in the name of fockery?

Shadden's old man is in my living room. I'm talking about K . . . K . . . K . . . K . . . Kennet. I can hear the focker's voice through the door.

He's going, 'Says I to him, "You're only a d . . . d . . . d . . . doorty screw basturd. You're only a doorty looken doort boord screw b . . . b . . . b . . . bastard." He was throying to goad me into hitting him a smack so I'd end up with anutter t . . . t . . . two year on top of me sentence – do you wonderstand me?'

I'm thinking, how the fock is he out? Did he escape?

He's there, 'So how's that b . . . b . . . b . . . bayooriful little gran thaughter of m . . . moyen?'

I push the door open a crack and I breathe a sudden sigh of relief. He's not out. He's talking to Shadden on Skype, presumably from his prison cell.

Technology is an amazing thing. It's allowed our prison population to break the law in ways that couldn't have been imagined a decade ago.

'She's great,' Shadden goes. 'She's getting big and bowult.'

He's there, 'And it's w . . . w . . . woorking out alreet, is it?'

'Yeah, thee've been great, so thee have.'

'Who, S . . . S . . . S . . . Surrogate?'

'Yeah.'

'And what about *him* – the fedda wears the sailing gear.'

'Ross has been great. Thee've boat been great, so thee have.'

Kennet won't be happy to hear that.

'M . . . m . . . m . . . make shuren not to forget yisser roots,' he goes. 'Or as me own fadder – Lorta Meercy on him – used to say, don't forget the b . . . b . . . bowl you were b . . . b . . . baked in.'

Shadden's like, 'What do you mee-un?'

'Look,' he goes, 'Ine not gonna l . . . l . . . loy to you, Shadden. Your mutter and me were veddy disappointhed wit your decision to go b . . . b . . . back to skewill.'

'Da, we've been troo it. I want to get me Leaving and then go to coddidge.'

'Filling yisser heads wit useless facts and f . . . f . . . figures. Let me tell you sometin, Shadden, I habn't a qualification to me nayum.'

He's talking to her from D Wing in Mountjoy Prison. They wouldn't be big on self-awareness, the Tuites.

'But one thing I am p . . . p . . . p . . . proud to say is that I was altwees theer for you kids when you were growing up. Well, that's if I wadn't in hee-er.'

'I know that, Da. And I appreciate it.'

'Look, I've s . . . s . . . s . . . said me piece. You're obviously deteermint to do whatever's in your head irregeerdless of what me and your m . . . m . . . m . . . mutter think abour it. Alls I'll say is make shoower not to get upset when you miss alt the big m . . . m . . . m . . . moments in your little babby's l . . . l . . . life.'

'What do you mee-un?'

'Ine just saying, if you have anutter woman reardon your b . . . b . . . b . . . babby . . .'

'She's oately moynding her while I'm at skewill.'

'There's a veddy good chaddence that you'll miss her foorst steps. Her f . . . f . . . f . . . foorst words.'

What a focking piece of work this dude is.

'I woatunt,' Shadden goes.

And Kennet's there, 'Feer denuff. Although you caddent say that for sh . . . sh . . . sh . . . shewer. Fact, she mireeven grow up forgetting who her real mutter is – you or bleaten Surrogate.'

Like I said, he's a piece of focking work.

JP gives me a shoulder nudge. And not a focking playful one either. Not the kind I gave Dave Kearney coming out of the Black Pig in Donnybrook two weeks ago, just to let him know, 'You're actually one of my favourite current Leinster players and one of the first names I'd have on the team-sheet every week – but in the back of my head you'll always be focking Clongowes.'

The one that JP gives me has none of that, like, begrudging

respect in it. In fact, he actually deliberately torgets the side where I famously damaged my rotator cuff muscle back in the day.

I'm like, 'Dude, I didn't say anything that everyone else isn't already saying behind your back.'

But it doesn't make him feel any better and it doesn't get me out of the doghouse. He just continues walking in the direction of the jacks.

'Asshole,' I hear a voice behind me go. A girl. Obviously Shoshanna.

I turn around to her and I'm like, 'Not everyone would agree with that particular assessment.'

She goes, '*Not everyone would agree with that particular assessment,*' and she says it in an idiot voice, except it sounds nothing like me, so the joke ends up being on her.

She's like, 'Trying to take away JP's joy at being a father – what kind of a friend are you?'

'That's the point,' I go. 'I don't think he *is* a father. And from what I hear, your last boyfriend was – I hate to have to keep saying this word – but black. He was a black man. A blackman. From what I hear.'

She goes, 'You stay out of our business and stay out of our fucking lives,' jabbing her finger at me.

I can't make that promise, though. I'd do anything for JP. Shoshanna wouldn't understand rugby. Why would she? She's American.

I pick up the drinks and I carry them over to our table, where Sorcha is telling Lauren that her legs are now so swollen that she can't zip up her over-the-knee boots – the Christian Louboutin ones that she, oh my God, *loves?* And Christian is writing the name of our team – the Quizzy Rascals – at the top of all of our answer sheets.

Sorcha is suddenly squinting at something over my right shoulder – the exact same shoulder that JP just tried to pretty much dislocate. She goes, 'Is that my sister?'

It is, by the way. I saw her come in.

She goes, 'Oh my God, *what* is she wearing?'

What she's wearing is half-nothing and her neeners are on full display.

The sister eventually comes over to our table. She's like, 'Hi, Ross!' in her usual flirty way, and, before I can even answer her, Sorcha goes, 'Do you think that's an appropriate way to dress for a table quiz?'

The sister's like, 'What are you, my mother?'

'You're dressed like you're going out to a nightclub.'

'Well, who says I'm not?'

The sister gives me a little smile, which Sorcha doesn't fail to notice. She goes, 'You needn't think you're joining our team. We've already *got* four?'

The sister looks around the bor – we're in Kielys, remember – and she goes, 'I think I'll ask Oisinn if he can squeeze a fifth onto the end of *his* table.'

Sorcha's like, 'Oisinn?' and I can see she's trying to make the connection – as in, how does she even *know* the Big O?

Off the sister flounces. I watch her wander over to where Oisinn is sitting, with the focking Snow Queen – my old dear, in other words – and two Michael's heads who Oisinn seems to be suddenly friends with. The sister leans over the table, giving Oisinn a good eyeful of Mulder and Scully, then I watch him look at each of the others in turn and ask them if it's okay – obviously for the sister to join them.

They all just shrug, although the old dear is a bit wary of her. She keeps, like, stealing sly little glances at her, her paranoid, probably coke-addled mind straight away identifying her as a threat. She can see that Oisinn can barely take his eyes off the girl, especially her num-nums.

Sorcha goes, 'Okay, I don't think I want to know what's going on over there.'

All of a sudden, roysh, Jenny steps up to the mic. She looks well, it has to be said.

She goes, 'Good oyvening, loydies and gintlemun – and think yoy all for coming aaht to Koyloys tonoyt to support thus toyble kwuz ivvint.'

'Yeah, no, it's my local,' I go, under my breath. 'I don't need a focking invitation from you to come here.'

She's there, 'We're gonna hipefilly royse a lot of monay tonoyt to hilp in the ongoying iffurt to foynd Fionn, whoys boyn hild kiptive for four and a half months noy, to wun hus reloyse and to bring hum hoym.'

I notice the famous Fred Pfanning, three tables over, sitting with Ewan and Andrea, then some old bird who I think Andrea used to play tennis with in Ashbrook years ago. Fred's supposedly heading off tomorrow to look for Fionn. He catches my eye – he doesn't like me, he's already made that much clear – and I try to stare him down, except he's better at it than I am and I end up having to look away.

Jenny's obviously going to be the quizmaster, because she goes, 'Okoy, lit's git on wuth the kwuz. Rahnd one is geographoy.'

I look at Christian and I roll my eyes. Geography isn't a table quiz round. It's a focking school subject. Fionn might not be *actually* here, but he very much is in spirit.

'Quistion one. In which osyhun is the oylund country of Madagascar situoytud? In which oyshun is the oylund country of Madagascar situoytud?'

Sorcha turns to Lauren and – almost in a silent whisper – goes, 'Is it the Indian Ocean?'

Lauren's like, 'I think it is, yeah.'

I'm there, 'Wait a minute, don't put that down. Think about it.'

Sorcha's like, 'What?'

'It's a trick question. Madagascar. It's from a cortoon,' because I've seen it, like, three or four times – most recently about six months ago, when Honor sat just staring at me while I watched it, throwing M&Ms at my head at, like, ten-second intervals and going, 'Lame . . . Lame . . . Lame . . .'

Lauren's like, 'I'll tell you what, Ross, why don't you save your brain power for the rugby round, if there is one?'

I'm there, 'Of course there'll be one – it's focking Kielys.'

She's there, 'Well, just pace yourself until then.'

She means shut the fock up because you're thick. As it happens, it actually suits me to do exactly that, because it allows me to keep an eye on how Sorcha's sister is getting on. The answer to that question is apparently *well?* She's laughing, I don't know, uproariously at everything Oisinn says and every time she laughs she also leans forward, to give him a flash of her Mulligans.

The old dear is giving her filthy looks and you can tell she's suddenly feeling the heat. Every female instinctively knows when another female has designs on her lunch and deep down she must realize that her little midge bites are no competition for the sister's thumpers – even *if* the air is going out of one of them.

I happen to notice also that the old dear's knee is going up and down like I don't know what – a sure sign that she's had a focking noseful before she came out tonight.

Snorting coke to go to a table quiz. It's like 2003 all over again.

'In the book *Moybe Duck*,' Jenny goes, 'what colour was the whoyle?'

We've moved on to apparently literature now.

'In the book *Moybe Duck*, what colour was the whoyle?'

Sorcha and Lauren stort, like, conferring with each other – 'Oh my God, I must re-read that book – it's definitely going on the list' – while me and Christian end up just sitting there like two spare knobs.

He's quiet, by the way. I say it to him as well. I'm like, 'What the fock is wrong with you?'

He goes, 'What do you think is wrong with me, Ross? I've just lost my focking business.'

Lauren goes, 'Come on, Christian, we said we'd forget about it for one night . . . I think the answer's white, Sorcha.'

Christian goes, 'Did I tell you the place got turned over last week?'

I'm like, 'What?' acting the innocent.

'Somone broke in. Trashed the office.'

'God, if I could get my hands on them. Did they take anything?'

'About four hundred euros that I stupidly left in my desk drawer. And for some reason all the security tapes.'

'The security tapes? What use are they to anyone? And I'm only saying that because it's all DVDs these days, isn't it?'

'I'm actually more concerned about the money, Ross.'

'I suppose.'

It's only then that it sinks *in* with me? I'm there, 'Did you say four hundred yoyos?'

He goes, 'Yeah, no, four hundred plus change.'

I'm thinking, the little focking wagon!

Lauren's there, 'Well, at least my dad is on the case now. If they think they can do this to us, they're going to have one hell of a fight on their hands.'

Sorcha goes, 'You're entitled to a full hearing and you're entitled to know every detail of the case against you – I told you, there's a girl in my pre-natal Pilates class who studied Constitutional Law. She has an apartment in Smithfield, although she's originally from Glenageary.'

'Well,' I go, 'let's just hope that this Footlong crowd just drop it and there's no need for a big major inquest into who did what and why. That'd be my genuine hope.'

I look over my shoulder. Sorcha's sister is flirting with Oisinn in a big-time way now, asking Oisinn to taste her drink – a trick she's pulled on me a hundred times before. She'll have been sucking on that straw and giving him the eyes for the last twenty minutes. She's good. And you can see that Oisinn is loving the attention.

Like I said, he's only ever with complete cronks.

We end up *not* winning the quiz? Although I probably don't need to tell you that. It ends up being won by four of Fionn's mates from Trinity, although Sorcha's successful challenge to the question about the exact duration of Aung San Suu Kyi's house arrest earns us the vital point that lifts us from joint nineteenth to outright eighteenth place.

At which point Sorcha decides that she's going to head home, because she's wrecked – triplets and blah, blah, blah – although she tells me that I should stay on, which is nice to hear, because I'm four or five pints down the road and I've got a serious goo on me.

Lauren offers to drive her home, then Christian – the focking wuss – decides he's going to head home as well. He's in shit form, which is portly down to me and that's the reason I don't force the issue with him.

I just go, 'Focking lightweight!' and then the three of them end up leaving me there on my Tobler, watching the raffle and wondering should I maybe switch to shorts.

'We have a guft vaahtcher,' Jenny goes, 'guven to us very koynd-loy by David Lloyd at Ruver Vyoy for toy froy Jukari *Fut to Flix* classes, an exercoyse roytoyn that's inspoyred boy the flying moyve-ments of Cirque du Suloy. And the wunner of that proyze is tucket number fufty-foyve.'

Oisinn slithers over to me like the focking snake that he is – his face is all flushed from the attention he's been getting.

He's like, 'Hey, Ross.'

I'm there, 'Is she *on* something? She *is* on something. Getting high for a focking table quiz – have we learned nothing as a nation?'

'She's fine. She can handle it.'

'Yeah, I remember you saying something similar about yourself.'

'Can I, er, get you a pint?'

'Like I told you before – I'm choosy about who I accept drinks from.'

There's, like, a moment of awkward silence. Amie with an ie wins a ninety-minute course in make-up application from Brown Sugar on South William Street.

Eventually, Oisinn goes, 'Dude, what's, um, Sorcha's sister's name?'

I'm there, 'No one knows. I mean, she possibly told me it years ago, but I've forgotten it. And I can't very well turn around and ask her all these years later.'

Especially since I've rattled her bors more times than I can count.

I'm there, 'She seems to definitely like you, though.'

He goes, 'What?'

He's embarrassed, but he's also, like, *interested?*

I'm like, 'Yeah, no, I saw her flirting her orse off with you.'

He goes, 'I don't know. I think she was possibly just being friendly.'

I laugh. I'm like, 'Come on, Dude. You know when someone's flirting with you. You've been with beautiful women before.'

Which is horseshit, of course. If you threw all of Oisinn's past conquests into a room, you'd have the cast for a Wes Craven movie.

I'm there, 'They're fantastic, by the way.'

He's like, 'What?'

'I'm talking about Sherlock and focking Watson – and I'm saying that as her brother-in-law. We're talking 36D. Can you believe that?'

'That's big.'

'You better believe that's big. Bail in would be my genuine advice, if you weren't in a relationship with someone.'

His eyes automatically turn to my old dear, across the other side of the bor. She has her little compact out, checking her nostrils and her upper lip for any bits of Shake 'n' Vac that she might have missed.

The sister is just staring at her with her lip curled up in, like, total contempt.

Arkadyevna or Darmstadtium or Triceratops – it's definitely a long name.

I look at Oisinn's face and I can instantly tell what he's thinking. It's the same face that Sorcha pulls when she's ordered a piece of fat-free carrot cake for dessert and then she sees my Death by Chocolate with extra ice cream arrive.

He's thinking, What the fock am I doing with my life?

I'm there, 'Do you know what, Dude, I think I'm finally storting to get my head around you and my old dear being together. I'm definitely going to make more of an effort to be more accepting of it.'

The seed has been well and truly planted.

'Our foynal proyze,' Jenny goes, 'is dinner for toy in Daniel's in Sendycoyve, which oy knoy is a huge foyvourite of Fionn's. He's a bug fahn of their grulled fillut of rid snipper thurmidor – at loyst he alwoys talked abaaht ut. And the wunner is tucket number twinty-toy – it's a punk tucket.'

Fred Pfanning suddenly stands up to claim the prize.

I shout out, 'Fix!' which is always a funny thing to do during raffles.

He just, like, glowers at me while Jenny is handing him the voucher.

Oisinn goes, 'He's off to Uganda in the morning.'

I'm there, 'So I heard. Fionn's old pair obviously handed over the shecks – a hundred Ks or whatever it was?'

'Their life savings. And they're selling their gaff, don't forget.'

'I just hope the focker is as good as he thinks he is – that's all I can say.'

All of a sudden, the dude storts walking to where we're standing. I'm thinking, Oh, shit.

'Is there sometheng that you wish to say to me?' is his opening line.

He's had it in for me from the very second he met me.

I'm there, 'Yeah, no, I was just saying it's great that you won the voucher for Daniel's,' trying to keep the conversation easy breezy. 'You and Fionn could have a celebratory dinner in there when you bring him back. Be a definite incentive for you. The Lobster Thermidor is also good.'

He goes, 'You knay, there's sometheng about you – every time you open your mouth I want to lay you out flet with a bunch of bloody well fives!'

'I'm just saying it'll be a treat for you.'

'I'm a professional. I don't need a restaurant voucher as an incentive to do anything.'

I stick out my hand and I go, 'Dude, we got off on the wrong foot. I'm prepared to let bygones be bygones and blah, blah, blah.'

'You're a bed day's work,' he goes. 'I knew it the very moment I set eyes upon you. I can size people up rather quickly, you see. I said to myself, now, there's a chep who's lecking in moral fibre.'

'Again, that's an opinion.'

'Yes, it is – and rather a good one, if I may say so.'

'All I was trying to say was good luck – as in, I hope you find Fionn.'

'I *will* find Fionn and it will have nothing to do with luck. And if you ever question my character again . . .'

'Dude, I always shout, "Fix!" at raffles. It's one of the things I'd be known for. Oisinn here will tell you that.'

'. . . I will subject you to tortures that would make a lifetime in Abu Ghraib seem like a welcome distraction. Do you understend?'

'Yeah.'

'I beg your pardon?'

'I said yes.'

He stares at me for a good twenty seconds, and I actually think he's going hit me again, except he doesn't. He goes, 'You're a bed lot,' and then he focks off.

Oisinn focks off as well, with the old dear in tow.

I stay for another hour or two. I chat away to the two Michael's dudes. They remember me playing rugby and the word phenomenal gets thrown into the mix, which is nice.

Around midnight, I decide to hit the road and I head outside to try to hail a taxi. One or two pass with their lights on, even though they've got actual people in them, which always pisses me off, and I obviously give them the finger.

And that's when I spot Jenny, in the little cor pork opposite Kielys, putting something into the boot of the Mazda she's been renting while she's here. I tip across the road to her, thinking, I'll see can I chorm her into giving me a lift out to Killiney, even though she despises me.

See, I love a challenge.

I'm like, 'Hey,' and I end up giving her a fright. She actually jumps. She was throwing the little pink cash box containing – I'm presuming – the proceeds of the evening into the boot.

I'm there, 'That seemed to go well. How much did you make?'

She goes, 'Abaaht foyve ind a hawf thaahsand yoyroys.'

'Well, they were good questions, in fairness to you. Some of them were real mind-benders. A lot of the brainiacs were even challenged.'

She goes, 'What do yoy want?'

I just shake my head. 'You know,' I go, 'when people give me a chance, they generally discover that I'm actually a lovely goy.'

She's like, 'Oh, royly?' in, like, a *sorcastic* way?

I'm there, 'Yeah, no, really.'

'Well, it's not the story *oy've* heard. Fionn's told moy tirruble stories abaaht yoy.'

'And I dare say they're all true. But the dude still loves me like an actual brother. And that's the exact same way I feel about him. He's the brother I never had.'

Something strange happens then, totally out of the blue. She looks away from me, roysh, then when she turns back, I notice that her eyes are filled with tears.

She goes, 'Oy muss hum, Ross – oy muss hum soy much. And oy'm thunking what if hoy . . . What if hoy . . .'

I'm there, 'Don't say it. Do not even say it.'

She goes, 'Oy moyt nivur soy hum agin,' and then she goes, 'Will yoy ployse hold moy?'

I'm like, 'Er, yeah, whatever,' and I put my orms around her and I give her a big hug, which is meant to comfort her, but then I stort petting her hair and rubbing her back and – I'm going to be honest here – tracing the outline of her bra with my right thumb.

This is what I meant when I said I always have difficulty finding the biting point.

There's a definite change in the atmosphere between us and she can sense it. 'What are yoy doying?' she goes.

I'm there, 'Nothing.'

'Yoy just kussed moy nick.'

'Well, you're not exactly pushing me away, Jenny.'

Which she's not, by the way. I know she's turned on.

I stort kissing her face then and I can taste the salt of her tears.

She goes, 'What koynd of a bahsturd moyks a moyve on his frind's girlfiend whoyle hoy's boying hild hustage?' but it's one of those questions that doesn't have an actual answer.

Rorratorical.

I kiss her on the mouth then and she finally responds in kind. She's a fantastic kisser, in fairness to Fionn. She really puts the work into it, although she also keeps stopping every twenty seconds or so to go, 'You're noy koynd of frind. You're a bahsturd – a rull bahsturd!' but in a kind of, like, *admiring* way?

I'm nothing if not a gentleman, so I'm going to draw a discreet veil over the rest of the proceedings. Suffice it to say that we end up doing the business there in the cor pork, in her little Mazda, with the front passenger seat pushed back – me going at it like a porn stor, and her digging her heels into my orse and screaming shit into my ear, alternating between compliments – 'Thus is soy good. Thus

148

is soy, soy good' – and insults – 'What koyd of a facking frind are yoy? What koynd of a frind?'

At some point in the transaction, I just happen to open my eyes. And that's when I see him. Fred Pfanning is staring at me through the rear window of the cor. He's looking me right in the eye. And his words come back to me.

A bad egg. Lacking in moral fibre.

5. FO'CKed Over

'What's she weerton?'

That's what Shadden wants to know when she arrives home from school. The answer is a pink butterfly dress and little baby ballet flats, although that's not really the question that she's asking.

Sorcha either doesn't cop the tone in her voice or she decides to basically ignore it.

'It's a pink butterfly dress and some little baby ballet flats,' she goes. 'You're a little fashionista, aren't you, Rihanna-Brogan? Yes, you are! Yes, you are!'

The kid looks delighted with herself, in fairness.

The only person in the room *not* smiling is Shadden.

She's like, 'Who toalt you to purr her in that?'

Sorcha finally cops what's going down here – or at least she stops pretending that there *isn't* an atmosphere in the kitchen?

'No one told me to put her in it,' she goes. 'I just happened to see it in BTs. It just reminded me how much I love the way Victoria Beckham dresses little Horper – always on trend, but she still looks like a little girl.'

Shadden's like, '*I* buy her clowiz,' and she basically spits the words out through gritted teeth. '*I* decide what she weers. Ine her mutter.'

'I'm well aware that you're her mother, Shadden.'

'Some toyums I wonther are you?'

It's at that exact moment that Ronan suddenly arrives home from school. It's like he picks up on the air between Sorcha and Shadden the second he walks through the door, because he drops his school-bag in the hall and literally sprints down to the kitchen.

He bursts into the room, giving it, 'What's the stordee?'

'Look at the wee *she* has her thressed?' Shadden straight away goes, lifting her baby out of her high-chair.

Ronan looks confused for a second or two. He's there, 'What's wrong wirrit?'

Shadden doesn't *answer* him, though? She just, like, fixes Sorcha with a stare – her eyes narrowed to little slits – and goes, 'She's not a bleaten doll for you to thress up and make a fooken howully show of!'

Ronan goes, 'Shadden, you're ourra oarter.'

Except Shadden's on a roll now. She's like, 'You can do that wit your owen babbies. You're not doing it wit moyen.'

I stare at Sorcha, thinking, Okay, just keep the von Trapp *dúnta* here, Babes – it's not going to do anyone any good if it all kicks off. Except Sorcha can't *not* speak out? It's all those Amnesty International newsletters she reads. Even now, she'll come to me every so often and tell me that this person is being tortured or that person has been executed and I can never understand why they don't just stop, you know, stirring the shit. But like a lot of those poor fockers, Sorcha prefers to say stuff rather than keep it in her head.

So she goes, 'Well, actually, Shadden, while we're on the subject of clothes, those trainers that *you* have her wearing aren't good for her little feet.'

Shadden's there, 'Soddy?'

'I'm talking about those little Nikes – or whatever they are. The soles are too thick. How's she ever going to learn to walk if she can't feel her feet on the floor?'

'*They* were a present from me Ma and Da.'

That says everything that needs to be said. She looks like a little focking joyrider in them.

'The tops are also too high,' Sorcha goes. 'Too much ankle support actually constricts movement and discourages a baby from taking its first steps. There's a whole orticle about it in *Practical Parenting and Pregnancy* magazine.'

Shadden ends up seriously flipping then. She's like, 'Who the bleaten hell do you think you eer?' and it's the first time I can see something of her old pair in her. 'Do *you* tink you're bethor than me or sometin?'

Ronan takes the baby off her, then sort of, like, hustles her out of the room, going, 'Mon, Shadden – joost leaf it!' and he brings her upstairs to try to calm her down.

Sorcha ends up just, like, shaking her head, going, 'It *has* to be post-natal depression, Ross. The mood swings. Sion Hill. It's like she's caught in some kind of downward spiral.'

Honor suddenly walks through the kitchen, swinging her piccolo case by her side, a big triumphant smile on her boat. 'I was the one who said it wouldn't work,' she goes. 'People like Shadden and that baby don't belong here. They're, like, *different* from us?'

Sorcha goes, 'Where are you going?'

She's obviously just passing through on her way down to the coach house. Our daughter is only ever passing through our lives these days.

Honor's there, 'I'm going down to practise my piccolo.'

Sorcha's like, 'Not down there, you're not. That place gives me the creeps.'

'It doesn't give me the creeps.'

'Honor, I don't want you going down there!'

'Er, when was the last time I listened to anything you said? Hashtag, you're not a role model to me – get over it.'

Honor walks out the back door and goes down to the coach house.

'Are you just going to stand there,' Sorcha goes, 'while people speak to me like that?'

I'm there, 'Like what?'

'Like the way Honor just spoke to me. Like the way Shadden just spoke to me. You just stood there with your mouth open.'

'I just think, I don't know, maybe there's something in what Honor says about Shadden not fitting in on the Southside. I was watching this thing on YouTube about these two dudes in – I don't know – maybe the 1960s, and they bought, like, a lion cub in Harrods. We're talking an actual lion cub. They put a collar around its neck and they used to walk it up and down to the shops.'

'Everyone's seen that, Ross. What's your point?'

'My point is that one day the cub became an actual lion. And these dudes knew that – as much as they loved the lion and the lion loved them – one day he'd probably turn around and just eat their focking heads, either out of boredom or just because he wanted to see what they looked like with no focking heads.'

'Okay, I still don't get what you're trying to say.'

That's often the way with people when I'm being deep.

'What I'm trying to say,' I go, 'is that Shadden is still K . . . K . . . K . . . Kennet and Dordeen's daughter. There's still a lot of the jungle in her. And maybe, like that lion, back in the jungle is where she belongs.'

I look to my right to see Ronan standing at the kitchen door. I'm wondering did he hear me. I'm hoping he didn't hear me.

'Ine soddy,' he goes. 'About Shadden.'

No, he mustn't have heard me.

Sorcha goes, 'It was just a dress and a pair of shoes, Ronan. I also bought her a rose-print beret and a Julien Macdonald tutu, but I'm afraid to give them to her now.'

'Like I said,' he goes. 'Ine soddy.'

That's when my phone all of a sudden beeps and it ends up being a text message from an unknown number. It's like, 'Ross we really need to talk,' and then underneath – fock it – it's like, 'Jenny'.

Christian is already wankered drunk when I arrive in Kielys. From the state of him, sitting at the bor, staring stupid-eyed at the lounge girl who looks like Florence Brudenell-Bruce, I'm guessing he's a good six or seven pints down the road, which for him is usually a kebab and a taxi home time.

'What's the point of arranging to go for scoops,' I go, 'if you're going to be already shit-faced when I get here? It means I'm going to have to stort throwing them down me now.'

I tell Florence to line up two pints of the Wonder Stuff for me, while Christian goes, 'I had a row with Lauren.'

I'm like, 'Dude, she's your wife. That's going to happen.'

'This was, like, massive, though. Massive, massive . . .'

The poor focker is falling aport.

I'm there, 'Dude, you're horrendufied.'

He goes, 'It's all . . . It's just too . . . Ross, do you ever have moments in your life when you think, fock it, I just don't have the strength to go on?'

'Of course I do. And do you know what I think about in those moments? I think about a certain thing that Father Fehily used to say. Heroism is endurance for one moment longer . . .'

'Endure, endure, endure.'

'Exactly. Never forget those words.'

'I told Lauren I wanted to give up.'

'Give up what?'

'This, you know, Footlong thing. Hennessy's talking about the High Court. Supreme Court. Europe, if it comes to it.'

Okay, that's a different story.

'Actually, I agree,' I go, 'I think you should let the whole thing go. Have you thought any more about my Centra slash Londis slash Spar idea? They're never focking empty, those places.'

He sort of, like, laughs, except in, like, a *bitter* way? He's there, 'What happened to endure, endure, endure?'

I'm like, 'Yeah, no, I definitely believe in that. But then Father Fehily also said that a dead horse isn't going to get any less dead if you keep whipping the focking thing.'

'That's what I'm trying to tell Hennessy. Even if they're forced to give us the franchise back, they can make it very difficult for us to operate. They could stop supplying us with logoed items. They could open another store next door.'

'It sounds like your mind is made up to drop it. Just tell Lauren you've decided to leave well enough alone. Then Hennessy can go back to the States and we can all get on with our lives . . . Like I said, Dude, those Centras are never focking empty.'

'No, her old man's determined to fight it all the way. He keeps saying we've done nothing wrong. And if we're being accused of something, then, under the Constitution, we're entitled to the full facts.'

'The only people you ever hear talking about entitlements and rights are the poor. And you don't want to go down that road, Christian. I'm saying that as your best friend.'

'I said to Lauren, I know your old man likes a fight, but we've got two children to support. Two mouths to feed. What are we going to do, spend the next two or three years and whatever money we have left chasing some focking fast-food multinational through the courts?'

'She's being focking ridiculous, Christian. And a bit selfish as well, if you don't mind me commenting. If you're looking for my opinion, you should stand up to her. You're the man of that house, not focking Hennessy.'

It's at that exact point that I become suddenly aware of someone standing at my elbow. Well, actually, first I notice Christian opening and closing his drunken eyes, trying to focus on whoever it is standing beside me. Then I just happen to turn to my left and it ends up being – oh, for fock's sake – Jenny.

'Hey, is there any word on Fionn?' I go, deciding to keep the conversation businesslike. 'Has Fred found him yet? I mean, he's been out there, like, a week.'

She looks actually well. I'm not saying this to be a dick, but I think I succeeded in putting a bit of colour back in her cheeks.

She goes, 'Can oy spoyk to yoy?' And then she quickly adds, 'In proyvut?'

Christian is out of his gourd, but he's not so far gone that he fails to pick up on the strangeness of this situation. Jenny's hated my basic guts from the very first second she met me. And I can almost hear the little cogs in Christian's head turning, thinking, Okay, what's the deal between these two? And of course it doesn't occur to him that I might have schtupped her. Christian always thinks the best of me – that's one of his major weaknesses.

'Yeah, no,' I go, 'let's go and talk somehere.' And then I turn to Christian and I go, 'It's probably about that Aung San Suu Kyi question that Sorcha queried the night of the quiz. New information. It looks like this one could run and run. Get them in while I'm gone, will you?'

Then I follow Jenny outside.

'He's off his focking tits in there,' I go, just to make conversation with the girl. 'Lauren will be along any minute to pick him up – you watch. Some boys' night out it's turned out to be.'

'Yoy dudn't reploy to inny of moy tixts,' is her opening line.

I'm like, 'Yeah, no, you obviously don't know me very well, Jenny. I wouldn't be a big one for the post-match chat.'

She seems confused by this. It's obviously a cultural thing.

She's like, 'Do yoy not want to talk abaaht whut hippened?'

I'm there, 'Do you mean in terms of analysis? All I can say is I enjoyed it.'

'Well, oy enjoyed it, toy.'

'Yeah, I gathered that. The noises out of you. Like a penguin at feeding time. Jesus.'

I suddenly cop that we're standing directly opposite the little cor pork where we did the deed.

It's the next line out of her mouth that causes a shudder of dread to run down my spine. She's like, 'So whut are we gonna doy?'

I'm there, 'Do? About what?'

'Well, abaaht us?'

'Us? What the fock are you talking about?'

'Yoy sid yoy loved moy.'

'Did I? When did I say I loved you?'

'Er, whin we were huving six in moy caahr.'

I laugh. See, I'm a shocker for just blurting out shit like that.

I'm there, 'Jenny, that's just something you say while you're doing it – adds a bit of atmosphere to the occasion. I'm, like, married with a kid and triplets on the way.'

'Yoy told moy your marriage was oyver – thit yoy were just stoying togither for the soyk of your kuds.'

'Again, that's just a line, Jenny. I was being romantic. I can't believe you took that literally.'

I watch her eyes suddenly water. Oh, for fock's sake.

'Well, oy dud take ut seriousloy,' she goes. 'Oy thought yoy mint ut.'

I just shake my head. I'm literally lost for words here. I'm like, 'Jenny, what did you think was going to happen?'

'Oy thought moy and yoy moyt – yoy knoy – git togither.'

That's when the tears really stort to come.

I'm there, 'Me and you? You're going out with someone, can I just remind you? You're going out with my friend, who's being held as a hostage in a foreign country, in case you've forgotten.'

And can I just add that I am focking disgusted with Fionn at that moment for ending up with a bird like this. A desperate bitch, in other words.

She goes, 'Oym suppoysed to boy moyting Inda Kinnoy tomorroy.'

I'm there, 'Okay, why is that name familiar?'

'Inda Kinnoy,' she goes. 'He's, like, the *Toyshock*?'

That'd explain it. His name keeps popping up everywhere these days.

She's there, 'Oy just doyn't knoy uf oy can moyt hum naah.'

'Well, just go ahead would be my basic advice.'

She goes, 'Oy feel loyk such a huppocrut. Oy was thunking thut moybe oy'd continue the campoyn for Fionn's releoyse as, loyk, his frind rather thin his *girlfrind*? Oy was thunking oy'd moybe put aaht a stoytmunt.'

I'm there, 'Don't do that!' and I say it straight away.

She's like, 'Whoy not?' crying even more now.

I feel like crying myself, I want to tell her, except some of us have a thing called dignity.

'Jesus Christ,' I go, 'it's only a few weeks ago that you were on the focking *Late Late*, telling the Tubster and the rest of the country that Fionn was the love of your life.'

'Oy thought he was. But oy doyn't foyle thit woy innymore.'

I was right about Lauren. She's suddenly coming this way, carrying little Oliver in one orm, with little Ross Junior holding her other hand and running along beside her. She doesn't look happy. I turn my head to try to, like, avoid her eye, except *he* ends up seeing me and goes, 'Hi, Roth! My mommy ith wearing chethnut Ugg booth!'

For fock's sake.

Lauren cops me then and she ends up just glowering at me. She's like, 'Where's *he*?'

I'm there, 'He's at the bor.'

She shakes her head at me – disappointed – like *I'm* somehow to blame?

'If it's any consolation,' I go, 'he was practically falling off the focking stool when I arrived.'

It's no consolation at all.

She goes, 'He needs to grow a pair of balls,' and then she turns her head and notices who I'm standing there talking to. She goes, 'Oh, hi!' and I see the confusion on her face – same as Christian – wondering what's going on and why is Jenny crying?

I go, 'We're having a private conversation here – would you mind?' and Lauren rolls her eyes and shakes her head and goes into Kielys with the kids to drag her husband home.

I tell Jenny that we need to go somewhere quieter to talk and I take her down that little laneway at the side of the Porty Shop.

'Look,' I go, 'you're confused at the moment. It can't be easy, your boyfriend – the love of your life, bear in mind – being kidnapped in Africa. But what you really need to do is focus on him. He's your priority now.'

'Oy doyn't thunk oy kin,' she goes. 'Oy thunk oym in love wuth yoy.'

'You're not in love with me, Jenny. You don't even know me.'

'Oy thought oy hoytud yoy whin oy first mit yoy. But oy can't hilp ut – oy loyk min who are bahsturds. And you're a comployt bahsturd.'

'I'm not going to deny that.'

'And yoy can't denoy thut there's something betwoyn us.'

'Like I said, I wouldn't base anything on what happened across the road that night. The whole thing was an act – certainly from my point of view.'

'Oy'll till yoy what wasn't an ict – the woy yoy moyd love to moy.'

She's obviously talking about the length of time I lasted. Girls are obsessed with that whole duration thing and this was up in the old fifteen-minute range, in fairness to me. I sometimes use various concentration techniques to stop it going off – naming the three Leinster XVs that won the Heineken Cup, just as an example, then the subs. But with Jenny, I didn't need to do any of that. The reason it took me so long to get there was because I couldn't get Fred Pfanning's face out of my mind after I saw him gawking in the focking window.

I'm surprised I managed to lead the horse home at all.

'Look,' I go, 'it was a one-night thing, Jenny. You were emotional. I saw an opening and I went for it. A lot of people would say fair focks to me for that. Some maybe not. But it meant literally nothing to me – you need to know that.'

She's like, 'Whoy would yoy huv six with someone if yoy didn't have feelings for thum?'

Oh, it looks like we've got a live one here.

I'm there, 'That's like asking why do dogs chase cars they have no intention of driving?'

She's like, 'Ross, oym in love with yoy.'

Like I said, I'm focking furious with Fionn.

'Whether that's true or not,' I go, 'you need to get over me – and fast. You got the Royal Command performance out of me that night. Be thankful for that and move on.'

Then I turn around and I leave her standing there, nursing her broken hort in the laneway, shouting, 'You're a bahsturd! You're a toytal bahsturd!' like the crazy stalker bitch that she suddenly obviously is.

Sorcha is rubbing her hands up and down her belly like she's playing an imaginary accordion. I ask her if she wants me to drive slower, but she says no, it's fine.

'It's just, they're really kicking hord this morning,' she goes.

Honor's there, 'They probably know what you're driving,' because it's the first morning we've taken her to school in what she calls the special needs bus. 'They were conceived in shame and they're going to be born in shame.'

Sorcha's like, 'Honor, that is not a nice thing to say.'

She goes, 'I'm calling it like I see it.'

That's a quality she gets from me.

'Oh my God,' Sorcha suddenly goes, 'what is going on with Jenny?'

I get such a fright, roysh, I end up driving straight through a red light at the crossroads in Ballybrack village.

I'm like, 'What do you mean, Babes?'

She goes, 'Did you see the coverage of her meeting with Enda Kenny?'

'Er . . .'

'She said in all of the papers that from now on, she wanted to be referred to as Fionn's friend rather than his girlfriend.'

Oh, fock.

I'm there, 'Fionn always struggled to hold on to women, in fairness.'

She goes, 'But why the sudden change of hort, Ross? She was on the *Late Late Show* not so long ago, talking about how he was the love of her life.'

'That can happen, though, when you're away from someone for a while. You think you like them more than you do.'

'What are you talking about?'

'It's like when you go to Irish college and you end up scoring some bird from, I don't know, Cahirciveen or Cloughjordan or one of those. And you go home and you tell all the goys about this absolute cracker you were with, even though she's from the country. Then you have your reunion six months later. You're standing outside McDonald's on Grafton Street and you see her coming and you think, Oh my God, look at the focking state of that. She's focking feral. The mind plays tricks. I think that's the moral of the story.'

'But they were thinking of getting engaged. That's what she told Ryan. Something must have happened to change her mind. I'd love to know what it . . .'

She all of a sudden jumps and goes, 'Owww!'

One of the babies has kicked her seriously hord. I like to think what they're saying is, Stop putting the dude under pressure and leave well enough alone.

We pull up outside the school. I get out and open the sliding door. I notice quite a few kids – boys, especially – pointing at the bus and openly laughing.

Honor goes, 'I can't believe you'd bring me to school in this. You've ruined my focking life.'

And then off she goes. I notice one of the boys – a kid of nine with the body of an adult – shout something in her direction, then the others all laugh as she passes, except Honor just stares straight ahead of her, totally blanking them, then disappears into the school building.

I climb back in and Sorcha goes, 'I hope she's not being bullied.'

I'm there, 'As far as bullying goes, I've always seen Honor as a perp rather than a victim, Babes. I'm proud to say that she's very much her father's daughter in that regard.'

'Those boys were saying mean things to her, though. I'm wondering is that why she's spending so much time down in that coach house? She seems a bit withdrawn to me. You know, a bit absent.'

'Absent can be good, Sorcha, especially when you're dealing with a kid like Honor. Breaks from her are important. Otherwise you'd go off your focking head. Look, I wouldn't worry. One thing we know for sure is that she can definitely handle herself.'

Just as I'm turning the key, there's a knock on the window on the passenger side. It ends up being Mr O'Fathaigh.

Sorcha winds down her window and she's like, 'Hello, Mr O'Fathaigh – it's lovely to see you.'

She's still a focking lickorse, even though she's out of school fifteen years.

He's there, 'Yes, likewise. You received Honor's report card, I gather.'

She's there, 'Yes. Oh my God, we were so proud, weren't we, Ross? I know it's awful that I sound so surprised. But Honor has never much liked school.'

'Well, Miss Maidin is an excellent teacher,' he goes. 'She has a real way with young people. Did Honor tell you that she's going to be playing her piccolo at our Christmas concert?'

Christmas concert. It's focking November. Let's at least get the autumn internationals out of the way before we stort thinking about Christmas.

Sorcha looks delighted and confused at the exact same time, if you can picture that face.

'She never said anything to us,' she goes. 'Did she, Ross?'

She might have said something to me. I think I was watching *I'm a Celebrity, Get Me Out of Here* at the time.

He's there, 'Well, she's going to be playing "O Holy Night" at our Christmas concert. She's been practising for weeks.'

Sorcha goes, 'We've heard her! We have a little coach house at bottom of our gorden and she goes in there to practise.'

A little coach house. You can nearly hear the dude thinking, What focking planet are these people living on?

'Mr O'Fathaigh, can I ask you something?' Sorcha goes. 'Do you think it's possible that Honor is being bullied?'

He's there, 'Bullied?'

'It's just, well, that boy over there said something to her when she walked past and it made all the other boys laugh.'

'Which boy?' he goes, looking over his shoulder.

She's like, 'The one with the, em . . .' trying to come up with a polite way of describing him that offends no one.

I end up just blurting it out. 'The one with the big bones,' I go. 'I'd be pretty focking stunned if that's not medication-related, by the way.'

He cops who I'm talking about pretty much straight away.

'Derek Drewery,' he goes. 'I shall have a word. Thank you for drawing it to my attention.'

Then, finally, off we go, back to the gaff again, Sorcha banging on about how she would have always believed that private education was – oh my God – so much better than public education, but she was possibly being a snob and maybe she owes Shadden an apology for being such a bitch about Sion Hill.

We're back in the gaff. I'm fixing myself a pot of coffee and Sorcha is chopping up a mango for Rihanna-B when she suddenly remembers something.

'Oh my God,' she goes. 'Put on Today FM.'

I'm like, 'Er, why?'

'Your mum is going to be on Ray D'Orcy.'

'Ray D'Orcy? Why does *he* have her on?'

She turns on the radio and shushes me. After twenty seconds of ads, it comes back to Ray and he goes, 'Now, Fionnuala O'Carroll-Kelly is many things . . .'

I'm there, 'He's got that right. I hope "dried-up old hag with a face like an empty sock puppet" is on that list.'

'Shush,' Sorcha goes.

Ray's like, 'A best-selling author, a TV chef, a screenwriter, a charity campaigner and a woman in the, shall we say, autumn of her life who still enjoys a full and active sex life.'

I'm like, 'Oh, for fock's sake!'

'This morning she's here to talk to us about what is going to become, I hope, a regular feature on the show concerning seniors sex. And actually, if you have any little kiddies in the room, you might move them out of earshot for the next fifteen or twenty minutes or so.'

I'm like, 'Turn it off.'

Sorcha goes, 'Ross, I want to hear this!'

'Yeah, no, you heard what Ray said – my *granddaughter* is in the room?'

'She won't understand a word of what they're saying. Shush, Ross, I want to hear this,' and she actually turns the volume *up*?

'Fionnuala,' Ray goes, 'you're very welcome to the programme. Sex. It's not just for young people, is it?'

The old dear goes, 'Well thankfully no the human need for intimacy is ageless and it doesn't diminish with time but perhaps other things diminish for instance our energy levels our sense of adventure and our contentment with our bodies and we fool ourselves into thinking that it's an issue with our libidos when in fact it's not because the desire for sexual intercourse remains as strong in us at seventy as it does at seventeen and that's why seniors sex is an issue we should all be comfortable speaking about because with better understanding and an open mind you can continue to enjoy a physically and emotionally fulfilling sex life well into your seventies eighties and nineties . . .'

Sorcha goes, 'Oh my God, what's wrong her voice?'

I laugh. She's so innocent, sometimes I wonder should she be out of the house at all.

'Possibly too much coffee,' I go.

She's there, 'It does sound like that. I sometimes end up talking faster if I have a second cup before eleven.'

Ray goes, 'You are, what, late fifties?'

I shout, 'And the focking rest – give her back that decade, D'Orcy!'

He goes, 'And you're in a relationship with a much younger man, which we've all read about in the newspapers. If it's not too intimate a question, what challenges does that present?'

She goes, 'There is no such thing as too intimate as far as I'm concerned and that's what I'm here to do which is to try to deconstruct these taboos that surround the sexuality of people in the autumn of their lives . . .'

'Winter!' I make sure to shout.

She's there, 'Of course there are challenges be they physical emotional or psychological many senior people may have hang-ups about their bodies or their performance but all of these things can be very easily overcome provided erectile dysfunction and vaginal dryness isn't a factor by simply reopening your mind to the emotional and sensual aspects of your sexuality and that's very much the message I'm trying to convey and the fact that sex at fifty-eight as I am can be even more enjoyable than sex at twenty-two because as we advance in years we are inevitably wiser and we're more aware of our bodies and we feel more self-confident or at least we should and we are freed from foolish notions about you know the ideal mating partner and we're released from our prejudices regarding aesthetic beauty and that's why more and more senior people need to realize that regardless of your age or your infirmity you can enjoy an orgasm and in fact it is your right . . .'

Sorcha's there, 'She is – oh my God – *so* brave, even though I'm struggling to keep up with what she's saying.'

The old dear's going, 'My message to older couples whose sexuality has perhaps been lying dormant for a few years is to take your time don't expect to be swinging from the chandelier this evening start with perhaps a romantic dinner or breakfast perhaps read some erotic literature together and my book *Fifty Greys in Shades is* still available from all good bookshops *and* as an ebook and make sure you connect with each other because sex without a connection is no kind of sex at all so don't forget to tell your partner that you love them and perhaps share with them some of your ideas for sexual experiences you might like to try together and then you can resume your physical relationship graduating to different sexual positions whether that's him on top or her on top or perhaps intimacy in your case might not necessarily involve vaginal penetration it could be oral sex or masturbation which can be very very fulfilling and don't be afraid of playfulness and when I say playfulness I'm talking about everything from tickling to battery-operated toys and lubricants . . .'

I'm there, 'Okay, turn it off.'

Sorcha goes, 'Ross, wait, I want to hear the end of this. An awful lot of what she's saying makes sense.'

I'm like, 'Okay, I'm going to find a bathroom and puke.'

I tip out to the hallway and the first thing I see is Sorcha's sister coming down the stairs in a very short dressing gown.

Her legs are God's work.

I'm there, 'The very woman. How are you getting on? With Oisinn?'

She's like, 'Oh my God, amazing. A lot of flirty texts going back and forth.'

I go, 'You need to take it up a gear. Forget flirty. You need to stort giving him filthy.'

And she's like, 'Okay, consider it done.'

Ronan will never understand rugby. He's just watched Johnny Sexton slice between two defenders and reach across the line for a try that I would have been proud to call my own and yet he sits there watching it like a cow reading graffiti.

'I'll nebber wontherstand rubby,' he goes.

He says it himself.

'Well,' I go, 'I'm the same with the whole Association Soccer thing.'

A few weeks ago, he took me to see his beloved Bohiz against Something Wanderers or Something Rovers and I had to ask what direction I should be facing.

It's nice to have him here, although it's weird being at the Aviva for an Ireland match without any of the goys. Fionn's not here for obvious reasons. Christian has too much on his plate, what with losing his business and – according to Sorcha – his marriage to Lauren being in supposedly trouble. Oisinn's off doing fock knows what with my so-called mother. And JP's seat is just empty.

'You alreet?' Ronan goes.

I'm there, 'Yeah, no, I'm cool.'

'It's joost you seemt a bit tense eerdier, when we were in the poob.'

'Ah, it's just that Orgentina are a bit of a bogey side for us. They always give us a hord game.'

'Is that it, yeah?'

'Yeah, no, there's one or two other things going on in the background as well. My life feels like a plate-spinning act at the moment – that's all. Look at Donnacha Ryan down there. He's making shit of their lineout.'

He goes, 'I wanted to say sometin to you, Rosser.'

I'm like, 'Yeah, go ahead,' at the same time thinking can this not wait?

'It's about Shadden.'

'Keep talking. I'm definitely listening.'

'I wanthed to apodogize again – over the way she's arthur been acton lately.'

I look at him. He's turned out to be one incredible kid. I hate patting myself on the back, but he's a genuine credit to me.

'You don't have to apologize,' I go. 'If anyone should be apologizing, it's Dordeen and K . . . K . . . K . . . Kennet. I heard *him* – Skyping her from the Joy – winding her up. I nearly rang the prison to tell them that he had an iPhone in his cell.'

'Look, you and Sudeka are arthur been so good to us. I wootunt be repeating me Junior Ceert if it wadn't for you two putting a roof over isser heads. And Shadden wootunt have been able to go back to skewill eeder. But you're reet. They're arthur getting into her head.'

'Focking scumbags . . . Good focking take, Donnacha Ryan! Again!'

'And she's teddified that she's gonna miss her foorst woords. That she's gonna come howum from skewill one day and Sudeka's gonna tell her that she took her foorst steps and she wadn't there to see it.'

'Look, we'll definitely record it for you if happens while you're at school – that's a promise to you.'

'You bethor fooken not, Rosser. If it happens while we're at skewill, you caddent fooken tell her, do you hear me?'

'Okay.'

'Ine seerdious, Rosser. Ine arthur promising her she'll be there when Rihadda-Burrogan leerns to walk. Even if it's not the foorst toyum, she has to think it is – do you wontherstand me?'

I understand him. And I'm happy to see that he understands women.

Something suddenly grabs his attention. 'Here's your mate,' he goes and I turn my head in time to see JP making his way up the steps towards our row, followed by Shoshanna, holding – I'm sorry but – their black baby.

I've got a big dumb smile on my face when I see J Town. And I don't think I'm imagining that his face lights up when he sees me as well.

She's not pleased, though. She's obviously surprised to see me sitting there. She actually goes, 'Are you *fucking* serious?' when she realizes who they're going to be sitting next to.

Someone behind us shouts, 'Sit the fock down!' which is fair enough, because Ireland are on the attack again – Richardt Strauss is playing out of his skin – and she's blocking about fifty people's view of the action.

She insists on taking the seat next to me – which is usually Fionn's seat, because he loves to hear my analysis during matches – and she sits there just to make sure there's a buffer between me and JP. She obviously realizes – even as an American – that rugby has the power to heal old divisions. You only have to watch Matt Damon and Morgan Freeman in *Invictus* to understand that.

Of course, JP isn't in his seat more than twenty seconds when he finds himself leaning across Shoshanna to go, 'What did I miss?'

He's actually forgotten that he's not talking to me. I love rugby so much that it makes me want to sometimes cry and that's not the drink talking.

'Two tries,' I go and it's just like old times. 'Craig Gilroy scored the first.'

He's like, 'Gilroy?' delighted for him.

It's his debut, to be fair.

'Gilroy,' I go. 'After a pop pass from Sexton that had to be seen to be believed, although Gilroy still had a lot of work to do. He beat three players. Sexton got the second. Class written all over it . . .'

Shoshanna says it again. She's like, 'Are you fucking serious?' except even louder this time. And then she turns around fully to JP – with her back to me, which is rude – and she goes, 'Are you seriously talking to this guy who said what he said about our baby?'

And it's like JP suddenly remembers himself and he turns his head and storts watching the match.

Shoshanna is bouncing little Ezra focking Dumpling up and down on her knee. I'm stealing little sideways glances at him. He's got a set of big green earmuffs on him that look like headphones. It's the first time since the hospital that I've been this close to him and it's obvious to me – though it makes me sad to say it – that there's literally nothing of JP in him.

I just so happen to turn to Ro, who nods his head and mouths the word, 'Black,' to me, as if to say, Yeah, no, you were right all along, Rosser, because he's heard me banging on about it for weeks now.

I go to have another sly look – I can't take my eyes off the little chap – except this time Shoshanna catches me in the act and goes, 'What the fuck are you looking at?' and then, 'Turn your fucking head! Don't you fucking look at my baby!'

JP tells her to calm down, except that makes her even *worse*?

She's like, 'Don't tell me to calm down! First, you bring me to this stupid game that I don't even give a shit about . . .'

Quite a few people in the crowd are suddenly listening. And of course, they have no sympathy for her after that comment.

She's like, '. . . and then I discover that I'm sitting next to this fucking idiot who said just about *the* most hurtful thing he could have said about our baby.'

JP goes, 'Look, I'm just here to see the game, okay?' totally losing it with her for a second.

It's nice to see.

I go back to watching the match with – I think this is the word – a *wry* smile on my face?

My phone beeps in my hand. It's a text message from Sorcha's sister, who's actually in my contacts book as 'Sorcha's Sister'.

It's like, 'U wundt believ wot oisinn just told me hed like 2 do 2 me!'

I'm just about to text her back to say fair focks when a huge roar goes up. I look up. Ireland have won a lineout and they're about five metres away from Orgentina's line. Suddenly, Strauss comes around the back of a ruck with the ball under his orm and makes a dive for the line.

He gets over.

I punch the air, then I turn to Ro.

'Is that anutter scower?' he goes.

I'm like, 'It's called a try, Ro – and yeah.'

Out of the corner of my eye, I notice that JP is looking at me – again, he's doing it subtly. So I turn my head slightly to the left and our eyes meet. He smiles at me. And that smile says, I'm actually delighted for Strauss, because he's a legend to me, but it also says something else – that this shit between us is possibly fixable.

And for a quiet little moment, I think to myself, Yeah, no, it's like things are storting to finally turn for the old Rossmeister. But of course as soon as you allow yourself to think that, well, that's usually when the Universe is lining up to deliver you an almighty kick in the town halls.

Fionn's old pair, his sister and *her* husband – the famous David – are standing at my front door and I can straight away tell from the serious looks on their faces that this is not a social visit.

My first instinct is to shout, 'Don't focking listen to her. Nothing happened. She's mad.'

But if experience has taught me anything, it's that you should never admit or deny anything until you've actually been accused – and then you should deny it anyway. So I play it cool.

I'm like, 'Hey, Ewan. Hey, Andrea. How's it going, David – are you still thinking about doing a triathlon?' because that was a story that went around.

'We'd like to speak with you,' Ewan goes – very formal. It reminds me of being arrested.

I'm there, 'Now is not a good time. Can you give me a hint as to what it's about?'

And that's when Sorcha suddenly appears behind me and blows my focking cover. She's like, 'Hello! Hi, Andrea! Hi, Eleanor! Come in! Ross, I can't believe you left them standing at the door!' and then, as she leads them into the hallway, she turns around, her face suddenly filled with concern, and goes, 'Oh my God, it's not bad news, is it? About Fionn?'

Ewan's like, 'No, we still haven't heard anything.'

'Nothing,' Andrea goes.

Sorcha's there, 'And what about that man who went over there to try to find him?'

Ewan's like, 'Apparently, he's still trying to make contact with the kidnappers. We get the distinct impression that we're not being told everything.'

Sorcha goes, 'Come in – we're down in the drawing room,' which is exactly where she leads the whole focking porty.

Sorcha's old dear is sitting on the floor, rolling a ball across the corpet to little Rihanna-B, then Rihanna-B rolls it back again.

Sorcha makes the introductions, then it's Eleanor who decides to dispense with the pleasantries and get down to business.

'We wanted to ask Ross something?' she goes.

I'm there, 'Hey, ask away,' although, beneath this cool exterior, I'm quietly shitting Baileys. I'm wondering do they know and, if so, how much do they know? 'Ask your questions, even though this all seems a bit random to me.'

Eleanor looks well. She's lost a bit of weight and it definitely suits her.

Andrea goes, 'Do you know what's wrong with Jenny?'

They don't know anything. They definitely don't know anything, because it's meant as a genuine question.

'Jenny?' I go. 'As in, Fionn's girlfriend Jenny?'

'Well, apparently not,' Ewan goes. 'I don't know if you saw the newspapers the day after she met Enda Kenny, but she asked to be referred to as Fionn's friend rather than his girlfriend.'

Sorcha has to go and stick her Shiva focking Rose into it then.

'Yeah, I was wondering about that as well,' she goes, 'wasn't I, Ross? Because she was saying on the *Late Late Show* that Fionn was definitely the one. She said she knew it from the very first moment she met him, because I remember thinking, Oh my God, that is, like, *so* lovely!'

Andrea – big serious head on her – goes, 'Do you know what's going on, Ross?'

Genuinely. This family used to be mad about me.

I stick out my bottom lip, shake my head and go, 'I really don't have a clue. I'm as mystified as the rest of you.'

Sorcha's there, 'Ross is hordly likely to know. It's no secret that he and Jenny didn't exactly hit it off.'

Of all my wife's amazing qualities, her unshakeable faith in me – despite everything she deep down knows about me – is the thing I love the most.

She goes, 'I think she actually hates you, doesn't she, Ross?'

'Yeah,' I go, 'she hates me in a big-time way.'

Sorcha's there, 'Have you asked Jenny herself what's going on?'

Eleanor's like, 'She won't talk about it. We've all tried. As soon as any of us brings up Fionn's name, she bursts into tears and says he deserves better than her. She hasn't been out of her bedroom for three days now.'

'Ross, you definitely don't know anything?'

It's Ewan this time.

I'm there, 'No, nothing. Although what I would say is that a lot of birds who go out with Fionn at some point down the line end up wanting to just be his friend. It happened a lot in school.'

That may have sounded horsh. They don't like it. Eleanor fixes me with a look, then goes, 'Did something happen?'

I'm like, 'Happen? What are you talking about?'

'I'm asking did something happen between you and Jenny?'

173

I don't believe this. She's asking me in front of my wife, my granddaughter and my mother-in-law whether I tupped her brother's girlfriend. They've some focking cheek, this family.

I can see Sorcha struggling to make sense of what's going on, although her old dear is a lot quicker on the uptake, from the way she's suddenly glowering at me.

I'm like, 'No. Of course nothing happened between us.'

They all continue just staring at me. It's hord to know who believes me and who doesn't. Sorcha does – I know that. Her old dear is fifty–fifty, although that's all she ever is when it comes to me. Ewan and Andrea believe me, I think. David doesn't, because he hates my guts. And Eleanor definitely doesn't, because I threw her about, once or twice, when she was on a break from David, and she can see that Jenny's symptoms are exactly the same as hers when I burned *her*.

'Oh my God!' Sorcha suddenly goes. And for a second or two, I think it's finally dawned on her what I've done. But when I turn my head, I notice that she's looking not at me but at Rihanna-B, who has managed to manoeuvre herself upright by holding onto the sofa, as I've seen her do before, except this time she's standing unaided and even though she's wobbling backwards and forwards a little bit, it's pretty obvious that she's about to take her first steps.

'This is it!' Sorcha goes. 'Oh my God!'

'Has she walked before?' Andrea wants to know.

Sorcha's like, 'No! Oh my God, I can't believe I don't have my iPhone to record this.'

She has a point. These are the precious moments. Suddenly, everyone in the room has put aside what I may or may not have done to Fionn's girlfriend and we're watching a tiny, little baby, her orms stretched out in front of her for balance, finally discover why she has feet.

She swings them like they're filled with concrete. First the right, then the left, then for about five seconds it looks like she's going to fall, but she manages to steady herself without touching any of the furniture, then she puts her right foot forward, then her left again.

She's suddenly making good progress. Sorcha's old dear stands about six feet in front of her with her orms open wide, going, 'Come on, Rihanna-Brogan! Come to me! Come to me!' giving her a torget to aim for.

The kid has a big serious *expression* on her face? She's a competitor, like her grandfather.

Eleanor and Andrea are going, 'Isn't this a wonderful thing to see!' and even Ewan and David have big ridiculous smiles on their faces.

Sorcha's going, 'That's it, Rihanna-Brogan! That's it!'

And it's at that exact moment that I hear the front door slam and Ronan shouts, 'We're howum!' as in home from school, and I instantly remember what he said to me at the Aviva about Shadden being terrified slash teddified of missing all the big moments in Rihanna-Brogan's life.

I have to think fast here.

I look down and I notice that she's walking on this, like, long, narrow rug.

'What the hell are you doing?' Sorcha roars at me.

I'm there, 'Ro said Shadden will have a shit-fit if she's not there to see this moment.'

'Oh! My God! She will!'

'We have to stop her.'

Before she gets a chance to say another word, I give the rug a serious tug with both hands and Rihanna-Brogan ends up flying about two feet into the air, then falling flat on her face.

She screams, then that scream turns into sudden hysterical crying. The door opens and in walks Shadden, followed by Ronan. They see their daughter lying on her face on the ground, roaring her head off, and Shadden goes, 'What the hell are yous doing to horr?'

She runs over to her and picks her up and talks softly to her, telling her everything's going to be okay. And Ronan – who's obviously copped what happened – smiles at me and gives me an incredible wink of thanks.

★

I'm sitting in Bucky's in Blackrock, knocking back a grande pumpkin spice latte while Sorcha is at her pre-natal Pilates class above the Central Café on the Main Street – and I'm plotting the final destruction of my old dear's relationship, if you could call it that, with Oisinn.

She answers on the third ring.

'Hello,' she goes, 'who's that is it Ross hold on Ross I'm just in Donnybrook Fair yes please can I have some of the *Affineur* no not that big piece that little one there and also some of the *Bleu de Gex* yes the *Bleu de Gex* hold on Ross I'll be with you in a moment and can I pay for my San Pellegrino here as well oh good yes you can put them all in the same bag hello Ross . . .'

I'm like, 'Hey, you!'

I end up having to swallow down what I *actually* want to say to her, which is, 'What, you can't even do your shopping now without snorting a few lines?'

'I'm wonderful,' she goes, even though I don't remember asking her how she was. 'Did you see that typhoon on the news this morning it was in the Philippines it's killed over a thousand but the death toll could be higher because there's the same number unaccounted for and you'd have to presume dead and I was thinking of organizing a ladies' golf day to raise money just like the old days they're bound to need things food blankets medication there'll be typhoid and cholera and all of those it's been years since I've done one of my charity events I used to be famous for them it's been so difficult to find the time in the last few years but suddenly I have all of this energy . . .'

I go, 'What are you doing Friday night?'

That puts a stop to her gallop.

She's like, 'Friday night what do you mean why are you asking me what I'm doing on Friday night . . .'

I'm there, 'I'm just wondering, did you want to do something together?'

'You're going to say something cruel now aren't you Ross you're not going to saying something cruel are you because I really don't think I could . . .'

'It's a genuine question. It's a genuine offer. Sorcha has tickets for Joshua Bell, but she obviously can't go because she can't sit in the National Concert Hall all night in her condition.'

'Oh I love Joshua Bell I was listening to *Romance of the Violin* in the car just the other day I love that CD it's one your father bought me and there's another one I have I think it's called *The Essential Joshua Bell* . . .'

'See, I remembered you liked him. So I was thinking we could have a bit of – what do you call it? – focking supper in the Gables, then head in to the Concert Hall. Make a night of it, in other words. We never really do shit like that, me and you.'

'It sounds wonderful Ross yes I think I'd really love that oh wait I'm going to need some charcoal crackers to go with the cheese . . .'

'Okay,' I go, 'I'll pick you up from your gaff at six o'clock.'

Then I hang up and I ring Sorcha's sister. She's in work.

'I can't stay on long,' she goes. 'My supervisor is being – oh my God – such a passive-aggressive bitch to me.'

I'm like, 'It's on. It's on like Maud focking Gonne. Friday night. I'm treating my old dear to a night out, the drug-addled bitch. I'm picking her up at six. She's probably already on the phone telling Oisinn – focking delighted with herself. You arrange to call around to see him at, what, half-six?'

'When do I get my money?'

'When you do the job.'

She sighs and calls me a wanker under her breath. I actually feel sorry for her supervisor.

'I'll do the job,' she goes.

I'm there, 'Happy days.'

I hang up and I end up just sitting there, quietly focking pleased with my lunchtime's work, when all of a sudden I become aware of someone staring at me. I look up and I end up nearly shitting myself, there in my comfy chair.

It's Jenny.

I'm like, 'What the fock?'

She goes, 'Helloy, Ross.'

'What, are you stalking me now?'

'Noy, it's just a hippy coincidunce, thut's all.'

Happy coincidence, my focking hoop.

'Jenny,' I go, 'you've got to forget this whole obsession thing you have with me. I had Fionn's old pair at my door the other day asking me questions. His sister and that focking goon she married as well.'

'What koynd of quistiuns?'

'Well, basically, whether I rode you – this was in front of my focking pregnant wife and my mother-in-law, can I just mention?'

'And what dud you till thum?'

'What do you think I told them? I told them nothing happened. But they think something did because of you telling the press that you wanted to be described as Fionn's friend.'

'Oy doyn't love hum. Oy've *realoyzed* thit?'

'Jenny, I'm not an option for you.'

'Oy'm hearing what you're soying. But oy've decoyded thut oy'm just not tyking noy for an aahnser.'

Jesus. She's mad as a bucket of piss.

I'm there, 'Er, the law says you kind of have to, Jenny.'

'Moyboy oy'll till Ewan and Andrea the troyth,' she goes. 'Moyboy oy'll till thum whut hippened. Thut we had six in moy caahr aahfter the toyble kwuz.'

'Look, I don't think that'd surprise them. They know I'm a dirty dog.'

'Oy'll till them tonoyt thin, thut oy stull want to doy everythung oy can to hilp foynd their son, but oy've fallen hid ivor hoyles in love with one of hus frinds. That's just an unfortunut fict.'

'Again, that doesn't automatically mean we're going to be together.'

And that's when she says it. She's there, 'Moyboy oy'll till your woyf as will.'

I'm like, 'What?'

She goes, 'Yoy doan't knoy hah miny toyms oy've nearly phined her in the last few doys.'

I'm there, 'Don't do that. No matter how tempted you are, please don't do that.'

I suddenly realize that I need to stall her, the mental cow. 'Look,' I go, 'can you just, I don't know, give me a week?'

She's there, 'A woyk?'

'That's all I need. Possibly two.'

'To doy what?'

'To arrange it so that we can be together.'

Her face lights up like a skobie with Christmas on Ice tickets. 'So you're sayin yoy doy love moy?'

I sigh, then I look away. I'm there, 'There's no point in denying it. I think you felt it that night . . .'

'Oy dud.'

'. . . when I lashed you out of it in the cor.'

'Oy filt ut alroyt. Moy hoyle bodoy was, loyk, *tingling*?'

'Well, mine was doing pretty much the same thing. There's a connection between us. So there's your proof.'

'So whut are we gonna doy?'

'Look, that shit I said to you – about me and Sorcha being on the basic rocks – that *was* actually true.'

'You're not just soying thit naah to stop moy tilling her abaaht us?'

'I'm a lot of things, Jenny. But one thing I'm not is a liar.'

'Oy'm soy hippy to hear yoy talk loyk thus.'

'I'd be a fool to fight these feelings. I've be a definite fool up until now. But look, Jenny, timing is everything in this case.'

'Whut do yoy moyn?'

'Like I said, I need a few days to break the news to Sorcha.'

'And you're soying we're difinitloy gonna boy togither?'

'No one is going to stop that from happening. And I mean no one.'

'Do yoy royly moyne ut? You're not gonna miss moy araahnd?'

The answer to those questions are no and yes. Jenny has to be taken out of the picture. The only question is, how do I do it? I'll need a day or two to mull it over. I'm an absolute master at focking people over, as my old dear is about to discover.

But even Superman can only do one job at a time.

I'm like, 'So what are you going to do tonight?'

And do you know what Oisinn has the actual balls to go?

He goes, 'I might just stay in and watch TV.'

I'm there, 'TV? Now I feel bad. Dude, why don't you come with us?'

He's like, 'Come *with* you?' horrified at the idea, his plans for a night of happy-happy with Sorcha's sister suddenly in jeopardy. 'No, I don't want to intrude . . .'

I'm like, 'Dude, I don't mind. Seriously. Look, I'm cool with it now – the whole you and her thing . . .'

He can't even look me in the eye. 'Er, okay,' he goes.

I'm there, 'I mean, she's entitled to a bit of happiness, isn't she? And it might as well be with someone I know would never hurt her.'

He's like, 'Er, thanks, Ross.'

He already feels bad about what he's about to do.

I'm there, 'Yeah, no, at first, I have to admit, I thought the whole thing was a bit warped. I thought you were only together because she's a desperate bitch and you like old dogs. But that was then. Nowadays, I think of you as a proper couple. As a matter of fact, I can see you two still being together when she's well into her seventies.'

He can't even listen to any more. He goes, 'I'll just go and see is she finished, em . . .'

And he doesn't even finish his sentence. Shoving coke up her ample hooter, I think to myself, as he disappears out of the kitchen and upstairs to get her. He's anxious to see the back of her. Sorcha's sister is due in fifteen minutes.

I spot the old dear's handbag on the island in the middle of the kitchen. Coco focking Chanel. No recession there, I think. I open it up and look inside. I'm looking for her glasses.

I find the little case right at the bottom and I slip it into my jacket, just as she arrives into the kitchen, botoxed to a fine sheen, followed by her very edgy, soon-to-be-ex-boyfriend.

He even looks at the clock on the wall behind me.

I do the whole air-kissing bit with the old dear. You've got to put on an act.

'You look great,' I go. Which she doesn't, by the way. She looks like someone beat a swarm of bees off Sharon Osborne's face using a running spike. 'Genuinely great.'

She's like, 'Thank you I picked this up today in that little boutique in Sandycove what's it called oh I can never remember the name Miss Something oh it's a gorgeous little shop you can always find something different in there a unique piece that you know you're not going to see someone else wearing . . .'

I'm there, 'That's focking great, that.'

I can't believe she's coked off her tits for an early bird in the Gables followed by a visit to the National Concert Hall.

I can see Oisinn getting more and more anxious. I decide to make him sweat.

'I was just saying,' I go, 'I don't know why Oisinn doesn't come with us. A bit of supper, followed by a bit of culture. A bit of violin or whatever the fock this dude plays.'

The old dear's like, 'I said that to him I said Oisinn why don't you come with us I don't want to think of you stuck at home I want to bring you out and show you off that's what I want to do I want to show you off . . .'

I stare at Oisinn and I'm like, 'There you are, Dude. Your girl-friend wants to show you off! Go and grab your coat.'

'No,' he goes, 'I'm, er, actually a bit wrecked. And a bit flu-y.'

I'm there, 'Flu-y?'

'Yeah, no, I'll probably end up just grabbing an early night.'

I finally decide to put him out of his misery.

'Come on,' I go, offering the old dear my orm to link. 'Let's go,' and we go out to the cor – so-called, because I'm driving Sorcha's Nissan focking Leaf again. It was either that or the special needs bus.

Ten minutes later, we're sitting in the Gables and I'm putting on one hell of a show, nodding away with a big interested look on my face while the old dear fills me in on the mind-numbingly dull comings and goings of her life while talking at two hundred kilometres per hour.

'There are three movie production companies three Ross bidding for the film rights to *Fifty Greys in Shades* and one of them wants Judi Dench to play Sally and Jake Gyllenhaal to play Gideon Ben Basat the young Israeli soldier with whom she enjoys a cross-generational fling I don't even need to look at a menu I know what I'm going to have I'm going to have the Arborio rice risotto it has crayfish in it it's such a tasty fish very underrated and I said Judi and Jake are perfect for the roles I can picture them together see can you catch that waitress's eye would you Ross . . .'

I'm there, 'Shit certainly seems to be going well for you.'

'And of course the other news,' she goes, 'is that I've agreed to help Delma and Angela out with this new campaign of theirs to stop this proposal to link the two Luas lines oh it's inhumane what they're proposing to do Ross connecting Ranelagh to Drimnagh and Milltown to Tallaght and Leopardstown to Fetter-bloody-cairn and Fortunestown I mean Fortunestown Ross it sounds like something from a bloody cowboy movie I said it to Angela I said our world and their world shouldn't even be on nodding terms with each other I mean that's why the economy is in the state it's in people from all these awful awful areas I mean God help them at the same time but they were given a glimpse of how the other half lived and they wanted to live like that too and they were encouraged to take on loans they couldn't afford . . .'

'That's actually an amazing point,' I go. 'I hadn't thought about things from that particular angle before.'

Anyway, this is how it continues for the next, like, forty minutes. We order and our food arrives and she ends up not even touching hers, she's talking so much and so fast. I horse into my Homemade Hereford Beef Burger, just asking the occasional question.

I go, 'How's everything going with Oisinn? Very well would seem to be the answer.'

And she's there, 'Wonderfully well is the answer I know what a lot of people are probably thinking Ross and I know Delma and Angela have their own concerns oh I could see it in their faces but what they don't understand Ross is that just because two people are close in age is no guarantee that a relationship is going to be happy quite the opposite in fact a young man and an older woman is statistically the most successful . . .'

She stops. Her nose is suddenly streaming like the Powerscourt focking Waterfall. She tries to cover it up by going, 'I think I'm getting Oisinn's flu how was your beef burger Ross I know that Delma's son always has the beef burger here he says it's wonderful . . .'

'Look,' I go, 'I just wanted to say to you that I'm cool with the whole you and Oisinn thing. I said this to Oisinn as well tonight. At the beginning, I was like, "That's sick and depraved. They're a focking embarrassment, not only to themselves, but also to me." But I've had a definite change of opinion since then.'

'I'm happy to hear that I really am Ross because we're very happy together . . .'

'I think one of my problems was that I thought, you know . . .'

'Say it Ross it's okay I don't mind you saying it I'd prefer if you said it if it's on your mind . . .'

'I was worried that you were maybe just a novelty for Oisinn. The older woman thing. Look, I've done it myself. Howl at the Moon. I'm known in all of those places. I was scared he'd get bored with you and maybe want to be with someone with – no offence – but a nicer face and body. I mean, you're not exactly easy on the eye, are you? I just don't want to see you get hurt.'

My phone suddenly beeps. It's a text message from Sorcha's sister. It just says, 'Come now!'

The old dear goes, 'Oisinn's not going to hurt me we care about each other Ross oh I know there are lots of pretty skinny little things out there who would just love to take him away from me and I notice the way girls look at him all the time . . .'

I'm like, 'Yeah, yeah, whatever – have you got your glasses, with you?'

She goes, 'What do you mean do I have my glasses of course I have my glasses what kind of a question is that . . .'

'Just double-check, will you? Because I don't want to get to the Concert Hall, then have you asking me every five minutes, "Who's that on the stage now, Ross?" Just have a look now.'

She picks up her bag, then storts rooting through it.

'Oh,' she goes, 'it seems I *don't* have them even though I could have sworn I put them in there it looks like I'm having one of what Oisinn calls my senior moments . . .'

I pretend to laugh. 'That's hilarious,' I go. 'Come on, let's go back to the gaff to get them – we'll still make it to the concert if we leave now.'

She pays the bill – well, *I* wasn't going to – and then we hop in the cor and head back to the gaff.

They're in the kitchen. I can hear them even before the old dear has put the key in the door. It's all swearing and compliments and threats and slaps and promises. She's a fabulous little rattle, in fairness to Sorcha's sister.

The old dear – hilariously – goes, 'Oisinn has that television on very loud, doesn't he?'

And I'm like, 'I don't think it *is* the TV because it's coming from the kitchen. Jesus, I hope nobody's broken in.'

I let her lead the way to the kitchen. And it's she who pushes open the door to be greeted by the sight of Oisinn standing with his back to us and his chinos around his knees, while Sorcha's sister, with her legs wrapped tight around his waist, rides him like Frankel.

The sister – there's badness in that girl – actually smiles at my old dear to let her know she's loving it.

I do the whole shock horror thing. I'm like, 'What the fock is going on here?' at the top of my voice and it's only then that Oisinn realizes that we've arrived back.

He turns around – as in, he turns *fully* around? – with Sorcha's sister still clinging to him, so that now we're looking at *her* back, and he tries to come up with something to say, an excuse for what he's been caught in the act doing.

But of course, there *isn't* one?

I hand the old dear her glasses. I'm like, 'Look what I just found.'

I don't want her to miss out on any of the details, for instance the scratches on Oisinn's back and chest.

She doesn't put them on her, though. She doesn't need to.

The funniest thing is that she doesn't even recognize Sorcha's sister. Her opening line is, 'What's your name?'

I notice that me *and* Oisinn both lean in closer in the hope of catching it.

'Never mind my name,' the sister goes, disentangling herself from Oisinn, as the dude pulls up his trousers and generally tries to tidy himself up.

The old dear doesn't know what to say. She's too in shock. Too upset.

So I go, 'Oisinn, I can't believe you'd do something like this. And *she* was only just saying how well things were going between you and how there's no way you'd be interested in anyone else. I genuinely don't believe this, although disappointment would be my main emotion.'

Oisinn looks at the old dear and goes, 'Fionnuala, I didn't . . .'

But he doesn't get to finish whatever it is he wants to say.

The old dear goes, 'Oisinn I want you to go I don't want you here I want you to leave this house right now all of you . . .'

6. O Holy Shite!

The old man takes a sip of his coffee, then he suddenly stops. 'Would you listen to that!' he goes. 'Is that my granddaughter making that beautiful, beautiful noise?' Sorcha smiles. She goes, 'It's "O Holy Night", Chorles! She's going to be playing it at her school concert in, like, two weeks' time! Oh my God, Chorles, you wouldn't believe the reports we've been getting from the school about her.'

He's there, 'Not to worry. She might settle down as she gets older, Sorcha. If not, well, there's always boarding school. That might straighten her out.'

Poor Honor. That's what she gets for seven years of bad press.

'No,' Sorcha goes, 'these are actually positive reports. She's, like, totally settled down. Her teacher – oh my God – loves her and she's top of her class in pretty much everything.'

He's like, 'Are you sure this is a non-fee-paying school you're sending her to?'

'It is – it's a national school, Chorles.'

'Good Lord! Isn't that extraordinary?'

'And there's this really amazing Principal, isn't there, Ross? Mr O'Fathaigh.'

I'm there, 'Yeah, no, he seems cool.'

'I forgot to tell you,' she goes. 'He rang here yesterday. He said he spoke to that boy, Denis Drewery or Derek Drewery or whatever his name was. It turns out he's been teasing her – about the minibus and about, well, other things. Mr O'Fathaigh said he's put a stop to it, though.'

The old man's like, 'Listen to that music! It's not coming from upstairs, is it?'

'No, she goes down to the coach house to practise.'

'Well, I'll have to go and see her. Tell her how much I'm admiring her playing.' He heads for the back door.

I'm like, 'No,' and I automatically block his way.

He's there, 'What's wrong, Ross?'

Obviously, I don't want him to know she's got an entire family of rats out there.

I go, 'Nothing. Just leave her alone. She likes her quiet time. She's playing her piccolo. The last thing she wants is the crashing focking cymbals of your voice drowning her out.'

He's there, 'Yes, you're quite right, Ross! Leave genius to its own devices! That's what I used to tell myself when I was tempted to go and watch you practise your kicking!'

'Yeah, whatever.'

'Of course, you know where she gets it from, don't you?'

I'm like, 'What?'

He's there, 'The music! She gets it from her grandmother, of course!'

Sorcha goes, 'Oh my God, Ross,' like this is some major revelation, 'your mom! Fionnuala is an amazing pianist.'

That's horseshit, by the way. If you got a chimpanzee pissed and sat him at a piano with a hammer, he'd get better sounds out of it than my old dear.

'Speaking of your mother,' he goes, 'I bumped into her in Sandycove this morning. She was coming out of Caviston's as I was walking in. She didn't look at all well.'

'She never looks well,' I go. 'She's bet-down.'

'And she has this cold that she can't seem to shake – oh, she's had it for weeks. Her nose was streaming. Also, well, I don't like to speak out of turn, but she implied that her relationship with what's-it had, um, burned itself out.'

Sorcha goes, 'Oisinn? Oh! My God!'

I'm there, 'It was never a relationship. They were just two desperadoes getting their focking thrills by rutting each other. I said he'd end up sleeping with someone else.'

'Is that what happened?'

'It's just an educated guess, Sorcha. It was focking obvious it was going to happen.'

The old man goes, 'Well, I think we all should rally around her at this time.'

My phone all of a sudden rings and I end up having to step out of the kitchen because it's Jenny.

I'm there, 'Hey!' except I say it in a bit of a flirty way. It's more like, 'Heeey!'

She goes, 'Oy'd a mussed call from yoy,' delighted with herself. 'Is ivverythung okoy? Have yoy lift your woyf yut?'

Left my wife! What a serious focking headbanger she is.

I'm there, 'No, not yet. But I have to see you.'

'Yoy doy?'

I'm there, 'Big time,' because I have a plan.

She goes, 'Fionn's peerunts are gonna be aaht all *doy* todoy?'

I'm like, 'Cool – I'm on my way.'

Jenny touches my face like she can't believe it's real. And what she can't believe, of course, is that I'm here, in her bedroom and that we're about to do the nasty-nasty for the second time.

'Yoy nivver aahnswered moy quistion,' she goes. 'When are yoy goying to loyve her?'

That's one of the things that I've never liked about women. It can never be just sex. They're always testing you to see how much of a shit you actually give about them. It becomes annoying.

'Not yet,' I go.

Her face goes instantly all pouty and she turns away from me.

No one ever said they weren't hord work.

'I just need a few more weeks,' I go. 'Like I said, we've got, like, triplets on the way. They're due in, like, four weeks. It's difficult.'

She's like, 'How oysey doy yoy thunk ut's boyne for moy? Luving here wuth, loyk, Fionn's *peerents*? Because lit moy till yoy, it hasn't boyne oysey – it's boyne soy, soy duffucult.'

'I can imagine.'

'They koyp asking moy why oy'm suddenly descroybing moysilf

as Fionn's frind rather than hus *girlfrind*? And oy just want to shaaht it from the bloody royftops that oy've fallen for somebody ilse.'

'Don't do that. Definitely don't do that.'

'Whoy not, Ross? Oy dudn't want ut to hippen – oy certainly dudn't plin for ut – but thit's what's hippened, loyk ut or not. And oy doyn't knoy hah much longer oy can goy on pretindung.'

'Just a few weeks more,' I go. 'Let's get the whole babies being born thing out of the way first. And Christmas. The New Year is actually a good time for announcing shit like this.'

'But oy want to boy with yoy naah.'

She's standing with her back to me, the crazy bitch. I walk up behind her, put my two hands on her shoulders and go, 'You *can* be.'

I kiss her ear and I feel her body suddenly loosen up. She smells of *Angel* by Thierry Mugler, which I must remember to wash off me later on, because – take it from a philanderer of long experience – it's one of those ones that tends to stick around for ages and give you away.

Love focking *Chloé* is another one.

I kiss her from her ear, right the way down her neck and along her shoulder blade and her breathing suddenly goes all, like, *trembly*?

Again, I'm going to do the gentlemanly thing and not give you the full blow-by-blow. Suffice it to say that I move my hands into position and treat her to a famous foreplay move of mine that I call the Double Bass.

After a sixty-second solo, she turns her head and goes, 'Moyke love to moy. Ployse. Moyk love to moy.'

Which is what I end up doing, roysh, like a focking sailor home on shore leave, with Jenny's heels digging into my flanks and her blaspheming loud enough to burst my ear drums and send us both to hell.

She ends up being surprised and possibly a little disappointed by how quickly the show is over.

She goes, 'Are yoy funished?' and I'm not going to deny that I can detect a slight criticism in her tone.

Let this be a warning to the rest of you about setting the bor too high early on.

'Yeah, I'm done,' I go, trying to get my breath back, then rolling off her. 'In a way, that's a compliment to you.'

She's like, 'Oy suppoyse ut us.'

There's no suppose about it. If I was hammering away for an hour and a half, the girl would nearly have a complex.

'I'll tell you what would be nice now,' I go. I always phrase it that way, then it leave it hanging for a few seconds, so it comes as almost a relief when I turn around and go, 'A cup of tea.'

She's like, 'Toy?'

I'm there, 'Yeah, milk, three sugars.'

'Mulk, throy sugars? Okoy.'

Then off she trots to get it.

Again, I can't tell you how disappointed I am with Fionn. He deserves better and I'm not just saying that because I feel guilty for taking her down to Hanky Town.

Anyway, I don't have time to think about that. As soon as she's gone downstairs, I hop out of the bed and I go to the first wardrobe. I stort pulling open the drawers and looking inside, underneath her knickers and her bras and her socks and whatever else.

There's no sign of it in there.

I open the second wardrobe. It's all, like, shelves with her jeans and trousers and jumpers and T-shirts piled up. I lift up every focking item in there, checking underneath.

Again, nothing.

I notice that the bed is one of those ones with, like, shelves built into the base. I open the first drawer and there it is – the little pink cash box with the five and a half Ks she raised the night of the table quiz.

The focking idiot has left the key in it as well.

I open it, then I pull the money out – just the notes, mostly fifties and twenties. Then I pick my chinos up off the floor where I dropped them and stuff the money into the pockets.

I put the cash box back, then I search the other three drawers in the base of the bed.

I find the next thing I'm looking for in the fourth one. It's her passport. It's, like, blue in colour, with some kind of crest on the cover, with a massive crown on top of it, then the words 'New Zealand' above it and then 'Passport' below.

I turn to the information page. I check out her photograph. She doesn't look great in it, it has to be said. I grab my phone and I key her passport number into it.

Then I put that back, too.

Her credit cords are easier to find. They're in, like, her purse, which is in her handbag on the vanity table.

She has two. She's got, like, a Visa cord and Mastercord. I put both numbers into my phone, including the expiry date and the three-digit security code on the back of each.

Then I put them back and I hop into the bed again – just in time, as well, because it's literally at that exact moment that Jenny reappears with my famous tea.

'Oy moyd ut just loyk yoy sid,' she goes, like she's expecting a focking round of applause or something.

I take a sip of it. She makes a good cup of tea, in fairness to the girl.

'Soy,' she goes, 'doy yoy full gulty at all?'

I'm there, 'Guilty?' nearly laughing in her face. 'Er, no. I never feel guilty about things I can't control. And attraction is one of those things.'

She loves that. Big focking grin on her.

'Do you know what I'm going to do now?' I go.

She's like, 'What?' her eyes all hopeful.

I'm thinking, yeah, no – not that.

I'm there, 'I'm going to make you some lunch.'

She goes, 'Oy'm not royly sure oy'm hungroy – not for foyd innywoy!'

I'm there, 'You will be when you taste what I'm going to make for you. You could call it my speciality.'

I hop out of the sack and throw my chinos on.

I'm there, 'Give me ten minutes. I'm going to cook you something incredible. Don't come down.'

She's like, 'Oy'll boy woyting royt here!'

I tip downstairs.

My speciality, hilariously, is scrambled egg in a cup in the microwave with pepper and focking salt on it.

I never said I was Donal Skehan.

I crack two eggs into a mug, then I whisk it with a fork – I might as well go through the motions, I think – then I stick it in the microwave and turn it on for a minute and twenty seconds.

Then I go looking for Andrea's laptop.

I find it on the coffee table in the living room. It's a different one to the one I took a shit on that time. I suppose it *would* be – I don't know how you'd go about cleaning a computer after something like that.

I open it up and the first thing that greets me is a photograph of Fionn on the desktop. It's from his graduation. One of his graduations. His big geeky face smiling under his mortar board.

I feel a sudden twinge of something, which may, in fact, *be* guilt? But then I cop on when I remember that this has to be done. I've got myself into a situation – portly due to my own stupidity – and I have to get myself out of it.

I open Safari and I type the word *cruises* into Google.

Then I click into one or two websites and I stort browsing.

There ends up being shitloads of them. We're talking India, Mauritius, the Maldives and the Seychelles. We're talking Malta, Italy, France and Gibraltar. We're talking Jamaica, Bermuda, St Kitts and the Bahamas.

These are all countries that I'm naming.

Eventually, roysh, I think, fock it, why not, and I end up choosing a seriously luxurious one – we're talking three and a half weeks, taking in Busan, Singapore, Tianjin and Fukuoka.

Seven focking grand.

I whip out my phone and I lash in Jenny's passport and credit cord details, praying that there's enough room on either her Visa or her Mastercord to pay for it.

Fortunately, it goes on the Visa first time.

I shut the laptop, then I go back out to the kitchen to grab that focking egg out of the microwave.

By now, it's cold and a bit rubbery-looking, plus I end up forgetting to put the pepper and salt on it.

Still, spending someone else's money is obviously a serious turn-on. Because, as I'm walking up the stairs, telling Jenny to prepare herself for a taste sensation, I realize that I'm actually feeling horny again.

I end up stortling Honor. She's stepping out of the coach house just as I'm about to walk in and she ends up getting a genuine fright.

She's like, 'What the fock do *you* want?'

Seven years of age and dropping the f-bomb on her old man just in casual conversation. Where *do* the years go?

'I was just popping in for a visit,' I go.

She's like, 'A visit?'

'Yeah, no, I just wanted to see how you were getting on down here.'

'I'm getting on fine, thank you.'

'Well, what about them? God, they must be huge now.'

'They're big, yes.'

'Because I haven't actually seen them in weeks.'

I try to look over her shoulder, except she quickly pulls the door shut and stands with her back against it.

'They're sleeping,' she goes.

I'm there, 'All of them?'

'Yes. And I don't want you to wake them.'

'I'll be quiet, Honor. I definitely won't wake them.'

'I know you won't. Because you're not coming in here.'

'Okay, could I maybe just stand here and have a look in.'

She totally loses it with me then. She goes, 'Why are you always trying to stick your nose in my focking business?'

She goes from calm to homicidal in 0.6 seconds.

I'm like, 'Whoa! Chillax, Honor!'

'Don't tell me to chillax!' she goes, again roaring at me. 'Why can't you just leave me alone?'

'I'm only taking an interest.'

'You're not taking an interest. You're like *her*. You can't just let me get on with my life. You have to keep trying to get involved, no matter how that focking affects me.'

I'm thinking, Okay, where the fock is this coming from? And that's when I notice her school jumper. The neck of it is all torn. From my previous life as one of Castlerock College's most feared bullies, it looks very much to me like someone has grabbed her by the scruff of the neck and swung her around.

I'm like, 'Who did that to your jumper? Was it that focking, I don't know, heavy-set kid? Focking Medication Time?'

She's there, 'Why?'

'I asked you a question and I want an answer.'

'Why, so you can make it even worse? Like *she* already did?'

'What do you mean?'

'She told the focking Principal that he was calling me names,' she goes. She grabs a fistful of her jumper. 'And this is what happens to *little fooken poshies* who can't keep their mouths shut.'

In that moment, I'm mad enough to literally kill someone. My beautiful little daughter – even though she's a complete cow – is being bullied.

I'm there, 'Okay, I'm going to go and sort this out once and for all.'

Except Honor's there, 'You're not! You're going to stay out of my focking business!' Then she opens the door, slips back into the coach house and slams the door in my face.

I walk back up to the gaff.

There's a lot of girly squealing going on in the kitchen. Sorcha is hugging Shadden and Sorcha's old dear is hugging Ronan and Ronan is holding Rihanna-B, who's laughing along and clapping at all the excitement.

I'm there, 'What's the story? What's going on?'

'Rihadda-Burrogan's arthur taken her foorst steps!' Shadden goes. 'She's arthur walken about ten steps wirrout falden over!'

Ronan gives me a look that tells me to play along.

I'm there, 'No way!' hoping that my face doesn't give it away, as sometimes happens. 'And you were there to see it, Shadden! Despite what Dordeen and K . . . K . . . K . . . Kennet were trying to claim. That's great news!'

'I have to tell you,' she goes, 'I was woodied, Sudeka. Woodied that I wootunt be hee-er when it happent. You toalt me to relax, ditn't you, Ro-Ro?'

He's there, 'I did, yeah.'

'I was joost doing me homewoork upsteers. I'd a lot of chemistoddy to do. Rihadda-Burrogan was on the flowur, playing wirrer toyiz. And I happened to look up at the clock and I taught it's past hoor bedtoyum. The next thing, I turdens – didn't I, Ro-Ro? – and she's stantin up on her owen. I says to Ro-Ro, "Get your phowun out and filum tis!" Show it to tum, Ro-Ro.'

We all stand around and we watch it twice, Sorcha, her old dear and me making all the right noises.

'Ine soddy again,' Shadden goes – aimed at Sorcha. 'I've been a birrof a wagon.'

Sorcha goes, 'It's fine, Shadden. You've been through so much this past year.'

I tell Shadden and Ro that I'm delighted for them, then I head upstairs. I'm still thinking about the whole Honor being bullied situation, but – even though I hate myself for saying it – Jenny is the more, I don't know, *imminent* danger?

I lie on the bed and whip out my phone. I call up Eleanor's number. She answers on the third ring.

I'm like, 'Hey, Ellie.'

She's there, 'Yeah, Ross, don't call me Ellie.'

I called her far worse than that the day I sired her cross-eyed in her gaff in Blackrock. She was pretty inventive with the names herself, as I recall. But now is not the time to point that out.

'Can I talk to you?' I go. 'In confidence?'

She's there, 'Are you suggesting meeting up?' and I can nearly, like, *hear* the hope in her voice. I actually laugh.

What is it about me that makes women want me so much?

I'm like, 'No, on the phone will do,' because between Honor, Jenny and this Christian thing that's still bubbling away in the background, I've got enough complications in my life right now. 'I'm going to level with you here. There was something I didn't tell you – the day you called here with your old pair and focking what's his face . . .'

'His name's David, Ross.'

'Yeah, I was going to say David, if you'd given me the chance. Look, Jenny said something to me the night of the table quiz that may or may not be relevant. You'll have to decide that yourself. She said the pressure was storting to get to her.'

'What pressure? What are you talking about?'

'Just the pressure of being the girlfriend of a hostage. *The Late Late Show*. Then having to go to meet that, is it Edna Kenny, guy? It was all too much. She said – okay, this is the thing I feel bad about telling you, because she actually told me this in confidence . . .'

'Ross, you have to tell me.'

'She said she was thinking about just running away.'

'That makes sense.'

'Sorry?'

'I'm saying it fits with what happened here this morning. My mum opened her laptop – I'm here with her now – and there were seven or eight windows open.'

'You'll have to explain that to me, Eleanor. I'm not much of a computer nerd. I barely know how to switch one on.'

That's called cleverly covering your tracks.

She's like, 'Someone had been looking up cruises,' and then I hear her turn to her old dear and go, 'Ross said Jenny was talking about running away.'

I crack on to be shocked.

I'm there, 'You're focking joking me! Are you saying you think Jenny was planning to go off on a cruise?'

She goes, 'Well, it wasn't my mum and dad. They've just handed over their life savings and they're trying to sell their house. They're hardly going to be looking at cruises.'

I hear Andrea go, 'Going away on holidays is the last thing on our minds!'

I'm like, 'But how would Jenny have access to that kind of money?' and I let the question just hang there.

I can almost hear the little cogs in Eleanor's head turning. Five seconds later, she goes, 'Hang on a second,' and I hear her running – running, presumably, through her old pair's hallway, then up the stairs to Jenny's room.

The girl mustn't be home, because Eleanor bursts straight in without knocking. And she clearly knows where the cash box is kept because it only takes about thirty seconds for her to go, 'It's empty!'

I'm like, 'Whoa, what are we talking about now? This doesn't sound good, whatever it is!'

'The box,' she goes, 'where she kept the table quiz money.'

I'm there, 'Jesus, Eleanor, you seem to be saying that she possibly spent it on a cruise.'

'Well, isn't that a reasonable conclusion to draw?'

'Fock, I suppose it is. Although I'm famous for always trying to see the good in people. This is a serious knock to that. Maybe she banked the money.'

'Well, we'll find out when she comes home.'

'Eleanor, do me a favour, will you? Please leave me out of it. I only mentioned it because it was weighing down on my conscience.'

She goes, 'I will,' and then she thanks me – she actually *thanks* me?

I hang up and I suddenly hear a girl's laugh. It's Sorcha's sister. She was obviously outside the door, listening to the entire conversation.

'Who are you focking over now?' she goes.

I'm there, 'It's a long story.'

She's like, 'Do you ever wish your life could be just simple?'

'Most days,' I go, 'yeah.'

She looks well. I'm beginning to find the Aldi uniform a little bit sexy.

She's there, 'Where's my money?'

I'm like, 'Money?' stalling for time, because I forgot to get it from my old man the last time I saw him.

She goes, 'We had a deal, Ross.'

I'm there, 'Okay, I'll have it for you when . . .' and then I stop, roysh, because I suddenly remember the massive wad in my chinos pocket.

This is me suddenly standing on my own two feet.

I reach into my trousers and I whip it out. I'm talking about Jenny's table quiz money.

Sorcha's sister's eyes go wide when she sees it. I count off five Ks and I hand it to her.

She's like, 'Pleasure doing business with you,' and then she laughs. 'I think your friend has it bad for me.'

I laugh as well. 'Who, Oisinn? Yeah, no, I told you – he's only ever been with dogs before. It's an actual focking syndrome. And, hey, maybe you're the cure.'

'Er, I don't think so. He's texting me, like, fifteen or sixteen times a day. That's way too clingy for my liking. The funny thing is, I don't think he actually knows my name.'

'What?'

'Seriously. He never called me by it when we were together. And I saw him put my number in his phone as Sorcha's Sister.'

'That's funny.'

'Anyway, I think he's sad about me breaking up his relationship, then giving him the brush-off.'

'I'll give him a ring,' I go. 'Hey, you did good,' and then I think, fock it, and I hand her the rest of the table quiz money.

Like I said, she earned it.

I'm in Kielys with Christian and Oisinn and, I'm going to be honest with you, they're about as much fun as a lap-dancer with a cough.

I try to get a bit of a debate going. I throw it out there that the order in which I'd ride the members of Little Mix is exactly the reverse order in which I'd have ridden them when they won *The X Factor* a year ago.

There's no takers.

All Christian wants to do is sit there staring into space and all Oisinn wants to do is to keep repeating that he focked things up.

I should have just stayed at home and drunk cans with my fifteen-year-old son.

'I really hurt Fionnuala,' Oisinn goes, tracing the H on his pint glass with his finger over and over again. 'Like, I really, *really* hurt her?'

So I just go, 'I know. I'll never forgive you for that, by the way.'

I can't make him feel any worse than he already does, but I owe it to myself to keep trying.

I'm there, 'It's something she'll possibly never get over.'

He goes, 'Dude, don't say that.'

'Hey, I'm just calling it. She thought you had genuine feelings for her. I was even – as you saw yourself – coming around to the idea of you two as an actual couple. Then we come home to find you giving Sorcha's sister the full cordio workout.'

He puts his hand to his forehead. 'Oh, fock,' he goes.

I'm there, 'I'm sorry, Dude, but you focking disgraced yourself. I'm no fan of my old dear, but I still think the woman deserved better than that, the focking orang-utan with lipstick.'

'I've made a complete fool of myself.'

'I said it from day one, if you cast your mind back.'

'I mean with Sorcha's sister. She's not even returning my calls.'

'She's a little bit out of your league, Oisinn. And I'm not just saying that to kick you while you're down. You got lucky. You just happened to lift your game at the same time as she lowered her standards. Be thankful for that.'

He nods. The poor focker. I'm not letting him out of the dog-house yet, though.

He goes, 'I just hope Fionnuala is going to be okay,' and I notice him – and this isn't my imagination – look sideways at me, as if trying to get my reaction.

I suddenly know that he doesn't mean emotionally.

I'm there, 'Are you talking about the coke?'

He just nods.

'Yeah,' I go, 'this coming from the man who said it was just the odd few lines.'

He's there, 'I mean, it *was* at the beginning . . .'

'How many times have we heard people say that? How bad is she, Oisinn?'

'She's bad.'

'I said *how* bad?'

He takes a breath, then he goes, 'Ross, she can't go two hours without it.'

'Jesus Christ.'

'Dude, I'm sorry.'

'You're sorry? You bang my old dear and then you get her addicted to drugs and you're sorry?'

He gets up off his stool.

He's there, 'I should go.'

I'm like, 'Focking right you should go.'

He walks out of there looking totally defeated. He even leaves half a pint. I'll have it, though. It's the focking least he owes me.

I turn to Christian and it's like he hasn't heard a word of the conversation.

I'm there, 'Every two hours? Can you focking believe that?'

He goes, 'What?'

Seriously. He's on Planet Christian tonight and he has the place to himself.

I'm there, 'Don't worry about it. We were just talking about how my mother is a basic focking drug addict – it's not a major thing.'

He's like, 'I'm sorry.'

'What's the deal with you anyway? Is Lauren still busting your balls?'

He laughs – like, bitterly – then goes, 'It's gone, Ross. It's over.'

I'm like, 'What's over? What are you talking about?'

'Me and Lauren,' he goes. 'We've separated.'

I'm there, 'Separated?' feeling suddenly shit, knowing that I set the whole thing in motion. 'Dude, you two can't split up. You've just had a baby. And what about little Ross?'

'I'll still see the kids.'

'You can't break up over a focking sandwich shop. Dude, that's ridiculous.'

'Ross, it's over. I'm back living with my old dear.'

That's when my phone all of a sudden rings. I check the screen and it ends up being Jenny. I was wondering how long it would take. I tell Christian that I need to take this call and I step outside.

I answer by going, 'I was just thinking about you. Who am I kidding? I'm always thinking about you.'

Oh, I'm good.

She's crying. It takes her a good ten seconds for her to say anything. When she does, she goes, 'Ross, ut's gone?'

I'm like, 'What do you mean? What's gone?'

She's there, 'The foyve and a haahf graahnd oy roysed frum the
toyble kwuz. Somebody's stoylen ut?'

'No focking way!' I go. 'What kind of a low life . . .'

'Fionn's mum and daahd and hus suster accuysed moy of
toyking ut.'

'You? No! I'm not having that!'

'They, loyk, confronted moy abaaht ut tonoyt. They sid that oy've
boyne icting royly stroyngeloy lateloy, then they sid, "Where's the
monoy from the kwuz?" And oy sid, "It's upsteers in moy *bidroym*?"
They sid, "Goy and git ut." And when oy went upsteers, Ross, ut
wasn't theer – ut's gone.'

'It's a genuine focking mystery, isn't it?'

I can tell she doesn't want to say what she ends up saying next.

'Ross,' she goes, 'yoy dudn't toyk ut, dud yoy?'

I'm there, 'How dare you!' and I really let her have it. I've always
found that indignation helps when it comes to selling a lie. 'I can't
believe you would ask me something like that.'

She's like, 'Oy'm royly sorry, Ross. Oy'm just soy confused here.
Fionn's suster staahtud soying that oy'd boyne onloyne looking at
croyses. Oy sid oy've nivver looked at croyses in moy loyfe. Oy've
noy unterest in goying on a croyse. She sid she knoy it was moy.'

'She's out of order there.'

'What am oy gonna doy, Ross?'

'Sit tight would be my advice.'

'How can oy? They told moy tonoyt that oy've got twenty-four
aahrs to give them the monay. Otherwise, they sid they're gonna
phine the poloyce.'

I'm just like, 'You poor thing. You poor, poor thing.'

The first thing I hear when I walk through the door is the sound of
sniffing coming from the kitchen. She's hoovering up lines like a
focking Dyson.

When I push the door, she's wiping down the surface of the

island with a Flash Wipe and dabbing at her nostrils with the back of her hand.

I go, 'Nine o'clock in the morning? Are you focking serious?'

She's there, 'I don't know what you're talking about Ross I have no idea what you're talking about and would you please ring the front doorbell instead of just crashing in here all the time . . .'

'I'm talking about you putting that shit up your hooter.'

'It's just a little pick-me-up not that it's any of your business but I didn't have a good night I haven't been sleeping at all well.'

She looks wretched, in fairness to her. Like someone stuck a hose up Donatella Versace's orse and filled her with custard.

I'm there, 'Why aren't you sleeping?' and then I laugh. 'Presumably because of the whole Oisinn thing?'

She goes, 'I don't want to hear you say I told you so Ross because I really don't think I could bear your sanctimony . . .'

'I wasn't going to say I told you so. I was just going to say there was no way you were going to be able to keep a young goy like Oisinn interested. The focking state of you. He was always going to go off with someone younger and thinner and less like something out of *Troll Hunter*.'

'I thought you and I were going to make a better effort to get along Ross I thought that was what we agreed in the Gables that night I thought we said we'd put all the unpleasantness of the past behind us . . .'

'Hey, I'm on your side. It actually upsets me that people are laughing their heads off at you and saying that you made a complete focking fool of yourself and not for the first time in your life either.'

'I don't have time to listen to your unpleasantness Ross I have a very busy day ahead of me I've been asked to write a treatment for a better-sex guide for seniors which I was thinking of calling *We Found Love with a Denture Plate* and I told Sorcha I wanted to buy something for the triplets something they'll always know came from their grandmother but I don't know what it's going to be yet so I might pop into town after lunch . . .'

She's talking so fast it's like her focking head is going to overheat.

She's there, 'Maybe BTs will have something or maybe some-where else I'm having lunch with Delma to discuss a campaign of civil disobedience in response to this connecting of the two Luas lines nonsense and oh I mustn't forget I promised Angela I'd dig out my recipe for pecan and apricot stuffing she's having sixteen for Christmas Day if you can believe that including her son's first wife what's her name it was Vanessa or Alexina I can never remember which I mean it's going to be awkward isn't it because the girl he's with now was one of her bridesmaids . . .'

I turn suddenly serious. I'm like, 'Mum!' which is something I never, ever call her, so she knows that whatever I'm about to say is coming straight from the hort. 'Will you shut the fock up for ten seconds and let me get a word in edgeways?'

She goes, 'What is it what do you want what are you trying to say . . .'

'What I'm trying to say is that you need to lay off that shit. The coke. You've got a problem.'

'How I live my life is my concern why is it any of your business . . .'

'Because I focking care about you,' I go. 'Is that okay?'

She just stands there staring at me.

'Well you don't need to worry because I'm fine like I said I haven't been sleeping well and I couldn't function if I didn't pep myself up it's like you with your morning coffee . . .'

I'm like, 'Where is it?'

She goes, 'What are you talking about where's what . . .'

'Your toot. Your dust. Your sneeze. Your candy. Where do you keep your stash?'

Her face suddenly hordens. She obviously has no intention of telling me.

I turn and I walk out of the kitchen, then I suddenly run up the stairs, taking them two at a time, a man on a definite mission. She comes running after me, screaming, 'Don't your dare you stay out of my room do you hear me stay out of my room . . .'

Suddenly, I'm the one not listening, though.

I burst into her room. I don't even need to look for the stuff. It's on her dressing table, I swear to fock, in a zip-lock freezer bag – there must be, like, two pounds of it.

I grab the bag just as she's running into the room behind me. She literally throws herself across the bed at me, trying to grab me around the waist. I flick my hips and ride the tackle beautifully and she ends up falling flat on her face and at the same she's screaming, 'Give it to give it to me give it back give it back . . .'

I run into her en suite and I slam the door and then lock it behind me. I lift up the lid of the toilet just as she storts hammering on the door with the palm of her hand, going, 'Ross please that's all I have left I need it I wouldn't know where to buy it . . .'

I open the zip, then I turn the bag upside down, tipping the entire contents into the toilet. I tell her what I'm doing as well. I'm there, 'I'm going to flush it down the jacks. But I'm only doing it because I care about you, you raddled old crone.'

She goes, 'Noooooo!!!' and she actually screams it, then bangs on the door and calls me a hortless bastard and one or two other things, then she drops to the floor and puts her nose under the door and – I shit you not – storts trying to sniff the bowl from the next room.

I grab the handle of the toilet and I go, 'I'm about to flush it. Five . . . Four . . . Three . . .'

I hear her jump up and move away from the door.

I'm like, 'Two . . .' at the same time wondering where the fock she's gone. Suddenly, she's back, because the next thing I hear is the sound of hord metal crashing against the door, once, then twice, then a third time.

That's when I realize that she's trying to break it down with the fire extinguisher she keeps on the landing.

I go, 'One!' and I flush the toilet, just as the door gives way under the weight of the fourth blow.

She drops the fire extinguisher, then bursts into the bathroom and slides across the tiled floor on her knees, like a kid on the dance-floor at a wedding.

The water is still swirling around in the bowl and – again, I'm not making this shit up – she puts her face over it, both hands gripping the porcelain and her mouth wide open, and storts trying to breathe in, I don't know, the mist of cocaine as it flushes away.

I stand there just looking at her, shaking my head.

I'm there, 'And you're saying you definitely don't have a problem, are you?'

She takes her finger and she wipes it off the inside the bowl and then – I feel like nearly throwing up here – storts rubbing it into her gums.

I end up having to leave. It's not something any son should see.

I'm there, 'Yeah, you can definitely handle it alright. You've proven that to me. I don't know why I ever doubted you.'

Sorcha says she's beginning to think it's definitely going to be three girls. This is while I'm painting the walls of the nursery in Arabian Sand.

I'm like, 'Why do you say that?'

She goes, 'I don't know. Intuition. It's like I knew that Honor was going to be a girl – oh my God – *way* before she was born . . .'

She's talking out of her orse, by the way. She was one hundred percent convinced that Honor was going to be a boy, although I don't point that out to her, because we're actually having a bit of a moment here. The triplets are due in, like two and a half weeks, we're both dressed in, like, old clothes that are covered in paint and – okay, I'm going to sound like a sap saying this – but my wife has never looked more beautiful, even though the Leinster training top from the 06–07 season that I loaned her is practically bursting at the seams trying to hold in her big, swollen Minka Kelly.

'I have to say,' she goes, 'I'm *so* looking forward to the Christmas concert tomorrow. Honor's first recital, Ross!'

I'm there, 'Yeah, no, she's certainly put the hours in.'

'Will we go down and tell her how proud we are of her?'

'What?'

'Down to the coach house?'

'Errr . . .'

'Come on, Ross!

'I don't know, Sorcha. I think we should maybe leave her to it. She had a bit of a strop on with me the other day when I tried to go in.'

'Oh my God, she's a bit of a prima donna, isn't she? The best musicians often are. I remember that from the time I auditioned for the National Youth Orchestra.'

'We'll leave it so, then.'

'Well, we'll make sure to tell her how proud we are of her tomorrow. Oh my God, did you hear about Christian and Lauren?'

'Yeah, no, it's shit for them, I'm agreeing.'

'I didn't think things had gotten that bad. Lauren said little Ross is devastated. He wanted a Flutterbye Flying Fairy for Christmas and a Lalaloopsy tri-scooter. He asked Lauren last night if they could write to Santa and cancel his presents and ask him to bring his daddy back instead.'

Jesus Christ. I think I'm about to burst into tears, so I end up just changing the subject.

I'm there, 'The house is quiet, isn't it? Where is everyone?'

'Mum has gone to Monkstown,' she goes. 'She's thinking of going back playing tennis. She's reclaiming her independence. And – oh my God – did I tell you about my sister?'

I'm like, 'Er, no,' wondering has she somehow found out about Oisinn tapping her.

She's there, 'She's going to England tomorrow to have her breasts fixed.'

I'm like, 'Were they broke?' playing the innocent.

'One of her implants had perished or something. Do you know how much it's costing her?'

'I wouldn't have a clue how much something like that would cost, Babes.'

'Five. Grand.'

'Five grand?'

'I don't know where she's getting the money. I mean, she couldn't have earned enough in Aldi to have saved that much.'

It's at that exact point that my phone rings in the back of my old jeans. My hands are, like, covered in paint, so Sorcha goes, 'I'll answer it!' and makes a grab for my orse pocket.

I'm like, 'No, leave it – let it go to voicemail!' knowing that about fifty percent of the phone calls and text messages I receive would constitute grounds for divorce.

Someone needs to invent an App that automatically disables a man's mobile phone as soon as his wife or girlfriend touches it. That person would become a billionaire.

Sorcha goes, 'No, I'll get it!' and she pulls it out of my pocket, studies the screen for a second, then goes, 'Oh my God, it's Eleanor!' and then answers.

She's like, 'Hi, Eleanor, it's Sorcha. Is everything okay?'

I'm suddenly shitting it. I'm thinking, okay, what fresh focking madness is this?

Sorcha's like, 'Okay . . . Okay . . . Okay . . . Okay, I'll tell him . . .' and then she hangs up.

I'm like, 'What was that about?'

She goes, 'Eleanor wants you to call around to her mum and dad's house.'

'When?'

'Now.'

'Did she say why?'

'No, she just said that they wanted to talk to you. Oh my God, I hope they haven't had bad news about Fionn. Oh my God, maybe that Fred man has found something out and it's bad news!'

I know it's not about Fionn, though. I know it's about Jenny. That's *my* intuition. I'm wondering did she tell them that I rode her?

'Ross,' Sorcha goes, 'you should go.'

I'm there, 'Yeah, no, there's no rush. I might try and get this wall and one other painted and then I'll drive out there.'

She's like, 'No, Ross, you need to go now,' and she takes the paintbrush out of my hand.

Arguing with Sorcha is like using public transport. It takes up a lot of time and all you feel at the end is tired and dizzy. So I throw a pair of old deckies on and I hop in the minibus and head to Ewan and Andrea's place.

I ring on the doorbell, genuinely not knowing whether I'm going to be greeted with a slap across the face.

It's Eleanor herself who answers. She's like, 'Hi!'

I'm there, 'Hey!'

There doesn't seem to be any threat of violence, or even hostility, unless she's going to unleash it on me when I step into the hall.

Thankfully, she doesn't. Instead, she lowers her tone to a basic whisper. 'We've had one hell of a day here,' she goes.

I'm like, 'Really?'

'We just wanted to talk to you before we left for the airport.'

'Airport? Oh my God, *has* Fred found Fionn?' My hort literally leaps.

She's there, 'No, not yet.'

I'm like, 'So what's the Jack?'

'Jenny's going home.'

'Home? To China?'

'To New Zealand.'

'Yeah, that's what I meant.'

'She's never been to China, Ross.'

'Yeah, no, I keep forgetting because, you know … Look, I'm afraid to talk here in case it comes out as racist. So what happened?'

'Remember I told you someone was looking up cruises on Mum's laptop?'

'Yeah, keep going.'

'Well, some tickets arrived here this morning – for a three-week cruise.'

'No!'

'Booked on Jenny's credit cord.'

'Jesus. Where was she going? Not that it's important.'

'Well, China, as it happens. And a few other places along the way.'

'Fock. Where did she get the money?'

'We're presuming that's where the table quiz money went.'

'God, I feel very let down to hear that. And I feel a lot of anger as well. I hope you called the focking Feds?'

'We said we were going to unless she put the money back. Then when the tickets arrived, my mum decided to contact her parents – find out what was going on?'

'I'm presuming from the way this conversation is going that they had a tale to tell.'

'Jenny has a form of Munchausen's syndrome, Ross.'

'Okay, what's that?'

'It's a psychiatric illness. It's, like, a compulsive need for attention?'

Inside, I'm suddenly punching the air.

'God, you'd have to feel sorry for her,' I go. 'That's what we're saying, I presume?'

'Of course. I mean, the poor girl. Her mum said she's a complete fantasist. She's been that way since she was about sixteen.'

I end up just shaking my head and going, 'Your brother sure can pick them!'

She gives me a look. She's right. It was probably unnecessary.

I'm there, 'Sorry, I'm just saying the poor dude never had any luck when it came to the ladies.'

'Jenny's parents asked us not to call the police. They said they'd give us the five grand themselves if we just put her on a plane home.'

'Yeah, no, that sounds like the best solution all round, so she's out of everyone's hair. So what am I doing here?'

'She said she wouldn't go unless we let her talk to you first.'

'Me? Why?'

'She says she's in love with you, Ross.'

'What?'

'She said you're in love with her, too. She said you had sex in her car after the table quiz and then here, upstairs.

'I don't know where the fock she's getting that from. I don't even find her remotely attractive.'

'Well, like I said, she's a fantasist.'

'Hey, there are some things that are far-fetched even for fantasy. Do you know what the worst thing is?'

'What?'

'People might have actually *believed* that about me.'

'It did cross my mind that it might be true.'

'Yeah, no, people might have actually believed it, if she hadn't turned out to be properly mental.'

She goes, 'Will you say goodbye to her?'

I'm there, 'I don't know. I'm kind of a bit freaked out here.'

And before I get a chance to actually back out, the kitchen door is suddenly thrown open and Jenny comes racing out into the hallway and throws her orms around me.

She's there, 'Ross, yoy heff toy till thum. Yoy heff toy till thum abaaht us.'

I let her hug me for a good ten or fifteen seconds. I let her hug herself out, in fact. Over her shoulder, I notice Ewan and Andrea step out of the kitchen with big, apologetic faces on them. They definitely feel for me.

It's nice.

Jenny eventually senses my lack of involvement in the hug and pulls away from me, holding me at orm's length and searching my face for something she's not going to find there.

She's like, 'Ross?'

I'm there, 'Jenny, what are you talking about? There *is* no us.'

'There uz an us,' she tries to go. 'Ross, ployze till thum. We fill un love. We boyth want toy continyoy looking for Fionn, excipt woy caahn't denoy the woy we foyle abaaht oych other. Till thum, Ross. Ployse till them the troyth.'

I'm like, 'Jenny, you and I didn't hit it off from day one. And I sensed that a lot of that may have been down to the fact that you had feelings for me.'

'Yoy baahsturd.'

'But nothing happened, Jenny, much as you would have liked it to happen and probably dreamed of it happening.'

'Yoy facking . . .'

'Because Fionn is a friend of mine. And that actually means something to me.'

The slap comes from nowhere – as in, I don't actually see it com-ing? It stings like fock.

'You facking baahsturd!' she goes, actually shouting it this time.

Ewan grabs the tops of her orms from behind and goes, 'That's quite enough of that! Come on – let's go to the airport.'

She's like, 'Oy'm not goying!'

'It's either the airport or it's Blackrock Garda Station,' Andrea goes. 'The choice is yours.'

That softens Jenny's cough.

'I, er, better get back to my wife,' I go, really rubbing it in. I should possibly feel sorry for the girl, except she focked with the Rossmeister General and threatened to take away everything I basically have. And I couldn't let her do that.

Andrea picks up what I'm presuming is Jenny's suitcase and we all walk outside.

I stand on the side of the road and I watch her get into the back of Ewan and Andrea's cor, alternating between calling me a baahsturd and telling me that shoy loves moy.

I'm just there, 'Yeah, in your dreams, Jenny. In your focking dreams.'

Eleanor rolls her eyes and shakes her head and tells me that she's sorry. I'm like, 'Look, I just hope and pray that she gets the treatment that she needs.'

She goes, 'At least now we can concentrate on finding Fionn,' and then she smiles at me.

I'd say I could definitely bail in there again if I picked the right moment.

I give her hug and I have a little sniff of her hair – making sure Jenny sees it – then she gets into the back of the cor with her and off they go to the airport, with me waving them off.

Honor is up to something.

I'm flaked out on the sofa watching an old rerun of *The Love Boat* when it hits me like a bucket of ice water.

Honor is focking up to something.

Why now? I don't know. But I suddenly know it as well as I know my own face.

I jump up from the sofa and run through the house, through the hallway, through the kitchen and out into the gorden. I'm still in, like, my stocking feet and the rain soaks through my socks, except I don't *give* a shit? I'm famously slow on the uptake, but all of a sudden, all I can think about is how she slammed the door in my face that day and how she definitely didn't want me to see what was going on behind it.

I reach the coach house and I put my hand on the handle of the door, then I take a second or two to, like, steel myself for whatever surprise is awaiting me inside.

I pull down the handle and give the door a shove, then I reach inside and switch on the light to reveal the full focking horror show of what's been going on behind my back.

There are rats everywhere. We're talking possibly a hundred or more. All in cages. All squealing and chewing the bors or fighting or riding each other.

The cages are on shelves. We're talking floor to ceiling, and right the way around the walls. I count twenty-five cages, each of which seems to hold an average of about four rats.

So we're talking twenty-five times four.

All of a sudden I hear a voice behind me in the dark. *Her* voice.

She's like, 'I was wondering when the penny was going to drop. Hashtag, *slow* much?'

I'm there, 'Honor, what the . . . what the . . . what the fock have you done?'

'I've just been raising a family,' she goes, as calmly as that. 'Raising a family, like you and Mom!'

'Are you saying you . . . Jesus Christ, are you saying you bred all of these?'

'Well, they kind of did the breeding themselves. I just created the right conditions. Heat. Lots of space. Plenty of food – seasoned with this . . .'

She holds up one of those little Schwartz bottles with *Saffron* written on the front.

'For rats,' she goes, 'this stuff is an actual *aphrodisiac*?'

I'm there, 'You're saying they bred with each other?'

'Er, yes, Dad!'

'But aren't they all, like, brothers and sisters?'

She laughs like her old man is some kind of idiot.

'Okay,' she goes, 'I don't *really* have time to fill in the gaps in your education right now?'

I'm still standing in the centre of the room, turning around and around on the spot, trying to get my head around the sheer focking number of them.

I'm there, 'How are there so many of them?'

'Female rats are ready to carry a litter of their own after five weeks,' she goes. 'The gestation period is only, like, twenty-one days.'

I'm there, 'Answer my question. How many are there?'

'There's ninety-four . . .'

I had a feeling it was in that ballpork.

'But some of the younger ones are already pregnant,' she goes.

Now that I think of it, Sorcha's been wondering where the saffron keeps disappearing to.

I'm there, 'Jesus, Honor, you're like some kind of evil *James Bond* villain.'

She goes, 'Thank you.'

'Well, you can't keep them all. I just want you to know that.'

She laughs. She's there, 'Oh my God, I have no intention of *keeping* them.'

I'm like, 'Good. Because we need to get rid of them before your old dear sees them. We're going to release them into the wild.'

It's the next thing she says that causes me to think, Oh my God, *what* have we raised?

'No,' she goes, 'we're going to release them into the school. We're going to bring them there tonight.'

She says it so casually, like it's the most natural thing in the world. I actually laugh. I'm like, 'Excuse me?'

'You heard me,' she goes. 'We're going to put them in the ventilation system. Oh, bring a screwdriver, if we own one, because we need to open one of the outside grilles.'

I'm like, 'Okay, bear in mind that I'm only humouring you here, but what do you think is going to happen then?'

'I haven't fed them since yesterday. That's why they won't settle. They're, like, *storving*? I always play my piccolo while they're eating, so they associate the sound with food.'

'Okay. So when you get up on the stage and stort playing your piccolo at the concert tomorrow morning, they're all going to come flooding into the hall?'

'Exactly. And the school will be closed down like it deserves to be. Come on, let's stort bringing these cages out to the special needs bus.'

I laugh. I'm there, 'Honor, I'd actually be impressed with the level of preparation you've put into this if the whole thing wasn't so – I don't know – focked up. But it's over now. You've been busted in a big-time way. It's not happening.'

She sighs, very dramatically, then goes, 'I didn't want to have to do this, but you haven't given me any choice. If you don't help me do this, then I'm going to tell the Gords that you made me break into Christian's office.'

I'm like, 'What?' my body going suddenly cold.

She puts on this innocent little voice and goes, '*My daddy said if I didn't do it, he'd be angry with me! I didn't want him to be angry with me!*'

Shit. She'd focking do it as well. She'd do it in a hortbeat.

I'm there, 'What makes you think you'd be believed? You're seven going on eight. I'll just say you have an overactive imagination.'

She holds up her hands, palms out, her fingers and thumbs splayed.

She goes, 'I put my fingerprints everywhere in that office.'

She smiles at me to let me know that I've been basically out-manoeuvred here.

'I'll call the Gords,' she goes. 'You know I will.'

Do you know what's weird? I get this sudden moment of clarity then – as in, it hits me that I'm the reason she's turned out like this. Because I'm thinking about Jenny – presumably on the plane now, on her way back home to New Zealand – and how I focked her over.

Then I'm thinking about this plan of Honor's and I realize that it's actually *my* style. As in, it's exactly like something *I'd* do?

We all hope to see our better qualities reflected back at us in our children. It's a frightening thing when you see your worst.

I'm there, 'Honor, please don't make me do this thing, I'm literally begging you.'

'Okay,' she goes, 'let's stop talking in the whiny child voice and stort carrying these things outside.'

And with a basic gun to my head, that's what I end up having to do.

I can't face my breakfast, which is panettone French toast, as it happens. My stomach is in knots. If I ate something, I'd probably spew everywhere.

Sorcha notices that it hasn't been touched. She's like, 'Are you okay?'

And I'm there, 'Yeah, no, I'm just a bit nervous.'

'She'll be fine, Ross. You've heard her play.'

'Er, yeah, I suppose.'

'My mum and dad used to get nervous for me. She's amazing, though, Ross. I really think she's going to bring the house down.'

There's a ring at the door and I literally jump.

Sorcha laughs. She's like, 'Oh my God, Ross, you are *so* on edge.'

I have to stort simplifying my life. Otherwise, I won't see fifty.

Sorcha opens the kitchen door, but Shadden comes running down the stairs, going, 'I'll gerrit!'

'That'll probably be her mum,' she goes. 'They're taking Rihanna-Brogan Christmas shopping this morning!'

I'm there, 'Christmas shoplifting – oh, that'll be nice.'

'Ross!'

'Hey, I'm just making the point. Her old dear's on first-name terms with practically every shop security gord on Henry Street.'

She shushes me then because in walks Shadden, followed by the famous Dordeen, wearing – there's no real surprises here – ski pants, humungous Nikes, a tracksuit top, then underneath a T-shirt with the words *Psycho Slut* on it.

'Weer is she?' is her opening line. 'Weer's tat gowergeous little granthaughter of moyen?'

Shadden goes, 'Ro-Ro's barringing her dowin now.'

'I caddent wheat to see her,' Dordeen goes – and you just know there's a dig coming. 'I habn't seen half enough of her. I wonther will I eeben reconize her.'

It sails totally over Sorcha's head, of course.

'Oh my God, you're right,' she goes. 'She is changing *so* fast.'

Dordeen's there, 'When are *you* due?' and she says it – I'm not imagining this – in a definitely resentful way.

'Two weeks,' Sorcha goes. 'They're being delivered by Caesarian on Christmas Day!'

Dordeen decides to change the subject to avoid saying something nice. She looks at my plate, turns up her nose and goes, 'What's tat – ferroyd bread?'

Sorcha's there, 'No, it's actually French toast, Dordeen.'

Dordeen laughs – bitterly. 'Fooken *posh* ferroyd bread, in utter woords.'

I end up having to just bite my tongue.

Sorcha goes, 'I can make you some, Dordeen, if you like.'

Dordeen's there, 'No, tanks,' and she pulls a Johnny Blue – I swear to fock – from behind her ear, holds it up and goes, 'Tat's my barreckfist theer.'

Ronan suddenly arrives down with Rihanna-B and Dordeen grabs her out of his orms in a big, stinking, nicotine hug, going, 'Theer she is! Theer's me bayooriful little granthaughter! Are we going to see Saddenty?! Are we going to see Saddenty Claus?!'

I always think that Northsiders could speak properly if they really wanted to.

I'm there, 'So you're all heading out shopping then, are you?'

'That's reet,' Dordeen goes. 'We're going to Thunthrum Shoppiding Centhor,' deliberately trying to make it sound like a ridiculous place, like Willy Wonka's Chocolate Factory or something like that. 'To be hodest wit ye, I'd radder go to Liffey Vaddey.'

I'm there, 'I doubt if that's news to anyone in this kitchen, Dordeen.'

She gives me a serious filthy. I'm just letting her know that I know what she's genuinely like, even if Sorcha doesn't.

'So,' she goes, 'I heerd she's walken and evvyting now.'

Shadden storts looking for the footage on her phone. She's there, 'Yeah, I haff to show it to you, so I do – it's amazing.'

'Me and your daddy were woodied you might miss it,' Dordeen goes. 'What wit you oately being a peert-toyum mudder.'

I'm there, 'Well, you were wrong, Dordeen. Because she was there to actually see it, so . . .'

Dordeen watches the footage, her face struggling not to seem impressed.

'Well,' she goes, 'as long as you doatunt miss her foorst woords now.'

I end up just shaking my head. It's impossible to please people like Dordeen unless you're handing them free money or things that are fried in grease.

I suddenly notice that Ronan is giving me eyes, then he looks at the back door. He obviously wants a word on the old QT.

I'm there, 'Ro, I must show you that thing outside that I was telling you about,' which is the cover story I come up with.

Out we go.

I'm there, 'Is everything okay? I swear to fock, if you told me that that was Brendan O'Carroll dressed up in there, I'd have to believe you.'

He laughs, in fairness to him. Then he goes, 'I need to talk to you about your ma.'

'My . . .'

'Your auld one, Rosser.'

'Okay, what about her?'

'Is she in some koyunt of thrubble?'

'Possibly. What do you know?'

'She reng Buckets of Blood last neet, aston him does he know wheer she could get coke.'

'Jesus.'

'Buckets wadn't happy. He's nebber been involfed in thrugs. The woorst he ebber was, Rosser, was a sthroker. He hates thrugs. It was thrugs what kilt he's brutter.'

'Tell Buckets not to take it personally. She thinks everyone who lives north of Westmoreland Street is a dealer of some kind.'

I actually do as well, although I don't say that.

He's there, 'What's she looken for coke fower?'

And I end up having to tell him the truth about his grandmother, tough and all as it will be for him to hear.

I'm there, 'The woman is a crack whore.'

He's there, 'What?'

Like I said, it's a lot for him to take in.

'Your grandmother,' I go, 'is a fiend for the old white powder.'

He's there, 'Moy Jaysus. She should be getting help, Rosser, not aston Buckets to supply her.'

'I'll talk to her again. I've just got, well, one or two things I need to deal with first. Thanks for mentioning it, though.'

We step back into the gaff. Honor is in the kitchen now, dressed as an angel – wings and everything – her little piccolo case swinging by her side. She sweet-smiles me and my hort storts beating instantly faster.

She goes, 'Come on, Daddy! I don't want to miss the concert!'

Sorcha stands up and she's like, 'Yes, we don't want to be late!' and she storts waddling towards the door.

And Rihanna-Brogan's orms – I swear to fock – shoot out in Sorcha's direction, then out of her mouth comes her first word, the worst word I can possibly think of at that moment in time, even worse than the C word or the B word or the F word.

She goes, 'Mom!'

Shadden bursts into tears and runs out of the room. And Dordeen – I don't think I'm imagining this – actually smiles, like her point has been somehow proven.

Me and Sorcha stand out amongst all the other parents, as you can imagine. Firstly, we're the only ones not wearing either tracksuits or leather Members Only jackets. Secondly, we're the only ones who keep turning to each other and smiling every time a kid on the stage says something in what I call a *real* Dublin accent.

A knackery accent, in other words.

At the same time, I've got this, like, sick feeling in my stomach. My knee is bouncing up and down and I'm literally chewing my fingernails.

Sorcha puts her hand on my thigh to stop it shaking. She's like, 'Oh my God, Ross, I've never seen you like this.'

I'm there, 'What?'

'This nervous – even before big rugby matches you played in. She's going to be fine, Ross. Just relax and enjoy it. When we're in our old age, we'll look back and remember this day.'

I really focking hope not.

Behind me, I hear a woman go, 'Thee should be up in the fooken royal box, that peer,' referring to us – presumably because we're wearing clothes that weren't designed for exercise or focking people out of nightclubs.

Up on the stage, Mary – or 'Ear Laity' as she's known in this port of the world – is limping around with a pillow up her shirt while her husband, Joseph, is looking for somewhere to stay.

You all know the story of the first Christmas. I don't know why I'm bothering my hole telling you.

Joseph, I notice, is being played by Something Drewery, the big-boned kid who's been giving Honor shit. He has a big, like, sneering look on his face, like he finds the whole thing hilarious.

'Yiz can stee in the staple,' the innkeeper tells Mary – who has hair extensions, by the way, and about fourteen coats of fake tan on her. 'You can have yizzer babby in there.'

Sorcha smiles at me. 'Staple!' she goes.

I try to smile back, except I can't.

I'm there, 'It's funny, yeah.'

She goes, 'I must dig out that CD we used to have of those inner-city kids telling Bible stories. Shocking holy saint. I think your mom actually gave that to us.'

'She definitely thought it was funny alright.'

'Shocking holy saint. And then the way the little girl said, "Brrroach!" I must see do we still have it.'

Someone – three seats down – shushes us. I lean forward. It's a scrawny little focker with a newsprint moustache who's recording the entire thing with a video camera. At a guess, I'd say he's this kid Drewery's old man. I give him a serious filthy.

All the kids stort singing.

> 'Soydunt night,
> Hody night,
> All is caddom,
> All is burroyt.
> Round John Veerchin,
> Mudder and choyult.'

The baby – Jesus, in other words – ends up being born and they wrap him in 'sawaddling' clothes and put him in a 'maincher'.

Sorcha gets a tap on the shoulder. We both turn around. It ends up being a woman in a pink cordigan – I, personally, think she looks like Kaya Scodelario, but then I'm sitting very close to her – who introduces herself as Noelle Maidin, as in Honor's teacher?

'We're all looking forward to Honor's recital,' she goes.

Sorcha's like, 'Oh my God, we are, too. I was just saying to Ross – sorry, this is my husband, Ross – that these are the moments, aren't they?'

'Oh, they are. And, may I tell you, you have raised a beautiful little girl.'

Sorcha's like, 'Have we?' like she actually needs persuading. 'Well, yeah, she can be good sometimes, can't she, Ross?'

I'm there, 'Hmmm,' not committing myself one way or the other. I already know she's in for a major focking land here.

I stort looking up at the air vents, wondering are they in there, scuttling around? Then I'm thinking, maybe Honor won't actually go through with it – as in, maybe she's changed her mind.

'I am aware,' this Miss Maidin one goes, 'of Honor's, shall we say, history. I know she didn't have a happy time of it in Mount Anville.'

Nor did anyone else, I think. They couldn't wait to see the focking back of her.

She goes, 'Teaching is all about creating an environment in which a child feels confident enough to grow. And that's certainly been my experience with Honor this year. Oh, there's the Three Wise Men. She'll be coming on next.'

We turn to face the front again. The three boyos hand over the gowult, frankiddensents and murr, then suddenly on walks Honor in her little angel outfit, holding her piccolo and smiling sweetly.

A woman a few rows back, at the top of her voice, goes, 'This moost be the little fooken snobby one that eer Tracy was tedding us about.'

Then her friend goes, 'That moost be her peerdunts sitting up theer at the ferrunt. The fooken stayra dum. Musta taught theed rowull out the red keerpit for thum.'

There's a small port of me actually wants this to happen now. It'll serve them right. Didn't God send down plagues of locusts and frogs to sort out fockers like these in the actual Bible?

Honor puts her lips to her piccolo and plays the opening notes. There is, like, literally silence in the school hall. That's how good the girl is on the thing.

I'm just sitting there, silently shitting it.

'Thee've probably spent bleaten tousands on lessons for her,' the dude with the video camera goes.

People like these can't admire you without hating you a little bit as well.

Sorcha puts her hand on top of mine, then storts rolling her head from side to side – *appreciating* the music, I think it's called – silently mouthing the lines, with her eyes fixed lovingly on our daughter.

Fall on your knees!
Oh, hear the angel voices!
O night divine!
Oh, night when Christ was born!

The first scream I hear comes from behind us, towards the back of the hall. It's the scream of a little girl. Then an adult – a man – goes, 'Jaysus fooken Carroyst, there's a rat!'

223

Suddenly, a massive clearing appears at the back of the crowd, as people try to move away from it.

'Theer's anutter one!' someone else shouts. 'Fooken two mower,' and it's amazing how quickly panic takes over the room.

There are women's and children's screams.

Then suddenly, over to our right, someone goes, 'Look at them! They're coming through the bleaten poyp theer! There's fooken middons of them!'

Throughout all of this, I should say, Honor continues to play, standing there with her angel wings and the sweetest little smile on her face.

Parents are storming the stage, grabbing their children, then running for the emergency exits, except there's rats in front of them. There's rats everywhere, in fact. So people are just running around in circles and bumping into each other in all the confusion.

Someone – it's Miss Maidin, would you believe? – screams, 'I've been bitten! I've been bitten!' and she jumps up on her chair, but then she's knocked off it by someone having a panic attack trying to get out.

I'm too fixated with Honor and the madness going on around me to even think about Sorcha. But suddenly she squeezes my hand unbelievably tightly and when I look at her she has tears streaming down her face.

'I . . . need an ambulance,' she goes. 'Ross . . . get me . . . an ambulance.'

It's at that exact point that the music stops.

I whip out my phone and I dial the emergency number as quickly as my shaking hands allow. While I'm waiting for an answer, I go, 'What is it, Sorcha? As in, what's wrong?'

She's in pain. I can see that.

She's there, 'I think . . . I'm losing them, Ross . . . I think I'm . . . losing our babies.'

No.

Fock, no.

I tell the emergency services bird the Jack and where we are and she says that an ambulance will be with us shortly.

I'm like, 'Shortly? What the fock does that mean?' except by that time she's already hung up.

'Go and get . . . Honor,' Sorcha goes.

I turn around. I can see her through the general pandemonium on the stage. I push my way through the heaving mass of bodies and rats running everywhere and I call her.

I'm like, 'Honor!' and I say it in a really angry way.

She's there, 'Coming, Daddy!' and she says it in a really *sarcastic* way?

I look to my right and I notice Joseph, Jesus's old man – in other words, this Drewery kid who's been bullying her – lying flat on his back, blood pouring from a cut in his head and Honor's piccolo lying on the floor beside him. His old man – it *is* the dude with the video camera – is trying to help him up.

Honor goes, 'I can't believe, in this day and age, there are schools infested with rats. Hashtag, *disgusting* much?'

I'm there, 'Your mother's not well. Something's happened,' and I notice the expression on Honor's face suddenly change.

She can tell from my voice that this is suddenly serious.

By the time we make it back to Sorcha, she's basically out of it – we're talking unconscious – still sitting in the chair, with her head back and her hands strapped across her stomach.

I kneel down beside her. There's rats all around me and yet I don't actually *give* a fock? I take Sorcha's hands as I hear a siren approaching and I stort talking to her stomach.

'Hang on, my babies!' I go, tears streaming down my face. 'Whatever you do, don't die. Please don't focking die!'

7. Get Him to the Geek

The midwife asks me to please stop shouting. I wasn't aware that I even *was*?

I'm there, 'Look, I'm sorry. I just want to know what the fock is going on.' I've been pacing the corridors of Holles Street for the past, like, two hours.

'Your wife has an incompetent cervix,' she goes.

I'm there, 'Okay, what the fock does that even mean?'

'It means that she's going into labour.'

'Labour? But she's not due for another, like, two weeks.'

'The neck of her womb has opened, which means we're going to have to carry out an emergency Caesarian.'

'When?'

'Right now.'

I'm thinking, oh shit – oh shit, oh shit, oh shit.

I'm there, 'Can I see her?'

'She's not in any condition,' she goes.

'But I want to see her.'

'Her blood pressure is very, very low.'

I hear my voice – all trembly – go, 'Is she . . . Jesus Christ, is she going to be okay?'

The midwife looks me straight in the eye and goes, 'We're not sure. Your wife is very, very sick. Which is why we have to deliver the babies and then . . .'

'Is she going to, like, *live*?'

'Like I said, we're not operating in a world of certainties here. The next twelve hours are vital.'

'Can you not just let me see her?'

'The best thing you can do, Mr O'Carroll-Kelly, is to remain calm and look after your daughter.'

My daughter. Jesus, I totally forgot about her. She's sitting on a grey plastic chair at the other end of the corridor and for once she's not texting or Tweeting or whatever else. She's just sitting there, staring sadly at the wall.

The midwife focks off.

I walk down the corridor towards Honor, who doesn't even look up at me. I sit down on the chair next to her.

I'm there, 'Are you okay?'

She just nods. Again, she doesn't even move her head. She looks on the point of definite tears.

I'm there, 'I just want you to know that I'm not blaming you – even though, looking at it from the outside, a lot of people would say that it *is* your actual fault?'

In the background, Mariah Carey is singing 'All I Want for Christmas is You'.

'I hated that school,' Honor goes, her voice sounding for some reason tiny. 'I hated it.'

I'm there, 'Well, you'll be happy to hear that I doubt they'll be taking you back.'

My phone all of a sudden rings. It ends up being Sorcha's old dear – she obviously got my message. She was playing tennis this morning.

She's, like, up the focking walls when I answer the phone.

She's like, 'What's going on? You said Sorcha was in hospital!'

I'm there, 'Yeah, no, she was rushed in this morning. They're delivering the babies now.'

'Now? What . . . What's wrong?'

'It's a long story. Basically, we were at Honor's Christmas concert slash recital slash whatever you want to call it and the hall was suddenly filled with rats.'

'Rats?'

She acts like it's the weirdest thing she's ever heard. Then again, it probably *is*?

I'm there, 'Yeah, no, there was suddenly pandemonium and Sorcha collapsed. All the talk now is of an incompetent cervix.'

She goes, 'Why am I only hearing about this now?'

I hear a cor door slam and then an engine stort up.

'I rang you,' I go. 'You had your phone switched off.'

She's there, 'Could you not have phoned the clubhouse and asked them to contact me out on the court?'

'I didn't think to. The last couple of hours have been pretty intense.'

'How is she?'

'I don't know.'

'What do you mean, you don't know? Have you asked?'

'Of course I've asked. They said there's no certainties.'

There's suddenly, like, silence on the other end of the phone, except for the sound of her breathing. She's obviously struggling to take it in. Then she just hangs up on me.

Honor goes, 'You don't need to worry, by the way.'

I'm there, 'What do you mean?'

'The rats. I'll say it was me.'

'It *was* you.'

'But I won't say you knew about it. I won't say you drove them to the school.'

'You focking blackmailed me into doing it.'

'I'm saying I'll take the blame. I'll leave you out of it.'

I could nearly cry.

I'm like, 'Yeah, no, I'd appreciate that, Honor. It'd be cool if you did.'

We sit there, neither of us saying a word for what must be an hour, listening to Christmas songs and waiting for news.

After a while – it *must* be an hour – Sorcha's old dear comes running down the corridor, as fast as her feet can carry her.

She sees me and Honor sitting there, except she doesn't acknowledge us. She runs past us, straight to the nurses' station and storts making a nuisance of herself, firing out questions.

What?

Why?

How long?

She gets pretty much the same answers as I did. Sorcha's in the labour ward. Her blood pressure is a cause for serious concern.

They're delivering the babies right now by Caesarian. Incompetent cervix and blah, blah, blah.

She eventually settles down, then sits opposite us. But she doesn't say shit. I can tell she's already decided that I'm to blame for this. She just hasn't figured out how yet.

I stare at the wall and I think about Sorcha and how I've treated her over the years – killing myself wth guilt, basically – how I've cheated on her and lied to her and broken her hort so many times. And how if I lost her, I genuinely don't know what I'd do.

I'd be half a person.

An hour passes. Then another. I ask Honor if she wants something to eat and she shakes her head in, like, tight little movements.

Sorcha's old dear stands up and says she'd better go and feed her meter. She goes, 'I suppose I should ring Sorcha's dad,' and I think, Yeah, no, he's entitled to know, even though he's a knob and also a dick.

Off she goes.

I turn to Honor and I'm like, 'Are you sure you won't have something?'

The last thing she ate was her breakfast and it's now six o'clock.

She goes, 'I'm not hungry,' but not in her usual fock-you voice. She says it, like, softly, even *gently*?

She's in shock. I can tell she's in shock.

A few minutes later, the midwife appears at the end of the corridor. I stand up. I go to speak, except no actual words come out.

'Would you like to meet your sons?' she goes.

I'm like, 'Sons?'

She smiles. She's there, 'Come on,' and then she leads me down to what turns out to be the intensive care unit, wth Honor following a few steps behind me.

They're laid out next to each other in three adjoining incubators. They're tiny and pink and beautiful. I suddenly feel like I've been punched in the solar plexus. That's the only thing that's happened in my life that I can actually compare it to.

I stand there, just, like, staring at them through the glass, lying on their backs, their little eyes scrunched shut, one of them wriggling around and roaring crying, the other two totally out of it.

'Are they okay?' I somehow manage to go. 'Are they going to *be* okay?'

The midwife is like, 'We're concerned about the one on the end. His heartbeat is very low.'

I look at him and I notice that he's got various wires coming out of everywhere. I also notice that he's got, like, a strawberry-coloured birthmork across the bridge of his nose.

He's beautiful.

I'm there, 'What about Sorcha? Is there any news?'

She smiles at me – I'm going to say *weakly*?

'She's not good,' she goes. 'The next few hours are vital for her. I'll, em, leave you two alone.'

Off she goes, leaving me and Honor just standing there, rooted to the spot, staring through an inch of glass at these three – Jesus! – baby boys.

My baby boys.

I suddenly hear the sound of crying and I'm surprised to discover that it's me. I'm crying and I'm doing it in great big heaving sobs. I cry so hord that it feels like I might not stop.

Then I suddenly feel Honor slip her hand into mine and she gently squeezes my fingers.

'You can go and see your wife now?'

I wake up with a sudden stort. I'm like, 'What?'

'You can go in and see her,' this nurse goes. 'But not for long. She's still very weak.'

I look around, trying to get my bearings. It's the following morning. Ronan and Shadden arrived just before midnight to bring Honor home and I must have just nodded off.

I don't know where Sorcha's old dear is. Maybe she's feeding her meter again.

I'm there, 'Is my wife okay?'

My neck is sore and I can feel saliva on my right cheek. Fock knows what I look like.

'Like I said,' the nurse goes, 'she's very heavily medicated. But she's a fighter.'

There's no doubt about that. I think about the twenty-six consecutive Saturdays she spent picketing that fur shop at the bottom of Grafton Street when she was in UCD. Dogged is possibly *more* the word?

She looks focking wretched, which is no real surprise considering what she's been through. She looks at me through two narrow slits and her face suddenly brightens.

'Hey,' she goes, 'we have three . . . three little boys.'

I sit down beside the bed and I take her hand in mine. I'm like, 'I know. They're beautiful, Sorcha. They're so . . . Jesus, so beautiful,' and I think about telling her that one of them is sick – as in, like, *really* sick? – but it turns out she already knows.

'How did *he* look?' she goes. 'The one they say might not make it.'

I'm there, 'Yeah, no, not great. He's hooked up to all sorts of . . .' and then I hear my voice suddenly crack.

Sorcha's eyes close. She's having trouble staying awake.

I'm there, 'He'll pull through,' even though I have no idea whether it's true or not. 'He's a fighter. Like his mother. Like his father as well, a lot of people would say.'

She smiles. She likes that thought.

She falls asleep for, like, five seconds and then wakes up. It must be the drugs. You see people doing that on the Nitelink.

'What are we . . . going to do?' she goes.

I'm there, 'Do? What are you talking about specifically?'

'About Honor.'

Her breathing is all, like, *laboured*?

I'm there, 'Honor? What about her?'

She goes, 'Ross, she infested . . . infested her school . . . with rats.'

I think deep down I hoped she'd forgotten the entire episode.

'She must have been . . . oh my God . . . breeding them . . .'

'It's possible, I suppose.'

'Down in the coach house . . . But how . . . Ross, how did she get them . . . to the school?'

'I suppose we'll never know. And maybe it's better that way.'

'There must have been . . . hundreds of them . . . How did she . . . get them . . . to the school?'

'Let's not think about that now, Babes. The important thing is that you rest and get better.'

'Of course it's . . . important. Ross, think about . . . the level of . . . planning and . . . and cunning that went into it.'

'Yeah, no, I'm agreeing with you. She's like some kind of evil genius. I'm on the record as saying that.'

'I'm . . . scared, Ross.'

'Scared?'

'Scared of . . . what else . . . she might do.'

The eyes close again for a few seconds, then they're back open. She goes, 'I'm scared . . . she might hurt . . . the babies.'

I'm there, 'No. No way.'

'Ross, let's be honest . . . We don't know . . . what she's . . . capable . . . of doing.'

'I don't think she'd do that, though. I genuinely don't.'

'Would you feel comfortable . . . leaving her around them?'

Jesus Christ. The truth is, I wouldn't.

She goes, 'She's a very . . . a very disturbed little . . . little girl, Ross.'

I'm there, 'I know. Through nothing *we've* done, I hasten to add. When you think about it, we've given that girl everything she's ever wanted. We've spoiled her, in fact. So we've no questions to ask ourselves.'

She doesn't respond to that. She just turns her head to one side, then turns back to me and smiles. She goes, 'Are they beautiful, Ross?'

I laugh. I'm there, 'Yeah, they're beautiful.'

'Who . . . who are they more like?'

'I think they're like you.'

'Really?'

'Yeah, no, *I* think so.'

'The doctor said I . . . said I might be able . . . to see them later . . . if I'm well enough . . . She said . . . She said they could bring me to the ICU in . . . in a wheelchair.'

234

'I'm going to say fair focks. But you probably should try to get some sleep now, Babes.'

'What . . . what are we going to call them, Ross?'

'What?'

'I'm talking about names.'

'Oh, yeah. Well, I'm very much veering towards Brian, Jonathan and Leo.'

'What would you think . . . of Aelhaeran . . . Addis . . . and Abracham . . . with a c?'

It might be the drugs.

I'm there, 'Don't overexert yourself, Sorcha. We've got ages to decide. I'm just mentioning – as someone who's actually seen them – that they do look like a Brian, Jonathan and Leo.'

'You look . . . tired, Ross.'

'Yeah, no, I'm banjoed.'

'Go home and get some . . . get some sleep.'

'I'm staying here until you're ready to go. You and the babies.'

'No. Go home, Ross. Get . . . Get your rest . . . Because I'm going to need you . . . to be strong.'

I'm there, 'Okay,' and I reluctantly stand up.

I lean over her and I kiss her on the cheek. She's, like, so pale.

'I love you,' I go, which is very unlike me. I just go with the moment.

She's there, 'I love . . . I love you, too.'

She's out of the game before I even leave the room.

I step out into the corridor and I decide to have one more peek at the boys before I go. I stort heading for the intensive care unit and that's when I end running into Sorcha's old dear in the corridor.

'She's awake,' I go, already on the big-time defensive. 'I've just been in with her. I was actually going to text you. I didn't know whether you were feeding your meter or what you were up to.'

She's there, 'I've been to the airport.'

I'm like, 'The airport?'

I look over her shoulder and I notice Sorcha's old man coming steaming down the corridor towards me, his eyes wild and his focking tache bristling furiously.

'What have you done to her?' is his opening line.

I'm prepared to be civil to the prick – you know what I'm like – and I go, 'She's going to be definitely happy to see you, Dude – you're going to make her actual day,' because despite the whole supposed divorce thing, Sorcha is still, at hort, very much a daddy's girl.

He shoves me out of the way – literally shoves me, with his hand on my chest – and goes, 'Where is my little girl? I want to see my little girl.'

The old dear is still in her dressing gown. This is at, like, one o'clock in the day. She's staring at the television with *Home and Away* on mute and she looks as ugly as ugly can get.

I go, 'Hey,' and she barely even turns her head to look at me.

She's there, 'What do you want, Ross?'

My own mother, bear in mind. She has a face on her like a gutted trout.

I'm there, 'Oh, nothing really. I just called in to tell you that the triplets were born. Three little boys.'

'Oh,' she just goes, 'how nice.'

I'm there, 'Yeah, no, they're a couple of weeks premature. Sorcha storted to go into labour, so they had to deliver them by emergency Caesarian. Two of them are fine. One of them has a weak hortbeat.'

'I said I'm happy for you, Ross.'

'Well, you don't sound happy. I called into the old man and he at least opened a bottle of Veuve Clicquot. I left him shit-faced and talking gibberish half-an-hour ago.'

'I'm feeling a little under the weather today, that's all.'

'Yeah, no, it's called going through the horrors. In other words, *drug* withdrawal?'

She finally looks at me, cracking on to be offended. She's there, 'I *beg* your pardon?'

'You're all out,' I go. 'Of coke. You rang Ronan's mate, Buckets of Blood, trying to score it from him.'

'I haven't the faintest idea what you're talking about.'

'Yes, you do. Look at you – not even dressed at, what, half-one in the day?'

I know I've a cheek to mention it. That was me in UCD.

'Like I said,' she goes, 'I'm not feeling myself.'

I'm there, 'You haven't even put up a Christmas tree.'

'I might see the doctor. I might need a little pick-me-up.'

'The only pick-me-up you're interested in is the kind that you can stick up that ample-sized hooter of yours.'

She suddenly jumps up out of the chair, as if she's been stung by something. She's there, 'What was that?'

I'm like, 'What are you talking about?' because I literally didn't hear a thing.

She goes, 'Someone's trying to break in, Ross. They're trying to kick the front door down.'

'So, what, now you're hearing things as well?'

'I'm not *hearing* things. Someone is trying to break in. There! Did you hear that?'

I roll my eyes, then I wander out to the front door. I open it. There's no one outside – surprise sur-focking-prise.

I go back into the living room to her. 'There's no one out there,' I go.

She's like, 'They're after my jewellery.'

I notice she's shaking – we're talking genuine fear slash paranoia.

'Who?' I go. 'Who's after your jewellery?'

She's there, 'Whoever's trying to kick down that door. They were here last night, too.'

I'm there, 'You need treatment. There's clinics you can go to – did you know that?'

That's when she suddenly loses it with me.

She's like, 'Get out! Get out of my house!' and – I swear to fock – she bends down and picks the poker up off the fireplace.

I'm there, 'Hey, I'm only trying to help you here.'

She holds the poker about three inches from my face and she goes, 'I'll use this. God help me, I'll use it.'

From the crazy look in her eyes, I don't doubt she would, so I decide to get the fock out of there, stopping on my way out the door to go, 'You've lost it. You've lost it in a major way. You need help, you crazy fock.'

Then I leave, because no amount of encouragement from me is going to *make* her look for treatment.

I stort the cor and I point it in the direction of Holles Street. I end up smiling to myself, even though I'm operating on, like, three hours of sleep. I'm thinking about my little baby boys and I'm thinking about Sorcha and how my life feels suddenly complete. And that's when my phone rings and – as usually happens – I'm brought suddenly crashing back to Earth again.

It ends up being Shoshanna. Her opening line, if you can believe this, is, 'You fucked her.'

'Yeah, no, in Ireland,' I go, 'we usually stort conversations with the word *hello*?' because I'm feeling a bit full of myself today – bulletproof even.

Silly focking me.

She goes, 'You had sex with Jenny!' and she sounds delighted to be saying it.

I'm there, 'Excuse me?'

'You had sex with her, then you told her you were going to leave your wife for her. Then you stole her money and you fucking set her up.'

I laugh. I'm there, 'Those are some pretty serious allegations, Shoshanna. And if you're going to be an allegator, you better make sure you have a certain thing called evidence.'

She's like, 'Well, how's this for evidence? Jenny told me everything.'

Again, I laugh. I'm there, 'Jenny?'

She goes, 'I phoned her. She's back in New Zealand.'

'Yeah – she's also as mad as a focking supermorket trolley.'

'She said you fucked her twice. Once in the cor pork opposite that stupid pub . . .'

'Careful now.'

'And then once in Ewan and Andrea's house. That was when the table quiz money went missing. She only worked it out on the flight home. You took it and you set her up.'

'And you're relying on *her* word? She's a focking fantasist. Her own family said that about her.'

'Just because she has issues, it doesn't mean she's lying.'

'Well, the problem is, who's going to believe her?'

'I believe her.'

'Well, you're in a minority of one.'

'For now,' she goes, sounding for some reason very focking pleased with herself.

I get a sudden sense that she has a cord to play. I'm there, 'What are you talking about?'

She goes, 'I asked her, you know, if you had sex with Ross, as you claim, tell me what was it like.'

'Why, are you jealous?'

'No, I was just looking for some little detail that might, you know, authenticate her *story*?'

'And?'

'Well, she said the second time you did it – she was very disappointed, by the way – you kept saying men's names, like you were naming a team, maybe a rugby team, by rote.'

Oh, fock.

'That's not something I do,' I try to go. 'She's obviously just made that up.'

Shoshanna's there, 'Well, maybe I'll mention it to your wife and see does she recognize it.'

I suddenly turn on her. I'm there, 'Sorcha's not well at the moment. She's just given birth. If you upset her, I swear to fock . . .'

'Not nice,' she goes, 'is it? When someone tries to fuck with your happiness.'

Then she hangs up. And I realize in that moment that Shoshanna is going to have to get her comeuppance, too – and she's going to have to get it before I get mine.

He's a little bit stronger tonight. That's the word from the intensive care unit. They're, like, more hopeful than they were. I can't take my eyes off him. I'm just, like, staring at him, trying to will him better. It sounds like crazy talk, but I would literally tear out my own hort and give it to him if I thought it meant he'd survive.

'What's that on his face?' Honor goes.

She's taking a photograph of him with her iPhone.

'Oh,' I go, 'that's a birthmork. They usually disappear after a while.'

I expect her to say something cruel, maybe 'Hashtag, *deformed* much?' or something along those lines. Except she ends up totally surprising me by going, 'I love *him* the most.'

I laugh. It's, like, an *unconscience* thing, if that's the word?

'Love?' I go. 'That's a strange word to hear you use. It's nice is what I'm saying.'

She looks at me with genuine – I'm pretty sure it's genuine – sadness in her eyes. She goes, 'If he dies, will it be my fault?'

I'm like, 'What?'

She's there, 'It's my fault. I know it's my fault,' and then she all of a sudden bursts into tears.

I'm like, 'Whoa, whoa, whoa,' and then I crouch down to her level and I take her by the shoulders and go, 'Your mother had an incompetent cervix, Honor. I don't know whose fault that is, but it's certainly not yours.'

It makes little or no difference.

'You're just saying that to make me feel better,' she goes. 'It *is* my fault. It *is* my fault.'

I'm there, 'Honor, your mother went into labour prematurely. It could have happened anywhere. In Saba on Clarendon Street. In the Morvle Room in BTs. It just so happened to happen at the exact moment you infested your entire school with rats.'

'But I said I didn't want little brothers. I kept saying in my head every night, "I hope they die. I hope they die. I hope they die."'

'Honor, you can't kill someone by just wishing them dead. At least I don't think you can.'

'But I don't want them to die, Daddy. I'm their big sister.'

I pull her close to me and I kiss her on the top of the head and I go, 'You are, Honor. And they're going to love you every bit as much as you love them.'

As she's crying in my orms, I think about the conversation that me and Sorcha had this morning and I think, no, there's no way that Honor would ever hurt the babies. I'd be eighty percent sure of that.

After a minute or so, I let her go, then with my two thumbs I wipe away her tears and I tell her not to worry. Things will work out. And that's when I hear *his* voice. I'm talking about Sorcha's old man.

He's there, 'I've come to see my grandsons,' and he puts – I'm not imagining this – the emphasis on the word *sons*, so as to distinguish them from his granddaughter, who he hates.

I try to keep things at least civil. I'm there, 'Sorcha seems well on the mend. Have you decided when you're going to head off back to England or what are your plans?'

He doesn't even answer me, the ignorant fock. He spends about five minutes grinning like an idiot through the glass at the three little goys – I decide to just go with Brian, Jonathan and Leo until I'm told otherwise – and then suddenly, out of nowhere, he goes, 'Did I ever tell you about the night of my fortieth birthday?'

For a minute, I'm not even sure he's talking to me – well, that is until he actually looks at me.

'Your fortieth?' I go. 'Er, no. Was it a good night?'

He's there, 'We went out for dinner. My wife and I, Sorcha and her sister . . .'

I think to myself, would somebody please, just once, say her focking name?

'We went to Daniel's,' he goes, 'in Sandycove.'

I'm there, 'Yeah, no, Fionn loves that place. They raffled a voucher for it at the table quiz.'

'Sorcha was, what, fifteen at the time? She couldn't take her eyes off the tank where they kept the lobsters.'

'That's what it'd be famous for, of course. You sometimes see Pat Kenny in there, don't you?'

'The waiter came to take our order and that's what she said she wanted. She even pointed out the exact one through the glass. So the waiter rolled up his sleeve, stuck his hand in the tank and pulled it out, then off he went to the kitchen to drop it in the pot. But Sorcha stopped him. She said, "No, no – I'm taking him to go."'

He has a little chuckle to himself. It's a good Sorcha story alright.

He's there, 'She wanted to liberate him. She decided to keep him as a pet.'

I'm like, 'Did it live long, do you remember?' just making conversation with the dude.

He doesn't answer me. He just keeps staring at the babies – Brian, Jonathan and Leo – then he goes, 'That's Sorcha, of course. She's sensitive and caring and thoughtful . . . I'm just hoping that her boys take after her . . .'

Then he turns and he glowers – I'm serious here – *glowers* at Honor and goes, 'And not – like you – after their father!'

It's a dig at me. And at Honor as well, I suppose.

I'm there, 'Whoa, Dude, you're out of order. You're actually *bang* out of order?'

He roars at Honor then. He's like, 'You stupid, stupid, stupid girl!'

Honor suddenly shrinks back. She's terrified of him. I am, too, although in my defence he has made two attempts on my life.

He's there, 'My daughter could have died because of you!'

'I'm not a hundred percent sure there's anything to be gained from pointing fingers at this stage,' I try to go.

He keeps his attention focused on Honor, though. He's like, 'Of course, your father will always defend you, because you're just like him! Twisted and conniving and utterly self-centred!'

That's when I decide that I've heard enough. I step in between them and I go, 'Dude, that's my daughter you're talking to.'

He roars in my face then. He's like, 'And that's *my* daughter downstairs! She nearly bloody died, you know!'

I'm there, 'Two words for you, Dude. Incompetent. Cervix. That's what the doctor said. It was fock-all to do with the whole rat thing.'

He goes, 'I don't care what the doctor said,' and then he turns around to Honor, who at this stage is, like, cowering behind my back, and goes, 'You nearly caused your mother's death, you stupid girl! And if that little baby in there dies, then it's on your head, too! You'll have to live with that for the rest of your life!'

I grab him by the lapels of his jacket and I slam him hord against the wall of the intensive care unit. I hold him there, my hands shaking and my blood basically *boiling*?

Behind me, I can hear Honor going, 'Hit him, Dad! Punch him in the face!'

'Go on, do it!' *he* goes. 'Hit me! And give me an excuse to have you removed from my daugher's life once and for all!'

That's what brings me to my all of a sudden senses – knowing how much it'd suit him to see me put away for assault, or possibly even murder.

I let go of him. He fixes his clothes while my breathing slowly returns to normal.

I'm there, 'Come on, Honor, let's go and see your mother.'

As we're walking away, he goes, 'You're peas in a pod, you two,' and you can tell he's delighted with himself.

Honor turns around, looks her grandfather up and down and goes, 'You're an asshole. You're actually a *bankrupt* asshole?'

And I know I shouldn't laugh, but I end up, like, having to.

I have a brainwave while I'm sitting at traffic lights on the Rock Road. I text Oisinn and I tell him that a friend of a friend is trying to get in touch with an ex of his – long story and blah, blah, blah – and ten seconds later he texts me back her number.

I'm the last person in the world she expects to hear from at, like, nine o'clock on a random Tuesday morning. She answers on the third ring, genuinely no idea who it could be.

I go, 'Hey, Speranza!'

She's like, 'Who's this?'

I'm there, 'A ghost from your past. It's Ross O'Carroll-Kelly?'

There's a good, like, ten seconds of silence on the other end. Then she goes, 'You wanker. You focking . . .'

It's the response I was kind of *expecting*?

I'm there, 'That's not very friendly.'

She goes, 'I'm hanging up.'

I'm there, 'Okay, wait, wait, wait. Look, I'm sorry I walked out on you in the middle of the night.'

'You know, I stopped my next-door neighbour from ringing the Guards that night. I actually wish I hadn't.'

'I had to get out of there, Speranza. I found myself developing feelings for you and it frightened me.'

'You told me that you and your wife had broken up'

'I didn't say that, if you cast your mind back. You said that's what you heard and I just didn't correct you.'

'You also didn't tell me that she was pregnant with triplets. I found the photograph from the scan in your wallet.'

'Well, she's had them now – three little boys.'

'I'm very focking happy for you.'

'Look, we could stay on the line all day trading insults. But it's not going to get us anywhere.'

'Why are you even ringing me, Ross?'

'Okay, you're a doctor, right?'

'So?'

'Well, I'm actually trying to get in contact with another doctor and I was wondering do you know her?'

She laughs.

She's like, 'Do you know how many doctors there are in, Ireland?'

I'm there, 'She's an American bird. Shoshanna.'

She sort of, like, laughs. 'Okay, I remember Shoshanna,' she goes. 'She was, like, two years behind me in Surgeons. She was always a bit strange. She became, like, a fat whisperer or something. She claimed she could communicate with people's fat cells and persuade them to leave the body.'

'What a chancer.'

'She had a clinic – actually on Morehampton Road. Why are you asking me about her? She's not another one of your . . .'

I'm like, 'No, no – I'm entirely innocent. No, it's a friend of mine is trying to get in touch with her boyfriend. He was a black dude.'

'Oh, Kevin,' she goes, suddenly remembering. 'Kevin Plessy. He's in the Galway Clinic. He's in cardiology. He was the year below me. I was friends with someone he was friends with, if that makes any sense.'

I scribble his name down and the name of the hospital and I even have a crack at spelling cordiology – that's how good a mood I'm in – while she continues blabbing on about nothing.

I go, 'Anyway, Speranza, it was good to catch up. I'll maybe see you around,' and then I hang up on her.

At the next traffic lights, I whip out my phone, go into the Facebook app and type the words *Kevin Plessy Ireland* into the search line. Up comes his page. He's black alright. Not that I expected him *not* to be? But in a weird way, it comes as a relief.

Then I call up the photograph that JP took of me holding little Ezra that day in the hospital. I study his little face, then I stare at this Kevin dude's profile picture – it looks like it was taken outside Bruxelles – and I look for similarities. And of course the most obvious one is that they're the same basic colour.

Someone behind me in a silver Nissan Primera beeps me and I realize that the light has turned from red to green. I wind down the window and give them the finger and, as I'm doing so, I figure out my next move.

Which is to pull into Blackrock Shopping Centre, print out the photograph of Ezra – cropping me out of it, obviously – then post it to the Galway Clinic, with a unanimous note telling Kevin the joyous news that he is someone's daddy.

I touch Sorcha's hand and she wakes up. She still looks like shit and I'm saying that, remember, as her number one fan. She's obviously still in a fair bit of pain.

She goes, 'How long have you been sitting there?'

I'm like, 'Fifteen, twenty minutes.'

'Why didn't you wake me?'

'I was watching you sleep. Are you okay?'

'A bit sore. But they're easing me off the morphine. They're going to let me go home this weekend. Did you see the boys?'

'Yeah, no, I was just with them for about an hour.'

'The doctors say there's been a huge improvement, Ross.'

She's obviously talking about the third little fella.

I'm there, 'Yeah, I know.'

She goes, 'They think he's going to be strong enough to come home with me.'

'This is going to be the best Christmas ever. Honor loves them, can I just say in her defence. She was going to come in to see you, but in the end . . .'

'I don't want to see her.'

'What?'

'I don't want her in here, Ross. I don't want to see her.'

This is the girl she used to call her Little Princess, bear in mind.

I'm there, 'Well, to tell you the truth, she's a bit nervous about seeing you again.'

She goes, 'I mean it, Ross. I don't want to see her until I've worked out how I feel about her – and, of course, what we're going to do about her.'

Her old man has obviously been in her ear.

As if reading my mind, she goes, 'It's been so nice having my dad here for the last few days. I think seeing his three little grandsons has put a lot of things into perspective for him.'

I'm there, 'That's great, Sorcha. When's he going back?'

She doesn't answer me and I notice a flicker of something in her eyes, which I straight away recognize as trouble.

I'm like, 'Okay, what?'

She's there, 'I was just going to say I want you two to make an extra-special effort to try to get along.'

'Er, why?'

'Because you're the two most important men in my life.'

'He's never been an admirer of mine and he made that pretty much clear from day one. And you didn't answer my question. When's he going back?'

I mean, he's supposed to be trying to establish residence in England. In which case, he possibly shouldn't even *be* here? I wonder could I report him. It'd be nice to fock him over.

You can possibly imagine my shock when Sorcha turns around to me and goes, 'He's not going back, Ross.'

I'm like, 'What are you talking about?' possibly already fearing the worst. 'What about the whole bankruptcy thing?'

'He's decided to do it here.'

'Here? But doesn't it take longer? Isn't it, like, years?'

'He doesn't care. He said his family comes first. He told me this morning that once he had the people he loved around him – including my mum – he was the richest man in the world.'

I can nearly hear him saying it as well, the focking sap.

I'm there, 'But what about the whole divorce thing?' the disappointment obvious in my voice. 'Jesus, don't tell me that's not going ahead either.'

She goes, 'They've decided to give things another go.'

'Fock.'

'Ross!'

'This is a serious focking let-down, I don't mind telling you. I think your old dear's mad taking him back, by the way. That's just me calling it. Where are they gonna live, can I just ask? I'm presuming their old place in the Beacon South Quarter is still vacant.'

And that's when Sorcha hits me with it. Square between the eyes. She goes, 'I said they could come and live with us.'

I'm like, 'What?' and I actually shout it.

I *roar* it, in fact?

Sorcha suddenly scrunches up her face and doubles over in the bed, clutching her stomach. And the worst thing is, I don't know if she's doing it because she's in pain or because she wants to avoid the discussion.

'Ross,' she goes, 'I'm going to have to ask you to leave me alone. I need to rest.'

And I step out of the ward and into the corridor, thinking that this day could not get any worse. And that's when I get a phone call from the Gords in Store Street, to say that my old dear has been caught in possession of €30,000 worth of cocaine.

*

I haven't seen the woman look so frightened since McCabe's off-licence in Blackrock opened an hour late one Sunday morning. Her cell door is heavy and it literally screams on its hinges as I push it open. She's sitting bolt upright on a bench that supposedly doubles as a bed.

It's obvious she's been crying.

'The focking state of you,' I go. 'You look like Steve Tyler with malaria.'

'I don't even know who that is,' she goes. 'But I'm already regretting telling them to ring you.'

'Oh, do you think I *want* to be here? I've got a wife and suddenly three babies.'

'I should have told them to ring Delma.'

'Oh, you want Delma to know you're a focking drug addict, do you?'

She stands up. 'I'm not an addict,' she goes. 'I was having a bad day. I needed a little filip.'

I'm like, 'Thirty focking Ks worth of a filip?'

'Well, I just presumed it was cheaper if you bought it in bulk.'

'Has all that shit you've had injected into your forehead over the years storted leaking into your brain?'

'I beg your pardon.'

'Er, stopping randomers on Talbot Street and asking them if they could get drugs for you?'

'Well, it only took six or seven people before someone said yes.'

'Talbot Street! Jesus Christ – anything north of the Molly Malone statue you used to call Caracas.'

'Are you just going to stand there shouting at me or are you going to get me out of here? Some of the things that are written on these walls are turning my stomach.'

I actually laugh. I'm like, 'The only way you're getting out of here is to be transferred to Cloverhill.'

That gets her definite attention.

She's there, 'What do you mean?' because she knows she won't last pissing time in there with that accent of hers. They'll kill her.

I'm like, 'What do you think I mean? You're being chorged with possession with intent to supply.'

'Supply? But I bought it for myself.'

'Doesn't matter. Once it's over a certain weight, you're automatically considered a dealer. That's how Ronan explained it to me.'

'You told Ronan I was in Store Street Gorda Station?'

'I focking had to. I needed directions.'

She storts pacing the floor. She's really storting to kack it now.

'Well,' she tries to go, 'could these people not just accept that I'm very, very wealthy. I mean, €30,000 wouldn't represent a great deal of money to someone like me. I've had cleaners who've stolen that amount of money from my purse and I didn't even bother to phone the Gords.'

'Yeah, no, I'd say that story would go down very well in here, especially with the way their overtime has been taken away from them. I would say it's definitely worth mentioning how focking well you're doing for yourself.'

'These things are relative – that's the point I'm trying to make.'

I'm there, 'Do you know what kind of a stretch you're looking at?'

She goes, 'No,' and she suddenly stops pacing. 'What?'

'Ten years.'

'Ten *years*? Ten years of what? You can't mean imprisonment?'

'Of course I mean imprisonment.'

And that's when she suddenly breaks in two. Her bottom lip storts trembling. 'Ten *years*?' she goes. 'I'd be . . . I'd be sixty when I got out.'

I'm there, 'I'm going to let that one go, because you're having a shit enough day as it is.'

The tears come then – first in a trickle, then in floods – as it finally dawns on her how much trouble she's actually in. She sits down again and puts her head in her hands.

She's there, 'I'll never come back from this. I mean, my career is over.'

'I don't know,' I go. 'People might buy your prison memoir in, what, 2023?'

'And the disgrace. Oh, Jesus – Delma! Angela! What are the girls going to say? And my grandchildren. Those little boys are going to grow up knowing their grandmother is in prison.'

'I don't know if I'd bother my hole mentioning you to them.'

'Why didn't I listen to you?'

'Because you're a dope.'

'I nearly went, Ross. The last day you spoke to me. When *was* that? I rang my agent in America. She told me about this facility in Malibu. I said okay, I'll go. And then I'm suddenly on . . . Jesus, Ross, Talbot Street! And you're right – I mean, that in itself is a sign of how sick I am!'

She cries for, like, ten minutes without stopping. I just lean against the wall and stare at her, feeling absolutely nothing, except possibly a bit sorry for her. When she's finally all out of tears, I go, 'What if I could get you out of here?'

She looks up at me. Her face has been lifted so many times that her mascara has run down the back of her head.

She's there, 'Get me out of here? Do you mean now?'

I'm like, 'Yes, I mean now. If I could talk Sergeant McDumbfock out there into letting you off with a warning, would you go to that place – the one in, what, Malibu?'

She wipes her face with her two palms. 'I'd go now,' she goes. 'I'd take a flight to London and then an overnight to Los Angeles. I wouldn't even go home to pack.'

I just nod, playing it cool like Huggy, loving the power I suddenly have over her. I'm there, 'Okay, let's go, then.'

She stands up, although she's *in* shock? She's like, 'What?'

I stort heading for the door. 'Come on, we're going?'

'Where?'

'To the airport – isn't that what we agreed?'

'Are you saying . . . are you saying they're going to let me go?'

I'm like, 'Yeah,' and then I turn around and I tell her what the dude on the desk told me when I arrived. 'You paid thirty Ks for three one-pound bags of baby formula.'

She's there, 'What?'

She stops and she stands there in the doorway of the cell.

I'm there, 'You were ripped off. So it's not just plastic surgeons who see you coming. Now, come on – you've got a plane to catch.'

The old man walks up to the desk and tells the duty nurse that he's here to see his three beautiful grandsons.

'Or, as I call them, Ireland's future numbers ten, twelve and thirteen,' he goes.

He turns around to me then and he's there, 'As Hennessy here is my witness, this very day I went to see Mister Patrick Power Esquire of bookmaker fame and wagered one thousand euros of my hard-earned money that all three of the little fellows would play senior rugby for Ireland by the age of twenty-five.'

I look at Hennessy, except he just stares at me. He's probably remembering that the old man placed a very similar bet on me.

The nurse tells us to fire ahead.

I lead them down to the ward, then in we go. The old man – in fairness to him – melts when he sees the three of them through the glass. I'm standing behind him and after, like, ten seconds of silent staring, I hear him go, 'Stupid bloody man!' and I realize that he's crying. 'Pull yourself together, old chap!'

I put my hand on his shoulder and ask him if he's okay and he says he will be in a moment.

I look at Hennessy and it's just about the most awkward I've ever seen him look. He's clearly uncomfortable around men crying, what with him having no emotions himself, apart from anger, which I'm not sure is an emotion as such.

'Oh, Kicker,' the old man goes. 'They're beautiful. They're the most beautiful bloody well babies I've ever seen in my whole ridiculous life.'

Hennessy goes, 'Yeah, very nice. Very nice,' like he's been asked by a waiter what he thinks of the Cabernet Sauvignon.

'Ross,' the old man goes. 'I'm very, very proud of you. And I'm sure if your mother was in her proper health, she'd tell you the same thing herself!'

He knows, by the way, that she's gone into rehab in the States. She rang us both before she had to surrender her phone.

'Three little beauties,' he goes. 'Dear, oh, dear.'

We eventually step out of the ICU. The old man decides he's going to go downstairs to see Sorcha, and Hennessy takes the opportunity to go, 'You do that, Charlie. I want to have a little chat with Ross here.'

The old man chuckles, the word would have to be *fondly*?

He's there, 'A little parenting advice, I shouldn't wonder! No one can say your godfather doesn't take his role seriously – eh, Ross?'

The old man disappears into the lift. The second the doors close, Hennessy pins me up against the wall, one hand around my throat.

'Okay,' he goes, 'I'm going to ask you one last time . . .'

I'm like, 'What . . . the fock?'

'Do you know anything about my daughter's shop?'

'I already told you that I . . .'

He tightens his grip.

He's there, 'Shut up and listen. I said shut the fuck up and listen . . . Me and Lauren, we had a good day today.'

I'm like, 'Okay . . . I'm going to say . . . fair focks.'

'We sought and obtained a writ of *habeas corpus* in the High Court. Do you know what that means?'

'Er, remind me again?'

'The judge has given these sandwich cocksuckers seven days in which to provide full details of the alleged infraction. Time and date it happened. The exact nature of the human matter involved. Every. Fucking. Thing.'

'That's . . . good . . . It'd be nice to have . . . closure, I suppose.'

'The only time in six weeks when both Christian and Lauren were away from the shop at the same time was the afternoon when Lauren went into labour. And Lauren says Christian left you in charge.'

'He . . . he did . . . yeah.'

'And?'

'What . . . what do you mean by . . . *and*?'

He puts his other hand around my throat as well then and storts seriously squeezing the life out of my windpipe. He goes, 'Did you spit in someone's sandwich?'

254

I'm there, 'N . . .'

'What's that? I can't hear you too good.'

'N . . . N . . . No.'

'Are you fucking sure?'

'Y . . . Y . . . Yes.'

'Because if you're lying, I will know. I will fucking know within seven fucking days. And then I will come after you and I will kill you. With these hands. In much the way I'm doing it now. Except I won't let go.'

'I . . . I didn't . . . d . . . do it.'

'You're telling me that?'

'Y . . . Yes . . . It's the . . . It's the . . . truth.'

He suddenly releases his grip on me. 'Well,' he goes, 'we'll soon know.' He fixes his clothes, calls the lift, then steps into it. 'Tell Charlie I'll call him tomorrow,' he goes.

I stand there for five or ten minutes trying to get my breath and my composure back, then I decide to head down to Sorcha to say goodnight to her.

I take the stairs, roysh, rather than the lift and it's *on* the stairs that I end up running into JP.

I'm like, 'Hey, Dude.'

He's there, 'Hey, Ross.'

In his hand, I notice, he's got three baby-sized Ireland rugby jerseys. He notices me noticing them, if you know what I mean.

He's there, 'I just wanted to . . . it's a baby-warming present . . . to say congratulations. I was going to just leave them with the nurses.'

I'm suddenly wondering has something happened. It feels like it possibly has.

I'm like, 'Thanks, J Town.'

He hands the three little jerseys to me – they're focking great – then he goes to turn away.

I'm there, 'Pint?'

He looks at me, as unhappy as I've ever seen him, and I feel instantly bad.

He goes, 'I thought if I could convince myself that Ezra was mine, then that was all that mattered.'

I'm there, 'Dude, I'm sorry,' even though, officially, I don't know what actually happened. 'Did the real father just suddenly randomly turn up out of the blue or something?'

He doesn't answer me. He just smiles sadly and goes, 'The older he got, you know, the harder it would have been to keep up the pretence.'

I feel bad and I actually *mean* that?

'Dude,' I go, 'it'll happen for you one day. I'm talking about for real. And believe me, there's no focking feeling in the world like it.'

He nods.

I'm there, 'Come on. Sorcha would love to see you. Then we'll go and get mashed.'

Honor wants to know if she can hold one of the babies.

This is when Sorcha and the babies have been home, like, a day or two.

She's standing in the doorway of the nursery, twisting the ends of her hair while giving me the old bloodhound eyes.

She's there, 'Can I hold one?'

And there ends up being this moment of horrible silence when I'm thinking about what Sorcha said – about not *trusting* her? – and I end up going, 'Er, I've just put them down for their nap, Honor. Maybe later, yeah?'

And she says fine, although I suspect that she knows the score.

I'm there, 'The thing is, Honor, it's very rare that you manage to get all three of them to sleep at the exact same time. If one of them wakes up now and storts crying, then he'll wake the others and, well, your mother and I have had about three hours of sleep in the last three nights.'

She's like, 'Okay,' and, as she turns away from me, under her breath, she goes, 'I'm not a monster, you know?' and – I'm going to admit it – in that moment, my hort breaks. Because I'm a sucker for my daughter. I don't care what she's done.

'Honor,' I go, at the same time lifting little Jonathan out of his cradle. 'Here.'

Her face lights up. I know she plays people, but this seems actually *genuine*?

I hand him to her and she takes this tiny little bundle into her orms so carefully and so gently that you just want to take out your iPhone and film it.

'Is this Jonathan?' she whispers to me.

I'm there, 'Yeah, no, that's my little number ten.'

'He actually *looks* like a Jonathan?'

'Yeah? Make sure to keep saying that around your mother. She's got all sorts of ridiculous notions in relation to their names.'

She plants the softest, gentlest kiss on his little forehead, then hands him back to me and I'm thinking how there is an actual *nice* side to Honor?

'How long is that focking man going to be staying in our house?' she goes.

I'm there, 'Are you talking about Sorcha's old man?'

'Yeah.'

'I'm still hoping not permanently.'

'I hate him.'

I put little Jonathan back in his crib.

I go, 'Yeah, no, the man is no fan of mine, although you've probably picked up on that. He thinks Sorcha could have done better for herself.'

She's there, 'He keeps asking me questions.'

'What kind of questions?'

'Where did I get all the cages for the rats?'

'Tell him to fock off. In fact, tell him to fock off back to England.'

'That's what I did say.'

'Bankrupt wanker. Sticking his hooter into our family's business.'

'Then he keeps asking me how I managed to get the rats to the school.'

'Here, you're definitely leaving me out of it, though, are you?'

'What?'

'You're not going to tell him it was me.'

'No.'

'Because that'd be ammo to someone like him. He'd use that. Twist it.'

'Don't worry. I'm not going to say anything.'

'Thanks, Honor. Look, I know your old dear's giving you a hord time at the moment as well. But I'll keep being nice to you and buying you loads of stuff behind her back – just to even it out.'

She smiles at me, then throws her orms around my waist and goes, 'Thanks, Daddy,' and, as I lean down and kiss her on the top of my head, I allow myself a little smile and I think, Now *that*, ladies and gentleman, is how you parent!

She goes back to her bedroom and I tip downstairs. Sorcha and her old pair are in the kitchen – as is the sister. No one acknowledges me when I walk in, by the way.

Sorcha's old dear is telling Sorcha that she really should be lying down and Sorcha tells her that she's – oh my God – *not* an invalid. She goes, 'I'm capable of making myself a cup of tea.'

I'll tell you something – they know how to make themselves at home, the focking Lalors.

Sorcha's old dear is like, 'We must go out and get a Christmas tree!'

And her old man goes, 'And I'll take the decorations down from the attic. We'll do up the house just like we used to when you two were little girls!'

I'm thinking to myself, Yeah, remember whose gaff this is now. Here's a hint. It's not focking yours.

That's when I spot his shoes on the mat in front of the back door, where I usually throw my Dubes when I come home. Childish as it might make me seem, I end up losing it and I kick them across the floor of the kitchen and that's the first time that any of them even notices that I'm even in the room.

'Oh, sorry,' I go. 'I didn't see those things there.'

He just stares at me, obviously considering saying something, except in the end he decides not to. He's only here because of my good nature.

'Ross,' Sorcha goes, in a suddenly serious voice, 'my dad has given us a list of people. We should look at them later.'

I'm there, 'People? What kind of people?'

And that's when the atmosphere in the room tightens.

She goes, 'Psychiatrists, Ross. For Honor.'

I look at *him*. I swear to God, he's got the tiniest hint of a smile playing on his lips.

'Edmund worked for thirty years in family law,' Sorcha's old dear goes – she was focking divorcing him a week ago, remember. Now she's his number one fan again. 'He knows a lot of very good people.'

I'm like, 'No,' because I'm not having him thinking he can stort taking over. 'That all sounds a bit heavy.'

'It *is* heavy,' Sorcha goes. 'Oh my God, Ross, she let a plague of rats loose in her school. The school might even be closed permanently.'

'Well, I still say it's something we can work out between us – as in, within the family. And I'm talking about me, you and Honor.'

He has to say something then. 'The girl is deeply disturbed,' he goes. 'I've *seen* cases.'

I'm there, 'She's not deeply anything,' because I'm going to defend her if nobody else is.

'She told my dad to fock off this morning,' Sorcha goes.

That doesn't get the shocked response she possibly expected from me.

I'm there, 'What were the circumstances?'

He laughs – except *bitterly*?

'Oh,' he goes, 'you mean there *are* circumstances, in your view, in which it's fine for an eight-year-old girl to address her grandfather in that way?'

I'm there, 'If her grandfather was giving her a hord time, yeah. If he kept cross-examining her about shit that was none of his basic business.'

'She called him a focking bell-end as well,' the sister goes. 'And a dick with ears . . .'

Her old man silences her with a look, then he turns his attention back to me. He goes, 'Maybe *you* should have been asking some questions, hmmm?'

I'm there, 'Excuse me?'

'Well, how does a little girl of that age manage to breed an entire colony of rats without her father once looking in on her?'

'Sorcha didn't look in on her either.'

I feel bad for saying it. But it's true.

'Sorcha,' he goes, 'was pregnant with triplets and looking after another baby – *your* granddaughter, I believe. So what were you doing?'

I'm there, 'I wasn't doing anything.'

'Exactly! You weren't doing anything! Do you think either of my two girls could have raised – what? – a hundred rats in this house without my knowing it? No. Because, as a good and responsible father, I made it my business to *know* what my children were up to at all times.'

'Well,' I go, 'that's where you're wrong then, because I actually *did* know.'

The words are out of my mouth before I've had the chance to even think about them. I realize straight away that I've made a serious focking booboo here. I can even feel my face get hot. He tricked me into saying it. He knew exactly what he was doing. Focking lawyers.

'You *knew*?' it's Sorcha who goes.

The sister's like, 'Oh! My God!' with a humungous focking smile on her face. Her old dear tells her to stay out of it.

I'm just there, 'Yeah, no, look, I knew *some* things?' trying to limit the damage. 'I know you said she had to get rid of – what was it, Pippa? – and then all of her little babies. But Honor was sad – again, just thinking of her and trying to be a good father – so I said that she could keep them, as long as they stayed down in the coach house.'

Sorcha goes, 'You encouraged her to lie to me.'

'Look, when you have kids,' I go, 'you try to be their friend.'

He doesn't say a word. He just lets me dig a hole for myself.

'You knew she was breeding them?' Sorcha goes.

I'm there, 'No. No, I didn't. Not until later. I walked in there one day and the focking things were everywhere. I had no idea they could reproduce like that. And brothers and sisters as well. I mean, it's actually sick when you think about it, isn't it?'

No one seems to want to get into it. That bit doesn't seem to bother them one way or the other.

Sorcha goes, 'Ross, I'm going to ask you something, even though I'm terrified of what the answer might be . . .'

I'm there, 'Okay, ask away.'

'Did you help her bring those rats to the school?'

I can't lie to the girl.

I'm there, 'No,' thinking, Fock it, I might as well give it a try.

But she knows I'm lying. You don't need to own a Derby winner to know what horseshit smells like.

She goes, 'You did, didn't you?'

I'm there, 'Okay, yeah, I did. But in my defence, I'd have to point out that I was blackmailed.'

'Blackmailed?'

'Yes, blackmailed. She had shit on me, unfortunately.'

Sorcha keeps looking at her old pair, then back at me, in the hope that someone else in the room might explain to her what the fock is going on.

'What are you talking about?' she goes. 'What did she have on you?'

I'm there, 'I'd prefer not to say – as in, I don't want to get into it?'

Sorcha's old man laughs. He's obviously loving this.

Under pressure, I end up losing it with him. I'm like, 'Why don't you stay the fock out of it?'

Sorcha's old dear goes, 'Ross!'

The sister goes, 'Oh! My God!'

I'm there, 'Better still, why don't you fock off back to England?'

He looks at Sorcha. He's there, 'And this is the man you told me had changed?' and then he sort of, like, tuts to himself.

I'm like, 'I know what you're trying to do, which is get your feet under the table again and then try to break us up. But you won't succeed. And the reason you won't succeed is because we're too strong.'

'I want you to leave, Ross.'

It's, like, Sorcha who says it. Of course, I'm suddenly in shock.

I'm there, 'What? Leave where?'

'Leave here,' she goes. 'I don't want you in this house.'

'What are you saying? Jesus, Sorcha, we've just had triplets.'

'I know that!' she goes. 'And despite all of that, I still can't trust your word. Get out.'

'Where am I going to go?'

'I don't care where you go. I need some time and I need some space to think about what I'm going to do.'

Her old dear goes, 'Ross, you heard her,' and I'm looking around the kitchen, in shock at how quickly it all just happened.

'Okay,' I go, 'I'll give you space. But I want you to know, Sorcha, that I still love you and I always . . .'

'Out!' her old man shouts, like he's talking to a dog.

'Can I at least say goodbye to our babies?' I go.

He's there, 'No you can't. My daughter has just asked you to leave.'

I give him a serious filthy, then I walk out of the kitchen, pulling the door behind me.

Honor, it turns out, has been listening to the conversation from the top of the stairs.

She's like, 'Daddy, don't go!'

She comes running down the stairs.

I'm there, 'It's only for a couple of weeks until your mother sorts her head out and decides what she wants.'

She throws her orms around me. She goes, 'Daddy, take me with you! Don't leave me with *them*.'

Much as it breaks my hort, I peel her off me and I'm like, 'I'm sorry, Honor.'

Sorcha's old man opens the kitchen door to make sure I've gone. And Honor looks at him and goes, 'I focking hate you! I focking hate you!'

I'll go back to the old dear's gaff. That's what I decide to do. She's going to be in the States for a while, so I'll stay there for two or three days and maybe hopefully talk Sorcha around. It won't take long for her to realize that, compared to some of the shit she's forgiven me for in the past – sleeping with her sister, sleeping with her friends, sleeping with practically everyone she knows – this is actually small change.

He'll be twisting the knife, of course, telling her that this time she needs to take the hint and kick me to touch once and for all. In fact, I'm suddenly cursing myself for leaving, rather than staying in the gaff, where I could at least work on winning her around. Loads of, like, sorrowful looks. The Leinster training top that showcases my upper body. I'm not passing the buck here, but hopefully, in time, she'll see that the entire thing was Honor's fault.

I get as far as Westminster Road – I'm driving Sorcha's Nissan focking Leaf, by the way – and I think about turning back, when all of a sudden my phone rings and the little screen says, 'Out of area'.

I end up answering it anyway.

There ends up being, like, five seconds of silence before anything happens, then there's a click, then all this static and then I hear a voice that causes me to nearly drive into the path of an oncoming Subaru Forester.

It's Fionn.

'Ross,' he goes. 'Ross, can you hear me?'

I'm there, 'Fionn!' struggling with the wheel. 'Dude, what the fock? Have you been released?'

He's like, 'No,' and he sounds like shit – *and* on the point of tears. 'Ross, just listen. I don't have long. Ross, they're going to kill me.'

'Are we talking about the kidnappers?'

'Yes, we're talking about the kidnappers. They're desperate, Ross. They're talking about cutting their losses.'

'Shit'

'They told me an hour ago, it's not worth their while keeping me alive for another six months if they're not going to see any money.'

'Jesus!'

'Ross,' he goes, his voice suddenly melting, 'they were going to shoot me. They put the gun to my head.'

I go, 'Dude, just hang in there a little while longer. There's a dude called Fred Pfanning who's over there trying to negotiate your release.'

'He's been kidnapped, too, Ross.'

My body turns instantly cold. I'm like, 'What?'

He's there, 'The same crowd. They have him. They're trying to get ten million dollars out of that security firm he works for.'

In the background, I can hear a voice – a male voice – shouting angrily in African, telling him that he's saying too much or maybe just telling him to hurry the fock up.

Fionn goes, 'Ross, do something. Please.'

I'm there, 'Er, okay,' wondering what the dude has in mind.

He's like, 'Father Fehily said to me once, "If ever you're in trouble, just pick up the phone and ring Ross. He'll know what to do."'

I'm going to admit it, I'm surprised – bear in mind, I'm a complete focking dunderhead and always have been.

I'm like, 'Dude, did he genuinely say that?'

'He's not as stupid as people think,' Fionn goes. He's really crying now. 'That's what he said. Ross, please. Do something. They're saying they're only going to give me another forty-eight hours . . . Ross, you're my last hope . . . I don't want to die . . .'

The line goes suddenly dead.

Father Fehily was actually right. I *do* know what to do.

I ring Andrea and I ask her if she and Ewan are home. She says they are and I tell her I'm on my way. Then I ring Christian, Oisinn and JP and I tell them to drop whatever the fock they're doing and meet me in Fionn's old pair's gaff.

I drive straight there, my mind trying to work out what forty-eight hours is in terms of, like, days. According to my calculations, it's just over two.

JP and Oisinn are already at the gaff when I arrive. Christian pulls up ouside in his 2009 Toyota Camry just as I'm ringing the doorbell.

'What's this about?' he goes, as he comes crunching up the gravel.

He looks like shit, by the way. He obviously couldn't be orsed shaving anymore.

I'm like, 'All will be revealed in a minute.'

It's Ewan who answers the door. He asks exactly the same question as Christian – as in, what's this about?

I'm there, 'Can I come in?'

He opens the door and in we go, into the sitting room, where I catch the tail end of Andrea telling JP and Oisinn that they haven't heard from Fred Pfanning or that company of his for weeks now.

'That's because he's been kidnapped as well,' I go.

All eyes turn to me in shock.

'He's been what?' it's Ewan who goes.

I'm there, 'He's been kidnapped. By the same crew that's holding Fionn. Except they want ten mills for him.'

'But why haven't we been told about this?' Andrea goes.

Ewan's like, 'Because it does nothing to enhance the company's reputation as international security experts. That explains why they haven't been returning our calls.'

Andrea looks at me. She's like, 'Who told you he'd been kidnapped?'

I'm there, 'Fionn.'

Her jaw just drops. 'Fionn?' she goes. 'You mean, you spoke to him?'

I'm like, 'About half-an-hour ago.'

'How is he?' Ewan goes.

I'm there, 'He didn't sound great. He said this crowd that took him are at the end of their rope. They're giving him two and a half days.'

'And then what?' it's Oisinn who goes.

I don't answer, because I can't bring myself to say the actual words.

Andrea bursts into tears and Ewan goes to comfort her.

I'm there, 'I called you all here because I wanted to tell you that I'm going. I'm going to Ungung Ganga. Right now. I should have done it months ago. Now, I'm not putting pressure on the rest of you . . .'

'I'm coming with you,' Christian is the first one to go. He doesn't even need to think about it. 'You're not going out there on your own. I'm coming with you.'

JP just shrugs. He's like, 'Well, what have *I* got to lose now? Count me in.'

We all turn and look at Oisinn.

I go, 'Like I said, Dude, there's no pressure.'

Oisinn turns – looking solemn – and storts making his way to the door. And at first, I think, yeah, no, it's understandable him not wanting to go. It's going to be possibly dangerous.

But he's just like, 'What are we waiting for? Let's go and get him – and bring him home.'

8. A Few Collars More

I come back from the bor with a round of Sambucas and JP looks at me like I've just suggested we drink the contents of his granny's urostomy bag.

'Ross,' he goes, 'what I said was, "If we're heading to Africa, then maybe we should have got shots."'

I'm there, 'And?'

'Well, by shots, I meant . . .'

Oisinn grabs his, as does Christian, so JP has no choice but to get over whatever the fock's wrong with him and knock it back like the rest of us.

I get the sudden urge to say something before we do, though. In a weird way, it feels like we're back at school and I'm their captain again, leading them into battle.

I hold up my glass and I go, 'Here's to friendship. And here's to – hey, I'm going to have to say it – here's to rugby. Now let's go and find our friend. And let's get him home for Christmas.'

We knock back our drinks.

I'm kind of still buzzing on what Father Fehily told Fionn. If you're ever in trouble, ring Ross. He'll know what to do. Even his line about me not being as stupid as everyone thinks was an amazing thing to say.

It's no wonder my confidence is so unshakeable.

'Christian,' I go, 'it's your focking round. Get them in. What do we think – baby Guinnesses this time?'

We're at Heathrow Airport, I don't know if I mentioned.

Christian goes, 'Ross, they're going to be calling our flight any minute,' trying to wriggle out of it.

JP goes, 'And I still need to book us a hotel.' He's staring at his phone. He's obviously on the old Internet.

'What about this one?' he goes. 'The Sheraton Kampala?'

I'm there, 'That sounds alright. Does it have a gym?' Not that I'm going to focking use it.

'It's got a gym,' he goes. 'It's got a restaurant called the Paradise Club, which looks nice. And a bar called the Equator Lounge.'

'The Equator?' Oisinn goes, then shakes his head. 'You suddenly realize how far from home we're going to be when we step off that plane.'

I don't. I've no idea where the Equator is – or even *what* it is? It's probably better that way.

'Book that hotel,' I go. 'Christian, I'll room with you,' because Oisinn and JP snore like focking bears. 'Stick it on my old man's credit cord.'

JP's like, 'Really?'

'Yeah, fock him,' I go. 'He's good for it.'

'We're only staying there for one night. Then we'll hire a driver to take us to Mbale.'

'Sounds like a plan.'

There's suddenly an announcement. 'Your attention, please,' a woman's voice goes. 'British Airways is happy to announce that Flight BA812 to Entebbe Kampala is open and ready for boarding.'

I'm there, 'I just need to make a quick call,' and I whip out my phone.

'Ross,' JP goes, 'they're going to be calling our seat numbers any second.'

I'd forgotten how focking moany he can be when he goes away. He worries about everything.

I'm there, 'Yeah, do you mind if I just say goodbye to my wife and my daughter?' and then I feel instantly bad for saying it. 'Dude, I didn't mean . . . Look, I'll be two minutes, that's all.'

I find a quiet corner of the terminal – between a Dixons and a Caffè Nero – then I dial the number, hoping that it's *her* who actually answers?

He's not going to let her make that mistake, though. He knows I'd only worm my way back in. After, like, five rings, it ends up being his voice I hear.

He goes, 'Hello,' and he says it full of confidence, like he's the man of the house again.

I think about just hanging up, but then I think, fock him, so instead I go, 'I'd like to speak to Sorcha O'Carroll-Kelly, please,' at the same time trying to disguise my voice.

I try to do a Northern Ireland accent. I don't know why. He just laughs.

He's there, 'Nice try, Ross.'

I go, 'This isn't Ross. I'm ringing from, I don't know, Amnesty International or one of those . . .'

'Your number has come up on the little screen here. What do you want? We're all rather busy.'

'I want to speak to my wife.'

'She's feeding her children at the moment.'

Her children. It's like a knife in my ribs.

I'm there, 'Well, could you still go and get her. It's kind of important.'

'She doesn't want to speak to you,' he goes. 'I thought she made herself very clear on that point yesterday.'

'I'm going away.'

'Oh, good.'

'I just wanted to say goodbye. I'm off to Umbom Penanga.'

He's either never heard of it or he pretends that he hasn't.

He's like, 'Where?' and at the same time he's, like, *laughing?*

I'm there, 'It's definitely Umbom something. It's where Fionn was kidnapped. Me and the goys are heading over there to try to – I'm going to use the word – *rescue* him? Even though it could be dangerous.'

He gives me fock-all back, though, just silence.

'So I'm just ringing Sorcha,' I go, 'to let her know that I'm going to be away and not to worry about me . . .'

'I doubt she will.'

'And we'll maybe talk when I get back.'

'Are you finished?'

'Well, maybe you'd put Honor on the phone.'

'No, I won't. You're not a good influence on her.'

'Who the fock do you think you are to decide that?'

'Goodbye.'

He hangs up. I end up kicking the milk and sugar station in Caffè Nero out of pure frustration. That's when I notice I've got six or seven missed calls from JP and Christian and I realize that they've possibly already boarded?

It turns out they have. And I'm the last.

'Your seat was called ten minutes ago,' the bird at the gate tries to go – with a focking face on her as well.

She's in bits anyway.

She tears my boarding pass, then on I go, down the gangway and up to the door of the plane, where two air hostesses try to guilt-trip me in the same way.

'You're delaying the entire flight,' one of them – who happens to be a complete focking ride – goes. 'We were about to take your bags out of the hold.'

I'm there, 'Kaya Scodelario.'

'I beg your pardon.'

'That's who you're a ringer for. Don't worry, it's a compliment.'

'Please take your seat.'

I walk down the plane towards the goys. We're sitting in the middle bank of seats – the four of us together.

One or two people tut and shake their heads when they see me coming, presumably pissed off with me for holding up the entire flight.

'Give over that tutting,' I tell one dude, 'or I'll fock you out the window as soon as we're airborne.'

JP goes, 'Well done, Ross. Way to make an entrance.'

At least it means I get an aisle seat. I sit down and buckle myself in. I've got Christian next to me, then it's JP, and then Oisinn, who, I notice, is resting his forehead on the back of the seat in front of him. He hates flying. His face is already green and we're not even on the runway yet.

Christian asks me how Sorcha reacted to the whole me going away and leaving her with three newborn babies thing. It's nice of him to ask. I haven't told him or any of the goys that she's focked me out.

I'm there, 'Yeah, no, she was surprisingly cool about it.'

He goes, 'Lauren didn't give a fock one way or the other.'

'Dude, I'm sure that's not true.'

'I rang from Dublin Airport. I said, "We're going to Africa to try to find Fionn." Know what she said? It was, "Do whatever you want, Christian. I'm done talking to you." Something like that.'

'She's got a lot on her plate.'

'She cares more about that sandwich shop than she does about me.'

I think about what Hennessy said – seven days to substantiate the chorge – and I hope to fock that I'm still out of the country when that particular shit-storm breaks.

I'm there, 'Yeah, no, she certainly seems to be obsessed. Let it go has been my point all along, if you remember.'

He nods.

'So how are you feeling?' I go.

He's there, 'About this? I don't know. Nervous.'

'Personally, I'm excited.'

'Really?'

'Dude, look at us. All of us. Back together. It's like old times.'

I look down and I notice that JP has kicked off his Dubes. In the old days, I'd have waited until he was asleep, then taken a shit in one of them.

Not on this trip, though. It's a different vibe. You could say that this is business.

The engines roar, then we're hurtling down the runway and then, all of a sudden, we're in the air. Oisinn vomits in his own lap. And, at the top of my voice, I shout, 'Hang on, Fionn! The Castlerock team of '99 is coming to get you!'

Christian nearly falls off the bed when he sees me. He's like, 'What the fock are you wearing?'

He's laughing for the first time in I don't know how long. I'm saying it's nice.

'It's a Lions jersey,' I go. 'They're playing Australia next year, in case you've forgotten.'

He's there, 'And what about the trousers?'

They're Gulf War II Desert Camo, which is in at the moment.

I go, 'I actually got them in that Hugo Boss store in Heathrow.'

He bursts out laughing again. I just let him. Like I said, it's nice to see him actually happy again.

There's a knock on the door. I check through the little spyhole and it ends up being Oisinn and JP, so I open it.

I'm like, 'Hey, goys, how did you sleep?'

Oisinn goes, 'Not great – focking air-conditioning,' and then he cops the trousers and goes, 'What the fock?'

I'm like, 'Yeah, whatever, I've already been through it. Camo is in at the moment. Plus, they're practical.'

'But they're *desert* camouflage. Where *we're* going, it's all jungle. You're going to stick out like a focking pork chop in a mosque.'

I'm like, 'Whatever.'

JP, I swear to fock, is *limping*. He's such a focking drama queen.

I'm there, 'Are you okay there, Dude.'

He's not a contented temporary tent dweller.

He's like, 'I can't believe you took a shit in my shoe.'

I'm there, 'Never leave your Dubes unattended. That saying is as old as the hills.'

'What are we, back in Irish college?'

'Hey, it's not my fault if you've forgotten the rules.'

'In front of a plane full of focking people as well.'

'Hey, I took it into the jacks to do it, in my defence.'

'I'm saying I put my foot in it in front of a plane full of people!'

'Yeah, no, that's why it was funny.'

'It wasn't funny.'

'Let's agree to differ on that point. What I'm saying now is that you've got to get over it. You cleaned your shoe out, didn't you?'

'Yeah.'

'And I gave you a fresh pair of socks.'

'That's not the point.'

'It is the point. Jesus, we've all shat in each other's shoes over the years. I've never seen anyone take it so badly, though – and that includes that limp that you're walking around with. It's focking ridiculous. You need to possibly grow up.'

He shakes his head. He's like, 'Okay, let's change the subject before I do something I regret.'

Oisinn goes, 'I've managed to get us a driver to take us to Mbale.'

Oisinn has always been a good logistics man.

I'm there, 'Fair focks. It's good to see someone's doing something other than having a focking moan.'

He goes, 'The hotel arranged it. It's a local dude called Lloyd. It's twenty-five dollars each – that's obviously US.'

'Lloyd,' I go. 'He sounds like a good goy.'

'He's downstairs now. And I've booked us into a hotel in Mbale. The Regency. It doesn't look much, but it's supposedly safe.'

I go, 'Okay, what are we waiting for?'

We tip down to the lobby, where we meet this Lloyd character, who ends up being a lot younger than I expected – twenty, maybe twenty-one – and a ringer for a young Will Smith when he was in the *Fresh Prince*.

He's one of those dudes who's always laughing and when he cops my trousers he can't focking stop. He keeps saying shit to himself in African, then giggling and shaking his head.

'Mbale?' Oisinn goes.

And Lloyd nods and goes, 'Mbale,' and then he has another look at my trousers and bursts out laughing again.

We follow him outside to his cor, which turns out to be a white Volvo Estate, I'm presuming from the 1970s – no hub caps, windows caked in mud, leopard-skin rug on the dash.

'Shotgun,' I go, then I climb into the front-passenger seat.

Christian, Oisinn and JP hop into the back, while Lloyd throws our bags into the boot.

It's, like, half-eight in the morning when we set off.

'How long?' I go. I say it in English, but with a foreign-sounding accent – the way you do when you're talking to, like, Spanish people or French people or whatever other countries there are.

'Three hours,' he goes. 'Little more.'

I turn around to the goys and I smile, delighted with myself for being able to communicate across the old language barrier.

I'm amazing in a lot of ways.

The Volvo pulls out of the grounds of the hotel and through the grimy, shit-covered windows of Lloyd's cor, Africa slowly reveals itself to us.

It smells of pipe tobacco and overripe fruit and smelly feet and burning tyres. And there's noises you never hear at home – parrots squawking in the trees and cor horns sounding the entire time.

The four of us sit there, silently taking it all in. Trees with things growing in them that might be coconuts. A man walks past us with a donkey. A boy of no more than six tries to sell us a monkey through the window. Then a little further on there's a woman who could be Beyoncé's sister carrying a massive basket of mangos literally on her head. There's a camel – at least it looks like a camel – dead and decomposing on the side of the road, its ribcage sticking out like part of a ship that's, I don't know, run aground. A man is sitting on a chair and having his hair cut – I swear to fock – in the middle of the street. A gang of children – black, and I'm saying that just as a statement of fact – run after the cor. In their bare feet, they chase us for about a mile.

It's kind of like Pornell Street, except a more *extreme* case?

After about fifteen minutes, the road turns into basically a dust-track with humungous potholes that you have to drive around, otherwise you'd be swallowed up and never seen again.

We're all too busy taking it all in to even say anything. It's Christian who eventually speaks first.

'So,' he goes, 'what happens when we get to Mbale?'

I'm there, 'We stort asking questions. And demanding answers, knocking focking heads together where necessary.'

And Christian stares out the window and goes, 'I don't know if it's just me. But I have a bad feeling about this.'

If you asked me to sum up Mbale in one word, that word would have to be total focking shithole. I know Fionn was a fan of the place – he supposedly raved about it in his travel blog, which I never read – but you'd have to wonder what the fock he was looking at.

The smiles on the faces of the children. I remember him

mentioning those when he was home. That'd be typical of him. Has to see the focking good in everything.

Again, there's no actual roads – that's obviously a thing in this country – just mud tracks covered in this, like, reddish-brown dust, which gets into your eyes and blinds you when the wind blows. The main drag – *their* O'Connell Street, if you want to call it that – is all, like, single-storey buildings, painted maybe twenty years ago in basic, paint-box colours, which have faded in the sun. Men on motorbikes that look way too small for them buzz past and some-times they slap the bonnets of cors that went out of production in the 1980s and the drivers have an argument, presumably about which of them is the worst driver on the road.

The streets are, like, teeming with people – just take it for granted that everyone is black, because it'll save me having to constantly say it – all just walking around without having anywhere specific to go.

An old man with hair like steel wool and a goatie and tiny teeth but humungous gums storts shouting something at me in African – possibly about my famous trousers – then he follows us for about fifty yords, hammering his point home, whatever his point even is. There's a focking cow with horns as long as my orms tied up out-side the local phormacy, like you'd see a dog tethered outside – I don't know – the focking Tesco Express in Donnybrook. And then there's a woman, who's maybe in her sixties, standing outside the launderette with just a vacant look in her eyes, wearing a yellow sar-ong around her waist and a yellow sort of, like, turban thing on her head and – I shit you not – nothing else. Her tooters are out for everyone to see and it's hord to describe how they look – it's like someone took a pair of brown tights and dropped a snooker ball down each leg. I stare at her for ages until Oisinn gives me a nudge and asks me what the fock is the plan.

I go, 'What do you mean? To keep doing what we're doing.'

He's there, 'What, you mean going from shop to shop, showing people pictures of Fionn on our phones and going, "Haff . . . You . . . Seen . . . Thees . . . Man?" at the top of our voices?'

'Have you got any better ideas?'

'No.'

275

'Then just trust me. Here, did you see the paw patties on your one back there?'

'I did, yeah.'

'They don't seem to mind, do they? Walking around with them out. We seem to have been the only ones who were actually scoping her.'

'They have different attitudes towards nudity. It's a cultural thing. I mean, that's what I'm presuming.'

'Well, they weren't great, it has to be said. But they're still worth a look. To me, they're always worth a look – that might be a cultural thing as well.'

He brings up my old dear then – seeing as we're on the subject of sixty-year-old women with tits like Chiquitas.

He goes, 'I hear she's gone into rehab.'

I'm there, 'Who told you that?'

'I just heard.'

'Yeah, no, she's gone to the States. There's a place in Malibu. Second Chances or Second Helpings or whatever the fock.'

'Dude, look, I'm . . .'

'You don't have to say it.'

'Well, I'm going to focking say it. I should have said it to you before and I don't want to – I don't know – die focking suddenly without having said it to you. I'm sorry. I'm sorry for, well, disrespecting you and putting our friendship second. I'm sorry for introducing your mother to – Jesus – that stuff . . .'

'Dude, forget it. It's in the past. Move on.'

He stops suddenly and sticks out his hand, presumably for me to shake it, which I do, even though it's unneccesary. Then he reels me in for a chest bump and a hug and – this is the lovely thing about rugby – that's us suddenly square and what happened between my friend and my old dear is instantly forgotten, although you can be sure I'll still bring it up from time to time, just to remind them how sick and focking depraved the entire thing was.

I spot JP and Christian at the bottom of the road. They're just, like, standing there, staring at something.

'Come on,' I go, 'let's see what these two benders are up to,' and we tip down to them.

I'm there, 'Any leads?' but neither of them answers me.

JP goes, 'Look,' and he nods at this, again, single-storey building, which looks newer than every other building on this street – and there's a reason for that. 'It's the school where Fionn taught. It's the school that Fionn helped to build.'

I suddenly feel unbelievably proud of him.

It's behind an eight-foot-high fence topped with razor wire. The windows are all barred and the doors are all chained.

'It's closed,' Christian goes.

I'm there, 'Yeah, no, I'm wondering is it a holy day.'

'It looks like it's closed permanently,' he goes. 'The crowd who built it obviously pulled out. I suppose if they can't guarantee the safety of the staff . . .'

I look at JP.

'So,' I go, 'anything to report?'

He's there, 'No – and I'm beginning to wonder are we just wasting our time?'

'You're saying no one remembers him?'

'Loads of people remember him, Ross. But no one knows what happened to him. I mean, we're walking up to complete focking strangers – what are we expecting them to say? "It's funny you should ask about him – he's been tied up in my basement for the last six months." I just think we're wasting our time.'

'Well, I don't,' I go. 'And that's a genuine belief of mine.'

He's there, 'I can't believe we travelled all this way without a focking plan.'

He kicks the ground, sending up a cloud of red dust. Then he just sits down on the dirty ground with his back to the school fence – like Honor when she's sulking.

I give the other two a look, as if to say, Leave this to the Rossmeister.

'I'll tell you what,' I go, 'let's swap portners. Oisinn and Christian, you do that street up there and we'll do this one over here. And,

Oisinn, make sure to bring Christian up there to see the auld one with the lob lollies – tell him what they're like.'

'They're not great,' he goes.

'Yeah, no, they're not great, but they're definitely worth a look – isn't that what we agreed?'

Oisinn nods, then off the two of them go. I sit down next to JP, with my back – like his – against the fence.

The dude just shakes his head. 'Like, what the fock are we doing here?' he goes. 'As a matter of fact, what the fock in general?'

I'm like, 'We're here to find our friend and to bring him home.'

'And you really think we're going to find him?'

'Yes, I do. I actually think we're going to find him today. And do you know why?'

'Why?'

'Because Father Fehily is going to lead us to him. He's watching over us.'

JP laughs. He goes, 'You say that with such, I don't know, certainty.'

I'm there, 'Hey, you're the most religious out of all of us. Don't tell me you don't believe he's up there guiding us.'

'I do . . . I mean, I do sometimes.'

I put my orm around his shoulder. I don't care how it looks. I'm there, 'Do you remember that time we played Pres Cork in a friendly?'

He laughs. He already knows where this is going.

I'm there, 'They were kicking the shit out of us – do you remember?'

He's like, 'Of course I remember.'

'Every area of the field. Half-time comes and Fehily just says one thing: 'To quote a famous American General: "They are in front of us and they are behind us. We are flanked on both sides by an enemy that outnumbers us by thirty to one. The bastards can't get away from us now!"''

He laughs, in fairness to him.

I'm there, 'It's one of my favourite of all his quotes.'

JP shakes his head. He goes, 'How the fock did we win that match? I mean, seriously, how did we win it?'

I'm there, 'A small thing called belief.'

I stand up and hold out my hand. He grabs it and I pull him to his feet.

'Come on,' I go, 'let's keep knocking on doors.'

'What is?'

The dude behind the counter grabs the crest of my Lions jersey and stares at it.

He goes, 'Is Manchester?'

I'm there, 'No, no – it's the Lions . . . Li . . . ons . . . They're a rugby team.'

He looks at me blankly. This is in, like, a mobile phone shop. Every second shop in Mbale seems to be a mobile phone shop. Like I said, in a lot of ways it's Pornell Street.

'Haff . . . you . . . seen . . . thees . . . man?' I go.

I show him the picture of Fionn on my phone. He looks at it, turns down his lower lip and shakes his head. He's obsessed with my jersey, though.

'You give me,' he goes, grabbing a fistful of it. 'Is gift.'

I'm there, 'I will in my focking hole give it to you. Are you definitely sure . . . you've never seen . . . thees man?'

'Robin van Persie,' he goes.

I'm like, 'Excuse me?'

'Robin van Persie. Paul Scholes. Nemanja Vidić.'

I turn around to JP. I'm there, 'Do you know what the fock he's talking about?'

He goes, 'No, not a clue. It think it's African.'

I'm like, 'Focking gobbledygook.'

The dude goes, 'Patrice Evra. Rio Ferdinand.'

I'm there, 'We can't . . . understand you!'

He goes, 'Javier Hernandez. Darren Fletcher.'

I'm like, 'I'm sorry . . . We haff . . . to go!' and we step out of the shop, back out onto the street.

'Waste of focking time,' I go.

That's when I hear the sudden screech of tyres, which doesn't strike me as particularly odd at first.

'We need to buy a phrasebook,' JP goes.

And I turn my head just in time to see a fist come sailing past my ear and hit me square on the temple.

I haven't been hit so hord since the night I was focked out of Flannery's in Limerick for heckling Ian Keatley on the TV.

My legs buckle and I go down like a detonated building. My hands are still by my side when my face hits the dirt. I don't get the chance to even turn around to find out what the fock is going on. There's suddenly, like, a knee between my shoulder blades and someone is pulling my two orms behind my back – really focking painfully – and cuffing my actual wrists together.

There's a lot of shouting – it's all in African – and I turn my head to the right and I notice that JP is pinned to the ground beside me, his face screwed up, like he's in severe pain. There's two, maybe three dudes on top of him. Their faces are covered with scorves – one of them, I notice, is Burberry print, probably fake – with just a little slit for their eyes. One of them is wearing heavy boots, another tracksuit bottoms with flip-flops, and that's all I end up seeing, because my neck is suddenly snapped back and a black hood is pulled down over my head, casting everything into sudden darkness.

I hear JP groaning in pain and then I'm lifted by three, maybe four, sets of hands and I'm carried for what seems like ages, but probably actually isn't. Then I hear what sounds like a van door slide open and I'm literally thrown inside, my forehead smacking off what I'm guessing is a spare tyre.

There are voices in the back of the van.

'Ross?' one of them goes. 'Is that you?'

It's Christian.

'Ross?'

And Oisinn.

I'm like, 'Goys, are you alright?'

Neither of them answers. Oisinn just goes, 'Dude, what the fock is going on?' and then someone shouts something in African – angry – and I'm punched again, this time on the back of the neck.

JP is thrown in on top of me, kicking and screaming. He's going, 'You mroke my heesh,' meaning presumably that they broke his teeth. 'You mroke my hocking heesh, you hocking . . .' and then he's suddenly silenced by three or four blows from what I'm guessing is the butt of a rifle.

The van storts and none of us says anything as it speeds off through the village with men's voices shouting and cheering. The four of us just lie there, all trussed up in a pile, as the van hurtles along at, like, a hundred and fifty miles an hour.

We seem to hit every focking pothole between Mbale and wherever the fock we're going and it crosses my mind that if we crash, or if the van just, like, turns over, we'd be dead, all of us. There'd be no focking walking away.

We drive for what seems like two hours, but is probably much less, then the van comes to a halt and the door slides open and there's all this, like, excited talk between the men and I even hear high-fives.

Someone grabs me by the legs and pulls me out of the van and my face smashes off the ground again.

I'm like, 'Focking take it easy!'

Then I hear a voice in English go, '*You* fucking take it easy!' and I'm kicked in the stomach before I get a chance to even flex.

I'm dragged to my feet, then my head is pushed down and I'm morched quickly across what I'm guessing is a courtyord. I can hear the others being pushed forward behind me.

A heavy-sounding metal door opens, then we're pushed inside, along what feels like possibly a passageway, then we're guided down two flights of stone steps. Then another metal door opens.

Someone behind me snaps the cuffs off me, freeing my hands, then I'm pushed forward into what I suspect is some kind of dungeon. The others – we're talking JP, then Christian, then Oisinn – are pushed in behind me.

I hear more shouting – again, African – then feet shuffling out of the room, then the steel door slamming and it's only then that I feel safe enough to pull the hood off my head.

We're in, like, a dungeon, twenty feet by twenty feet, with high, black, stone walls. It's hot and muggy and it smells like a focking toilet. The only light in the room comes from a small vent in the ceiling maybe thirty feet above our heads. There's, like, water trickling down one of the walls, which I'm presuming accounts for the smell of unflushed toilet. There's a mattress on the ground in one corner.

In another corner is what looks like a sack of some sort. Except then it suddenly moves and I can make out an orm, two orms, two legs and I realize that it's, like, an actual person, just sitting curled up in the – I think it's a word – *fecal* position?

'Who's that?' I go.

A head pops up and I see a pair of glasses and a line of teeth where his mouth has dropped open in, like, pretty much *surprise*?

He's like, 'Ross?'

My hort literally flips. The others take off their hoods and we find ourselves staring in shock – but happy shock – at a very pale and half-storved-looking Fionn.

'Are you real?' Fionn goes, properly pawing at my face.

I'm like, 'Jesus Christ, Fionn,' even though at the same time I'm laughing. 'Yes, I'm real!'

He's studying my face like he's about to throw the lips on me.

'You don't understand,' he goes. 'I've dreamt this – this exact scene – so many times. And then I always . . . I always wake up.'

'Well, this time it's real,' I go and I throw my orms around him.

I'm not ready for how thin he suddenly is. He's got shoulder blades like a Chinese gymnast's tits.

'For fock's sake,' I go, 'have they even been feeding you?'

He's there, 'The food isn't great,' as Christian, JP and Oisinn take their turn in hugging this sad bag of bones that used to be one of the most exciting players in Leinster schools rugby.

They're all going, 'It's good to see you, Dude! It's good to see you!'

And Fionn goes, 'I knew you'd come for me. I knew you'd find me.'

He's shivering cold, I notice, even though it's like a focking sweat box in here. That'd be the lack of food.

I'm like, 'Dude, are you saying you've spent the last six months in this focking room?'

He nods.

He's got a Band Aid wrapped around the bridge of his glasses, holding them together.

I want to focking deck someone.

'Five months, three weeks and four days,' he goes, then he nods at the wall next to the mattress. 'I've been marking the days off with a piece of flint.'

I'm there, 'What do you do all day? I'm presuming they're throwing you the odd book?'

Fionn without books is like me without sex. It's the mental equivalent of blue balls.

He goes, 'No, but I've spent the time trying to stay physically, psychologically and even intellectually strong. I walk three times a day. From corner to corner. Two kilometres in the morning. Two in the afternoon. Two in the evening. Then I set myself little mental challenges. I name all the elements in the periodic table based on their atomic numbers, electron configurations and recurring chemical properties. Then I arrange the ninety-eight naturally existing elements in alphabetical order using their chemical names. Then I separate all of the elements into metals, metalloids and non-metals, again using their chemical names, but this time I tabulate them in reverse alphabetical order . . .'

I suddenly see red. I take a run at the heavy steel door that we came through and I kick it hord.

'You fockers!' I shout. 'You've turned him into a gibbering focking imbecile. You focking . . . focks!'

'Mastards hocked out me hocking heesh,' JP goes.

I turn around and I look at him in the, I don't know, fading light. He's right. All of his front teeth are missing. And that's when my relief at finding Fionn still alive gives way to the sudden realization that we're now in exactly the same boat.

I'm there, 'Okay, we need to find a way to escape,' and I stort patting the walls, expecting – I know it sounds ridiculous – but one of the bricks to be a lever that opens up a secret passageway.

I possibly play too many computer games.

Fionn goes, 'Ross, what do you think is out there, beyond these walls?'

I'm there, 'I don't focking know.'

'If we made it out of here and we got to, say, the nearest village, who could we trust?'

'Again, I don't know. What point are you trying to make?'

It's Oisinn who answers for him.

'He's saying these walls aren't our prison,' he goes. 'Uganda is our prison.'

He goes over to Fionn's mattress and sits down on it, his back to the wall. A few seconds later, Christian joins him.

'So what's happening at home?' Fionn goes. 'I'm dying to hear news.'

'It looks like Leinster are out of the Heineken Cup,' I go.

He's like, 'What? But it's only December.'

'Well, Clermont Auvergne did us home *and* away. And, yeah, Sorcha had triplets!'

He's there, 'Triplets?' because he wouldn't have known she was even pregnant. 'Are they . . .'

'Mine? Yeah, no, definitely.'

'Yeah, I was going to say are they boys or girls?'

'Oh, yeah, they're boys – all of them.'

'Triplets. My God. What are their names?'

'Brian, Jonathan and Leo are what we're going with for now, although that could have possibly changed by the time we get home.'

Fionn turns to JP then. 'And Shoshanna?' he goes. 'Did she have . . .'

'Heah,' JP goes, 'mut mit's mot mime.'

'He's saying it's not his,' I go – I don't know why *I'm* the one translating. 'The baby ended up being – I hope it's okay to say this, JP – but black as those focking walls there.'

284

Fionn's there, 'Oh,' struggling to take it in. 'And Christian, what about Lauren? She was due.'

'A little boy,' Christian goes. 'Oliver Fionn . . .'

Fionn's in obvious shock. He's like, 'Oliver . . .'

'Fionn,' Christian goes. 'We named him after you.'

JP's there, 'Erryone's meen ho hurried habout hoo.'

'Everyone's been so worried about you,' I go. 'He's saying that everyone's been so worried about you. It's true. You've been in all the papers. *The Late Late* did a whole thing. Blah, blah, blah.'

'What about Jenny?' Fionn goes. 'Is she okay? I mean, how's she bearing up?'

'Er, yeah, no, she's fine,' I go, because we all agreed it was best not to tell him about her having a basic meltdown. 'As a matter of fact, she organized a table quiz for you.'

He's there, 'A table quiz?'

'A focking table quiz. And you'd have been proud of her if you'd heard some of the questions. Real mind-benders, weren't they, Ois?'

Oisinn goes, 'Er, yeah, definitely.'

'What's the capital of this? What's the capital of that?'

Fionn has a little smile to himself. He's there, 'I knew she'd be working for my release. She's great.'

None of us knows where to look.

He goes, 'The morning I was taken, we were actually lying in bed talking about maybe getting engaged.'

I'm there, 'I'd, er, keep my options open, Dude, if I was you.'

'What do you mean?'

'I'm just making the point that you're going to be getting a lot of sympathy sex when you go home. Birds who wouldn't have looked focking twice at you in the past because of your glasses and whatever else. You're going to be suddenly hot. It's a limited window is all I'm saying. Oh, and the other major news from home is that my old dear gave Oisinn there the flick. She caught him lashing Sorcha's sister out of it. Up to his focking nuts in her, he was. So the big so-called romance is over. Isn't that right, Big O?'

Oisinn can be a sore loser. He tries to straight away change the subject.

'What are they like?' he goes, meaning presumably our kidnappers. 'I mean, who even are they?'

'They're just criminals,' Fionn goes with a shrug. 'I mean, that was a relief finding that out. I was worried they might have been, you know, religious fanatics.'

I spot something out of the corner of my eye. Something scuttling across the floor.

'Jesus Christ,' I go. 'Was that a focking mouse?'

Fionn laughs. He's there, 'It was a cockroach. Although there *are* mice as well.'

I'm there, 'Mice and cockroaches?'

'And lizards. The floor comes alive at night. You get used to it.'

He sits down on the hord ground. He makes a face like it causes him pain. 'Ooow,' he goes. 'I can't tell you how sore it is to sit down when you've no fat on your arse.'

JP goes, 'How hany o hem hare her?'

'He's saying how many of them are there?' I go. 'I'm presuming he means how many kidnappers rather than cockroaches and mice?'

Fionn's there, 'About ten altogether. But they come and go. I've got nicknames for them all. The leader is a guy – I call him Julius. He's seriously unstable. Laughing and joking one minute, then sticking a gun barrel in your mouth the next and telling you to suck it.'

'What?'

'Yeah. He's got good English. Like, he's educated. He told me he went to university in England, which I actually believe. And he chews khat pretty much all the time.'

'What the fock is khat?'

'Oh, it's a plant. Like tobacco, but stronger. You chew it and it's like cocaine. And actually, yeah, that probably explains the mood swings.'

Oisinn goes, 'And what about the others?'

Fionn's there, 'The two I see the most – they're always in the house – are Benjamin and Rolly. Again, they're just names I made up. And those two are just . . . I hate using this word, but they're animals.'

I'm like, 'Does one of them wear flip-flops?'

'Yeah, that's the one I call Rolly.'

'I'm pretty sure that's the dude who decked me. It was some focking punch. I think, to be fair, even BJ Botha would have gone down to that one.'

'There's an older guy. I call him Ibrahim – he's maybe in his sixties. I don't know what his role is. I know he cooks for them. I think he just keeps the house. And then there's a woman . . .'

I'm there, 'A woman?' suddenly interested.

In some ways, I suppose, I'll never change.

'I call her Forest,' he goes, 'because she looks like Forest Whitaker.'

We all laugh.

I'm there. 'Yeah, no, Jenny mentioned her when she told us about the day you were taken. She sounds like a complete focking dog.'

'I shouldn't be unkind,' he goes. 'She does look like Forest Whitaker, though. You'll see that for yourselves. She never smiles. I think she may have English. Or at least she understands it. I've never heard her speak, though. Then there's various others – mostly just boys who hang around the house. I think I'm more frightened of them than I am of Julius or Rolly or Benjamin . . .'

Christian goes, 'Scared? Why?'

'They're, like, eight, nine years old. They've got guns and they're high all the time.'

He's just described my son's friends back in his primary school days.

He goes, 'To Julius and the others, I'm an investment. I mean, I'm of some worth. But these kids – I think they actually *pay* them in khat – they're so off their heads, they could pull the trigger and not realize they'd done it.'

A scream suddenly pierces the air. A man's scream. It's, like, *blood*-curdling?

JP's there, 'Mot ha huck hoz hat?'

'It's Fred,' Fionn goes, meaning presumably Fred Pfanning. 'Benjamin and Rolly sometimes torture him. They do it just for sport.'

I suddenly have difficulty swallowing. I don't know how the

others feel, but what I'm thinking is, What the fock have I walked myself into here?

It's, like, the early hours of the morning when the door suddenly swings opens with a loud screech of metal, sending a beam of light shooting across the floor of the cell to the wall opposite, where I'm sitting and being eaten slowly alive by bugs.

Two boys walk in. And Fionn was right – they *are* boys? We're talking not that much older than Honor. They're holding AK-47s – focking *actual* ones? – and, yeah, it does occur to me that, even though my daughter can sometimes be a bitch, there's always someone else's kids who are worse than yours.

I'm kind of patting myself on the back when two more kids enter – these ones unormed – each dragging a mattress behind him. They dump them in the middle of the floor, then they go outside and drag in two more.

One of the boys who *has* a gun points at me and makes this noise with his mouth. It's like, 'Tat-tat-tat . . . Tat-tat-tat . . . Tat-tat-tat . . .' and I can tell he's imagining what it would be like to shoot me.

I'm going to be honest, roysh, I'm focking kacking it.

Then a man appears in the doorway behind him and hits him the most unbelievable slap across the back of the head, and, as the kid falls to the ground, all I can think is, I hope he has the focking safety catch on. The man roars something and the kid scuttles out of the room, as do the others, leaving just him and us.

The man goes, 'Good evening, gentlemen. You are very welcome. I have here beds for you.'

It's obviously Julius – or the dude that Fionn calls Julius. In other words, the leader. He's not much older than we are – at a guess, roysh, I'd say mid-thirties? – and he's built like a dumpster. He's black, roysh, and when I say black I don't mean Barack Obama black. He's, like, black-black – we're talking so black he's nearly blue. He's also, like, totally bald, or possibly just shaven-headed, and he's got all this, like, scorring on his face – a bit like Seal, except it's all down his left cheek and his neck, like he was, I don't know, scalded with water when he was, like, a *baby* or some shit?

288

Oh, and he's wearing two bullet belts across his chest – left shoulder to right hip and right shoulder to left hip.

'My good friend,' he goes, 'who works in Mbale, he phone me today and he say there are men in the village asking about this missing Irish. I say, do they bring fucking money with them? He say, no, they say they are here to rescue him.'

He laughs like it's the most hilarious thing he's ever heard. It was actually *me* telling people that? Probably stupidly. He obviously knows it was me as well because, when he stops laughing, he suddenly fixes me with a stare.

He goes, 'So you are here to bring your friend home, yes?'

He takes what looks like a little freezer bag out of his pocket and it's stuffed with, like, green leaves. He pulls some out – like it's popcorn at the cinema – and he shoves them into his mouth.

I go, 'Yeah, we are actually,' deciding that I'm not going to let him see how scared I am.

He stares at me for ages, chewing like a focking giraffe. Then he's like, 'So how does the rescue go so far?' and then he laughs again, in long, machine-gun focking bursts.

Christian stands up and goes, 'I need the toilet.'

I think I mentioned already that he's rotten these days. He's already let one or two rip in here that'd curdle focking milk.

Julius looks at Fionn. 'Tell your friend,' he goes. 'Where do we do our toilet?'

Fionn's there, 'In that thing there,' and he points at this – I swear to fock – plastic bucket, one of those big ones they use for the mayonnaise and the coleslaw in the likes of O'Brien's.

'I'm not going in that,' Christian goes.

Julius is like, 'Then you don't go at all. And perhaps you burst in your fucking sleep, yes?'

His language is terrible. I know that makes me possibly a hypocrite.

'Sleeping on the floor and shitting in a bucket,' I go, still putting a brave face on shit. 'I always imagined this is what boarding in Clongowes must be like.'

At least Oisinn laughs. But that's when Julius's mood takes a sudden turn for the worse.

He's like, 'You are funny man, yes?' and he's no longer smiling. 'You have much to say. I think, yes, I will shoot you first.'

He points his focking Kalashnikov at me. It's, like, six inches from my nose.

I'm like, 'What?' and inside I'm thinking, Oh shit, oh shit, oh shit.

'Yes, your face,' he goes, sounding suddenly outraged, 'it makes me angry, so I will fucking shoot you and I will hang you in the trees. And do you know what will eat you? Fucking baboons will eat you. Come on. Come on, pretty boy, let's go,' and he puts the point of the gun to my right temple. 'Outside.'

There's no doubt he focking means it. I stare into his enormous bloodshot eyes and I look for some sign of, I don't know, humanity. But there's nothing there. His eyes are, like, dead.

I'm there, 'Dude, can we possibly talk about this?'

'No fucking talk!' he shouts. 'I fucking kill you now!'

The goys – especially Christian and Fionn – are trying to calm him down. They're going, 'There's no need for this! Please! There's no need!'

But Julius grabs me by the front of my jersey and throws me towards the door. He's like, 'Let's go. Let's go. Let's go.'

And my life – I swear to fock – flashes before my eyes. I'm thinking it can't end like this – what, here? On my first day in Omba Bomba Ging Ging?

I'm suddenly thinking about Sorcha and Honor and Ronan and those three beautiful babies that I didn't even get to properly know and all the people I'm not going to get the opportunity to say goodbye to.

Julius shoves me through the door and goes, 'Baboons will fucking eat you!'

And that's when I suddenly blurt it out. I'm like, 'Ring my old man! Please! Just ring my old man!'

He's there, 'What?' and he sounds – again – furious.

'My old man!' I go, my two hands joined in prayer. 'He has money! Just ring him!'

It's amazing how instinctively those words always come to me when I'm trouble – whether it's being arrested for pulling handbrake turns on the supposedly sacred turf of Blackrock College or being arrested for wrapping Johnny Ronan's Merc in clingfilm in the cor pork of the Powerscourt Hotel three or four Christmases ago.

Julius goes, 'Who the fuck is this *old man?*'

I'm like, 'No, I'm talking about *my* old man. It's what we say in Ireland for father. The old man. My old man. Blah, blah, blah.'

I'm just, like, babbling now out of fear.

'You say he has fucking money?' Julius goes.

I notice the life has come back into his eyes.

I'm there, 'Yeah, no, he's loaded.'

'How much?' he goes. 'How much does he fucking have?'

'I've no idea. But he's never short. He's as crooked as fock.'

'And he will pay for you?'

'He will. He'll definitely pay. I'm his only son.'

'And these other fucking assholes?'

'Yeah. But not if you shoot us. That's what I'm trying to tell you, Dude. Definitely not if you shoot any of us.'

He stares at me for a good, I don't know, thirty seconds. Then he goes, 'Okay, I fucking phone him. You fucking come.'

I'm there, 'Okay.'

'You fucking come with me.'

He shouts something in African and the two boys with the guns suddenly reappear and I'm pulled out of the cell and into a bright passageway. The light hurts my eyes. The door slams behind me and Julius pushes me up the stairs.

'I do not tie your hands,' he goes. 'If you escape, I will shoot your friends – do you understand?'

I'm there, 'Yeah, no, I do.'

'I will fucking kill every one of them. Now, we will phone this fucking asshole you call your father.'

We're in, like, a house, I'm noticing – we're talking someone's actual *gaff*? – although it's a bit of a shitbox, if I'm being honest. There's very little furniture in it. The floors are just, like, bare cement and the plaster is coming off the walls, exposing the original brickwork.

Even Felicity Fox couldn't put a positive spin on it.

Julius shoves me into this sort of, like, living-room area, where two big bruisers, both six-foot-plus, are sitting around on ormchairs made out of bamboo, both of them with their tops off. It's not a gay thing. It's just so focking hot in here.

One of them has, like, a square head and – I swear to fock – *the* flattest nose I've ever seen. He's, like, shorpening a stick with a knife that looks like it could probably cut a man in two. The other dude has an old must-dash and a look of pure focking hatred about him. He's taking aport his Kalashnikov, then putting it back together again, like he's timing himself. I look down and I notice the flip-flops.

It's Benjamin and Rolly.

They both stop what they're doing when they see me. Julius says something to them in African. I'm presuming he's explaining what's about to happen, because Rolly – focking flip-flops – indicates for me to sit at a table in the middle of the room, then storts shouting something at someone in the next room.

Ten, maybe twenty seconds later, in she focking walks.

I'm telling you, Fionn was bang on when he said she looked like Forest Whitaker. She's a focking ringer for him – when the dude was still fat, that is – we're talking – *my* guess? – twenty to twenty-two stone in weight. She's also got, like, a skinhead, ears like Graham Rowntree and a bottom lip that sticks out like a focking grouper. And she's wearing green combats, a matching jacket and then just, like, *ormy* boots?

You get the idea. A focking hippo wouldn't take a run at her.

She's carrying a phone the size of a borbecue brick, which she puts down in the middle of the table. I'm looking at it and I'm sort of, like, inwardly chuckling at it, although in fairness it's probably no bigger than the Nokia I had in my Senior Cup year. I just happen to look up at that point and I notice that Forest is just, like, staring at me.

Now, I'm pretty good at picking up on the vibe when a bird looks at me and likes what she sees. I've had it all my life. And this girl, I can straight away tell, likes me. She's focking staring at me like a dog in the window of Hick's.

Julius picks up the phone and asks me for my old man's number. I rhyme off the old digits and he dials.

'What is this fucking asshole's name?' he goes.

I'm there, 'Er, yeah, no, it's Chorles?'

'Charles?'

'Yeah, Chorles.'

He nods and goes, 'Yes!' like he approves of this, then, a few seconds later – in this, for some reason, fake upper-class accent – he goes, 'Helloooh. May I speak with Chooorles, please?'

It's like he's talking to focking royalty or something.

I don't hear what gets said at the other end, but Julius goes, 'I have your son here with me, Chooorles. He would like to speak with you, if he maaay . . . Just a moooment . . .'

Julius hands me the phone.

'Now fucking speak,' he goes, like he thinks I've never used one before.

I hold the receiver up to my ear and I'm there, 'Hey!'

I can't tell you how great it is to hear the old man's voice. 'Ross,' he goes, 'it's one o'clock in the morning! You haven't been arrested again, have you?'

I'm like, 'Shut the fock up, will you, and just listen. I'm in Oon Gan Gun.'

'You're where?'

'Oon Gan Gun. Something, something. Where focking Fionn was kidnapped.'

'Do you mean Uganda?'

'Yes . . . And now *I've* been kidnapped.'

'Kidnapped?'

'Yes – focking kidnapped.'

'This isn't one of your famous practical jokes, is it, Ross? Like the night you phoned me pretending to be Silvio Berlusconi, inviting me to one of his famous bingo bingo parties?'

'No, it's not.'

'You know how how much I admire that man, Ross. I stood in the garden for an hour, waiting for the helicopter.'

I'm like, 'Dude, this is not a focking joke. Me, JP, Christian and

Oisinn came over here, kind of on a whim. And we've ended up being taken by the same crew that's holding Fionn.'

'Good God!'

He's suddenly taking it seriously. I hear him turn to presumably Helen and go, 'It seems Ross and his chaps have been kidnapped in Uganda.'

I'm there, 'Dude, will you ring Sorcha and tell her not to worry. I'm okay. We're all okay. And tell her – I don't know – I love her. And say the same to Ronan. And to Honor. No, maybe not to her. No, do – say it to her. And my babies. Jesus, my beautiful babies . . .'

Julius suddenly loses it again. 'What the fuck is this?' he goes. 'No fucking messages. You tell your father we want five million dollars or we fucking kill you.'

I go to repeat it, except the old man goes, 'Don't worry, Ross, I heard every bloody word of that. Don't say another thing. I'm going to place this in the hands of a professional.'

I'm like, 'What?'

'A skilled negotiator, Ross. That's what this job calls for. Put me back on to your chap there. And don't worry about a thing.'

I'm there, 'Dude, I *am* worried? You've got to get me the fock out of here.'

He goes, 'This will all be resolved very quickly. Hand the phone back to the chap, Ross.'

Which is what I end up having to do.

Julius takes it off me and goes, 'Hellooo, Chooorles,' with the focking voice again.

He listens for a few seconds, then storts having an actual eppo. 'What?' he goes. 'What fucking negotiator?' and then, after another pause, 'Who the fuck is this Hennessy Cockalan?'

I'm thinking, no. Please focking no.

'Okay,' Julius goes, switching back to polite again, 'I will ring this number in twelve hours and I will speak to Hennessy Cockalan. It was a great pleasure to speak with you, Chooorles.'

He hangs up and he thumps the table. He's like, 'What the fuck is this Hennessy fucking Cockalan bullshit?'

I don't get a chance to say anything. The dude that Fionn calls

Benjamin says something to Julius in African and Julius looks at Forest focking Whitaker, who's still staring at me, by the way.

Julius laughs. He goes, 'I think my sister is in love with you!'

His sister. Jesus.

Rolly and Benjamin both laugh and Forest suddenly snaps out of it. She shouts something presumably uncomplimentary in Benjamin's direction, which makes him laugh even *horder*? Then she makes a run at him and storts slapping him around the head and Benjamin tries to cover himself with his orms, but Forest keeps raining blows down on him and Benjamin keeps laughing until Julius finally shouts something that I presume is *their* equivalent of, like, *stop*?

Forest shouts one final insult at Benjamin, then she storms out of the room and we all watch her orse go, like the boulder that nearly killed Harrison Ford in the first *Indiana Jones* movie.

'Now I take you back to your friends,' Julius goes. 'And tomorrow your father gives me five million dollars or I fucking kill you.'

'Who else is awake?' I go.

Oisinn's like, 'Me.'

And Christian's there, 'Me.'

And JP goes, 'Meh.'

And Fionn's like, 'Me.'

It's the itching that's stopping me sleeping, even more than the sound of mice, cockroaches and whatever the fock else scuttling across the floor of our basic *cell*? Even more than the smell from when Christian took a dump in the bucket in the middle of the night. Even more than the prospect of being shot some time in the next twenty-four hours.

'I'm being focking eaten alive,' I go, then I pull up my Lions jersey and I pull down the waistband of my famous camo trousers and I give my skin a good clawing. I can feel these just, like, massive lumps under my fingers. 'What the fock is eating me?'

'Mosquitos,' Fionn goes – as casually as that. 'Or Dengue flies.'

Christian's like, 'What time is it?'

It's impossible to say, of course. They took our focking phones when they lifted us off the street.

Fionn's there, 'It's about ten o'clock in the morning. I can tell from the quality of the light coming through the vent up there.' He climbs to his feet.

I'm there, 'Has anyone else been bitten?'

'Yeah, me,' Christian goes. 'Jesus, I hope I don't end up getting malaria.'

I'm there, 'Malaria? Are you saying there's an actual chance of that?'

He goes, 'I don't know, Ross, I'm not a focking doctor.'

With his Leaving Cert results, you may bet he's not a focking doctor.

We're suddenly all distracted by the sight of Fionn setting off on his morning walk, his right hand touching the wall as he makes his way, on little matchstick legs, from one corner of the room to the next. I think we're all a bit in awe of him and feeling suddenly a little bit guilty about all our pissing and moaning. We've only been here, like, a day – not even. He's been here for, like, six months.

'Dude,' I go, 'I genuinely don't know how you've survived in here.'

JP's like, 'Boo hoo know hot halked acoss my hace in ba mihull of ma might? A hocking hmider! Ma hize ob a hocking gat.'

A spider the size of a cat. Walked across his focking face.

I'm tempted to go, Yeah, no, First World problems, Dude. First World focking problems.

Fionn goes, 'When you're in captivity, it's not where you are that drives you mad. It's where you're not.'

And it's deep. There's no doubt that it's deep. Even JP stops moaning for five focking minutes.

'You should all exercise,' Fionn goes. 'It's important to keep mentally and physically sharp.'

We all stay where we are, in our flea-ridden – literally – beds.

Christian goes, 'I'm hoping we won't be here that long. What time are they ringing Hennessy?'

I'm there, 'Yeah, no, they didn't say. My old man just said he'd get him to handle the negotiations. I'm presuming it'll be some time today.'

'Good,' Christian goes, like this is straight away *good* news?

I try to get him to lower his expectations. I'm there, 'You're separated from his daughter, bear in mind?'

He goes, 'So? Jesus Christ, Ross, I'm still the father of his grandson. He's not going to leave us to rot in here just because me and Lauren are having problems.'

'He can be a dick,' I go. 'That's all I'm asking you to bear in mind.'

I go back to scratching. I've never felt anything like this itch and that's coming from someone who's had eighty percent of the sexually transmitted diseases out there. My fingers feel suddenly wet and I realize that I've drawn blood.

Christian goes, 'Hennessy will come through for us. I'm telling you. Between his money and your old man's money, Ross – and JP, your old man's not exactly skint – look, he'll make them an offer and I genuinely think we'll be out of here by tonight. Tomorrow morning at the very latest.'

The door all of a sudden opens and it's Julius who steps into the room. Fionn stops walking.

'I trust you slept well,' the dude goes – then he cracks his hole laughing. He'd definitely want to lay off the drugs.

'Do you have any Sudocrem,' I go, 'or whatever the equivalent is over here?'

But he just blanks me. He goes, 'Breakfast is served,' and in come the kids – and they *are* just kids – and they hand us each a plate.

Oisinn goes, 'Okay, what the fock *is* this?' referring to his breakfast and it's only then that I happen to look down at mine. It's, like, mashed potato – we're talking grey and we're talking runny – and two tablespoons of what looks very much to me like tinned tuna.

Fionn goes, 'Oisinn, eat it. There won't be much else,' and it suddenly makes sense to me why the poor focker is as thin as he is.

One of the kids picks up the piss and shit bucket to bring it outside to empty it. When he gets the hum off it, he slaps one hand over his mouth and storts walking with the thing at orm's length. Julius tells him to wait and he has a look inside it.

'Who does this?' he goes.

299

Christian at least owns up. He's there, 'Yeah, no, I have a bowel issue.'

'In Uganda,' Julius goes, 'you know what fucking shits like this? A fucking elephant shits like this!' and then he tells the kid to take it outside.

Forest Whitaker arrives then, carrying two Castrol GTX cans containing, I'm presuming, *water*? I stand up and I take one of them from her. I notice that her hands are slightly trembling and she can't look me in the eye.

A lot of girls get it bad for me.

I'm porched, so I open the cap and I knock back a mouthful. It tastes vaguely of petrol, but I swallow it down anyway.

'Eat your breakfast,' Julius goes. 'Then I ring Hennessy Cockalan.'

The morning goes slowly. And so does the afternoon. We pass the time talking about old times, matches we played in – actually reconstructing events from memory – and birds we rode.

It's, like, the early evening – Fionn has become a pretty good judge of time – when Julius suddenly reappears at the door, holding his AK-47, with Benjamin and Rolly either side of him. They're also *packing*, as Ronan would call it.

Julius does not look like a happy camper.

'This focking Hennessy Cockalan,' he goes, 'he is a fucking asshole.'

No one attempts to contradict him, including Christian, who's obviously related to him through marriage.

All Christian *actually* goes is, 'Did you speak to him?'

'I fucking phone your father this morning,' Julius goes, talking to me. 'He says this is the cell number for Hennessy Cockalan. I phone it and I say I would like to speak to Hennessy Cockalan please and I say it like that – yes? – in a nice voice. Hennessy fucking Cockalan says he is going out to play golf. Fucking golf. And he tells me to fucking phone him back.'

That sounds like Hennessy alright. He's obviously decided to dick him around for tactical reasons and now Julius is taking out his frustration on us.

'I ring him back,' Julius goes, 'and now he wants proof of life.'

I'm there, 'Proof of life? What the fock does that mean?'

We're all just sitting there on our mattresses with our backs to the wall.

Julius goes, 'He wants proof that you are all still alive. Fucking asshole. I say I cut off all their fucking ears and I post them to you. How is that for proof of life, you fucking motherfucker? He says to me I am going to sit down now and smoke a big fucking cigar. If you don't put them on the phone to me by the time I finish it, then you can fuck off.'

See, that would be very much Hennessy's style. He's a complete wanker when it comes to negotiations. That's why my old man has had him representing him for the past thirty-whatever years.

'Upstairs,' Julius goes, pointing the gun at each of us in turn. 'Fucking all of you.'

Rolly and Benjamin stort – I suppose – manhandling us to our feet. Then they push us out of the room and up the stairs, with Julius screaming at us to keep our heads down the entire way.

We're shoved into the living room – the exact same one that I was in last night, except this time we're pushed over to the two bamboo sofas – they're the kind you sometimes see in B&Q – and we're ordered at gunpoint to sit down, which we do.

Again, my eyes struggle to adjust to the light after however long in that cell. When they do, I notice this old dude standing there – he's another black man, with grey, Morgan Freeman-type hair – and it's obviously Ibrahim, the old dude who Fionn said does the cooking.

There's no sign of Forest tonight.

Ibrahim dials a number on the same humungous brick they used to call my old man and while it's ringing, he hands the phone to Julius. Hennessy must answer, roysh, because Julius goes, 'Okay, your proof of fucking life is here. Now, I fucking want five million dollars, you fucking . . . No, you listen to me. No, *you* listen to fucking *me* . . . What? Which one? Yes, but which one is that? Which one of you fucking assholes is Ross?'

I'm there, 'Er, yeah, no, *I'm* Ross?'

Julius rolls his eyes and shakes his head. 'He wants to speak to you,' and he hands me the phone, at the same time going, 'Fucking Hennessy Cockalan.'

I take the phone from him, not knowing what kind of reception I'm going to get. I hold it to my ear and I'm like, 'Hennessy, how the hell are you?'

'You little fucking turd,' he goes – that'd be one of his pet names for me. 'You spat in that fucking sandwich.'

I'm like, 'Er, yeah – now is possibly *not* the time to stort debating that?'

'There's no fucking debate,' he goes. 'I got the date it happened. I got the time it happened. I even got a full account of how it happened, including a very detailed description of you, right down to your stupid, gormless fucking face.'

I'm looking at the others – especially Christian – wondering can they hear him.

JP's like, 'Hot's he haying?'

He means what's he saying? They can obviously only hear *my* side of the conversation?

I try to go, 'Like I said, Hennessy, let's pork that for another day. We're in serious S, H, one, T, here. Can you give JP's old man a ring and also Oisinn's old pair . . .'

He goes, 'I've already done it. I don't need directions from you, you little prick.'

'Well, that's good news. Between them, then obviously Fionn's old pair, my old man, Christian's old pair and possibly even you – even though I know things aren't good between Christian and Lauren right now – you should be able to put together the moo to get us out of this mess.'

That's when he says it.

He's there, 'You're not getting out of anything.'

I'm like, 'What?'

'I said I'd have my revenge, didn't I? The day you burned my fucking boat.'

'Okay, Dude? This is not a time for settling old scores.'

'Who fucking says?'

'Hennessy, you can't just leave us here to rot.'

Fionn, JP, Oisinn and especially Christian are all looking at me with seriously worried looks on their faces.

'I'm not going to leave you *all* to rot,' Hennessy goes. 'I'm going to get the others out. In fact, you can tell them they're going to be on a plane home first thing tomorrow morning.'

I'm like, 'What do you mean?'

'I mean I've got two million dollars. It's here. Ready to be wired. I'm sure they'll take that. But I'm going to tell them that you ain't included in the deal.'

Christian goes, 'Ross, what the fock is going on? Is he saying he won't pay it?'

I look at Christian and I nod.

Hennessy's like, 'The two million is for Christian and the others. I'm going to pay them to keep you for another six months.'

I'm there, 'Dude, you can't do that.'

'Yeah, you fucking watch me.'

He might be bluffing. He might not be bluffing.

I'm like, 'Dude, I'm focking begging you. Ask my old man for the moo. He'll give it to you.'

He goes, 'Put that fucker – whatever he's called – on the line.'

And I just think, Fock it, no, I can't take the chance. I don't want to be left in that cell on my Tobler for even one night. I wouldn't survive six months. So I just go, 'Fock you! You're a focking dick!' and I hang up on him.

Oisinn is like, 'What happened?'

And Christian's there, 'I can't believe he won't pay.'

Julius is even more in shock. He goes, 'What the fuck is this shit?'

And then, before I can make something up, he lifts up his foot and he kicks me full in the face with the sole of his boot. I fall off the sofa and the phone goes flying across the floor.

'Motherfucker!' he shouts, then he stamps – literally stamps – on my ribs, once, twice, then three times. 'You fuck it up, you fucking motherfucker,' until Benjamin and Rolly end up having to drag him off me.

I'm lying on the ground, holding my side. My head feels like it's about to explode. Julius shouts something at them in African, then he translates it, I'm presuming for *our* benefit?

'So no one will fucking pay for you,' he goes. 'That's okay. Bring them downstairs. I will fucking shoot them in the morning.'

9. No Country for Old Tens

A hush descends on the Aviva Stadium. I turn to Father Fehily and I go, 'What's happening? Father, what's happening?' because I'm blind – as in, I literally can't see a thing.

His voice is, like, calm and soothing. 'It's okay,' he goes. 'It's just the haka.'

I focking hate the haka. I've always hated the focking haka.

'The boys,' I go. 'What are they doing?'

He's like, 'They're facing it down, Ross.'

'Are they?'

'And they're smiling. No, no – they're laughing!'

'That's what I told them to do. I said it to them in the hospital the day they were born. I said if you ever end up playing against the All Blacks and they're doing that ridiculous focking dance, don't be intimidated.'

'No tree is too tall for a short dog to piss on.'

'That's exactly it. I love that quote of yours. I love all your quotes . . . Will you tell them that I'm proud of them?'

'They know.'

'Whatever the score ends up being. I'm proud of my boys. I want you to say that to them.'

I feel a hand on my shoulder. I know that it's a steward. His voice is firm and businesslike. He's there, 'Let's go.'

And I stand up and I'm helped out of my seat and I somehow know that I'm being taken off to be, like, executed. And that's when I wake up with my face wet with tears and my breathing all – I don't know – *uneven?*

Christian, I discover, is holding my hand. He's there, 'Hey, you were having a nightmare.'

I'm there, 'I never even got to know them, Christian.'

'I'm the same,' he goes. And he shakes his head – I think I've heard this word used – *ruefully*? 'Oliver won't have any memory of me. And Ross Junior. God knows how messed up he's going to be. Fock, I've just remembered, I was supposed to go to see his Nativity play today. He was playing the Virgin Mary.'

There's things I could say, but it's neither the time nor the place.

I just wipe my cheeks with the palm of my hand and I go, 'Hennessy. He's always been a dick.'

My face hurts like fock. *Both* sides? Where Rolly punched me and Julius kicked me. My face is all lumpy, like a bag of onions.

Christian seems suddenly uncomfortable. I know him well enough to pick up on it straight away. 'Dude,' he goes, 'I know what happened – in that phone call.'

And I look sideways at him, wondering *does* he? As in, does he *actually*?

I'm there, 'Go on, let me hear what you think happened.'

He goes, 'He didn't say they wouldn't pay the ransom. He said they wouldn't pay the ransom . . . for me.'

I hate myself for this. I really do. But I end up going, 'Yeah, no, he said he'd actually pay them to keep *you* here for another six months.'

He goes, 'I knew it.'

'He just feels you very much betrayed his daughter,' I go. 'He said the rest of us could have been on a plane home tomorrow morning. But you could rot in here for all he cared.'

'What a focker.'

'But that's Hennessy, isn't it?'

'My own father-in-law.'

'And I just thought, you know, there's no way I'm walking out of here if it means leaving Christian behind. No focking way. So I just hung up on the focker.'

Oisinn goes, 'You did right, Ross.'

But Christian's there, 'I feel terrible.'

I'm like, 'Don't feel terrible.'

'Jesus Christ,' he goes, 'it's because of me that we're all going to be killed this morning.'

And I'm there, 'Hey – what movie was that where they said,

"Leave no man behind"? I focking loved that movie. Or more that expression. I didn't actually see the whole thing.'

JP is praying. He's going, 'Mail Mary, hull of hrace, ha Lord his hit hee. Hessed art how hamong mimmin . . .'

And Fionn's there, 'Enough! I can't listen to another decade of the Rosary!' and JP stops – we're talking mid-prayer – and he goes into a bit of a sulk.

'I'm sorry,' Fionn goes, 'but I don't want this to be how we spend our final hours – praying for our lives.'

Fionn wouldn't be a big believer in the whole God thing.

The door suddenly opens and we all look at each other, all thinking exactly the same thing. This is it. This is focking it. I realize that I'm shaking.

Julius walks in – his AK at the ready – and goes, 'So which one of you fucking assholes will I shoot first?'

He's chewing that shit again – his mouth working away like a cow you might see in the Irish countryside.

'Perhaps you,' he goes, looking at Christian.

And Christian, who obviously feels guilty for landing us in it, goes, 'Yeah, no, I'll go first,' and he stands up – he was always unbelievably brave on the rugby field – and he storts walking towards the door. He's there, 'Goys, again, I'm sorry.'

And his voice sounds so sad and depressed. And I think, No, I can't let my best friend die thinking that he's responsible for this. And I'm right on the point of telling him the truth when Julius all of a sudden storts laughing.

He goes, 'Sit the fuck down.'

And we all look at each other again, thinking, Holy fock, is this a reprieve? Did JP's prayers have an actual effect or is that just crazy talk?

'For six months I keep this fucking asshole alive,' he goes, referring to obviously Fionn. 'I want some fucking money for him. His employer will not pay. Fucking Hennessy Cockalan will not pay. Who will fucking pay?' and then he storts kicking Oisinn on the side of his legs, going, 'Who will fucking pay? I am sick of this shit!'

'I don't know,' Oisinn goes.

The dude screams it this time: 'Who will fucking pay?'

Oisinn's there, 'What about Fred – that dude you're torturing?'

'Mister Fred?'

'Fred Pfanning or whatever he's called. He works for some big private security crowd, doesn't he? I mean, they must have money.'

'Mister fucking Fred?'

He looks at Oisinn, roysh, totally incredulous. Then he walks over to the door and he shouts something up the stairs, presumably to Benjamin and Rolly, because the next thing we hear is them coming down and then a metal door further up the passageway opening.

'Mister Fred,' Julius goes. 'I will tell you about Mister fucking Fred,' and, literally ten seconds later, the dude is dragged into our cell by the two focking goons and dropped face down on the floor in front of us.

He looks up. He looks like shit – I'm just calling it. They've obviously been working him over on a regular basis for whatever reason. His face looks like the proverbial burst melon.

He's like, 'Hellay, cheps.'

Julius bends down, grabs him by the hair and pulls his head back. He's like, 'Hellooo, cheps,' trying to impersonate the dude. 'And how are you on this very fine day, Mr Fred?'

Fred just shoots him a look of basic contempt and Julius lets go of his hair.

'Shall I tell you,' Julius goes, 'about your Mister Fred? You say he is private security. Will I tell you what Mr Fred is?'

Fred's like, 'Dayn't listen to a word he says, cheps!'

'He is a fucking criminal. He is like we are.'

'Thet's a demned lie!' Fred goes – and he gets a kick in the stomach from Benjamin for his troubles.

Julius goes, 'That is the truth . . . . cheps. You think he comes here to try to win your release? This is fucking bullshit. He comes to us and he says this man that you have kidnapped has a family in Island – your country – that has a house they are happy to sell. Also, a sister who will sell her house if she must. They also have savings. Altogether, they can raise perhaps half a million pounds sterling.

Mister fucking Fred says if you release this boy into my custody, I will divide this money with you. Fifty fucking fifty.'

Me and Fionn and Christian and Oisinn and JP all just look at each other. Shock doesn't even come close to covering it.

Fionn's there, 'I don't believe it,' and then he turns to me. 'Did my mum and dad sell their house?'

I'm there, 'They definitely put it on the morket,' because I saw it on Daft dot ie.

He's like, 'And Eleanor?'

'I don't know. I know she said she was happy to sell it if that meant getting you safely home.'

Fred, by the way, doesn't try to deny any of this.

Julius laughs and goes, 'I will leave you here to fill them in, Mr Fred,' and then him and the two goons leave, pulling the door closed behind them.

Fionn flies into a sudden rage. He goes, 'How much money did they give you?' and he actually roars this at Fred. Fred says nothing. It's Christian who actually tells him.

'They gave him a hundred Ks,' he goes. 'Sterling. As, like, an upfront fee. Then it was half a million sterling if he brought you home alive.'

Fionn just shakes his head. 'And this was the money you were going to split with them?' he goes. 'The proceeds from my mother and father's house? And my sister's?'

Fred goes – I swear to fock, I'm not making this up – 'What the hell does it metter? Your parents were prepared to pay half a million pindes to get you home. Why do you care who the money goes to?'

'Because that makes you an accessory!' Fionn, again, roars at him.

'Yeah,' I go, 'and a wanker. And you had the balls to say that I was a bad egg? That I was lacking in moral fibre?'

And I see a sudden change of expression come over his face, like he's suddenly remembering me and Jenny bumping zippers in the cor pork opposite Kielys. He's about to say something to Fionn about it, so I quickly jump to my feet and I kick the focker hord in the ribs and he curls up into a ball, winded.

Fionn's there, 'So that's what the work of a security consultant involves, is it? Taking advantage of people's desperation?'

'Yeah,' Oisinn goes, 'then going splitsies on the proceeds.'

I kick him again and he storts gasping for breath and goes, 'Please! Please stop! Those bastards have . . . have already broken my ribs!'

JP's there, 'Moo moo mexpect hus moo heel horry hor hoo?'

Do you expect us to feel sorry for you?

Happily, Fred has forgotten what he was about to tell Fionn. Instead, he's suddenly looking for sympathy.

'I can help you,' he goes. 'Please.'

I give him another kick. Moral fibre. That actually hurt.

'Look,' he goes, 'I can help you. They have plens for us. I know what they are.'

Fionn goes, 'Ross, stop!'

I stop kicking him. I was only going to give him two or three more anyway.

Fred rolls over onto his back.

Oisinn gets up and stands over him. He goes, 'Well? What *are* these plans?'

Fred struggles to get his breath back. 'Look, I speak a little bit of the lenguage . . . I overheard them, perheps an hour ago . . . They were talking abite . . . They were talking abite selling us.'

'Selling us?' it's Christian who goes.

He's there, 'This is Efrica. Hostages are . . . are bought and sold like . . . like pineapples or maize or goats.'

Fionn's there, 'But selling us to who?'

'Thet I don't know, I'm afraid . . . Another geng . . . Maybe even Al Qaeda . . .'

I'm there, 'Al Qaeda?'

Now they're *serious* dicks. I don't know much about world affairs, but I do know that much.

Oisinn goes, 'What the fock would Al Qaeda want with us?'

'What do you think?' Fred goes. 'We're Westerners . . . We're royal game . . . Maybe they'll behead us . . . Put it on YouTube . . . I just dayn't knay, I'm afraid . . .'

The door opens and Julius is suddenly standing there in the frame.

He goes, 'Now, Mister Fred, you will return to your cell.'

And Fred looks at Fionn and goes, 'I know you're probably med at me . . . And perheps you have just cause . . . But we need to stick together . . . And we need to come up with an escape plen.'

Breakfast ends up being – I shit you not – eight pieces of *tinned* pineapple?

'If my old dear knew I was eating tinned fruit,' I go, 'she'd fly over here and kick that focking door down herself.'

The goys all laugh, except Oisinn, who just smiles and sort of looks guilty. He possibly still *feels* guilty? I think I can live with that, though.

'Jesus Christ,' Christian goes, 'it's hot,' which it actually is. 'I think I'm going to pass out here.'

Fionn goes, 'You've got to keep drinking the water.'

'I can't drink it. It tastes like, I don't know, petrol or something.'

'It doesn't matter. You have to stay hydrated, especially in this heat.'

He knows, I suppose. He's managed to survive nearly six months here.

Oisinn goes, 'Yeah, no, we want to look our best when Al Qaeda are chopping our focking heads off.'

And JP laughs – bitterly – and goes, 'Mi'm gomma mook midiculous,' meaning he's gonna look ridiculous, what with having no focking teeth. He's probably right. 'Hesus Hrist, my mout hurts – my meed a hentist.'

He's saying he needs a dentist.

Christian goes, 'They wouldn't sell us to Al Qaeda, would they? I mean, are they even based here?'

Fionn – who's forgotten more about world affairs than I've ever bothered my hole learning – goes, 'They're based everywhere. And, yeah, this happens a lot. I mean, Al Qaeda don't go around snatching Westerners off the street. Generally, it's criminal gangs that do the kidnapping, then they sell them on.'

Oisinn's there, 'I don't know. I think that focker was just trying to frighten us. As in, Fred. He got caught double-dealing and he's trying to put the shits up us to get us back on his side.'

It's time for me to suddenly say my piece. I actually stand up.

'So,' I go, 'are we just going to sit around like focking muppets waiting for them to sell us?'

I have to admit, there's a real Ross-back-in-the-day vibe to it.

Christian goes, 'Well, what the fock do you suggest we do, Ross?'

He wouldn't have been allowed to speak to me like that back in our rugby-playing days. I'm just stating that. But I'm prepared to put it down to the fact that he's suffering from possibly heatstroke and he's missing his kids and probably even Lauren.

'What I'm suggesting,' I go, 'is getting the fock out of here. What I'm suggesting is escaping.'

Christian's there, 'But how?'

'By using a certain thing called my brain. What did we do back in the day? We looked at the opposition and we looked for weak points. Jesus, we were probably the first school to use video analysis.'

The rugby reference does the trick. I can see it in one or two of their faces. They're suddenly prepared to place their trust in my leadership, just like they did so many times in the past.

'Okay,' Oisinn goes, 'you're saying they have a weak point?'

I'm there, 'You better focking believe they have a weak point.'

I love the feeling of sudden power.

Christian goes, 'So what is it?'

I'm there, 'It's Forest. She's the weak point. She's got a bit of thing for me.'

They all groan – predictively enough – including Fionn. The focking cheek of *him*. Six months he's been here and he hasn't come up with a single plan for getting out, other than ringing me and begging me to come and get him.

I'm there, 'Goys, I know it sounds big-headed, but I'm only stating it as a fact. I picked up on a vibe yesterday. And then again when she brought us our breakfast. She's into me in a major way.'

Christian shakes his head. 'So supposing you're right,' he goes. Focking *supposing*? How many exes of his have I ridden over the years? Jesus, I rode his mother. I could remind him of that, but I don't. 'What are you going to do about it?'

I'm there, 'What do you think I'm going to do? I'm going to make a move on her. My assets against her liabilities. Blah, blah, blah.'

'And she's going to fall so helplessly in love with you that, what, she lets us all go?'

'That's the general idea, Christian, yeah. Jesus focking Christ, have you looked at the girl? I wouldn't say she gets many offers. Especially from people like me – and again, I know that's going to make me sound possibly full of myself.'

JP – fair focks to him – is the first one to back me up. He's there, 'Has manyone hot a metter hi hee are?'

Has anyone got a better idea?

The answer is no. And that's when we hear the sound of banging on the pipes that run through our cell at, like, skirting level, then the sound of Fred Pfanning's voice, going, 'Cheps! Cheps! Can you hear me?'

We're all like, 'Yeah, whatever.'

He goes, 'Cheps, put your ears to the pipe. Thet way, I won't have to shout so lidely.'

We all just look at each other, thinking, Will we? Then we think, Fock it, what is there to lose?

We all wander over to the wall and kneel down with our ears against the black painted metal of the pipe. He's right. His voice does carry better, without the need to actually *yell*?

He's there, 'Cheps, I have a plen . . .'

Fionn puts his lips to the pipe and goes, 'Give me one good reason why we should we trust you?'

Fred's answer comes back straight away.

'Because you dayn't have a lot of choice,' he goes. 'Neither do you have a lot of time. They've gone ite.'

Christian's there, 'Who? Who's gone out?'

'The men. I heard them talking. They've gone out to do the deal – to sell us on to whatever bend of bloody well brigands is going to hold us next.'

Christian goes, 'So who's *in* the actual house?'

'Just thet awful eyesore of a woman. And maybe one or two of the young ones. But they've been chewing khat since early morning. I can hear them giggling and slurring their words. They'll be easily overparred.'

Fionn goes, 'Okay, so how do we get out of our cells?'

That's when he says something that causes hope to suddenly rise up in all of us.

'One of those young boys,' he goes, 'he came in here abite fifteen minutes agay, pointing his gun at me, trying to scare me. He gave me a bit of a kicking. Well, like I said, they've been chewing that stuff for arrs and arrs. He was so ite of his head thet when he left my cell . . . he left the key in the beck of the door.'

We're all there, 'Whoa!' at the same time looking at each other in – again, that word – *hope*?

Fred goes, 'The key to *your* cell – I'm almost certain – is on the same keychain. One of you needs to try to get ite of there.'

That's when I all of a sudden step up. I put my lips to the pipe and I go, 'This is Ross O'Carroll-Kelly speaking. It's going to be me. I have a plan to get out of here.'

'Okay, let's hear it.'

'She likes me. That big focking manster you're talking about. Forest Whitaker, we call her. I'm usually pretty good at picking up when there's an attraction and in this case there's a definite one.'

'So what are you propasing?'

'I'm going to let her think she has chance. And I'm going to do that by probably using one or two of my lines on her.'

'Excellent,' he goes. He's a prick and a snake in the grass, but at least he believes in me. 'With a bit of luck, she'll take you up to her bedroom. When you're passing my door, just turn the key. As soon as you've gone upstayers, I'll open your door and let you other cheps ite. Then we can go upstayers, overparr that woman – if thet's what she even is – and make good our escape using my special forces training.'

'My question still stands,' Fionn goes. 'How do we know we can trust you?'

And the dude goes, 'You dayn't. But we have a window of opportunity here that might not be aypen to us again. I suggest we take it.'

It's at that exact moment that we hear footsteps coming down the stairs and along the passageway and we can tell from the heavy tread of boots that it's *her*.

We quickly return to our places, sitting on our mattresses, scratching ourselves and swatting away mozzies and picking fleas and whatever else out of our hair.

'Okay,' Oisinn goes, 'what are you going to say?' and I get this sudden flashback to when we were in Annabel's back in the day and I would always set my sights on the most beautiful girl in the place and the question then would be exactly the same. 'What are you going to say?'

I go, 'Watch and learn.'

She obviously has her own set of keys, because I hear one go into the lock, then it turns and the door opens with a screech. It *is* Forest – here to collect our breakfast things. She points at our little plastic bowls with her gun and mumbles something in African and I stand up and I collect them all for her – ever the gent – then, when she goes to take them from me, I hold onto them tightly, so she can't *actually* take them? It's a thing I sometimes do to lounge girls back home when they're collecting glasses – just to let them know that they have my attention.

I eventually let go and she pulls the bowls from me.

I go, 'Thank you. That breakfast was fantastic,' and I smile at her. She's thrown by it – I can straight away tell – obviously wondering is she imagining the vibes I'm giving off.

Like I said, I wouldn't imagine she gets a lot of men throwing themselves at her. If you rode her in a dream, you'd wake up loathing yourself.

'I hope you don't mind me mentioning it,' I go, 'but you look beautiful today. I hope that doesn't come across as sarcastic. I'm actually talking *genuinely* beautiful?'

She doesn't say anything, just stares at me, really intensely. I think the girl is a little bit bowled over. I decide to up the ante by checking

315

out her doodads with my tongue in my cheek, then giving her a filthy little wink.

I can hear her breathing quickening. She swallows hord. She definitely has it bad for me.

'So,' I go, 'where do you tend to do your socializing?' and at the same time I reach out to pick a non-existent eyelash off her check. It's another famous move of mine, but in this case it proves to be my undoing.

Forest obviously thinks I'm making a move to disorm her and she takes a step backwards and lifts her Kalashnikov and points it at my face and storts roaring at me. It's all shit I don't understand, although I think it's safe to presume that she's telling me to get out of her face and sit the fock back down.

So that's what I do.

She shouts some more shit at me – she should be focking flattered, the dog – and then she backs out of the room, as angry as I've ever seen a woman. And I've seen them angry.

She pulls the door shut and locks it behind her.

'Where do you tend to do your socializing?' Christian goes.

There's, like, a mocking tone in his voice as well.

I'm there, 'Yeah, no, she mustn't speak English.'

He says it again. He's like, 'Where do you tend to do your socializing?'

He's pissing me off now.

'That wasn't going to be my entire routine,' I go. 'That wasn't even an actual chat-up line. That was me just getting warmed up. It was, like, an introductory line. I was going to follow it up with loads of others. Like I said, I don't think she understands a word of English. I mean, she couldn't.'

We listen to her feet retreat up the stairs, then Fred calls out from along the passageway. 'What heppened?'

It's Fionn who goes, 'Mission abort.'

I'm crushed. We're, like, *all* crushed? JP takes his disappointment out on a cockroach who gets a bit full of himself – showboating his way across the floor – and ends up flattened until the sole of a Dube, the cheeky fock.

'No!' Christian roars at him. 'Don't they say that if you stamp on a cockroach, it releases eggs?'

JP wonders is that not an urban myth. He goes, 'Is mat mot a murmban mit?'

Everyone looks at Fionn. He's the brains. He just shrugs and goes, 'We're in Africa. What's six cockroaches more?'

I'm just sitting there, beating myself up over blowing it with Forest Whitaker.

'I possibly went a bit early,' I go, 'with the whole physical contact thing. I was possibly thrown by the fact that she was holding a gun. Then there's the whole – again – language barrier?'

Fionn's there, 'You tried, Ross. At least you did that.'

I'm like, 'Yeah, no, but I still stand by my statement that she fancies me in a major, major way.'

No one comments and we end up sitting there basically bored for ten, maybe twenty minutes, breathing in each other's BO, before Oisinn – totally out of the blue – goes, 'Back home, I had this idea for, like, an adult cartoon. I was going to pitch it to maybe RTÉ. It's called *Rob the Builder*.'

Christian's there, '*Rob the Builder*? As in, like, *Bob the Builder*?'

'Yeah, no,' Oisinn goes, 'he's *kind* of like *Bob the Builder*? The difference is that Rob is never busy. In fact, he does pretty much fock-all, because his business is in the hands of NAMA, who pay him €250,000 a year to manage his own portfolio – in other words to sort out the mess that *he* made?'

We all laugh. In fairness, Oisinn always was an ideas man.

'Mot hus he hook hike?' JP goes.

He means, what does he look like? JP's obviously into the idea because of the whole property thing.

'He wears a hard hat and high-viz jacket,' Oisinn goes. 'I suppose a bit like Bob. But he also has a ponytail and a goatee and he fancies himself as a bit of a player. He's married to Maeve, but he also has a mistress called Amaris. And he leads the high life because he managed to transfer his house and most of his wealth into his wife's name. He also has properties hidden all around Europe and Eurasia. And the banks have hired private investigators who are always trying to find them. His best friends are Fiachra the TD and Bastard the Solicitor.'

'Hennessy!' Christian goes. 'He's definitely based on my focking father-in-law.'

Oisinn's like, 'Any similarities between these characters and persons living is entirely coincidental.'

Everyone laughs.

'Oh,' Oisinn goes, 'and like Bob the Builder, Rob the Builder has his mechanical friends, who also do fock-all. There's Sluggish the JCB, Slothful the Crane, Shiftless the Dump Truck and Slack the Roller.'

Again, they all laugh. They're all seriously into it. I suppose it's a way to take their minds off being sold to possibly lunatics.

'So come on,' Christian goes, 'give us the first episode.'

Oisinn's there, 'Okay. Well, the opening credits are a montage of images of Rob – drinking a cocktail, groping a woman's orse, giving the finger to the viewer, getting tested for venereal disease. And the theme tune is like:

> "Rob the Builder!
> Does he build things?
> Rob the Builder!
> Does he fock!
>
> Sluggish and Slothful,
> Shiftless and Slack,
> The taxpayer pays them
> For having the craic
> Rob and the gang have so much fun,
> They're meant to be broke,
> But they've plenty of mun!"'

Christian joins in. And so does JP – even *with* his focked mouth?

'Rob the Builder!
Does he build things?
Rob the Builder!
Does he fock!'

Oisinn goes, 'Okay, I have a storyline, but, bear in mind, I'm doing this off the top of my head. So picture the scene. Rob the Builder was standing on a building site slash unfinished ghost estate with Sluggish, Slothful, Shiftless and Slack. "I'm bored!" said Sluggish. "Me too!" said Slothful. "Are we ever going to finish this ghost estate, Rob?" Rob laughed. "Are we fuck!" he said. Shiftless was sad. "We used to build things, Rob." Slack nodded. "That's right," he said. "Houses, apartments – even destination spa hotels! Why don't we build things any more?" Rob scratched his balls. "Because the economy is banjoed!" he said. "Ireland is now what's known as a Third World country!" Slack looked sadly at the others. "That's terrible news!" he said. Rob laughed. "Not for me," he said. "I'm off to the races now with Bastard the Solicitor. The helicopter will be here any minute." '

Christian goes, 'A helicopter? Hennessy is definitely going to sue,' and we all laugh.

Oisinn's there, 'Slothful looked shocked. "You're going to the races in a helicopter?" he asked. Rob nodded. "That's right," he said. "We've a horse – *Bellini Boy* – running in the 3.30 at Fairyhouse!" Sluggish was confused. "But I thought you said Ireland was a Third World country!" Rob laughed. "It is for most people," he said. "But the Government set up a thing called NAMA to make sure the public pays the debts of people like me!" Slothful laughed. "Wicked!" he said. Just then, the helicopter arrived. "Anyway," said Rob, "I'm out of here." Sluggish waved. "Give our best to Maeve," he said. Rob laughed. "Oh," he said, "I'm not going with Maeve. I'm going with Amaris, my mistress slash prostitute. She's half my age and she's got tits like Pilates balls. She's a cracking little ride as well." Slack laughed. "Well," he said, "let's hope we can say the same thing for *Bellini Boy*!" They all laughed. Cue the closing credits.'

We give him a cheer and – in fairness – a round of applause.

JP goes, 'Mat meeds ha me on ma hebby,' meaning that needs to be on the telly, which it quite possibly will be if we ever get out of here.

We're all too busy laughing to hear someone coming down the stairs and the key being turned in the lock. But the next thing that happens is that the door opens – again, with the squeaky hinge – and Forest is standing there, silhouetted by the light of the passageway behind her.

She steps into the cell and she shouts something in the local lingo that seems to be directed at me. Whatever it is, she does not sound like a happy rabbit. She's, like, furious, if anything. She takes another step forward and she points her gun at me.

'You,' she goes, then she shouts something in – again – African, which I take as an order to stand up and walk outside. Which is what I do. She just nods as she watches me step out of the cell, holding my two hands up. She follows me and pulls the door closed, locking it behind her, then trousering the key.

I throw a subtle eye in the direction of Fred Pfanning's cell door and I notice the key still in it, with three or four more dangling from the keyring.

Forest punches me – I swear to fock – square in the chest, knocking me against the wall and basically *winding* me? Then she grabs me by the scruff of my Lions jersey, pulls me to her and – in broken English – goes, 'What does this mean when you say to me where am I socializing?'

I'm actually caught a little bit on the hop.

I'm there, 'Yeah, no, what I actually said was where do you tend to do your socializing, which I suppose is the same thing.'

'What does this mean?'

'Where do you tend to do your socializing? Well, it's a chat-up line, isn't it? Although it's probably fairer to call it an opener. Or an *hors d'oeuvre*, as we call it back home. More stuff would have definitely followed. That's the point I'm making.'

'Why do you look at me in this way?'

'What way?'

'You lick your lips and you make your eyebrows go up and down like this. And you look at my breasts.'

'Look,' I go, 'I can't believe you haven't worked it out by now. I like you.'

She's there, 'What?'

'I'm attracted to you. Yeah, no, it's cords on the table time.'

'Yesterday, you did not like me. When you see me for the first time, you make a face like you are going to be sick.'

I probably did. I'm a shocker. That's just, like, an *unconscience* thing?

'Sick?' I go. 'Hordly. You're one of the most beautiful women I've ever seen.'

That does it. With the hand that isn't holding a Kalashnikov, she grabs me by the back of the head and she pulls my face close to hers and her lips look for mine like I'm a Hallowe'en apple on a length of focking string.

Her kiss is surprisingly soft and gentle – especially for a big bird – and she gets really into it, making a bit of a meal of me, then coming up for breath every fifteen or twenty seconds to grab me by the jaw, stare into my eyes and go, 'Pretty boy. You are pretty boy.'

I make a grab for her mausers, which she seems to enjoy, whispering attaboys in African into my ear while I take them for a bit of a spin.

Fred's door is behind her – about ten feet behind her, as it happens – so I decide to seize the initiative then. I put my orms around her waist – I can just about clasp my hands around her – and I walk her backwards – it's like being in a rolling maul – until her back is to the wall, with the door just to my left.

'You are so pretty,' she goes, out of breath. 'You are pretty boy.'

One thing I *will* say in the girl's favour is that she knows how to pay a goy a compliment.

'You're not so bad yourself,' I go, then I reach out my left hand to turn the key in Fred's door. Just as I get my thumb and forefinger on it, she goes, 'Stop!' and she puts her hand on my chest and pushes me backwards. For a second I'm wondering has she copped.

'You think I am pretty?' she goes.

She smiles. All her Christmases.

She's there, 'No one says to me that I am pretty.'

I'm there, 'I find that very hord to believe. You're like something from a movie.'

I'm trying to think of the name of that film: *You did not persuade me, Nicholas!*

I take another run at her and we stort going at each other again – kissing and fondling and paying each other compliments. This time, I'm happy to say, I do manage to turn the key in the door. And not a second too soon either. Because as soon as it's done, Forest grabs me by the hair – by the hair! – and storts literally dragging me up the stairs behind her.

I'm there, 'Jesus Christ!' because it genuinely hurts. There's, like, tears in my eyes as she pulls me – doubled-over and nearly running to keep with her – up those stairs, through the hall and through the living room, where I notice the young boy soldiers, or whatever you want to call them, are all lying around, flaked out, two of them on the actual floor, presumably off their faces on that shit they've been chewing.

She drags me through the gaff like she's pulling a suitcase through the airport and she's late for her flight. She opens the door to her bedroom, hauls me inside, then throws me down on the bed.

Which is a new experience for me, because I'm usually the one in control.

She leans her Kalashnikov against the wall, then puts a foot up on the bed, rolls up the leg of her combats and pulls a knife – I swear to fock – at least fourteen inches long from a sheath strapped to her lower leg. It's, like, a shorp knife, but it's also got teeth like a saw and I'm lying there thinking, Okay, Fred, if there's going to be a rescue, now would be a good time for you to make your entrance.

She lies down on the bed beside me, grabs me by the hair again, then holds the knife, like a dagger, to the side of my head.

She goes, 'You do not try to escape.'

I'm there, 'I couldn't, even if I wanted to.'

She's like, 'Take off my boots,' still with a firm grip of me.

I unlace her boots and I take them off her and drop them on the floor, then I do the same with her socks.

She's goes, 'Next, my trousers,' and I'm thinking, Okay, Fred, you should have let the goys out by now. Where the fock are you?

'My trousers!' she shouts.

I'm there, 'Yeah, no, slow down. The mad thing is that I have all these feelings for you and I don't even know your name,' basically just stalling for time.

'My name is Judith,' she goes, tearing open the buttons of her fly, possibly scared that I might change my mind, then pulling her trousers down herself.

Now, when it comes to women, if there's one point I've been consistent on over the years, it's never divulging what goes on between the sheets – firstly out of respect to myself, but then also out of respect to the girl involved. It's, like, an actual principle for me and I'm not going to break it in this case, other than to tell you of my surprise, even shock, when Judith – hilarious – pulls down those thirty-eight-inch-waist combats to reveal that she's not wearing any knickers. She's commando. Actually, she's *literally* commando, given that that's her AK-47 leaning against the wall over my right hammer.

Again, without talking out of school, she grips my hair tightly and tries to pull my head closer to her – okay, let's just say the word and get it over with – vagina, which, by the way, looks like the proverbial ripped-out fireplace.

I move up her body. I help her out of her T-shirt and bra and I have another crack at her McGillicuddys, which are humungous, in fairness to the girl. Every cloud! She strokes the back of my hair while I have a little play with them – still holding the knife next to my head, by the way – and goes, 'That is nice, pretty boy. Oh, yes, pretty boy.'

I'm a sucker for positive feedback.

But suddenly she's adamant that I'm at the wrong end of her and she tightens her grip on my hair again, puts the point of the knife shorp against my temple and goes, 'No! This! This! This!' and she storts pushing my head south again.

325

I'm thinking, Okay, goys, where the fock are you? This is taking, like, way too long. She moves my head into position and – with no sign of the focking cavalry arriving – I'm forced to suddenly comply.

Discretion – again, I don't need to keep saying it – is sacred to me. But I *can* probably mention, just for the purposes of the story, that going down on Judith is like licking piss out of the doorway of Supermac's.

She ends up being a real fiend for the preliminaries as well. I'm down there a good ten minutes, drawing letters with my tongue – I do the entire alphabet, A to Z, fifteen or sixteen times – while listening to her praising the Lord in a sing-song voice.

That's when, all of a sudden, I hear the sound of, like, laughter coming from somewhere. I swivel my eyes to the right. The boys have obviously woken up, because they're suddenly standing outside, staring in the bedroom window at us. I get an actual fright.

I'm like, 'What the fock?' but Judith is too lost in the moment for embarrassment.

'No,' she goes, tightening her grip of my hair to hold my head in place, 'keep, keep, keep!' and there ends up being, like, more tittering and wolf-whistling and then banging on the window before Judith roars something at them in African, which presumably means, go away, or fock right off.

But they don't. They stay there, enjoying the show, whooping and hollering and high-fiving each other.

Judith puts her head back and orches her back and I'm thinking, Okay, this could possibly be the final phase, thanks be to fock.

And that's when I suddenly feel *the* most savage pain I've ever felt rip across my back. I hear a scream, which I know straight away has come from me. My head goes up and I notice Judith staring at something over my shoulder with a sudden look of fear on her face. There's a man in the room shouting, again, in the local lingo. I roll over – my back is stinging like you wouldn't believe – to find Julius bearing down on me, holding a whip in his hand.

Judith makes an effort to cover her shebas and her other various bits. It's her brother, in fairness. She's talking at, like, ninety Ks an hour, I'd imagine apologizing, but he's obviously calling her every slut under the sun.

He gives me another crack of the whip, this one across the front of my legs and I genuinely howl.

Judith pleads with him – this is my guess – not to hurt me. It's fair to say I've made an impression on the girl.

'Mister fucking Loverman,' Julius goes. 'Mister fucking Lover. Where the fuck is he?'

I'm there, 'Who?' but I'm pretty sure I know who he means.

He gives me another crack – again, across the legs. Same place. It's one of the sorest things I've ever felt.

'Mister fucking Fred,' he goes. 'Mister fucking Fred is gone,' and then he grabs me by the collar of my Lions jersey – I actually hear it rip – pulls me off the bed and drags me through the house.

He obviously wants me to see for myself.

At this stage, roysh, I'm thinking the poor focker doesn't even know the half of it. Wait till he finds out that Fionn, JP, Christian and Oisinn are also gone. They possibly heard Julius and the others coming back, which is why they never came for me, although I imagine they're alerting the local Feds to where I am at this very minute.

Julius shoves me in the back as I'm going down the stairs and I end up nearly losing my footing. When I reach the bottom, I can see that the door of Fred's cell is, like, *ajor*? Julius pushes me into it, going, 'He is gone! Mister fucking Fred is gone!'

He drags me back out again, just as Benjamin and Rolly come tearing down the stairs in an obvious hurry. And that's when I notice that the door of *our* cell is still shut, and a horrible feeling comes over me.

Benjamin puts a key in it and pushes it open. Julius shoves me inside. The goys are all still sitting there.

'He focking pegged it,' Oisinn goes. 'We were shouting at him. We were going, "Fred! Open the focking door!" but he just pegged it. Took the stairs two at a time as well. That must have been the special forces training he mentioned.'

I'm there, 'What a wanker!' and that's when I feel my orms pulled

327

behind me – by presumably Julius – then cuffed together, then a black cloth bag is pulled over my head again.

From the muffled noises in the room, I'm presuming the goys are getting the same treatment.

'Now, we must fucking leave,' Julius goes, turning me around. 'You fucking walk, Mister fucking Loverman.'

We're lying on top of each other – still cuffed and hooded – in the back of a pick-up truck, with the torpaulin pulled over us. We've been driving for, like, five or six hours, on potholed roads, through what I imagine to be just scrubland – I'm picturing it as a kind of hot Cavan? – and I've still got the taste of Forest Whitaker slash Judith in my mouth.

Fionn is talking about – I shit you not – a dude he read about in one of his science magazines who managed to cut a steel frying pan in two using six slices of prosciutto and it's a measure of how bored we all are that I end up going, 'Okay, explain that to me.'

'It's actually quite simple,' Fionn goes – you can tell he hasn't had anyone to talk to for the past, like, six months. 'He used the prosciutto to make a thermal lance – the same thing they use to cut people out of car wrecks.'

I'm there, 'Go on, keep going.'

The whip morks on my back and legs are stinging like fock, by the way.

'Okay,' Fionn goes, 'a thermal lance works by essentially blowing pure oxygen through a pipe packed with iron and magnesium rods – metals that are highly flammable in pure oxygen and release an enormous amount of heat as they are consumed. So you get this jet of superheated iron plasma coming out of the end of the pipe that can cut through metal, even concrete.'

I'm there, 'Yeah, no, but how did he make one of them using prosciutto?' I'm getting focking annoyed now.

'Well, prosciutto contains a huge amount of chemical energy in its proteins and obviously its fat. We release that energy when we eat and digest it. But you can also release it by burning it with a healthy supply of oxygen, which is what this guy did. He wrapped six or seven slices into thin tubes and baked them in a warm oven overnight, to get rid of the water. Then, the following morning, he bundled them up, wrapped them in a few more slices, then baked them again until the entire structure was hard and dry . . .'

'I've never heard anything so ridiculous. I'd love to focking deck this dude. Is he local?'

'Hang on, Ross. Then, to make an airtight outer casing, he wrapped the entire fuel core in uncooked prosciutto. Then he attached one end of it to an oxygen hose, shot the oxygen through it and the flame that came out the other end . . . cut a frying pan in two.'

JP's like, 'Mat's hamazing!'

I'm there, 'It's a waste of good prosciutto is what it is. A waste of my focking time as well. Fionn, can you just move about five inches to your right there so I can kick you in the focking head?'

And that's when I hear the sound of sobbing, here in the back with us.

I'm like, 'Who's that? Which one of us is crying?'

It ends up being Christian.

Oisinn goes, 'Dude, what's wrong?'

And Christian goes, 'We were on Ballinclea Road . . .'

'Who?'

'Me and Lauren. And the kids. Lauren was driving. She went down into first gear coming up to the first ramp . . .'

Stick shift. Jesus Christ. I'm sometimes surprised that the ormy hasn't just moved in and taken over Ireland.

'Christian,' I go, 'everyone in the country has had to adjust. That's what you hear people on TV say all the time.'

'She went over the ramp,' he goes, 'but she just left it in first. Like, she drove to the next ramp, thirty Ks an hour, in first gear. And I said to her, "Lauren, would you not move up to second? Or even third?" and she said, "What's the point if I'm going to be dropping back down to first again before the next ramp?" and I said, "The point is that I don't want to have to shell out for a brand-new focking gearbox – that's the point, you stupid bitch!" Then she storted crying and little Ross storted crying. And . . . little Oliver was even crying.'

I'm like, 'Dude, calm down.'

'That was . . . the day I moved . . . out,' he goes, between sobs. 'I never got to say . . . sorry. I never got . . . to say sorry . . . I never got . . . I never got . . .'

'He's hyperventilating,' Fionn goes. 'He's having a panic attack.'

I'm like, 'Christian, listen to me. You need to breathe . . .'

I'm back feeling guilty again, because deep down, I know that they'd possibly still be together, making meatball melts and whatever else, if it wasn't for me.

He goes, 'I never got . . . to say sorry . . . . I never . . .'

I'm there, 'Christian, name the fifteen who storted against Leicester. Come on. Nacewa, Horgan, O'Driscoll . . . Say it with me, Christian . . . D'Orcy, Fitzgerald, Sexton . . .'

Fionn storts kicking the torpaulin and shouting, 'Pull over! Pull over!' and whoever's doing the actual driving must eventually hear him, roysh, because after thirty seconds or so the truck comes to a sudden stop.

The torpaulin is pulled back and I hear Julius go, 'What the fuck is this bullshit?'

By now, Christian is basically hysterical, going, 'We're going . . . to die . . . We're going . . . to die . . .' in, like, a high-pitched voice.

Fionn's there, 'He's having a panic attack.'

'This fucking bullshit,' Julius goes. Then he opens the low door at the back of the actual flatbed and the five of us – we're talking me, we're talking Christian, we're talking Fionn, we're talking JP, we're talking Oisinn – are pulled out and literally dropped on the side of the road.

'Take the handcuffs off him,' Fionn goes. 'And the hood.'

Julius – or someone – does it. Then they do exactly the same for Fionn. Then my hood is pulled off, then Oisinn's, then JP's – although not our cuffs.

It's actually Ibrahim – the old dude – who does the actual pulling. There's only him, Julius and Judith slash Forest Whitaker, who seems to be the one doing the driving. There's no sign of the other two heads. They shot off in another cor to look for Fred.

Yeah, no, good luck with that, I think.

We're in the middle of this, like, open prairie. I can see what I'm presuming are wildebeest in the distance. It's my first sight of proper Africa. Let's call it *Lion King* Africa, for the sake of argument.

Fionn has Christian sitting down with his back to the rear wheel of the truck. He has his orm around his shoulder and he's using the hood as a bag, which he's telling Christian to blow into it to try to get his breathing back under control. And he's talking nicely to him and I think, Fionn can bore the ears off you with his ridiculous focking stories, but he's a stand-up goy who you'd always want on your side in a crisis.

'How long?' Julius shouts.

Fionn's there, 'Give him a few minutes, will you? Can we get some water as well? He's very badly dehydrated.'

'Maybe I don't have a few minutes. Maybe I just fucking shoot him and leave him here.'

I stand up – my hands still cuffed behind my back, bear in mind – and I go, 'If you shoot him, the bullet will have to pass through me first.'

'I fucking shoot you happily,' he goes and he points his gun at me.

I've scored a lot of people's sisters – including one or two amongst the present company – but I've never known anyone to take it as badly as this dude.

He notices Judith slash Forest staring at me – I think someone's fallen in love – and he flies into a sudden rage. 'Don't you fucking look at him!' he goes.

This is, like, six or seven hours after the event, bear in mind.

Then he turns to me. He's there, 'How can you do this to her? She is fucking pig . . .'

The poor girl is still standing there.

He's there, 'She looks like a wild boar. You understand wild boar? Fucking oink, oink, oink.'

Oisinn goes, 'I need to piss.'

And I'm there, 'Yeah, no, so do I. Come on, be fair. We've been on the road all day.'

Julius looks over his left hammer and points at this area of, like, random bush. 'Go there,' he goes. 'Two and two and one,' meaning me and Oisinn first, then the others after us.

Judith goes, 'I will bring them,' and Julius shouts something at her in the local lingo, then he storts making this, like, braying sound, which is similar to the sex noises she was making when he walked into the room and caught me, as they say, dining at the Y.

It's a pretty good impression – I have to give it to him – but then you'd have to worry about the poor girl's confidence going forward.

In the end, it's decided that Ibrahim should be the one to bring us, which he does. He uncuffs us and we both end up having just a hit and miss. I *could* shit if I wanted to, but I decide not to chance it.

Oisinn looks at me sideways – this is *as* we're pissing? – and he says something that actually surprises me.

He goes, 'Thanks, Ross.'

I'm like, 'Why are you thanking me? I thought you'd be blaming me. I was the one who dragged us all over here.'

'We came here because our friend needed us. And you put your neck on the line to try to get us out. And I'm saying thank you.'

I finish up and put it away. We both do. We turn to walk back to the truck and, just randomly, I go, 'What is a mighty oak but a little nut that held its ground?'

That's when Ibrahim suddenly goes, 'Stop!'

Me and Oisinn both turn. I'm like, 'What's the deal?'

He's there, 'What is this you say?'

I didn't even know he understood English. It's the first time I've heard him even talk.

I repeat it for him. Then I go, 'It's a phrase back home. It's one of Father Fehily's most famous ones – in other words, our old rugby coach.'

He stares at us for a good twenty or thirty seconds until Julius shouts something in African – presumably, 'What the fock?' – and Ibrahim shouts something back – presumably, 'Yeah, no, it's cool!' – and then we walk back to the truck.

Christian has calmed right down. He's, like, sipping water and he seems okay again. Fionn and JP go off to piss. When they come back, we're put back into the truck, our hands cuffed to the front of us this time, and no hoods. The torpaulin is pulled over our heads again and a few seconds later we're back on the road to fock knows where.

I end up falling asleep. We *all* do? Which is amazing. We're, like, piled on top of each other here – we're talking orms and legs everywhere – and yet we all manage to somehow get off.

It *was* a long day.

We end up driving through the night. This I know because I wake up once or twice and I end up hearing them changing drivers.

When I finally wake up – as in properly wake up – I've no idea what time it is, but we've stopped and all I can hear are crickets and the sound of Oisinn snoring and JP muttering gummy threats at someone in his sleep.

Eventually, another cor – although it sounds more like an actual SUV – pulls up alongside us and I hear cor doors slam, then voices, excited voices, shouting back and forth, first Julius, then the gruesome focking twosome, we're talking Benjamin and Rolly, then I smell their cigarettes and I hear them talking furiously in African and then I smell cooking and I realize it's breakfast time.

Fionn wakes up first, then Oisinn, then Christian, then poor JP.

Oisinn goes, 'What time is it?'

I'm like, 'No idea. Just that it's the following day. The other two have just rocked up.'

'Menjamin and Molly?' JP goes.

I'm there, 'Yeah. I'm wondering did they catch Fred.'

Fionn thinks not. He actually scoffs.

'Not with *his* training,' he goes. 'And his instinct for self-preservation.'

I ask Christian if he's okay. We look out for each other. When one is weak, the others stay strong. It's how it's always been. It's how we were raised.

'I feel like I slept for sixteen hours,' he goes. 'Something smells good. Well, edible.'

He's right. It's *actual* food. Not pineapple and tuna, but food that's being actually cooked over a *fire*?

I'm focking storving. I haven't had a hot meal since the so-called lamb biryani that British Airways served me on the flight. None of us has.

After a few minutes, the torpaulin is suddenly pulled back. We're all expecting it to be bright out, but it's still dork. My guess is that it's, like, five or half-five in the morning.

'Good morning,' Julius goes. 'Rise and shine. Today we have delicious breakfast for you,' and I look over and I notice that Ibrahim has two pots on the go on this little, like, *camping* stove?

We climb out of the truck and we sit on the ground. Rolly goes around opening all of our cuffs. Even if we tried to run, there's nowhere to go. To our right is – again – just open scrubland. To our left is what, from this distance, looks like jungle.

Ibrahim brings us our – I'm going to call it – breakfast. It's spaghetti and a meat that he says is, like, *goat*? I don't actually *give* a fock, I'm that hungry. I'd eat a horse and chase the jockey.

'Where are we?' Fionn goes, directing it at Julius.

He's like, 'Near to border.'

Fionn's there, 'Which border? Well, I doubt if you're taking us into South Sudan. Or the Congo. Or even Rwanda. I'm guessing it's Kenya.'

He's there, 'Yes, it's Kenya. Hurry – eat,' and then he stands up, like he has something major to tell us. Sure enough, he goes, 'Gentlemen, I have a fucking surprise for you this morning. You think you say goodbye to Mister fucking Fred yesterday. Many tears. Boo hoo. So now I am happy to say to you . . .' He walks over to the SUV. He's there, 'He is fucking back!' and he opens the back door.

Fred is lying on his stomach, with his hands and legs tied behind his back – I think the phrase is *hog-tied*? – and his mouth is taped up.

Julius claps and goes, 'Hooray!' and then pulls Fred out and drops him on the ground and goes, 'Mister Fred – how we have missed you!' and kicks him a few times in the stomach and face.

I'm thinking, Good enough for the focker. I could actually watch a good hour of this. But then Julius orders Rolly to untie his legs and Benjamin to clear up the stove and all of our breakfast shit and I horse down the last of the goat spaghetti before he can take my plate.

'Good!' Julius goes. 'Today, you have special breakfast because we have long, long walk ahead.'

I'm like, 'Walk?'

I notice that Benjamin is packing the stove and our plates into the SUV. He gets into the driver's seat and storts it up. Judith slash Forest Whitaker gets into the flatbed and does the same.

'Stand up,' Julius goes, snapping a pair of what look like night vision goggles onto his head. 'All of you.'

We climb to our feet. Benjamin and Rolly, I notice, are both holding torches. Benjamin has a map and a compass, while Rolly has a massive rucksack on his back, which Julius is filling with bottles of water and Tracker bors.

Behind us, Ibrahim and Forest drive off in the SUV and the flatbed.

'They're going to drive through the border into Kenya,' Fionn goes. 'I'm presuming we're going to be marched through this area of jungle and they're going to meet us on the other side.'

Julius is like, 'Let's go, let's go, let's go.'

I'm there, 'Whoa, whoa, whoa! I'm not focking walking in there,' because it's still pitch dark, bear in mind.

And, by the way, you haven't seen dark until you've experienced night-time in Africa.

But we're suddenly shoved towards the mouth of the jungle. Julius is at the front, then it's me, Fionn, Christian, Benjamin, JP, Oisinn and Rolly, in that actual order.

I'm going, 'Is this definitely wise? Should we not wait until it's maybe daytime?'

'No time,' Julius goes. 'Today, we walk for fourteen hours.'

I'm there, 'Excuse me?' and it's at that exact point that I hear it.

Were you ever driving through the Phoenix Pork and you heard a noise coming from the zoo that caused you to basically shit yourself and nearly drive into a focking deer? You know the noise I'm talking about. *Oooh-oooh-oooh aaah-aaah-aaah* is probably the best way that I can describe it. When you're in Dublin, your first instinct is, Okay, I don't know what the fock made that noise, but I hope it's in a cage. But when you're in Africa, there are no cages. We're about to walk into its focking gaff.

I'm like, 'I'm not going in there. End of.'

I'm genuinely shitting it like I've never shat before.

Julius takes the night vision goggles off his head and fixes them to my face. He's like, 'You will go in there first, Mister Loverman,' and he gives me a shove forward. 'You will lead the fucking way.'

The next three hours are – I swear to fock – *the* most terrifying of my life. The insanity of it. We morch blindly into that dork, dork jungle with me – focking me! – navigating our way along a pathway that, despite what the map says, doesn't seem to even exist.

All I have is, like, a metre of branch to beat my way through the thick, I suppose, *foliage*? Branches snap back and hit me full in my still bruised face, or across the tops of my legs, which are stinging like fock from the whipping I took. And though you'll probably think I'm imagining this, vines appear out of nowhere and wind themselves around my neck and my ankles.

And that's not even the most frightening thing.

Night-vision goggles allow you to see everything in green and every focking step on that walk I curse my luck that I was the one who ended up having to wear them. Ignorance, in my experience, is not a bad thing. There are things in this world that are best experienced with your eyes closed and, take it from me, the African focking jungle is one of them. At least in the dark, you don't know what's looking at you from the trees above you, or the undergrowth below you, and sizing you up for breakfast. The goggles allow me to see not only the shapes and outlines of things, but, even more terrifyingly, the whites of eyes, and, three or four times in the first fifteen minutes, I literally scream with fear.

I'm like, 'There's something up ahead. Oh my God, we're going to be eaten, we're going to be focking eaten.'

Julius just shoves me forward and goes, 'Colobus,' which is apparently a type of monkey, although there's no way he could be possibly sure.

'Just keep going,' Fionn – directly behind him – goes. 'The quicker we walk, the sooner we get to where we're going, wherever that is.'

I'm like, 'That's easy for you to focking say. I'm the one at the front. I'm the one who gets eaten if we walk into, I don't know, a lion or a tiger.'

Fionn laughs. He's like, 'There are no tigers in Africa, Ross.'

I'm there, 'That's one of the most ridiculous things I've ever focking heard. Think about what you just said, Fionn.'

He goes, 'Tigers are native to Asia, Ross, not Africa.'

That doesn't sound right. But then he does know a lot of stuff.

I'm like, 'Dude, let's just agree to differ. Let's just agree to focking differ,' and I go back to chopping a path for us through the trees, the branches continuing to snap against my various bruises and welts, and eyes, left and right, watching this procession – like you or I might stare at those little coloured bowls passing on the conveyor belt in YO! Sushi – thinking, Would *I* eat that funny-looking thing? Yeah, fock it – why not?

Every step of those first three hours is a minor focking hort attack and the sight of the sun announcing itself through a gap in the trees makes me as happy as I was when my children were born.

Birds are suddenly trilling and cawing and whatever-elseing above our heads. And now that the danger of something jumping out in front of us and eating us on the spot has passed, Julius decides that he wants to lead the group, which he's more than focking welcome to do.

I even let Fionn go ahead of me, just to create a buffer, and the dude storts trying to engage Julius in conversation. 'What is this route?' he goes.

Julius is like, 'Smuggling route. Old. Very old.'

I turn around to Christian and ask him if he's okay and he nods and says sorry for losing it and I tell him not to be focking stupid. It's totally understandable with the shit we're in. He says thanks and I put my orm around his shoulder and – this isn't gay, by the way – I kiss him on the top of the head.

Christian is such a great goy and – again – I have to swallow down my guilty feelings about ruining the poor focker's life.

JP, who's next behind me, tells me I did great this morning ('Moo did bate, Moss!') and presumably he means leading us through the jungle in the pitch dark.

I'm there, 'It's nice to get that recognition.'

Christian suddenly gasps, then points out this bird sitting on a branch, literally six feet above our heads, and he's, like, all sorts of colours, we're talking orange and blue and green and one or two others, and he's got a beak that's nearly half the size of his body, then a black strip across his eyes that looks like a Zorro mask.

And I feel suddenly, I don't know, *lighter*? It's not that the danger has gone away. The three goons are still carrying Kalashnikovs. It's just that it's, I don't know, shifted. Walking through this jungle, with fock knows what lurking behind the next tree, it feels like we're all in the same boat – the kidnappers and the kidnapped. Suddenly, it feels like no one is in control. No, what I actually mean is that the jungle is in control – the jungle and whatever it decides to do to us.

I know that sounds possibly deep.

Oisinn all of a sudden bursts into song.

> 'Rob the Builder!
> Does he build things?
> Rob the Builder!
> Does he fock!'

We all laugh. We're obviously *all* feeling the same sense of relief. Suddenly, we're not scared of Julius, who's still leading the way, or Benjamin, who's now walking just in front of me, or Rolly, who's walking – still in flip-flops, the mad fock – at the very back of the group, keeping a close eye on Fred, who's the only one of us whose hands are cuffed and whose mouth is still gagged.

I'm there, 'Come on, Oisinn, give us a story!' like I said, suddenly feeling a bit giddy.

And Oisinn – fair focks to him – has one ready for us.

He goes, 'It was a quiet morning on the ghost estate. Rob noticed that Sluggish, Slothful, Shiftless and Slack seemed a little down in the mouth. "What's up, fellas?" he wondered. Slack shook his head.

"Nothing," he said. But Rob knew that something was wrong. "Come on," he said. "You can tell me." It was Shiftless who broke the news to him. "It's your friend, Fiachra," he said. Rob scratched his head. "You mean Fiachra the TD?" he wondered. Shiftless nodded sadly. "Yes," he said. "He's been saying things about you in the newspapers, Rob! He said it was unacceptable that the very people who brought this country to its knees were still living the high life while the ordinary people of Ireland were paying for the greed and recklessness of others with increased taxes and cuts in vital public services!" '

Julius – I swear to God – turns around with, like, a big grin on his face. 'Keep telling this story,' he goes. 'I like this fucking story.'

So that's what Oisinn ends *up* doing?

He's like, 'Slothful shook his head sadly. "What a snake!" he said. But, just at that very moment, Fiachra arrived. "Here he comes," said Slack. "You can ask him yourself!" Fiachra was smiling. He was clearly happy about something. "Hello, Rob," he said. But Rob was in no mood for pleasantries. "Is it true what you've been saying," he asked, "in the newspapers?" Fiachra nodded. "Yes," he said. "The time has come for a new kind of politics! We must start serving the people!" Rob was almost speechless. "The people?" he said. "What do they matter? They're not clever like property developers." Fiachra nodded and tried his best to look understanding. "Well," he said, "they're still the people who elect us! And they're tired of seeing the likes of you drinking cocktails on your yacht as if nothing happened. Flying your helicopter down to Ballybunnion to play nine holes of golf. Collecting your six or seven grand a week from NAMA for doing nothing. There's genuine suffering out there! And when we return to Government, we will make sure that the people who created this mess will finally start picking up the tab!" Sluggish, Slothful, Shiftless and Slack gasped, for they had never heard Fiachra the TD talk like this before. Rob was downcast. "Do you really mean that?" he asked. There was a moment's silence. "Of course I don't!" said Fiachra suddenly. "It's just something we have to say to get dopes to vote for us!" Rob and Fiachra laughed. Sluggish and Slothful laughed. Shiftless and Slack laughed, too. "Fiachra," Rob said, "I'd like to make a generous contribution to your next political campaign." Fiachra nodded. "Thanks, Rob," he said. "I'll *vote* for that!"'

I laugh. We all laugh, but no one laughs horder than Julius.

'This is a funny story,' he goes. 'Rob the Builder. I fucking love this guy!' and he's still chuckling away to himself – I shit you not – half an hour later when we stop walking to have our lunch.

Lunch, by the way, is a litre of water and three Trackers each, roasted nut rather than the chocolate chip.

'Rob the Builder,' Julius goes. He's sitting cross-legged on the ground – as we all are – in this, like, *clearing*? 'He is your friend?'

Oisinn goes, 'What, Rob? No, no, he's just a character I made up. I invented him.'

Julius is obviously disappointed. His face just drops. He's like, 'Oh.'

I'm there, 'But there's loads of fockers like him back home, aren't there, Oisinn?'

Oisinn's like, 'Oh, yeah. I mean, JP's old man would be friends with a lot of them.'

Julius nods. He's happy to hear it.

I notice that JP has his head down and he hasn't touched his bors. His mouth is obviously still hurting him.

I'm there, 'My old man would be friends with a lot of them too. Practically half of his mates are in NAMA.'

Julius lights up a cigarette, then throws one each to Benjamin and Rolly. He's like, 'What is NAMA?'

It's Oisinn who ends up explaining it to him. 'It's, like, an organization that was set up to bail out property developers,' he goes. 'People like Rob the Builder.'

'I fucking love Rob the Builder. What is *bail out*?'

'Well, basically, a lot of developers in Ireland lost everything – billions, in some cases – when the economy collapsed. So NAMA pays them six or seven thousand euros a week.'

'They pay them?'

'Yeah.'

'These rich people who lose their money?'

'Yeah.'

'Is like charity?'

'Yeah, no, it kind of *is* a charity, yeah.'

Julius looks confused. He's like, 'But where does this NAMA get this money?'

'Well, I suppose, from the people.'

'From the people?'

Julius looks around him. Benjamin and Rolly both say something to him in African and he storts explaining NAMA to them. Their eyes and mouths go wide. They've obviously never heard anything like it. They're clearly impressed. When he's finished explaining it, Julius laughs, then the other two join in. When a bunch of gun-toting African gangsters admire the way your country does business, you've got to seriously wonder about the place.

'JP,' I go, because I'm still watching him, 'are you okay?'

He looks up and he nods, but he's got, like, tears streaming down his face.

I turn to Julius, and since he's in such good form, I go, 'Dude, can you give him something? His mouth is in agony.'

Julius goes, 'What is wrong with his mouth?'

'Well, your two goys there kicked his focking teeth down his throat.'

Julius takes two long drags off his cigarette, then stands up, goes to his rucksack and pulls a hipflask out of the front pocket, which he then hands to JP.

'Brandy,' he goes. 'Rémy Martin. Very good. A gift for you.'

JP takes it and knocks back a lungful, while I pick up one of his Tracker Bors and stort breaking bits off it and focking them at Fred, who's sitting about ten feet away. It's funny the way the bits bounce off his focking head.

There's still a bit of the school bully left in me, I'm happy to say.

Julius goes, 'I would like to hear more of the adventures of Rob the Builder!'

But then Benjamin tells him to suddenly shush, like he's *heard* something? Now, I have to admit, roysh, that *I* didn't hear a thing, but he jumps to his feet, then so does Rolly, and the two of them stort spinning around, with their guns raised, trying to work out where this sound – which none of the rest of us can hear – is coming from.

Julius all of a sudden points to the area of bush that's immediately behind me. He nods at the other two, then he quietly attaches the banana-shaped magazine to the gun and slips the safety catch.

Then, without any warning – and with the cigarette still in his mouth – he suddenly opens up, firing off round after round into the bushes about six inches above my focking head. Now, I don't know how many of you have ever heard a Kalashnikov in full voice. But ask anyone who's done the whole year-out-travelling-around-Thailand thing and shot a cow or a wildebeest at a firing range. The noise is deafening and very focking frightening.

I hit the deck, in fact, with my two hands cupped around my ears. I possibly even scream. Then suddenly the shooting has stopped and Julius is stepping over me and pulling back the bushes behind me.

There's some kind of animal back there – I can see it from where I'm lying – shot to focking pieces, blood and guts everywhere and flies already arriving on the scene for the buffet.

'Wild pig,' Julius goes, then he looks down at me and wipes his bloodied hand on the front of my Lions jersey. 'It look like my sister, yes? You want to fuck this? You want to fuck this, Mister Lover Lover?'

I tell him no, even though it's not a serious question. Then he laughs and goes, 'Okay, time to go,' and we get to our feet and we pick up the trail again.

It's just getting dark when we reach the end of the jungle. We can pick out the SUV and the flatbed truck in the distance, across an area of just scrubland, then as we get closer we can see Ibrahim and Judith slash Forest Whitaker. Her face lights up when she sees me.

Our lives were obviously in far greater danger than we even realized, roysh, because Ibrahim greets Benjamin like he thought he'd never see him again and even Julius seems relieved, patting me, Fionn, JP, Christian and Oisinn on the back and telling us that we did good.

The men stand around and smoke and Julius tells Ibrahim the story of shooting the boar in African, then also the punchline of me wanting to possibly ride it. Forest doesn't rise to it. She just keeps staring at me, then every time I catch her eye, she sort of, like, orches her back, to make her palookas stick out even more.

It's clear I made a big impression on the girl.

We're handcuffed again and loaded onto the back of the flatbed – this time *with* Fred? – although he's still gagged. The torp is pulled over us again, although none of us complains. We're, like, banjoed from the walk. Christian, especially, looks wrecked, having had the permanent squits for the last four hours of the walk, while JP is hammered on the brandy.

It's not long before we're asleep and we stay that way for most of the next twelve hours – until it's suddenly morning again.

The truck pulls to a stop, but they don't come near us. They're obviously just changing drivers. I'm pretty sure it's Julius who takes over from his sister.

'What date is it?' Christian goes.

And Fionn – who *was* counting the days off, remember – goes, 'It's the fourteenth of December.'

I'm like, 'Don't worry, Christian. We're going to be home for Christmas. I guarantee it.'

Fionn's like, 'We might not be, Ross. I don't think you should be making promises like that.'

'Dude, I've just guaranteed it,' I go, 'which means it's going to focking happen.'

Oisinn's there, 'What's everyone's first meal going to be?'

'Mishkanners,' JP goes.

He means Iskanders. He's mullered as well as toothless. We all laugh.

I'm like, 'Sorcha does these, like, mustard pork chops, although I wouldn't be a hundred percent certain she didn't rip the idea off from Kevin Thornton. She maybe added something or took something away.'

It's nice what we're doing. Visualizing being home. I think we're a lot more positive than we were about getting out of this alive. Surviving the jungle was, like, massive in terms of our confidence and you could even say self-belief.

'I'll tell you what I'm going to do,' Fionn goes. 'I'm going to take Jenny somewhere really nice. L'Ecrivain or somewhere like that. Cured salmon. Carpaccio of beef. All the courses. Scallops. And then I'm going to propose to her properly.'

I feel the sudden need to say something. I'm a focking idiot, of course. I should keep the old von Trapp shut, but I can't.

He's a mate.

I'm there, 'Like I said, Fionn, I wouldn't be a hundred percent sure that Jenny is the one for you. I'd stay out of Weirs for another while yet.'

There's, like, silence – a good thirty seconds of silence, when all I can hear is the belch of the truck engine and the occasional bang when we take a dip into a pothole.

'Oh my God,' Fionn suddenly goes, 'you rode her!'

I'm there, 'Excuse me?'

This is, like, under the torpaulin, remember, where he can't see my face.

He goes, 'You had sex with Jenny.'

I'm there, 'I can't believe you would think me capable of something like that.'

'You did, didn't you?'

I take a breath. I'm like, 'Yeah, no, okay, I did.'

I hear the others even gasp.

I'm there, 'But she was wrong for you, Fionn.'

He's like, 'I knew it. I focking knew it. I said to myself, I hope Jenny heads to Ireland because I know the goys will look after her. As long as Ross doesn't try to ride her.'

'Dude, what kind of a girl has sex with the friend of her kid-napped supposed fiancée? I'm asking that in all seriousness. Not the kind of girl I want to see one of my best mates end up with, put it that way.'

He's like, 'You bastard!' and you have to remember that Fionn hordly *ever* swears? 'You focking . . .'

'Dude,' I go, 'I never planned it. Chinese or Chinesey-looking birds do very little for me. It just came up one night – you could say the opportunity presented itself – and I took full advantage. But she's not all there, Fionn. I'm wondering did you know that?'

'She has issues, yes.'

'See, there you are, admitting it.'

'I was helping her. She'd finally found a medication that suited her.'

It's Oisinn who comes to my defence. He's like, 'Fionn, what Ross did was totally despicable. But he's right. She stole your table quiz money.'

Fionn's like, 'What?'

I sit tight and say fock-all. It's the kind of shit that sounds better coming from others.

'She was about to go off on a cruise,' Oisinn goes. 'Dude, your parents ended up having to put her on a plane home to New Zealand.'

Fionn goes, 'I'm going to kill you, Ross.'

I'm there, 'Dude, you've just had the facts laid out for you. I don't understand how you can still blame me.'

He's like, 'I'm going to kill you.'

That ends up putting a bit of a dampener on the day. We're mostly silent for the next – whatever – twelve hours or so, even when we stop for water, Tracker Bors and toilet breaks.

Under the torp, it becomes impossible to tell the time, or even differentiate between night or day, especially with all the sleep we end up doing. But if you were to ask me to guess, I'd say we end up driving for, like, a day or a day and a half minimum.

I wake up from a pretty deep sleep and I notice that Fred Pfanning's head is, like, four or five inches away from my foot, so I stretch out my leg and I accidentally on purpose kick him in the face a couple of times with the sole of my Dube.

I'm like, 'Oh, sorry!' but unfortunately what ends up happening is that I manage to somehow loosen his gag and, ten seconds later, he's managed to work himself free of it.

'Cheps,' he goes, trying to catch his breath, 'you have to listen to me . . .'

Christian's there, 'We don't have to listen to anything you say, you focking traitor!'

'There wasn't time to let you ite,' he tries to go. 'I heard the cars pulling up iteside.'

'So, what, you just pegged it.'

'I'm here now, aren't I?'

I go, 'Yeah, no, only because you got picked up again.'

He's there, 'I got picked up deliberately, you fool!'

'Do you want the word *Dubarry* printed backwards on your fore-head permanently?'

'I went beck to the hotel where I'd been staying. I knew they'd come looking for me there. All my things were there. Passport, money . . .'

Oisinn goes, 'So why did you run away if you wanted to be caught? This is horseshit.'

He goes, 'I had to collect something.'

'What?'

'A GPS device.'

'Excuse me?'

'We're being trecked. By my colleagues – who *will* effect a rescue, I can guarantee thet much.'

The truck suddenly stops. I hear voices. Julius and Forest and, I think, Rolly. A few seconds later, the cover is pulled back and the light is suddenly blinding. It's the middle of the afternoon – that's my guess – nearly two days since we left the jungle.

Julius seems tense, even angry. And he looks wrecked. 'We are here!' he goes. 'The fuck out! Quickly, quickly!'

We're all dragged out of the back and we're put standing in, like, a parade line and that's when I notice something that I haven't seen since I left Ireland.

The sea.

And not only the sea. We're also looking at a beach of white sand and palm trees that wouldn't look out of place as a screensaver.

'Where the fock are we?' Christian goes, speaking for – I think – many of us.

Fionn's there, 'Unless I'm very much mistaken, that's the Indian Ocean. In which case, we've driven right the way across Kenya.'

'Got it in one,' Fred goes, out of the corner of his mouth. I'm thinking, where the fock is this escape committee he was banging on about ten seconds ago? 'We're in the north-east of the country – by my estimate, four or five miles south of the border. And I trust you know what border I'm referring to.'

Fionn's like, 'Somalia.'

It's a new one on me, but it actually sounds beautiful.

'Silence!' Julius shouts.

Christian's there, 'I don't understand – who the fock has bought us?' as two dots suddenly appear on the horizon, dots which get bigger and bigger until they eventually turn into speedboats, heading in our direction.

Fred goes, 'It's obvious, isn't it? Pirates.'

10. Shiver Me Basic Timbers

We're divided up. Me, Fionn and Christian are ordered into one boat, along with Julius and Judith slash Forest Whitaker. In the other boat is JP, Oisinn and Fred along with Rolly, Benjamin and Ibrahim. The two boats are being driven by dudes – yes, black dudes – who don't look any older than sixteen. They're both, like, bare-chested, with denim cut-offs and so thin you wouldn't know whether to say hello to them or boil their bones for stock.

It's, like, awkward stepping into the boat with our hands cuffed behind our backs and Julius is shouting at us to hurry – 'fucking hurry!' – but a few minutes later we're sitting on the wet floor of the boat, the water soaking through the orse of our trousers and the smell of engine oil in our nostrils, watching the beach behind us shrink away to nothing.

I'm the first one of us to actually acknowledge what's happening. 'Pirates,' I go. 'That is so focking random.'

Christian's like, 'Why are you smiling, Ross?'

I'm there, 'I don't know – probably *because* it's so random?'

'He's thinking about *Pirates of the Caribbean*,' Fionn goes – still pissed at me for taking Jenny to the shake shop.

I'm like, 'No, I'm not.'

'Yes, he is. He's imagining Johnny Depp in eyeliner and a bandana.'

I actually am, although I wouldn't give him the pleasure of letting him know he's right.

I don't know how you actually measure sea, roysh, but we're a good ten- or fifteen-minute drive out into it when the water becomes all of a sudden choppy. We're, like, hitting these big waves head-on and the boat is lifting into the air and that's when I get all of a sudden scared again – thoughts of Jack Sparrow and all of the rest of it totally banished – because if the boat was to tip over it would mean certain death. I famously can't swim. And even if I could, my hands are literally tied here.

The sea throws us about like a – I'm going to say rugby ball – for a good ten or fifteen minutes and with every lurch of the boat I feel like I'm going to genuinely spew. Judith smiles at me once or twice and that doesn't help my stomach either.

But that's when Christian suddenly spots it in the distance – a ship.

It's, like, a funny-shaped ship as well. It's not like the ships you see in – yeah, no – movies like *Titanic* and blah, blah, blah. It's, like, square. Or *oblong*, I think is the *actual* shape? So it's hord to know when you look at it which is the actual front and which is the actual back.

It's painted, like, two colours – the top half is, like, white and the bottom half is, like, blue. And it's focking humungous as well. As we get closer and closer to it, it looms over us like, I don't know, something.

Of the two speedboats, ours is the first one to reach it. Our driver kills the engine, then catches onto a rope that's thrown from somewhere up above us and he pulls the boat closer to the ship until their two sides are basically touching. There's, like, shouting, again from up above us, presumably the actual *deck* of the ship, and our dude shouts something back. It's all in African, so it's basically just nonsense to me.

I'm staring up at this big metal cliff face in front of us, wondering how the fock we're going to get up there, when a rope ladder is thrown over the side and this fear suddenly grips me. Julius unlocks my cuffs. He unlocks all of our cuffs, in fact, then he goes, 'Okay, up this fucking ladder. You are first, Mister fucking Lover.'

Now, I wouldn't be a major fan of heights and the idea of climbing thirty feet up a rope ladder with the big lapping sea below gives me the pretty much instant squits.

'I can't,' I go. 'I actually can't. I'm very much scared of heights.'

He's there, 'Are you very much scared of a bullet in the fucking head?'

He drags me to my feet and shoves me over to the side of the boat. I put my two trembling hands on the sides of the ladder and

349

my right foot on the first rung, then I stort climbing the thing, my eyes firmly shut, feeling like the ladder above me is about to peel away from the side of the ship at any second, throwing me backwards into the sea.

The sixty seconds it takes me to reach the top are – I swear to fock – the longest sixty seconds of my life and I can't even begin to tell you the relief I feel when I put my right hand on the ship's metal gord rail. I climb up onto it, throw my leg over it and tumble onto the deck of the ship

I look up, roysh, and there's, like, ten – or possibly as many as fifteen – men standing in a horseshoe shape, looking down at me.

Again, they're not pirates as you'd *expect* pirates to look? Hats that curl up at the sides, wooden legs and parrots – there's literally none of that. These dudes look like gangster rappers and that's not me shitting you. It's all, like, big muscles and tattoos and shades and chunky gold. And Glocks. Yeah, no, there's no Kalashnikovs here. It's all Glocks.

I feel like I'm in a Rick focking Ross video.

The others climb over the side then, one by one, at sixty-second intervals, first Christian, then Fionn, then Julius, then, with a surprising amount of grace, given that she's a big, fat balooba, Judith slash Forest Whitaker. The pirates – it feels weird calling them that, because they're, like, *not*? – they laugh and nudge each other at the sight of her and they say shit to each other out of the corner of their mouths, which I take to be *their* equivalent of, 'I don't fancy yours much,' or, 'I wouldn't ride her into battle.'

One of the pirates steps forward – he's obviously the pirate leader – and, I swear to you, in English, he goes, 'Yo, I be Amadeus.'

Julius is there, 'Hello, my name is Emeka,' which is the first time I've heard his real name mentioned, although I'll probably go on calling him Julius, because it's kind of stuck now.

They greet each other like two stors of hip hop, the low five, which then turns into a chest-bump, then a hug, with lots of shoulder- and back-slapping on the way, as well as calling each other cousins, even though I doubt if they *actually* are?

Africa seems to be a pretty big place.

Amadeus is built like a focking Abercrombie model. He's black – again, obvious – and his hair is shaved tight, maybe a mork four, and dyed red, we're talking full-on Ronald McDonald red here. His two eye-teeth, I notice, are gold and he's wearing aviators, as well as a white vest, camo trousers – not unlike mine, except they're three-quarter length – and more gold chains than Thomas focking Gear would see in an average year.

The two dudes are still exchanging pleasantries when the rest of our porty arrives over the gord rail – first Oisinn, then Benjamin, then JP, then Fred, then Rolly.

Julius grabs Fred and leads him over to Amadeus like he's a prize horse. Which I suppose in some ways he *is*?

'This,' Julius goes. 'This is the fucking asshole. He has high friends. MI6. Fucking asshole.'

Amadeus smiles, his gold teeth winking in the sun. 'Yo,' he goes, 'me get five million large for a whiff of that dicksuck. Else the game be rigged – you feel?'

Julius goes, 'Er, yes, yes,' even though he hasn't a focking clue what the dude is saying.

Amadeus looks at the rest of us. He's like, 'Yo, nigga – who be the civilians?'

'They're British,' Fred – quick as a flash – goes. 'These cheps are all British subjects. Just like me.'

We possibly should correct him, but his information seems to definitely please Amadeus, for whatever reason.

He's like, 'That be tight, yo.'

He takes off his aviators and I see his eyes for the first time. They're horrible, clouded with cataracts, which I recognize from the time Sorcha's granny had them. He looks actually blind even though he's obviously not.

'Yo, nigga,' he goes, directing at it me, 'you know where I learn English?'

I'm there, 'Was it from *The Wire*?'

I hear JP groan. I mean, what the fock am I supposed to say? Amadeus walks right up to me, so close that for a second I'm convinced he's going to knee me in the balls.

I'm a bit taken aback – we possibly all are – when he goes, 'That be it, yo! This be one clever nigga. You like *The Wire?*'

I'm there, 'Er, yeah, no, the first series was alright. The one that was all set in the docks, though, I found that pretty hord to follow. I gave up on it after three or four episodes. I was going to stick the subtitles on, but then I just thought, fock it, sure you might as well read a book as do that.'

He nods like I've just made some, I don't know, big important point. Then he goes, 'This nigga don't like involving no taxpayers in the game who ain't already *in* the game – you feel me?'

I'm there, 'Er, yeah.'

'That ain't how this nigga carries. Ain't got no beef with no working man. This be just binniss – you feel?'

I'm there, 'Er, yeah – again, yeah.'

He nods. I kind of think he likes me. I don't know. Maybe he respects me for calling it in relation to *The Wire*.

He turns around then to his, I don't know, fellow pirates – the lower-ranking Mackenzie Crook-types – and he goes, 'Put them with the other niggas, yo,' and then all these hands suddenly seize us and shove us down a flight of metal stairs, below deck, then into a room where six men, all of them in sailor suits, are already sitting, tied up.

Our new cell is only about thirty feet by thirty feet and it seriously stinks of fish. Even so, it's a definite improvement on our cell back in Yung Gun Ganger – and even the back of that flatbed truck.

The sailors, it turns out, are from France and this is, like, *their* ship that's been hijacked? Fred storts banging on to them in French and of course Fionn can't resist the temptation to embarrass those of us who never did a focking tap in Madame Chauliac's class.

He's focking fluent obviously.

'*Bleu bleu bleu bleu bleu,*' he goes – not literally. I'm just telling you what it sounds like to *my* ears?

But *they* obviously understand him, roysh, because they're straight back with a bit of, '*Je je je je,*' of their own, then he turns around to us – the normal ones who even failed *pass* French – and makes a big deal of translating what they said.

He's like, 'They took over the boat about a week ago. They want six million dollars to release the ship and its cargo.'

He had a thing for Madame Chauliac as well, even though she wasn't great. I always thought she looked like Eric Elwood and that's not me being a bastard.

Oisinn's like, 'What are they carrying?'

Yeah, no, *I* was actually going to ask that?

Fionn's like, 'Apparently, a bit of everything. Food. Car parts. Electronics.'

'How do they think they can get away with it?' Christian goes, sounding seriously pissed off. 'What, board a ship, hold everyone to ransom – and then what?'

Fionn goes, 'Hop in their speedboats and return to Somalia. I mean, it's a lawless country. There's no government to speak of. No police force.'

'Pack of dicks,' I go, I think speaking for us all.

Fionn's there, 'The way *they* see it, Christian, is that they're just taking back what the West stole from them. The communities along the Somali coast used to live on fish, until the big Western trawlers came and plundered the seas around here. These pirates see themselves as heroic figures, stealing back what was rightfully theirs.'

'Well,' I go, 'I'm still calling them dicks.'

JP goes, 'Mot hoo hey mont mi *hus?*' meaning, what do they want with *us?*

It's another good question.

It's, like, Fred who this time answers. 'Their interest in me,' he goes, 'is purely finencial, I expect. Security consultant with a military beckground. Well, you heard the chep earlier. They think they can get a lot of money for me. With you cheps, I suspect they're plenning to use you as some type of human shield.'

Er, human shield? Okay, that does *not* sound good?

'Whoa!' I go. 'What the fock are you talking about?'

'Well, according to these cheps, both the British and French navies have ships in the region. The pirates know they won't fire on them if there are British and French netionals on board.'

I'm like, 'Whoa, horsey! We're not even British. I don't even know why you told them we were.'

'Because if they knew you were Irish,' he goes, 'you would be of nay importance to them whatsoever, at least from a strategic point of view. They'd have shot you dead and dumped your bodies overboard.'

I'm just like, 'Yeah, whatever.'

Christian goes, 'Six million dollars, though. I mean, how likely is it that the shipping company will pay?'

Fred's there, 'I would say pretty likely. Well, it's in their interests. A hijecked vessel like this one could run up a hundred thousand dollars a day in operating costs and penalties for late delivery. Thet's not even taking into account how much of the cargo ends up spoiled. It makes sense to pay up and pay up quickly. That's what makes it such a viable business for these bloody pirates. Some of these gengs are making up to twenty million dollars a year.'

That's not bad, I suppose.

Oisinn goes, 'Well, let's just hope they do pay and then just let us go.'

Fred's there, 'Well, at least we're being trecked,' and then he says something in French – *'le le le le le le le'* – which I presume is about the GPS device he's, like, supposedly carrying about his person.

Then Fionn weighs in with a bit of, *'Oui oui oui,'* and the dudes all nod.

I try to get a bit of, like, *proper* conversation going then?

I'm like, 'Here, Fionn, do you know who'd be actually proud to hear you gibbering away like that? Madame Chauliac. Do you remember in third year she asked you to stand up and read something and you had a big focking horn on you?'

He just blanks me, though. I can't believe he's still sore at me.

I'm there, 'Fionn, do you remember?' because I always make the effort to fix shit. 'It was like you had a can of Lynx in the front of your trousers.'

He turns on me all of a sudden. He's like, 'Ross, I'm not focking talking to you, okay?'

I'm there, 'Yeah, no, can I just remind you that you talked to me in the speedboat? It was when you said that I expected all the pirates to be like Jack Sparrow. And I actually *did*, in fairness to you. I'm admitting that.'

He turns around to JP and he's like, 'Hopefully, once the ransom is paid, they'll realize that we're no longer of any use to them,' making a massive point of blanking me. 'Although I wonder what will happen to the gang that originally took us?'

Fred's there, 'The pirates will kill them, of course. They're not going to gay sharing their plunder with some strangers they've never met before. They'll kill them. I'm rather surprised that they didn't do it the instant we arrived.'

I end up suddenly losing it with Fionn. I'm like, 'Fock you, Fionn.'

He tries to go, 'Ross, I've made my position clear. I've no interest in speaking to you.'

'Yeah, no,' I go, 'it suits you to blame me, of course, because it means you don't have to ask yourself the hord questions.'

He's like, 'Hard questions? What are you talking about?'

I'm there, 'I can't believe you'd end up with someone like that girl. Focking Jenny. God, you really know how to pick the winners, don't you, Fionn? I'm disappointed with you. I'm letting you know that.'

If he wasn't sitting flat on the floor with his back to the wall and his wrists handcuffed, he'd throw a definite punch at me – or at least he'd try.

He's like, '*You're* disappointed with *me*? Are you focking serious?'

I'm there, 'Yes, I am serious.'

He goes, 'I'm torn away from the life I knew and loved. I endure six months of enforced isolation and starvation and despair at the hands of armed men who threaten my life almost every day, sometimes just for the sport of it. And while that's happening, my so-called friend is back home, having sex with my girlfriend.'

Fred goes, 'Well, I can vouchsafe for thet! I saw them!' trying to come across as the – all of a sudden – hero. 'They were in her car, opposite that pub.'

Fionn goes, 'You did it in the car park opposite Kielys?'

'They were going at it like animals,' Fred goes.

I'm there, 'So you're actually my proof – that Jenny was into it as much as I was.'

I notice the sailors shaking their heads, then whispering furiously amongst themselves. I'm not going to be judged by French people when it comes to shit like this. I know that sounds possibly racist. They'd get up on a borbershop floor if it had enough hair on it.

I go, 'You don't know the circumstances, so keep your big French noses out of my bee's wax. You're a country of horn-dogs anyway.'

It's Oisinn who, again, comes rushing to my defence. 'Fionn,' he goes, 'Jenny wasn't right – you know that – mentally. Five grand, Fionn. She was going off on a cruise.'

Fionn goes, 'She must have stopped taking her medication or something,' still determined to see the best in her.

Then Christian gets in on the act. 'Whatever you think of what Ross did,' he goes, 'he came for you. He walked out on a wife and three newborn babies to come here and try to rescue you.'

And it's at that point that something passes over me, like a wave of nausea, which I recognize straight away as the stirring of my conscience.

The food ends up being great. That has to be said. All *we've* had in the last twenty-four hours, bear in mind, is Tracker Bors and I'm storving. Dinner ends up being a chicken curry and it's incredible, we're talking Kingsland-in-Glasthule-incredible. And there's, like, bread – loads of it – and Coca focking Cola, if you can believe that.

I horse mine into me, then I sit there with my back against the wall and my two hands resting, cuffed, but content, on my stomach.

Fionn and Fred continue chattering away in French to the sailor dudes. It's getting very annoying at this stage.

I pick up my dessert spoon – no knifes or forks, by the way – and

I lick it clean, then I check out my reflection in the back of it. It's the first time I've seen my boat race in a few days and I end up being pretty shocked by it. I'm, like, puffy around the eyes and still bruised on both cheeks, although the bruises have storted to turn yellow, like my teeth, by the way, which also feel actually *furry*? The lower half of my face is, like, covered in stubble, except in two or three spots, where it could qualify as actual beard.

Oisinn pushes his plate out of the way with his feet, then stretches out on the floor and storts doing – I shit you not – sit-ups. Seeing this, Christian storts doing the exact same thing.

I'm there, 'What the fock is this? I could blow the two of you out of the water if *I* storted doing them, by the way.'

'Well, I've just decided,' Oisinn goes, 'to use whatever time we're on this ship constructively.'

Fionn goes, 'That's a good idea, Oisinn. The only way I survived those six months back in Uganda was by putting a structure on my days, setting aside time for physical and mental exercise,' and then he translates what he just said into focking French.

I'm having to bite my tongue, of course.

I go, 'I still say if I storted doing sit-ups now, you'd all be blown away.'

I look over at JP. He hasn't touched his food. His mouth is obviously at him again. I'm there, 'Are you okay, Dude?'

He just gives me a little nod. His eyes are half closed and his face is wet with tears.

I'm there, 'This is a focking disgrace. We need to get you a drink.'

JP goes, 'Hi meed hum hing,' meaning he needs something.

And I'm like, 'We'll get you more brandy. Or rum. Pirates always have rum, don't they?'

It's at that exact point that the door of our cell opens and in walks Ibrahim with our dessert, which turns out to be – hilariously – an actual Mors Bor each. While he's giving them out, I go, 'Dude, can we get some alcohol. JP's mouth is at him again,' and, because I don't know if he actually understands me, I point at JP, make a 'glug, glug, glug' noise and then a kind of, like, *drunk* face?

He says something briefly in African, then he points at me, JP,

Fionn, Christian and Oisinn and indicates for us to stand. When we do, roysh, he walks to the door and sort of, like, beckons us to *follow* him?

We look at each other briefly, then that's exactly what we end up doing. I slip my Mors Bor into the old sky rocket and out we go after him. He locks the door behind us, then we follow him through this, like, maze of narrow corridors with magnolia-coloured walls, no idea where he's bringing us or why.

When we turn one corner, we suddenly hear the music – it's Kanye, followed by a bit of Jay-Z – and then the laughter and the shouting and it's suddenly obvious to us that there's, like, a *porty* in full swing?

We're not invited, as it turns out. Just as I'm getting my hopes up of having an actual drink myself, Ibrahim shoves us into this room, which turns out to be a kitchen. One of the pirates – one of the Mackenzie Crooks really – is sitting at a long table with, like, an *iPhone* in his hand?

He sort of, like, indicates for me to sit on this chair opposite him and that's when I realize that we're about to have our photographs taken, presumably so they can warn *whoever* that there's, like, innocent civilians on board and don't stort firing focking torpedoes at us.

I'm up first, then Oisinn, then Christian, then Fionn, then JP, and the dude asks each of us to key our names into the phone. When we're done, I turn around to Ibrahim and I remind him about the drink for JP – 'Some rum?' I go.

He's there: 'Some rum?' – and, after thinking about it for a few seconds, he indicates for us to follow him again, this time to the room where the music and laughter are coming from.

It turns out to be the officers' mess. And mess is very much the word.

Julius, Rolly and Benjaim are drinking with Amadeus and the rest of the pirates and they are shit-faced – we're talking totally here. One or two of the pirates are waving their Glocks and pretending to actually *be* Jay-Z, mouthing the lyrics and all the rest of it. Julius and Amadeus are laughing together, as thick as literally thieves.

The expression on Julius's face changes when he suddenly sees *us* all standing there? He shouts something at Ibrahim, who then says something back to him. It's all in African, so I can't help you, but Ibrahim obviously mentions that JP needs some pain relief, because Julius turns around to Amadeus and goes, 'Can this fucking asshole have something to drink?'

'Most def,' Amadeus goes, then he turns to one of his underlings, who's a ringer for Usain Bolt, and he's like, 'Yo, Dawg, get these niggas somepin.'

We're, like, herded over to the bor area, where the famous Usain takes our orders. JP asks for – and gets – a whole bottle of Sea Dog Dork Rum. I ask for a pint of Heineken, but I end up being given a bottle. Christian, Oisinn and Fionn have the same.

I'm just lifting mine to my lips when all of a sudden I hear this roar from Amadeus, then this, like, laughter and applause from everyone else. I turn around and I notice that JP is – I swear to fock – necking the rum. We're talking literally throwing it down his Jeff Beck like it's lemon-focking-ade.

'Yo,' Amadeus goes, seeming to definitely approve, 'bring them niggas over here, yo,' and we sort of, like, shuffle over to the corner of the room where they're sitting, bringing our drinks with us. Amadeus, who's drinking Jack Daniel's straight from the bottle, nods at the empty chairs around him and goes, 'Sit, niggas. Sit, yo.'

He actually seems like an alright dude, although my judgement is never reliable when free alcohol is being factored into the equation.

'Rob the Builder!' Julius goes, staring at Oisinn. 'Tell my friend about Rob the Builder.'

Oisinn's like, 'Er, yeah, no, he's, like, a *character* I invented?'

Julius shouts, 'Tell him how much money this fucking asshole makes!'

So Oisinn ends up having to go right the way back to the stort. NAMA and blah, blah, blah. Bust developers. Toxic loans. One or two actual people get a mention. Six or seven Ks a week for doing fock-all except helping a bunch of civil servants straighten out the fock-up they created.

Amadeus listens to this with what can only be described as an expression of misty-eyed wonder.

He's like, 'This for real, nigga?'

I honestly wish Enda Kenny and all that crew could see his face.

Oisinn tells him it's true, every focking word.

Then Julius storts singing.

'Rob the Builder,
Does he build shit?
Rob the Builder,
No, he fucking doesn't.'

Then he nudges Oisinn. He's like, 'Tell a story about this fucking asshole. Rob the Builder. A fucking *new* story.'

JP, I notice, is still tanning the rum.

'Er, okay,' Oisinn goes. 'Yeah, no, you've done the theme music, so it's . . . Okay. One morning, Rob the Builder was sitting in his jacuzzi, enjoying a quiet soak. Suddenly, his wife, Maeve, appeared, carrying a lot of shopping bags. "Hello!" Rob said. "I see you've been spending NAMA's money again! Don't go too mad, though. It's coming from the taxpayer, don't forget!" But Maeve didn't laugh. "I want a divorce!" she said. Rob was shocked. "A divorce?" he said. "Now, what's put that in your head?" Maeve stared at him angrily. "You've been seeing that slut again." Rob shook his head. "Amaris isn't a slut," he said. "Amaris is my bit on the side, Love. Sure doesn't everyone have one!"'

Amadeus cracks his hole laughing, like it's the funniest thing he's ever heard. He's very, very off his tits.

Julius puts his orm around his shoulder. 'I tell you! Rob the fucking Builder! I love this asshole! But this is not the end of the story, I think.'

He looks at Oisinn again. All the other pirates are now listening, too.

'Maeve remained unconvinced by Rob the Builder's assurances,' Oisinn goes. ' "You bought her an apartment in Portugal," she said, "and you paid for her to have her tits done! Maybe I want *my* tits done!" she said. Rob laughed. He had to. "Why would *you* need your tits done?" he wondered. "I don't think of you in that way any-more!" Maeve continued to stare him down. "Maybe you should!" she said. Rob laughed again. She was being silly now. "Come on," he said, "that's crazy talk! You've been a wonderful wife to me, Maeve! And you did a terrific job raising our . . . is it *two* children? I mean, that's the reason I'm happy to stay married to you! But when it comes to the job of sexually gratifying me, I'd prefer to leave it to a professional!" '

Amadeus laughs again. And this time he also claps, even though the story's not yet over.

I look over to my right and I just happen to spot Judith sitting at a corner table on her own, sipping what I'm guessing is a Pernod and black or something like that. Even on a ship full of pissed and testosterone-maddened men, there's no takers for her. She smiles at me – still one smitten kitten – and I sort of, like, smile back, then nod at her.

Oisinn finishes his story.

He's like, 'Maeve was furious. "You can tell Bastard the Solicitor to prepare for war!" she said. Rob the Builder laughed. He knew women, you see. "Look," he said, "I think I know what this is about. It's about your self-esteem, isn't it? Well, it can't be easy for you. Husband running around town with 23-year-old looker while you're mouldering your way through middle age. I'll tell you what – why don't *you* have *your* breasts done, too!" Maeve was suddenly thrilled. "Thank you!" she said. "I'll go and ring the clinic!" Rob chuckled to himself. "Hey, Maeve," he said, "I was just thinking – that really was just a storm in a D cup, wasn't it?!" '

All the pirates clap and cheer, though none more enthusiastically than Amadeus. 'Nigga, you bringing it!' he tells Oisinn. 'You bring-ing it, yo,' and then he turns to Usain Bolt and goes, 'Yo, get these niggas mo drinks – feel me?'

Julius goes, 'When this is over, you should fucking keep him,' talking about Oisinn like he's a focking chimpanzee or something.

'Most def,' Amadeus goes. 'That nigga be off the hook, yo.'

We're then each handed another bottle of Ken – although JP

361

sticks with the rum – and there ends up being a porty, a massive, unexpected porty, where we all drink and tell stories and sing and laugh. And for four or five hours, as night falls, it's easy to forget that we're basically hostages here – we're talking shit-faced dot com – and that there's probably a very good chance that we might not get out of this alive.

They turn out to be seriously wussy drinkers, certainly for pirates, and in the early hours of the morning, one by one, they all stort to fade. Amadeus – who *can* actually put it away, in fairness to the dude – is clever enough to cop that *we're* suddenly the soberest in the room, aport from JP, who's passed out on the floor.

'A'ight, niggas,' he goes. 'Time for bed, yo,' and Ibrahim and a couple of the Mackenzies grab us and we know, great as it was, that this porty is suddenly over for us. 'Yo, don't put them niggas in gen pop,' Amadeus goes. 'Them niggas be guests. Put them in a suite, feel?'

Judith picks JP up and throws him over her shoulder. Then we're led out a different door to the one we walked in through, along a corridor, up two flights of stairs, then along another corridor, to a nicely decorated dorm, with actual beds in it – the first beds that most of us have seen in however long it is since we left Ireland. And as Ibrahim locks us into the room, we all flop onto those beds, gloriously pissed and for one happy moment forgetting about the trouble that we're still in.

I'm asleep for, like, an hour – although it's impossible to put an *exact* figure on it? – when I wake up very suddenly with the horrible sense that someone is standing over me. I open my eyes, but before I can make a sound, a big strong hand is put over my mouth and storts pressing down hord, to the point where I can't even move my head, never mind scream for help slash mercy.

But then my eyes slowly adjust to the light of the room and I recognize the face of Judith, her eyes looking into mine with the same dreamy dumbness that I remember from a thousand girls whose names I don't.

She removes her hand from my mouth, then puts a finger to her lips to shush me. She throws back my duvet, grabs a hold of the cuffs that are connecting my wrists in front of me and literally pulls me to my feet. Then – again, without a word being spoken – she pulls me out of the room, locking the door behind her, then along a corridor, left turn, then another corridor, then a left again. Then suddenly, I realize, we're out on the deck of the ship.

'Are you sure we should be out here?' I go.

Except she doesn't answer. She shoves me up against the wall, then kisses me five or six times on the mouth. She tastes of liquorice – see, I knew it was Pernod.

'Soon,' she goes, 'this will be over. Will I see you again?'

I'm there, 'Definitely leave me your e-mail address. We can keep in touch that way.'

But she's suddenly holding my sore face between those big lion paws of hers, going, 'When you go home, you take me with you?'

I'm like, 'What? To Ireland?'

I'm caught a bit on the hop.

'Yes,' she goes, 'to Island.'

I'm there, 'Er, yeah, no, maybe.'

This seems to definitely please her. Her face lights up and she sort of, like, hugs me, applying a serious amount of pressure to my spine. I'm looking over her shoulder – a little bit grimacing in pain – and it's the first time I notice just how perfect the night is. The sea is, like, totally calm. It looks like a sheet of glass. The sky above us is a deep blue and there are more stors out than I knew even existed. And all I can hear is the sound of water gently licking the side of the boat.

She releases me from the death grip of her hug. She's there, 'You are really taking me to Island with you?'

I'm like, 'Yeah, no, definitely – that one's nailed on,' and as I'm saying it, I can suddenly feel her hands fooling around below-stairs.

I'm like, 'Whoa!' and I mean it in a good way.

Judith – I'm not going to call her Forest Whitaker anymore, because it's possibly disrespectful – drops to her knees and opens my fly buttons like she's opening her Christmas presents.

I rub my hands over the tennis ball surface of her perfectly round head, then I look down and I just so happen to notice the Mors Bor from last night, sticking out of my pocket. I grab it with my tied hands.

I don't want the girl getting distracted.

I lean against the wall behind me and she pulls out my under-stuff. I put my head back as she sets about her work – for which she has a rare gift and I'm saying that to be fair to her – and I look up at the dark, storry sky and I listen to the water splish-splashing against the side of the boat and – yes – I take one or two bites of the Mors Bor and I close my eyes and for the first time in a week I think how focking wonderful life can sometimes be.

Those twenty minutes of – I'm admitting it – bliss, end up being followed by the worst night's sleep I've had in years, full of nightmares that are all the more terrifying for the fact of seeming real.

I'm trapped in a house in, like, Tallaght, which is as frightening a prospect for me as being held captive on a focking pirate ship. I've just ridden this single mother called Roberta – three kids under the age of five by three different men and I'm not saying that in a judgmental way – and I'm pulling my usual stunt of trying to get out of there without waking the welfare-hungry bitch.

The front and back doors are both locked, as are all the windows, and there's no sign of keys anywhere. I can feel the panic rising in my chest – it's like actual claustrophobia – because I can suddenly hear the sound of footsteps – we're talking *children's* footsteps? – on the stairs.

There are few situations in life more awkward than the kids of the woman whose toes you've just wiggled taking you for their new step-dad and asking you to fix them breakfast the following morning.

But there's no way out. I watch as the handle of the kitchen door turns and then the door is thrown open and there's three kids standing there, we're talking big, medium and small.

I don't even look at them. I go, 'You'll have to get your own Coco Pops, kids. This is not my scene,' and I go to brush past them, except that's when I *do* look at them? I make the mistake of just glancing at their faces and I get the fright of my literally life.

The oldest one is little Ross Junior. He's wearing a Cinderella costume and his mother's mascara, although that's not particularly relevant to the story. The next kid down is very definitely black. And I straight away know that he's basically Ezra in two or three years' time. The baby, I realize, is little Oliver Fionn and he's crying, because he misses his father.

I know I have to get out of there. I shove past them into the hall, deciding to go up and wake their mother. It takes an eternity to get up the stairs. There seems to be, like, a thousand of them. But finally I reach the landing and I push her bedroom door – what did I say her name was, Roberta? – and there she is, roysh, lying on the bed with her back to me.

I go, 'It was only a one-night thing. Jesus, is that window open?' but then I notice that she's wearing – I shit you not – a strait-jacket and she's, like, wriggling around, desperate to get out of the focking thing.

I go, 'Roberta? Roberta?' and she turns around and I look at her face and I see that it's not Roberta at all.

It's Jenny.

She goes, 'Get moy aaht of thus stroyt-juckut.'

And I scream – as in, I literally scream – and I sit bolt upright in the bed. Christian and Oisinn are standing either side of me, telling me in soothing voices that I just had another nightmare, not to worry, totally understandable in the circs.

But I know it wasn't *just* a nightmare? It was my conscience, which is now fully awake and tapping me on the shoulder to remind me what a complete and utter dick I am.

I'm there, 'It just seemed . . . so real.'

Fionn, I notice, is lying flat on his bed, looking unimpressed. 'You were screaming Jenny's name,' he goes.

I'm there, 'What?'

Oisinn's like, 'Fionn, leave it.'

But Fionn's piss is still boiling over the whole thing. He's there, 'You were screaming my girlfriend's name.'

She's still technically his girlfriend, I suppose, although I don't know how he could ever trust her again. I don't say that, though.

365

I'm feeling raw and weirdly – I don't know – *remorseful*? It's one of those times when I daren't open my mouth for fear of what I might say – or, worse, what I might admit.

Oisinn's like, 'Come on, let's try to all stay friends.'

Fionn laughs. 'He's not my friend,' he goes. 'He's a disease that I can't get rid of.'

I look at JP, still flaked out on his bed, clearly hungover to fock. He must have put away the best part of a bottle and a half of rum.

'*He* looks like *I* feel,' Christian goes. 'That was some porty, wasn't it?'

I've had worse nights, I have to admit.

It's at that exact moment that Ibrahim steps into the room, looking like shit, it has to be said, even though I don't think he was even, like, *drinking* last night?

'Are you okay?' Oisinn goes, because the dude seems seriously agitated, pacing the room and muttering African words to himself, which could be possibly prayers. He's clearly been spooked by something.

Fionn's there, 'What is it? What's wrong?' and Ibrahim rolls his eyes in Fionn's direction.

'Godfrey is dead,' he goes.

It's the first time any of us has heard him speak actual English.

Oisinn's there, 'Who's Godfrey? Dude, who the fock is Godfrey?'

'Godfrey!' he goes. 'My cousin.'

'The dude with the flip-flops or the other one?'

'Flip-flop, yes.'

'Whoa, whoa, whoa,' Christian goes. 'What do you mean he's dead?'

'In bed. I find him. Shot. By pirates.'

He's in, like, shock.

Fionn stands up. He goes, 'Fred said it would happen, didn't he? He said they'd kill them.'

I thought Amadeus seemed cool. It shows you what a bad judge of character I can be.

Fionn steps in front of Ibrahim and stops him pacing. 'We need to get off this boat,' he goes. 'You have to undo these cuffs.'

Ibrahim shakes his head. He's, like, crying now.

Fionn goes, 'Listen to me! Listen to me! We can all help each other. But not if our hands are tied. Please!'

Ibrahim is, like, properly *bawling* now? He stares into space for a good thirty seconds, then he suddenly composes himself. He shouts something at Fionn – *in* African – then at me, for whatever reason, then he pushes past Fionn, opens the door, looks left and right, then slowly goes out, pulling the door closed and locking it behind him.

It's fair to say that the craic we had last night is instantly forgotten. We're in the clutches of bad bastards.

'We need to get off this ship,' Fionn goes. 'And fast.'

Christian is the one who ends up falling to pieces first. He goes, 'Oh, Jesus, no! Oh, Jesus, no! Oh, Jesus!'

Oisinn goes, 'Christian, calm down. Let's not panic yet.'

JP wakes up. He's like, 'Mots hoing on?' which is 'What's going on?' to those of us with teeth.

Christian goes, 'We're going to die! We're going to die!' He's actually, like, screaming it.

Fionn's like, 'We don't know that!'

'They're going to kill us! They're going to kill us all!'

JP's racing to catch up. He's like, 'Mot?'

'They apparently shot Flip-Flops,' Oisinn goes. 'In his bed.'

'And now we're all going to die,' Christian goes. 'And I won't have said sorry to Lauren. I won't have said sorry to Lauren.'

'Christian,' I hear myself suddenly go, 'shut the fock up,' because *I'm* actually tearing up here as well.

'I walked out on her over something so stupid. So focking stupid.'

'It only seems stupid now, Christian. There was a point of principle at stake. She was being a dope.'

'I'm never going to get the chance to apologize to her. It was my fault. It was all my fault.'

'It wasn't your fault!' I hear myself go. 'It was me! It was all me!'

That gets everyone's attention. Christian even stops crying. He's like, 'What are you talking about?'

I'm there, 'Dude, I spat in that goy's sandwich. The day you had to rush off to Holles Street.'

'You?'

'He wasn't giving you the respect you deserved as a rugby player. The respect you earned.'

His face is suddenly full of, like, confusion. He's there, 'You let me think the whole thing was all . . . all a big misunderstanding.'

I'm like, 'I know.'

'You watched my marriage break up over it.'

'Dude,' I go, 'that's not all,' and I turn to JP, because my focking conscience is on a bit of a roll now. 'I told Shoshanna's ex about the baby. I tracked him down and sent him a photograph of little Ezra. That's why he suddenly showed up.'

JP goes, 'Hoo hucking mastard . . .'

I'm like, 'Hang on . . . Oisinn, I set you up. I paid Sorcha's sister – no idea what her name is – to throw herself at you, then I brought my old dear back to the gaff deliberately.'

Oisinn goes, 'Shit the focking bed, Ross.'

'I paid her five grand,' I go. 'And I took the money . . .' I pause, roysh, because this is the hordest one of all. I turn and I look at Fionn. 'I took the money from Jenny. It was the money from the table quiz. Sorcha's sister needed it to get her left momma fixed. No, her right. No, left.'

Fionn roars at me. He's furious. He's entitled to be. '*You* took the money?' he goes.

I'm there, 'Dude, I had to. She was threatening to tell Sorcha that we, you know, did the deed. I couldn't let that happen. So yeah, no, I stole the five Ks and I sort of, like, booked cruise tickets using her credit cord details.'

'I can't believe even you would stoop so low.'

'Well, if it's any consolation, I'm actually feeling much better for having got all this shit off my chest.'

I look at my friends. They're all, like, staring at me like they want to basically kill me.

'Christian,' I go, 'the dude was being a dick to you, if you remember. He was lucky I *only* gobbed in his sandwich,' and that's when I suddenly remember Hennessy. 'Actually, there's something else.'

Christian's like, 'Something *else*?'

I honestly think the only reason they haven't torn me limb from limb is because they're all still reeling.

I take another breath. It's good to get this shit out. The Jesuits were always big believers in the whole Confession thing.

I'm there, 'When I was talking to Hennessy the other day, he knew about me gobbing in the sandwich – as in, he found out. When I told you, Christian, that Hennessy said he'd negotiate to free all of us except you – well, that wasn't exactly true.'

Christian shakes his head in total disgust. He's there, 'He said you, didn't he? He'd get us home, but they could keep you.'

I just nod. I'm like, 'I can't tell you what a load off my mind this is.'

Christian springs at me like a focking panther. His wrists are cuffed, but that doesn't stop him fixing his two hands around my throat and trying to strangle me. He pushes me back on the bed, straddles me and storts literally trying to choke the life out of me, his two thumbs pressing down hord on my windpipe.

I'm going, 'Goys!' looking for Oisinn or JP or Fionn to drag him off me. 'Goys! Goys!'

But they all just ignore me.

What actually stops my best friend in the world from murdering me in cold blood with his bare hands is the sudden sound of a voice booming out from somewhere in yet another language I don't understand.

'Who the fock is that?' Oisinn goes, looking around him, trying to work out where the voice is even coming from.

Fionn's there, 'It sounds like Russian.'

He actually studied it in Trinity – I *think* port-time?

'It *is* Russian,' he goes. 'It must be coming from another ship.'

Christian loosens his grip on my throat. He's like, 'Another ship?'

Fionn listens for a few more seconds. He goes, 'They're threatening to torpedo the ship unless the pirates surrender.'

JP's there, 'Horpedo mit?'

Fionn's Russian ends up being spot-on, roysh, because the dude ends up repeating the message then in English, French, Spanish and African.

It's the English version I understand.

'Surrender thees vessel,' he goes, 'or we wheel fire on you.'

Christian suddenly climbs off me. I rub my throat where he tried to throttle me. It feels almost burned.

We hear a key in the lock. The door flies open and in comes Ibrahim, bleeding from a wound to his shoulder. He's, like, clutching it hord and wincing as the blood spills between his fingers.

Oisinn goes, 'What the fock?'

'They are shooting,' Ibrahim goes. 'Pirates. They try to kill us.'

Oisinn shows his wrists to the dude. He goes, 'You've got to take these cuffs off us. We could swim to the other ship. If you take them off us, at least we have a chance.'

But Ibrahim just sits down on the end of my bed and his eyes take on this sort of, like, *distant* look? When he eventually speaks, he says something that stops us all dead in our tracks. He goes, 'Father Fehily was my teacher, too.'

We're all, like, stunned into silence.

'In Uganda,' he goes. 'When I was a little boy.'

We're talking, like, sixty years ago.

'I hear you say this thing. What is a mighty oak but a little nut that held its ground? I say to you, where do you hear this? And you say Father Fehily was your teacher also.'

Fionn nods, roysh, like he's finally worked something out. 'I thought I recognized you,' he goes. 'You were in the bar one night. I visited the little village where Father Fehily used to work. I saw you in the bar.'

Ibrahim flashes a half-smile at him, although he looks ashamed.

'What I hear you say,' he goes, 'is that you are building a school in Mbale. I tell my cousin about you. And he says charity will pay good money for him. We take him. He talks to Emeka . . .'

Emeka is Julius, remember.

'And Emeka,' he goes, 'says yes, it will be easy. Charity has lots of money. Will pay perhaps five million. Emeka has guns. He is the boss. He says it will be easy.'

The ship is rocked by a sudden explosion. We've been hit by a Russian torpedo. We all know it. No one needs to even say it. The room shakes. The lights flash. A siren goes off somewhere.

Ibrahim's there, 'Father Fehily will be ashamed of me. I did not know he was your teacher also.'

I stand up. I decide to take chorge of the situation. The mention of Father Fehily reminds me how much he actually believed in me, even though I was useless at pretty much most things.

I'm there, 'Dude, you can't let us die. Father Fehily definitely wouldn't want that.'

He goes, 'You see him?'

See him? He obviously doesn't know he's dead.

'Yeah, I see him,' I go. 'I see him all the time.'

Ibrahim is still clutching his shoulder, grimacing. The blood is still pouring out of him.

He's there, 'You say sorry. You tell him I am sorry I do this thing. I do not know he is your teacher also.'

'Dude,' I go, 'I'll tell you something Father Fehily used to also say. He used to say it's never too late to do the right thing. He definitely wouldn't want to see us die.'

I hold out my hands, presenting my cuffs to him. He thinks for a few seconds, then he fishes a set of keys out of his sky rocket. He tries a few keys on mine. The fourth one ends up being the right one. He uncuffs me. His hands are trembling, so I end up taking the keys from him and freeing everyone else.

There's a real sense that this is suddenly game time. Cometh the hour, you know the rest.

I run to the door, just as another torpedo rocks the ship. I end up having to grab on to a wardrobe to stop myself from falling orse over tit.

'We are dead men,' Ibrahim goes. 'We are all dead men. Finished.'

And I'm like, 'Finished? I wouldn't even know how to spell the word.'

I actually do know how to spell it, although I wouldn't be a hundred percent sure about the number of Ns.

There's a gun battle raging down on the deck. I can hear it the second I pull open our door. The tap-tap, tap-tap-tap of Kalashnikov fire and the poom, poom, poom of the Glocks.

'Come on!' Oisinn, behind me, goes. 'What are we waiting for?'

I hold up my hand. I'm like, 'Hang on until the shooting stops.'

After about twenty more seconds, it does, and I tell them to follow me, which they do – Fionn, then Christian, then Oisinn, then JP, and then, at the very back, poor Ibrahim, still bleeding like a rare tenderloin.

We reach the bottom of the stairs and my plan is to find a focking lifeboat.

There's a hell of a lot of smoke in the air – the ship is obviously on fire – and our visibility is reduced to, I don't know, whatever it happens to be.

'This way!' Fionn goes, suddenly deciding that *he* wants to lead? He turns left and storts making his way to the back of the actual ship. But then he suddenly slips, as in his legs go from under him and he goes three feet in the air and lands on his back. And I laugh – it's kind of comical the way it happens – until I notice that what he's slipped on is a giant pool of focking blood and literally two feet away from where he's lying is the bullet-riddled body of Benjamin.

Fionn storts having a panic attack. He's got the dude's blood all over his back. He tries to stand up, except he slips – the thing's like a focking oil slick – this time on his face. I end up having to offer him my hand and I pull him out of it. But then he won't move. Like I said, he's having some kind of panic-related episode. He stands there just shaking his head and going, 'He's dead! He's dead! He's dead!' and I turn around to the goys and I tell them to go on and see can they find the lifeboats.

Oisinn, JP and Ibrahim go, but Christian stays with me and we try to calm Fionn down.

'He's dead!' he keeps going. 'He's dead!'

And I'm like, 'Yes, he's dead. But he was also a dick. He kept you locked up in a basement for six months, remember. He got what was focking coming to him.'

I suddenly realize that I'm also covered in the dude's blood.

I manage to calm Fionn down by slapping him in the face seven or eight times, the last five or six of which Christian considers unnecessary. At least we manage to impress upon him the importance of getting the fock off this ship.

I notice Benjamin's bullwhip – random, I know – beside his body and for some reason I pick it up. I lead us along one corridor, then another – blinded by smoke – until I can just about make out the side of the ship. They have different names, of course. Star bird and something else. I'm going to say left, whichever one that is. I run for the rail, with Fionn and Christian behind me, but just as we reach it, the boat suddenly – I'm going to say – *lists* to one side, so the floor below us suddenly becomes a wall in front of us, and we're, like, sliding back across the deck.

Then it suddenly rights itself again

As I'm trying to, like, re-gather my bearings, I hear the sound of gunfire again. I look to my right and – again through the smoke – I can make out three pirates, including Amadeus, standing at various points on the deck and firing up at Julius, who's three floors above them, shooting down at them from a window, then taking cover between bursts of fire.

The ship lurches again. We may have been hit by a third torpedo, although I can't say for sure. In the confusion, Julius leaves his head exposed for a second too long and Amadeus hits him – or as Amadeus himself puts it while he's high-fiving his two pirate colleagues: 'That little poop butt nigga – I took his Kangol *and* most his dome, yo!' – and we watch his body fall nearly thirty feet onto the deck with a thud that would have to be described as sickening.

It's possibly the relief at seeing Julius dead – and no longer in a position of control over him – that causes Fionn to let out a sort of, like, squeal of relief, which Amadeus and the other two somehow hear over the sound of steel groaning and fuel exploding and sirens sounding and more warnings being shouted in Russian.

One of them storts firing at us. A bullet hits the floor right in front of Christian's feet and I push him over, then I hit the – literally – deck, pulling Fionn down with me and we crawl along a passageway, until we're satisfied that we're out of the line of fire. Then we climb to our feet again. And with the smell of oil burning and black smoke blinding us, we run to where we think the Russian voice is coming from.

Eventually, the smoke clears and we find ourselves at what turns out to be the back end of the boat. The French dudes are all free – even though I've no idea how – and they're throwing themselves over the rail and into the sea slash ocean slash whatever you want to call it.

I can see the Russian ship in the distance, maybe a kilometre away.

There's, like, a speck in the sea – between us and it – and I know, as sure as I know my own name, that it's Fred Pfanning, first off the boat, and not so much swimming as thrashing the sea to a fine foam, in an effort to save his own skin.

I watch Oisinn swing his leg over the top rail and then jump into the water below, while JP stands on the rail and does an actual swan dive into it.

Me, Christian and Fionn rush over to the edge, where Ibrahim is hesitating. At first, I think he's scared.

Fionn goes, 'Jump!'

But Ibrahim's like, 'No!' and he shakes his head. 'I don't want to go to prison. Too old.'

Christian's there, 'Dude, this ship is going down. If you stay here, you'll die.'

And Ibrahim just nods, like he's happy with that, then he walks back in the direction we came, to where Amadeus and the others are waiting with their Glocks to kill him.

I'm like, 'Fionn, jump,' which he then does, first putting his glasses into his pocket, then climbing over the rail and entering the water feet-first.

I'm there, 'Christian, go!'

But he's like, 'No, you first!' because he knows I can't swim and he thinks I'll possibly bottle it. In the end, I have to grab him and practically shove him through the middle rail and he falls head-first over the side of the ship, managing to turn it into a kind of dive before he hits the water.

As it happens, I'm not scared. Well, I am, but I know I have no alternative but to get off this burning focking coffin.

But just as I'm about to go over the side, my instinct tells me to turn around and look to my left, which is exactly what I end up doing.

About thirty feet away, through a cloud of smoke, I spot Judith standing with her back to a wall, apparently cowering from someone. I stort walking towards her, but I've only taken four or five steps, when a pirate steps between us – with his back to me – and raises his gun, getting ready to shoot her.

I remember the whip, which I'm somehow still holding. I have no focking idea how to use it, but I've seen all the Indiana Joneses and I think, fock it, how hord could it be?

I run forward, at the same raising my orm, then I bring the whip down, cutting the air between us. The dude lets out a scream as the whip cracks around his wrist and he drops his gun.

Judith takes a step forward and she sees me through the smoke. She smiles – my hero! – and that's how I will always remember the girl, standing there with a look of total and utter love on her face.

And then her head suddenly explodes. A pirate leans out of a window up above her and – before I can even shout a warning – empties his gun into her brain from, like, four feet away. Her big Pacman head opens up like a dropped watermelon. She didn't even see it coming.

I hear a scream. I look around and I realize that it came from me. I turn and I run back to the rail, before the dude has a chance to reload. I throw my leg over the top and I look down at the sea, feeling a shiver of fear, but at the same time knowing that to stay here for even ten seconds more means certain focking death.

So I close my eyes and I jump.

What happens next is a blur. I don't remember being under the water and I have no idea how long I am. All I remember is bobbing on the surface, with my mouth pointing at the sky, trying to suck as much air into my lungs as I can. This is suddenly my priority, and, while I'm actually doing it, I have no idea how I manage to stay afloat.

It's only when I'm properly breathing again and I remember that I can't actually swim that the panic storts to set in. I'm suddenly thrashing around in the water, my orms looking for something to hold onto, then suddenly I spot this, like, yellow oil drum floating on the surface, and I somehow manage to make it as far as that, then I hold onto it for dear life.

I look back at the ship that I've just jumped off. It's – again – *listing* to the side and about half of it is already below the waterline.

Suddenly, the oil barrel – the only thing that stands between me and being swallowed by the sea – storts turning upright and I realize that it's, like, filling up with water and any second now it's going to sink.

It takes about ten seconds. One moment I'm wrapping my orms around it, trying desperately to stay up, then it suddenly drops from between my outstretched orms to the bottom of the ocean.

I think to myself, this must be it. It *must* be? And I think about Sorcha and Honor and Ronan and the babies I never got to know. I think about my old man and even my old dear and I kick my legs and I think, Why the fock did I never learn to swim? And that's when I see them, maybe ten feet away: four heads bobbing in the water.

Christian, Fionn, JP and Oisinn.

They watch me for about thirty seconds, my orms flailing in the air, my legs working like a focking duck's legs under the water. None of them makes a move.

I'm like, 'Goys! Help me! Help!'

They look at each other – I swear to fock – and I can tell that a thought passes between them, a thought that I don't even want to put *words* to?

I'm there, 'Fionn, you said it yourself. I'm like a disease – you can't get rid of me.'

He goes, 'I didn't mean it as a compliment, Ross.'

And still not one of them makes a move towards me.

My body feels suddenly heavy. My chin goes under, then my mouth, then my nose. I'm sinking. I'm sinking faster than that barrel. With one last, desperate kick, I manage to get my mouth above the water again and I go, 'Goys, please! This can't be how it ends!'

Epilogue

It's Christmas Eve. But it's also Thanksgiving. That's Sorcha's line anyway. She even stuck it on the e-mail invitation.

The gaff is full. There's, like, people everywhere. The sound of laughter and 'Waltz of the Snowflake' from *The Nutcracker* and the smell of Sorcha's cranberry and chestnut falafel and her *Bûche de Noël* makes me feel warm and safe. Upstairs, Honor is opening her Christmas presents, even though she's been told that Santa won't be bringing them for another five or six hours.

I think what I'm saying is that it's good to be home.

I'm holding two of the boys, one in either orm, then Sorcha walks into the living room with the other. She was changing his nappy. She looks beautiful in a red dress and a real – as in, professionally applied – fake tan.

She goes, 'Hey,' and it turns into a smile.

I'm like, 'Hey, yourself.'

'They're *so* like you,' she goes, wiping drool from the mouth of the one in my right orm. 'Oh my God, three little Ross O'Carroll-Kellys. That's, like, *terrifying?*'

I laugh along – deep down, though, I think it's a compliment.

I'm there, 'It's going to take me a while to remember which one is George, which one is Anthony and which one is – what was it again?'

She's like, 'Spencer.'

This happened while I was out of the country, I should mention. They're all, like, Lalor family names, going back through the generations. *His* influence, of course.

He's staring at me across the living room, by the way, an Amaretto sour in his hand, which he's not even drinking. He's just giving me daggers. It's killing him to see me back with his daughter.

Sorcha follows my line of vision and goes, 'I told him, Ross, that if he and Mom are going to live here with us, then he has to accept that you're my husband and you always will be.'

She kisses me on the cheek. She does it deliberately for her old man to see.

Birds are funny.

I can hear my old man, somewhere in the room, going, 'That wasn't a budget! That was an outright assault on the middle-income earners who are this country's bloody well lifeblood!'

I just smile. I can't believe I'm saying this, but it's actually nice to hear his voice.

We had a Christmas cord from my old dear from rehab, with a little note, which was all about her. She didn't even mention the triplets. It's like her drug-addled mind has forgotten they were even born.

There's no sign of Hennessy, by the way. The word is that he's back in the States.

Christian and JP arrive. It's high-fives. It's hugs. It's everything.

JP's got his Taylor Keith fixed – or least he's got a set of falsies to tide him over until the New Year. We can understand the focker – that's the important thing.

'Look at these little goys!' he goes. 'Three little Ross O'Carroll-Kellys! Good luck!'

I laugh – as do Sorcha and Christian.

I'm like, 'Yeah, no, everyone seems to be saying that.'

Christian goes, 'So which one is which? I hear there's a George and a Spencer.'

And, while I'm trying to remember who's who, Sorcha takes a deep breath, then says something I'm not expecting.

She's like, 'No. Spencer, George and Anthony are going to be their middle names . . . This is Brian, this is Jonathan and this is Leo.'

I'm speechless. I'm genuinely speechless.

I'm like, 'Are you sure?'

She smiles at me and nods.

'Because they're heroes to me,' I go. 'My three all-time heroes.'

She's like, 'Brian, Jonathan and Leo,' and, as she says it, I couldn't be a hundred percent sure that she doesn't have a subtle look over at her old man. 'I better put them down. It's way past their bedtime.'

She sort of, like, summons her old dear with a nod of her head and the two of them take them off to bed.

JP goes, 'Dude, you're the luckiest man in the world,' and I feel instantly bad for *him*?

I'm like, 'Look, I'm sorry again about . . .'

But he cuts me off. He's there, 'Ross, someone had to do it. I was living a lie. So was Shoshanna.'

I turn to Christian and I go. 'And I'm sorry again about, you know, honking in that dude's roll and costing you your business.'

And Christian doesn't get a chance to answer because Lauren suddenly appears at his elbow. It's nice that they're back together, but I can't even look her in the eye.

I'm like, 'Do you want a Lycheeni, Lauren? There's also Poinsettias and then also, like, *non*-cocktaily drinks?'

You can't bullshit her, though. She's one of those birds who just refuses point-black to be bullshitted.

She fixes me with a look and goes, 'There's something I need to say to you, Ross. I will never forgive you for costing us our business and almost our marriage. But I'm prepared to never bring it up again because you saved my husband's life and you brought him back safely to me.'

I just nod.

I'm there, 'That's not a bad deal. I'll take it.'

All of a sudden, Honor appears in front of me. She goes, 'Most of what you got me is lame. I've arranged everything into two piles – the things I'm going to *reluctantly* keep and the things you better have focking receipts for.'

Lauren, Christian and JP all just look at her in horror. But I go, 'Okay, Honor,' and I stroke the top of her head and go, 'Merry Christmas.'

And do you know what she does? She wraps herself around my right leg and hugs it really tightly. The welts on my thighs sting like fock, but it's a small price to pay for knowing that my little wagon of a daughter loves her daddy.

There's still no sign of Fionn, although I spot Oisinn across the room, chatting away to Sorcha's sister, no doubt telling her the story of how he saved the Rossmeister from drowning – pulling me for practically a kilometre to the Russian ship – while at the same time stealing the odd look at her stacks.

I think they'll probably get it on tonight. I must remind him to get a name, if it comes up.

I spot Ronan. Or rather Ronan spots me. He's like, 'Stordee, Rosser?'

I'm like, 'Hey, Ro – how the hell are you?'

And he hesitates before he answers and I instantly know that he's got something to tell me, something I'm possibly not going to like hearing.

He goes, 'Rosser, we're mooben out – me and Shadden.'

I'm like, 'What? Where are you going?'

'We're mooben back to her ma's.'

'Back to Finglas?'

'Back to Finglas, yeah.'

I can't hide my disappointment and – I'm going to admit it – disgust. I'm there, 'This is *her* doing, isn't it? Focking Dordeen, putting in the focking poison. And focking K . . . K . . . K . . . Kennet.'

Ronan just shrugs. He goes, 'It hadn't woorked, Rosser. We throyed living hee-er. We gev it ear best shot.'

'Is this because Rihanna-Brogan thought Sorcha was her mother?'

'It's not just that. Shadden feels like she dudn't firrin. We're joost diffordent is all.'

I nod my head. I just have to accept it. I'm there, 'What about school?'

He goes, 'Ine staying in Castlerock. Ine still sitting me Judiniour Ceert in Jewin. But Shadden's thropping out. She wants to be a full-toyum mudder. She dudn't want her thaughter growing up a sthranger to her.'

'What'll you do for money?'

'Her ma says there's all sowurts of muddy she could be clayumen.'

'Yeah, no, I'd say Dordeen knows her social welfare entitlements like she knows her way to the chipper.'

'Ine soddy, Rosser. You've been veddy good to us, so you haff.'

'Jesus, Ro, I'm your father.'

'Eeben so.'

'When are you leaving?'

'Arthur Christmas.'

'That soon?'

I just nod. I can feel my eyes filling up and I can't trust myself to open my mouth. I'm there, 'Don't be a stranger. That'd kill me.'

He goes, 'Leave it out, Rosser. You'll see me as much as ebber.'

A hush suddenly goes through the house then and I know straight away that Fionn has arrived. I make my way through the throng of people out to the hallway, where I notice that Chloe and Amie with an ie are telling him that he's, like, oh my God, *so* brave.

He's nodding away, being nice and then he cops me. No words end up being spoken. I know it's going to sound gay – and I'm not sure I even care – but we move towards each other and I take him in my orms.

It's *not* gay? I'm just saying it possibly sounds it.

I'm there, 'It's good to have you back, Dude.'

He goes, 'There were times, Ross – well, you know – when I thought I'd never . . .'

I'm like, 'I *always* thought we would. I kept saying Christmas. Do you remember I said Christmas?'

'I do.'

'I had that belief. I've got incredible belief.'

He goes, 'That's why Father Fehily chose *you* to be our captain.'

It's an amazing thing to hear.

I hold him at orm's length. He looks good, it has to be said, given where he's been for the past six months.

'Dude,' I go, 'I've got this deal with Lauren where she's agreed to never forgive me for what I did to them but not to keep banging on about it either. I was wondering could me and you come to a similar arrangement about the whole Jenny thing?'

He's there, 'Ross, you are without doubt the lousiest, shittiest excuse for a human being I've ever met.'

'I'm accepting that.'

'But you're also the best focking friend a man could ever want.'

'There's good *and* bad, isn't there? I'm always thinking if I could just get the balance right between the two.'

'You came for me, Ross. You saved my life.'

'Castlerock über alles,' a voice behind me goes. It's Oisinn's voice. I turn around and the three of them are standing there. We're talking Oisinn, we're talking JP, we're talking Christian.

We end up forming a little circle, orms around each other's shoulders, like a pre-match huddle, except no one says a word. No one needs to say a word. We take a little moment for ourselves before we rejoin the porty and before we're pulled by different people in various different directions.

See us five? We're unbreakable. That's the word for us.

'It's Christmas,' JP goes, eventually slipping the circle. 'Let's get focked up.'

Acknowledgements

I would like to express my grateful thanks, as ever, to Rachel Pierce, 'whom' I'm very fortunate to have as an editor; to my very wonderful agent, Faith O'Grady, who helps me stay positive at all times; to the artist Alan Clarke, who just keeps raising the bar for himself and for me; to Michael McLoughlin, Patricia Deevy, Cliona Lewis, Patricia McVeigh, Brian Walker and all the staff of Penguin Ireland for your unwavering support and for the fun we continue to have producing these books; to editors past and present, especially Ger Siggins and Paddy Murray; to my father and my brothers for the great grounding in comedy that you gave me; and to Mary, the joy in my life.